"The Aspern Papers *is a great reverberating story on the themes of art, time and passion. . . . It is first-rate on all points, and so thoroughly realized that it rather defies definition.*" —F. W. DUPEE

"*For swift, unhalting, onward movement, there is nothing in James—there is perhaps nothing anywhere—like* The Spoils of Poynton." —JOSEPH WARREN BEACH

HENRY JAMES was born in New York in 1843 and died in London in 1916. A celebrated writer during his own time, he has come to be even more widely read after his death. He is regarded by contemporary literary critics as a supreme master of English prose and one of the great novelists in modern literature.

R. P. BLACKMUR, distinguished literary critic, poet and teacher, provided the introduction to this edition of *The Aspern Papers* and *Spoils of Poynton*.

The Aspern Papers

The Spoils of Poynton

HENRY JAMES

With a general introduction
by R. P. BLACKMUR

THE LAUREL   *HENRY JAMES*

Published by
DELL PUBLISHING CO., INC.
750 Third Avenue
New York 17, N.Y.

The texts for *The Aspern Papers* and *The Spoils of Poynton* are those of the original editions, published in 1888 and 1896.

First Dell printing—February, 1959
Second Dell printing—March, 1961
Third Dell printing—December, 1962
Fourth Dell printing—October, 1963
Fifth Dell printing—January, 1965
Sixth Dell printing—April, 1966
Seventh Dell printing—November, 1967
Eighth Dell printing—October, 1969
Ninth Dell printing—September, 1971

Printed in U.S.A.

INTRODUCTION

When I was first told, in 1921, to read something of Henry James—just as when I had been told to read something of Thomas Hardy and something of Joseph Conrad—I went to the Cambridge Public Library looking, I think, for *The Portrait of a Lady*. It was out. The day was hot and muggy, so that from the card catalogue I selected as the most cooling title *The Wings of the Dove*, and on the following morning, a Sunday, even hotter and muggier, I began, and by the stifling midnight had finished my first elated reading of that novel. Long before the end I knew a master had laid hands on me. The beauty of the book bore me up; I was both cool and waking; excited and effortless; nothing was any longer worth while and everything had become necessary. A little later, there came outside the patter and the cooling of a shower of rain and I was able to go to sleep, both confident and desperate in the force of art.

Such are the advantages and the energies of boyhood. By great luck I had been introduced simply and directly, and had responded in the same way, to what a vast number of people have thought an impossible novel by an impossible author and a vast number of other people have submitted to the stupefying idolatry of both gross and fine over-interpretation. In short, I was unimpeded.

Appreciation never heightened. But of course appreciation deepened, with many readings of the novel itself and of the rest of James's work. As my ignorance became compounded with familiarity and with the contingencies of art and life, there were reservations and recognitions and even enlightenments, and I got to know how to speak of what had so deeply affected me on my first reading with so little knowledge compacting my hungry sensibility. Perhaps I thought and experienced it all to begin with, for thinking is very different from knowing and saying. I did not know, for example, how James had worked on me with the "coercive charm of form," or how I felt, with him, the beautiful incentive of the deep difficulty braved. I think I saw but did not catch the force of the phrase that the relations between Merton Densher and Kate Croy, as they felt the spread of the wings of the dove, was a deep "contention of adverse wills." I did not know how to speak, that is, of that central adversity of the human condition which rises from the "otherness" of every individual from every other individual. It is aliens who make every commerce there is, and every intimacy. Not knowing, but seeing, I could not say how it was that the moral image of the American princess, Milly Theale, could both separate forever Merton Densher and Kate Croy and also give a marred substance of intimacy which would bind them forever together. It is the story of how Milly Theale could do this to Merton Densher and Kate Croy that constitutes *The Wings of the Dove* as a novel, as a psychology of human action and behavior.

To speak ordinarily is to make cries or to take up the time or to echo what once has properly been said. To speak well is to make a poem or a novel, to give form to the cry and a psychology to him who cried, a form and a psychology which can be used again, filled out or erected, as need be, by the reader. That is why when we seem to speak well we speak with voices not our own saying more than we knew we meant, and with a form—a style—into which we seem to have broken through, as into raw air. Henry James gives us such a voice and such a form whenever we need to use them. The voice is that of the psyche speaking and makes a psychology quite as much as Freud does. The form gives resonance to the voice so that it can reach our ears.

James first reached durable form—and his characteristic theme—in *The Portrait of a Lady* (1881) in which the charming sketch of *An International Episode* (1879) and adumbrated lyric tragedy of *Daisy Miller* (1878), were transformed from a living feast on the work of George Eliot, Dickens, Balzac, and Turgenev into something altogether his own. It is the *Portrait* which shows us what the others are about, and it is the others who grow up into the full fate of Isabelle Archer in the *Portrait*. The same could be said for *The Europeans* (1878) and *Washington Square* (1881). One could not imagine that they existed, or their characters (though an exception should be made a little for Catherine Sloper in *Washington Square* because her delicacy is greater than her weariness, and for Daisy Miller because she began it all, the very first of the American princesses) if they were not pendants about the neck of the *Portrait* and Isabelle Archer and Ralph Touchett. *The American* (1877) and *Roderick Hudson* (1876), the first brilliant with wit and sincerity and the second fairly somber with promise, do not come into it at all. In both the forms are ragged and the characters are constantly losing their roles with nobody and nothing to pick them up again except the reader out of the conventions of his own life; they are early works which we read now because James wrote them then, and we look in them to see the first hint of what only actually happened later—as Newman of *The American* is perfected as Strether in *The Ambassadors* a quarter of a century afterward: the American only goes home intact, the Ambassador, wholly ravaged, goes home all Europe within him. There are certain tastes in travel which still prefer to travel light, but these should not include those who have read and have liked *The Portrait of a Lady* and Isabelle Archer. We see in that young lady, as Carl Van Doren long ago remarked, the dawning knowledge of what life is like and the gradual creation—not at all a construction—of a psychology adequate to meet that dawning even if it destroys her in the process. The difference is easy to state. In *Daisy Miller* that young lady is "at once the most exacting in the world and the least endowed with a sense of indebtedness." Isabelle Archer, no less exacting, pays even her own life. Later, in *The Wings of the Dove*, Milly Theale who had no life to pay paid out her own death.

The curiosity is that after *The Portrait of a Lady* James fell into an uncertainty of intention, of form, and of psychology: his tentacles wavered, trying one surface and one substance after another without ever either grasping firmly or being wholly seized up. *The Princess Casamassima* and

The Bostonians, for example, reached, and touched, the undersides of things in official society and private morals, and *The Tragic Muse* imposed a glittering surface on both in the forms of stage and parliament. But it is clear that none of these absorbed or commanded his talents. None either broke through into form or created a psychology. Besides, he wrote also at this time his stories of the artist and his ghost stories, where though the interest is great and the finish exquisite, the effect—the thing made—is thin, and the magnitude, compared to *The Portrait,* is shrunken like an Argentinian skull. The artist was testing life, the ghosts dissolving life: though both were seeking to tap the force that is under or overwhelmingly within life. All of them tried and all of them had to do with his role—in the phrase made many years ago, I forget by whom—as "the historian of fine consciences" that either might or ought to exist. It is no wonder that he turned to the drama for relief and found there a brilliant collapse.

The economy, the essential housekeeping, of James's talent could not reach the outward concentration of the theatre where the action commands the meaning. He was at home only where the meaning, closely grasped, specifically interwoven, commanded the action. This economy he found in his late work where life was testing the artist and where he enlarged his role of the historian of fine consciences and became the creator of conscience itself and, what is even more remarkable in this largely unmotivated world, the creator of genuine motive as well. In the three great novels conscience and motive unite. Considered in this way Lambert Strether in *The Ambassadors,* Maggie Verver in *The Golden Bowl,* and Milly Theale in *The Wings of the Dove* are conscience and motive for everybody else taken separately and, taken together, for the human action as well. Each, naturally, is destroyed.

Before returning with this in mind to *The Wings of the Dove,* it may be as well to turn first to these other works: to *The Aspern Papers,* which one might say is an early, or primitive, form, to *The Turn of the Screw,* which is a kind of parallel form, and to *The Spoils of Poynton,* which is a direct preparation for the great novels. In each a conscience is created which achieves a deep human action, and from one to another there is a rising level of intensity and a rising degree of involvement. The heroine is in each case the seat of the conscience; each acts to the degradation or destruction of others; and each acts in result of a simple and direct nature—with the force of naïvety. Naïvety is intelligence at work for itself alone, but in response to deep principles of being which only gradually emerge from their hiding in nature. Henry James was the master of naïvety in the sense that Dante was the master of disgust, and each author showed his mastery by creating new forms for his insight—as Dante with Ugolino and James with Milly Theale, to take only the strongest examples. That James understood very well what he was up to is clear if we remember his remark that the value of naïvety was very like the value of zero in a number; it depended on the digit that preceded it. His heroines are witness to this in a rising series; and the figure of Miss Tita,* the small one, in *The Aspern Papers* (1888), is, if not the highest, still a very high example of this force. It is her naïvety which is the heart and target of the story. Without her full and unconsidered offer of herself—her meager, shabby, impregnable self—as the rich equivalent of every other value named of literature, romance and habit, there would have been no story, and the pursuit of the "papers" (as one should say, lost love letters of Shelley) would not have had even the mistaken value of the blackguard evil of the avid collector.

For what happens in *The Aspern Papers*? A damned publishing scoundrel—something very near a professional biographer—uses more than every needful fraud and deceit to work himself into the house and almost the confidence of a very old woman who has the relics of a love affair, two generations since, with a very great poet. The old woman—the Juliana, almost the Juliet, of the poems—has with her in her Venetian *palazzo* a niece, Miss Tita, into whose possession upon her aunt's death the papers fall. The papers—the vital papers of a vital love, a very scandal of history—have already cost our anonymous publishing

*"Miss Tina," in the revised version of *The Aspern Papers*.

scoundrel (even his *nom de guerre* is never told us, let alone his "real" name) a good deal of what ought to have been his honor and decency, and more money than he could afford besides. He has in effect even, as the least of his basenesses, committed murder, for the old woman dies in the smother of them. He has been the rogue in the fairy tale, a confidence man with a rage to tamper outrageously with the real humanity—the naïve conscience—of the middle-aged Cinderella who is Miss Tita. Were it not a fairy tale, a mere moral allegory, we would think him a puerile vampire or emasculated werewolf; and perhaps he was, for in Henry James you can never tell to what baseness his vision of evil descends—it is for the reader's own abilities to discern, as the tales begin to signify for themselves. I will only say here that our publishing scoundrel moves with energy and vivacity less than human.

At any rate, the pursuit of the papers has cost him a great deal which he has paid with willingness and assiduity, but when he comes to claim them from Miss Tita he finds that instead of plundering her he has brought her alive—the vital image of the vital love the papers had stood for, a very scandal of life itself. She proposes that to gain the papers he should become a relative and, so to speak, become bound by the family restrictions upon them, by the values they themselves were supposed to represent as they were now enacted in her. This, after all, was what he must have been, or ought to have been, seeking. She proposes to him the marriage her conscience had created for him and on the moment destroys in him every power but flight, distraction, and the repudiation of every motive he thought had driven him. At their last interview "she smiled strangely, with an infinite gentleness. She had never doubted that I had left her the day before in horror. How could she, since I had not come back before night to contradict, even as a simple form, such an idea? And now she had the force of soul—Miss Tita with force of soul was a new conception—to smile at me in her humiliation."

Force of soul is what we see when great naïvety is joined with conscience, and it has something to do with that reality which T. S. Eliot says we cannot bear very much of, but which we must seek, and when we find it must find destroyed.

Sometimes, in ourselves, we find it evil, as in *The Turn of the Screw* (1898). That novel, which for years has been the puzzlepiece in James for Freudians to play with (it would be more intelligent to apply the drama of the psyche as construed in Jung), is rather a magnificent creation of a bad conscience—a conscience vitally deprived, but vitally desperate to transform its hallucinations into reality. It is by that conscience and its vision of evil that the governess destroys the two children, and having done so escapes into another life. The ghosts she sees are the agents of her conscience, and their malevolence is her motive. In chapter twelve, the very center of the story, the current of evil begins to flow not only from the general outside in, as in the beginning, or just through Quint and Jessel (the ghosts) where it had seemed to concentrate for outlet, but also and spontaneously from the souls of the children themselves. Our heroine feels the evil in their unnatural goodness, which she had herself invented, along with the evil, and is therefore prone to feel it as everywhere developing. It is as if innocence is the looking glass for evil. It is only for her to tell *them*, the children, that they are possessed, and so to tell them that they will believe it; and indeed that is what happens. Meanwhile our heroine has begun to show herself quite above any merely primary infatuation, whether with herself or her bachelor employer remote in London. She is now driven by an energy which is suited to this solitary and friendless place and which mustn't be interfered with. She has taken hold; she has pushed along; she has dragged everything; nothing must stop the energy within her, for that energy is creative. So she goes on until she creates "the white face of damnation" and by it succeeds in killing the little boy—but not before he has identified the governess as the Devil. The abyss over which he fell at the moment of death is that of the intolerable consciousness which may often be brought best to us by human cruelty become conscience and motive in a personality driven, possessive, possessed.

Either James's tale is frivolous and the ghosts are "real,"

or they are actual, the governess's other selves, actual hallucinations by which the moral depravity of the unnaturally "good" parson's daughter is exacerbated and enacted, to the mutilation of one life and the demolition of another. Or it may be that there is a combination of the light-hearted gruesome and the dark-hearted moral apologia, with the second running away with the first, and the first covering up the worser inner cysts of the second. We have in any case the record of the governess's gradual damnation. She reabsorbs her specters, and any respectable servant a hundred and fifty years ago would have known her as a witch and have called on the vicar to exorcise her if not hang her. For us she is as near as the evil conscience can come to creating and enacting the motives of a witch. Yet, either way or both, at the end some part of our heroine, our twenty-year-old girl, should have tumbled after the little boy into the abyss: her ghosts, her other selves, those parts of ourselves.

Our third example, *The Spoils of Poynton* (1897), contains as many ghosts or specters as *The Turn of the Screw*, and exhibits a witch, in the figure of Mrs. Gereth, as evil in what we call the "sane" world as the poor governess was in the world of her possession. Mrs. Gereth has a houseful of fine furniture (the "spoils" of the title), a son, Owen, and a young girl companion, Fleda Vetch, who loves both the furniture and the son. The son breaks his engagement to Fleda and marries a big horse of a girl, Mona, who has no love for the furniture unless for its price. The contest is for the furniture and through it for Fleda's soul. Almost the witchcraft wins, almost it loses; it depends on the reader's taste, for the story ends in a conflagration in which the house and all its furniture are destroyed. James was still uncertain of his intention.

Who will say it is right or wrong that this novel which belongs to Fleda Vetch's fullness of action should have begun in the consciousness of Mrs. Gereth, or that the scenes all through the first hundred pages should be constructed as drawing-room comedy with every real stake ignored or horsed, and with everybody, even Fleda, seen pretty much as a type or a character part? The thing reads like a well-made novel trying to be a well-made play about trifles, about manners with the men and women left out; but with the distinction that rather a cynical fable is about to be unfolded in an atmosphere of sheer brutal brilliance: moral humiliation without moral compassion. Then the story deepens and the stakes begin to show larger at the point when Fleda discovers that Mrs. Gereth has stolen the furniture from her son and crowded it into a small cottage. Then Fleda begins to perceive. She has to fill the conventions, including the stage conventions, with the life and richness of which they had become only the demeaned manners: but somehow not letting go of the furniture, the "things," and the disposition of them, whether in rancor or generosity, since they have become, by the attrition of life, the central symbol of meaning and fate: the spoils of them.

In this contest of adverse wills Fleda is weaker than Mona, than Owen, than Mrs. Gereth. If Mona has no morals and Owen merely craves morals, Mrs. Gereth merely uses morals. That is the effect of turning her interest into disproportionate passion. Mrs. Gereth is one of those personal fanatics who will use morals for her own sake even if she burns for it. She is not a free spirit. Fleda supplies her with value after value and Mrs. Gereth heaps them one after another on her bonfire till she has a general conflagration, and in the end wetted ashes in her mouth. She does not exhaust Fleda so much as abuse her: the values Fleda provides become more and more desperate as she chucks them to her, faggots of love and hope, one after another. If the spirit has a body, the body of Fleda's spirit is pretty well wasted by the time Mrs. Gereth is done with her.

The process of that waste is the whole story of the last fourth of the book, and as we watch it we feel the menace, and then the act: the actual wastage under the open vampirage of unspecified evil: the plain waste of Fleda's otherwise indestructible human goodness. Fleda is smothered under the expansion of Mrs. Gereth's will; she submits like a sick animal to her embrace. In the end, when everything is gone, they have ravaged each other in terms of the spoils, for Mrs. Gereth, too, collapses. Yet Fleda has grown. If you like, Fleda in her intelligence and her free spirit has responded to the awful, attractive force of the spoils by creating a conscience for all the spoils, human and otherwise, for the people and the things. Her created conscience was her spoils—beautiful beyond markers and periods, let alone price; and her spoils have been taken away from her. It is quite fitting and right—it is poetic justice, it is the created justice of the free spirit—that when Fleda is brought by a last temptation to redeem at Poynton, in symbol, some one of its spoils, at the very moment of her coming all the spoils should have been lost or saved in flame.

It is matters like these that achieved magnitude when James broke into form and made a psychology in his three great late novels, and for me especially, in *The Wings of the Dove*, with its hope and its horror, its image of moral beauty and its actual waste of moral devastation—for which, as I should have known since I had been a choir boy, there were archetypal images in the Book of Psalms, though I did not connect them for many years. There is this from the 68th Psalm: "Though ye have lain among the sheepfolds, yet shall ye be as the wings of a dove that is covered with silver wings, and her feathers like gold." And there is this from the 55th Psalm: "The enemy crieth so, and the ungodly cometh on so fast; for they are minded to do me some mischief, so maliciously are they set against me. My heart is disquieted within me, and the fear of death is fallen upon me. Fearfulness and trembling are come upon me, and an horrible dread hath overwhelmed me. And I said, O that I had wings like a dove! for then would I flee away, and be at rest." This last is the voice of the American princess, Milly Theale, and the first is the acknowledgment of her power by those who betrayed her, Kate Croy and her lover, Merton Densher—a beautiful panther of a woman and her sensitive young man. For those who have read the story these lines from the Psalms will re-expand the whole book. For those who have not read it they should make a promise certain to be kept.

The story is simple. Kate Croy and Merton Densher wish to marry but are prevented because of Densher's poverty and because Kate's aunt wishes her to marry money and position. When Milly Theale, a millionaire American princess, appears in London and is discovered to be mortally ill,

Kate plots that Densher shall marry Milly, inherit her money when she dies and then marry Kate. Milly learns of the plot, but at her hastened death leaves Densher her money just the same. Densher refuses the money and also refuses to marry Kate. It is a melodrama of renunciation and remorse, of blessings confounding betrayals, of beauty casting too sharp a light to be borne upon the ugliness in which the human spirit struggles. It is also the story of the creation of conscience and the creation of genuine motive in Densher.

There are many other things of importance, but I want to fasten on Densher, for it is only on Densher that the Wings can spread or give the effect of their beat on others. Densher is both the sacrifice offered to the Wings and the test of their power. It is true that the others needed an "ideal" of some sort to reject or abuse, or evade or overcome; only Densher could deeply use Milly without at the same time losing her. Densher comes out not with a bad conscience or a good conscience; the one ought to be for Kate, the other for the titled adventurer, Lord Mark, who "reveals" the plot to Milly. Densher comes out with created conscience—the very "agen-bite of inwit"—and the assertion of conscience is his form of action. He struggles with his own odium and discovers his own self, longing to embrace Kate but unable to do so. This is the stroke of conscience: "As to their final impulse or their final remedy, the need to bury in the dark blindness of each other's arms the knowledge of each other that they couldn't undo." Densher's conscience prevents at the same time that it invites. His weakness is that he is incapable of his own conscience when it is confronted with the conditions of life. This is the course of the last two hundred pages of the novel: the realization and assertion of conscience in the name of, and at the same time destroying, the joy of life. And the conscience is good in every case but Milly.

Kate makes poetic versions of reality, she makes ideals smack of her own needs, and promotes steady action, but her poetics cannot dispel Densher's awkward conscience. Milly, on the contrary, makes disconcerting poetry which gives form to his awkward conscience, and her highest effort is when she tells him, just after he has perceived her to be either divine in trust or inscrutable in mercy, "If I *want* to live I can." This she generates in her spirit and by it she generates spirit in others; it represents pretty nearly all the substance she has. It is this poetics which teaches Densher that loyalty might be another kind of lie, an uncandid profession of motive, and that their fates are mixed. He knew her life was in his hands and that he might kill her.

Thus Kate uses her body because it was the very form of her will. Milly resorts to her spirit and when it fails of aims appropriate to it, she turns her face to the wall. Densher, confronted with both, wrestles waiting in his darkness, building his conscience, forcing Milly toward her death, forcing Kate to a full declaration of herself, of her sublime talent for life no matter what, and forcing himself finally to that assertion of conscience which destroys the incentive of his adventure. It becomes glib, and foul. Densher by his act makes the book a testing of Kate, not of good or bad, but of what she is: of the truth in her. Milly stands, or floats, above all she *dies* behind him: a test of what she stands for when she is not there. It is so we can see this fully that Densher is made to wrestle so long between decency and loyalty: wrestling with Kate's strength in his loins, not his own which she has taken from him in her embrace; wrestling then with his own condition, his own abjectness and with the ideal strength of the girl in white, Milly, who will no longer see him until at the last feasible moment she makes him the permanent accursed gift of the strength of her forgiveness. So Densher pays for his conscience by succumbing to the last temptation of enacted goodness: to go in for forgiveness under the image of inscrutable mercy.

In taking such views of James's novel several precautions ought to be taken so that other values will not be overlooked or forgotten. There are many things in the novel without which the conscience and the motive would be worthless: things that are there and that in their own way make an extraordinary amount of giving and doing and seeing. There is the sequence of the images of seas, tides, and waves. There is the ever renewable series of detached lyric reflections on the feel of morals and on the feel of life under the convulsive distortions afforded by living with people in any discriminating stage of consciousness at all. And there is in this novel, beginning exactly in the middle, the image of Venice, at first attached to Milly, then to Densher, in phase after phase of what the book is about. I select only these: The Venice of the joy and the dread of life; the Venice of all evil; and the Venice profaned and bewildered, in the first sea-storm of autumn, during Densher's three days of temptation. All these are joined, I think, in Densher's emergent rock in the gray expanse of straightness; and together they make a form for the novel where the things are their own meaning beyond any conscience.

But there is another or final precaution which has to do with the estimation of the fable of good and evil which is the book's conceptual form. What does this fable think of its three characters at the end? We see Kate sitting by the wakened evil of her father and of her sister's family. Milly is dead and has taken the posthumous action of her absolute goodness and beauty. Densher is the image of absolute weakness, all that cannot live, but which judges life not quite up to what it is. In Kate there is some nobility; she got or will get some of the money and some of the strength. In Densher there is some odium, but he can never again be so weak, for he has found under Milly and in Kate a measure for his weakness.

I think it all depends on the Christmas letter from Milly: the unread vision in the higher dream; it depends, that is, on your reasons why neither Kate nor Densher would open it. Densher was equal only to the idea of it. Kate could learn anything; she was equal to everything but the idea, she could survive everything but the ideal. Densher had to make himself a hero as Milly had to make herself a martyr, but Kate had to make out of herself nothing but the best of what life is. The curiosity is that it is the Kates who are uncommon everywhere; the Millys and Denshers are common enough in type—only the riches, the excesses, are uncommon, and those only perhaps because we are not usually allowed to see them. But Milly is a princess as well as a dove, and she guards Kate always for her sublime talent for life, in the face of which her mere corruption does not matter. Yet the wings spread; there is the vision in the higher dream, and although we do not know what it is, it is nevertheless read in the beauty of the perception.

It is exactly like—and so we come full circle in James's tour of human sensibility—what the publishing scoundrel saw in the eyes of Miss Tita in *The Aspern Papers*, force of soul, or what we all hear in Fleda Vetch's silent cry at the conflagration in *The Spoils of Poynton*.

R. P. BLACKMUR

The Aspern Papers

CHAPTER I

I HAD TAKEN Mrs. Prest into my confidence; in truth without her I should have made but little advance, for the fruitful idea in the whole business dropped from her friendly lips. It was she who invented the short cut, who severed the Gordian knot. It is not supposed to be the nature of women to rise as a general thing to the largest and most liberal view —I mean of a practical scheme; but it has struck me that they sometimes throw off a bold conception—such as a man would not have risen to—with singular serenity. "Simply ask them to take you in on the footing of a lodger"—I don't think that unaided I should have risen to that. I was beating about the bush, trying to be ingenious, wondering by what combination of arts I might become an acquaintance, when she offered this happy suggestion that the way to become an acquaintance was first to become an inmate. Her actual knowledge of the Misses Bordereau was scarcely larger than mine, and indeed I had brought with me from England some definite facts which were new to her. Their name had been mixed up ages before with one of the greatest names of the century, and they lived now in Venice in obscurity, on very small means, unvisited, unapproachable, in a dilapidated old palace on an out-of-the-way canal: this was the substance of my friend's impression of them. She herself had been established in Venice for fifteen years and had done a great deal of good there; but the circle of her benevolence did not include the two shy, mysterious, and, as it was somehow supposed, scarcely respectable Americans (they were believed to have lost in their long exile all national quality, besides having had, as their name implied, some French strain in their origin), who asked no

favours and desired no attention. In the early years of her
residence she had made an attempt to see them, but this
had been successful only as regards the little one, as Mrs.
Prest called the niece; though in reality, as I afterwards
learned, she was considerably the bigger of the two. She
had heard Miss Bordereau was ill and had a suspicion that
she was in want; and she had gone to the house to offer
assistance, so that if there were suffering (and American
suffering), she should at least not have it on her conscience.
The "little one" received her in the great cold, tarnished
Venetian sala, the central hall of the house, paved with
marble and roofed with dim cross-beams, and did not even
ask her to sit down. This was not encouraging for me, who
wished to sit so fast, and I remarked as much to Mrs. Prest.
She however replied with profundity, "Ah, but there's all
the difference: I went to confer a favour and you will go
to ask one. If they are proud you will be on the right side."
And she offered to show me their house to begin with—to
row me thither in her gondola. I let her know that I had
already been to look at it half a dozen times; but I accepted
her invitation, for it charmed me to hover about the place.
I had made my way to it the day after my arrival in Venice
(it had been described to me in advance by the friend in
England to whom I owed definite information as to their
possession of the papers), and I had besieged it with my
eyes while I considered my plan of campaign. Jeffrey Aspern had never been in it that I knew of; but some note of
his voice seemed to abide there by a roundabout implication, a faint reverberation

Mrs. Prest knew nothing about the papers, but she was
interested in my curiosity, as she was always interested in
the joys and sorrows of her friends. As we went, however,
in her gondola, gliding there under the sociable hood with
the bright Venetian picture framed on either side by the
movable window, I could see that she was amused by my
infatuation, the way my interest in the papers had become
a fixed idea. "One would think you expected to find in them
the answer to the riddle of the universe," she said; and I denied the impeachment only by replying that if I had to
choose between that precious solution and a bundle of

Jeffrey Aspern's letters I knew indeed which would appear to me the greater boon. She pretended to make light of his genius and I took no pains to defend him. One doesn't defend one's god: one's god is in himself a defence. Besides, to-day, after his long comparative obscuration, he hangs high in the heaven of our literature, for all the world to see; he is a part of the light by which we walk. The most I said was that he was no doubt not a woman's poet: to which she rejoined aptly enough that he had been at least Miss Bordereau's. The strange thing had been for me to discover in England that she was still alive: it was as if I had been told Mrs. Siddons was, or Queen Caroline, or the famous Lady Hamilton, for it seemed to me that she belonged to a generation as extinct. "Why, she must be tremendously old— at least a hundred," I had said; but on coming to consider dates I saw that it was not strictly necessary that she should have exceeded by very much the common span. None the less she was very far advanced in life and her relations with Jeffrey Aspern had occurred in her early womanhood. "That is her excuse," said Mrs. Prest, half sententiously and yet also somewhat as if she were ashamed of making a speech so little in the real tone of Venice. As if a woman needed an excuse for having loved the divine poet! He had been not only one of the most brilliant minds of his day (and in those years, when the century was young, there were, as every one knows, many), but one of the most genial men and one of the handsomest.

The niece, according to Mrs. Prest, was not so old, and she risked the conjecture that she was only a grand-niece. This was possible; I had nothing but my share in the very limited knowledge of my English fellow-worshipper John Cumnor, who had never seen the couple. The world, as I say, had recognised Jeffrey Aspern, but Cumnor and I had recognised him most. The multitude, to-day, flocked to his temple, but of that temple he and I regarded ourselves as the ministers. We held, justly, as I think, that we had done more for his memory than any one else, and we had done it by opening lights into his life. He had nothing to fear from us because he had nothing to fear from the truth, which alone at such a distance of time we could be interested in establishing. His early death had been the only dark spot in his life, unless the papers in Miss Bordereau's hands should perversely bring out others. There had been an impression about 1825 that he had "treated her badly," just as there had been an impression that he had "served," as the London populace says, several other ladies in the same way. Each of these cases Cumnor and I had been able to investigate, and we had never failed to acquit him conscientiously of shabby behaviour. I judged him perhaps more indulgently than my friend; certainly, at any rate, it appeared to me that no man could have walked straighter in the given circumstances. These were almost always awkward. Half the women of his time, to speak liberally, had flung themselves at his head, and out of this pernicious fashion many complications, some of them grave, had not failed to arise. He was not a woman's poet, as I had said to Mrs. Prest, in the modern phase of his reputation; but the situation had been different when the man's own voice was mingled with his song. That voice, by every testimony, was one of the sweetest ever heard. "Orpheus and the Mænads!" was the exclamation that rose to my lips when I first turned over his correspondence. Almost all the Mænads were unreasonable and many of them insupportable; it struck me in short that he was kinder, more considerate than, in his place (if I could imagine myself in such a place!) I should have been.

It was certainly strange beyond all strangeness, and I shall not take up space with attempting to explain it, that whereas in all these other lines of research we had to deal with phantoms and dust, the mere echoes of echoes, the one living source of information that had lingered on into our time had been unheeded by us. Every one of Aspern's contemporaries had, according to our belief, passed away; we had not been able to look into a single pair of eyes into which his had looked or to feel a transmitted contact in any aged hand that his had touched. Most dead of all did poor Miss Bordereau appear, and yet she alone had survived. We exhausted in the course of months our wonder that we had not found her out sooner, and the substance of our explanation was that she had kept so quiet. The poor lady on the whole had had reason for doing so. But it was a revelation to us that it was possible to keep so quiet as that in the latter half of the nineteenth century—the age of newspapers and telegrams and photographs and interviewers. And she had taken no great trouble about it either: she had not hidden herself away in an undiscoverable hole; she had boldly settled down in a city of exhibition. The only secret of her safety that we could perceive was that Venice contained so many curiosities that were greater than she. And then accident had somehow favoured her, as was shown for example in the fact that Mrs. Prest had never happened to mention her to me, though I had spent three weeks in Venice—under her nose, as it were—five years before. Mrs. Prest had not mentioned this much to any one; she appeared almost to have forgotten she was there. Of course she had not the responsibilities of an editor. It was no explanation of the old woman's having eluded us to say that she lived abroad, for our researches had again and again taken us (not only by correspondence but by personal inquiry) to France, to Germany, to Italy, in which countries, not counting his important stay in England, so many of the too few years of Aspern's career were spent. We were glad to think at least that in all our publishings (some people consider I believe that we have overdone them), we had only touched in passing and in the most discreet manner on Miss Bordereau's connection. Oddly enough, even if we had had the material (and we often wondered what had become of it), it would have been the most difficult episode to handle.

The gondola stopped, the old palace was there; it was a house of the class which in Venice carries even in extreme dilapidation the dignified name. "How charming! It's gray and pink!" my companion exclaimed; and that is the most comprehensive description of it. It was not particularly old, only two or three centuries; and it had an air not so much of decay as of quiet discouragement, as if it had rather missed its career. But its wide front, with a stone balcony from end to end of the *piano nobile* or most important floor, was architectural enough, with the aid of various pilasters and arches; and the stucco with which in the intervals it had long ago been endued was rosy in the April afternoon.

It overlooked a clean, melancholy, unfrequented canal, which had a narrow *riva* or convenient footway on either side. "I don't know why—there are no brick gables," said Mrs. Prest, "but this corner has seemed to me before more Dutch than Italian, more like Amsterdam than like Venice. It's perversely clean, for reasons of its own; and though you can pass on foot scarcely any one ever thinks of doing so. It has the air of a Protestant Sunday. Perhaps the people are afraid of the Misses Bordereau. I daresay they have the reputation of witches."

I forget what answer I made to this—I was given up to two other reflections. The first of these was that if the old lady lived in such a big, imposing house she could not be in any sort of misery and therefore would not be tempted by a chance to let a couple of rooms. I expressed this idea to Mrs. Prest, who gave me a very logical reply. "If she didn't live in a big house how could it be a question of her having rooms to spare? If she were not amply lodged herself you would lack ground to approach her. Besides, a big house here, and especially in this *quartier perdu*, proves nothing at all: it is perfectly compatible with a state of penury. Dilapidated old palazzi, if you will go out of the way for them, are to be had for five shillings a year. And as for the people who live in them—no, until you have explored Venice socially as much as I have you can form no idea of their domestic desolation. They live on nothing, for they have nothing to live on." The other idea that had come into my head was connected with a high blank wall which appeared to confine an expanse of ground on one side of the house. Blank I call it, but it was figured over with the patches that please a painter, repaired breaches, crumblings of plaster, extrusions of brick that had turned pink with time; and a few thin trees, with the poles of certain rickety trellises, were visible over the top. The place was a garden and apparently it belonged to the house. It suddenly occurred to me that if it did belong to the house I had my pretext.

I sat looking out on all this with Mrs. Prest (it was covered with the golden glow of Venice) from the shade of our *felze*, and she asked me if I would go in then, while she waited for me, or come back another time. At first I could not decide—it was doubtless very weak of me. I wanted still to think I *might* get a footing, and I was afraid to meet failure, for it would leave me, as I remarked to my companion, without another arrow for my bow. "Why not another?" she inquired, as I sat there hesitating and thinking it over; and she wished to know why even now and before taking the trouble of becoming an inmate (which might be wretchedly uncomfortable after all, even if it succeeded), I had not the resource of simply offering them a sum of money down. In that way I might obtain the documents without bad nights.

"Dearest lady," I exclaimed, "excuse the impatience of my tone when I suggest that you must have forgotten the very fact (surely I communicated it to you) which pushed me to throw myself upon your ingenuity. The old woman won't have the documents spoken of; they are personal, delicate, intimate, and she hasn't modern notions, God bless her! If I should sound that note first I should certainly spoil the game. I can arrive at the papers only by putting her off her guard, and I can put her off her guard only by ingratiating diplomatic practices. Hypocrisy, duplicity are my only chance. I am sorry for it, but for Jeffrey Aspern's sake I would do worse still. First I must take tea with her; then tackle the main job." And I told over what had happened to John Cumnor when he wrote to her. No notice whatever had been taken of his first letter, and the second had been answered very sharply, in six lines, by the niece. "Miss Bordereau requested her to say that she could not imagine what he meant by troubling them. They had none of Mr. Aspern's papers, and if they had should never think of showing them to any one on any account whatever. She didn't know what he was talking about and begged he would let her alone." I certainly did not want to be met that way.

"Well," said Mrs. Prest, after a moment, provokingly, "perhaps after all they haven't any of his things. If they deny it flat how are you sure?"

"John Cumnor is sure, and it would take me long to tell you how his conviction, or his very strong presumption—

strong enough to stand against the old lady's not unnatural fib—has built itself up. Besides, he makes much of the internal evidence of the niece's letter."

"The internal evidence?"

"Her calling him 'Mr. Aspern.' "

"I don't see what that proves."

"It proves familiarity, and familiarity implies the possession of mementoes, of relics. I can't tell you how that 'Mr.' touches me—how it bridges over the gulf of time and brings our hero near to me—nor what an edge it gives to my desire to see Juliana. You don't say 'Mr.' Shakespeare."

"Would I, any more, if I had a box full of his letters?"

"Yes, if he had been your lover and some one wanted them!" And I added that John Cumnor was so convinced, and so all the more convinced by Miss Bordereau's tone, that he would have come himself to Venice on the business were it not that for him there was the obstacle that it would be difficult to disprove his identity with the person who had written to them, which the old ladies would be sure to suspect in spite of dissimulation and a change of name. If they were to ask him point-blank if he were not their correspondent it would be too awkward for him to lie; whereas I was fortunately not tied in that way. I was a fresh hand and could say no without lying.

"But you will have to change your name," said Mrs. Prest. "Juliana lives out of the world as much as it is possible to live, but none the less she has probably heard of Mr. Aspern's editors; she perhaps possesses what you have published."

"I have thought of that," I returned; and I drew out of my pocket-book a visiting-card, neatly engraved with a name that was not my own.

"You are very extravagant; you might have written it," said my companion.

"This looks more genuine."

"Certainly, you are prepared to go far! But it will be awkward about your letters; they won't come to you in that mask."

"My banker will take them in and I will go every day to fetch them. It will give me a little walk."

"Shall you only depend upon that?" asked Mrs. Prest. "Aren't you coming to see me?"

"Oh, you will have left Venice, for the hot months, long before there are any results. I am prepared to roast all summer—as well as hereafter, perhaps you'll say! Meanwhile, John Cumnor will bombard me with letters addressed, in my feigned name, to the care of the *padrona*."

"She will recognize his hand," my companion suggested.

"On the envelope he can disguise it."

"Well, you're a precious pair! Doesn't it occur to you that even if you are able to say you are not Mr. Cumnor in person they may still suspect you of being his emissary?"

"Certainly, and I see only one way to parry that."

"And what may that be?"

I hesitated a moment. "To make love to the niece."

"Ah," cried Mrs. Prest, "wait till you see her!"

CHAPTER II

"I MUST WORK THE GARDEN—I must work the garden,"
I said to myself, five minutes later, as I waited, upstairs, in
the long, dusky sala, where the bare scagliola floor gleamed
vaguely in a chink of the closed shutters. The place was
impressive but it looked cold and cautious. Mrs. Prest had
floated away, giving me a rendezvous at the end of half an
hour by some neighbouring watersteps; and I had been let
into the house, after pulling the rusty bell-wire, by a little
red-headed, white-faced maid-servant, who was very young
and not ugly and wore clicking pattens and a shawl in the
fashion of a hood. She had not contented herself with opening the door from above by the usual arrangement of a
creaking pulley, though she had looked down at me first
from an upper window, dropping the inevitable challenge
which in Italy precedes the hospitable act. As a general
thing I was irritated by this survival of mediæval manners,
though as I liked the old I suppose I ought to have liked it;
but I was so determined to be genial that I took my false
card out of my pocket and held it up to her, smiling as if
it were a magic token. It had the effect of one indeed, for
it brought her, as I say, all the way down. I begged her to
hand it to her mistress, having first written on it in Italian
the words, "Could you very kindly see a gentleman, an
American, for a moment?" The little maid was not hostile,
and I reflected that even that was perhaps something
gained. She coloured, she smiled and looked both frightened
and pleased. I could see that my arrival was a great affair,
that visits were rare in that house, and that she was a person
who would have liked a sociable place. When she pushed
forward the heavy door behind me I felt that I had a foot in

the citadel. She pattered across the damp, stony lower hall
and I followed her up the high staircase—stonier still, as
it seemed—without an invitation. I think she had meant I
should wait for her below, but such was not my idea, and I
took up my station in the sala. She flitted, at the far end of
it, into impenetrable regions, and I looked at the place with
my heart beating as I had known it to do in the dentist's
parlour. It was gloomy and stately, but it owed its character
almost entirely to its noble shape and to the fine architectural doors—as high as the doors of houses—which, leading into the various rooms, repeated themselves on either
side at intervals. They were surmounted with old faded
painted escutcheons, and here and there, in the spaces
between them, brown pictures, which I perceived to be
bad, in battered frames, were suspended. With the exception of several straw-bottomed chairs with their backs to
the wall, the grand obscure vista contained nothing else to
minister to effect. It was evidently never used save as a
passage, and little even as that. I may add that by the time
the door opened again through which the maid-servant had
escaped, my eyes had grown used to the want of light.

I had not meant by my private ejaculation that I must
cultivate the soil of the tangled enclosure which lay beneath the windows, but the lady who came toward me
from the distance over the hard, shining floor might have
supposed as much from the way in which, as I went rapidly
to meet her, I exclaimed, taking care to speak Italian: "The
garden, the garden—do me the pleasure to tell me if it's
yours!"

She stopped short, looking at me with wonder; and then,
"Nothing here is mine," she answered in English, coldly
and sadly.

"Oh, you are English; how delightful!" I remarked, ingenuously. "But surely the garden belongs to the house?"

"Yes, but the house doesn't belong to me." She was a
long, lean, pale person, habited apparently in a dull-
coloured dressing-gown, and she spoke with a kind of mild
literalness. She did not ask me to sit down, any more than
years before (if she were the niece) she had asked Mrs.
Prest, and we stood face to face in the empty pompous hall.

"Well then, would you kindly tell me to whom I must address myself? I'm afraid you'll think me odiously intrusive, but you know I *must* have a garden—upon my honour I must!"

Her face was not young, but it was simple; it was not fresh, but it was mild. She had large eyes which were not bright, and a great deal of hair which was not "dressed," and long fine hands which were—possibly—not clean. She clasped these members almost convulsively as, with a confused, alarmed look, she broke out, "Oh, don't take it away from us; we like it ourselves!"

"You have the use of it then?"

"Oh yes. If it wasn't for that!" And she gave a shy, melancholy smile.

"Isn't it a luxury, precisely? That's why, intending to be in Venice some weeks, possibly all summer, and having some literary work, some reading and writing to do, so that I must be quiet, and yet if possible a great deal in the open air—that's why I have felt that a garden is really indispensable. I appeal to your own experience," I went on, smiling. "Now can't I look at yours?"

"I don't know, I don't understand," the poor woman murmured, planted there and letting her embarrassed eyes wander all over my strangeness.

"I mean only from one of those windows—such grand ones as you have here—if you will let me open the shutters." And I walked toward the back of the house. When I had advanced half-way I stopped and waited, as if I took it for granted she would accompany me. I had been of necessity very abrupt, but I strove at the same time to give her the impression of extreme courtesy. "I have been looking at furnished rooms all over the place, and it seems impossible to find any with a garden attached. Naturally in a place like Venice gardens are rare. It's absurd if you like, for a man, but I can't live without flowers."

"There are none to speak of down there." She came nearer to me, as if, though she mistrusted me, I had drawn her by an invisible thread. I went on again, and she continued as she followed me: "We have a few, but they are very common. It costs too much to cultivate them; one has to have a man."

"Why shouldn't I be the man?" I asked. "I'll work without wages; or rather I'll put in a gardener. You shall have the sweetest flowers in Venice."

She protested at this, with a queer little sigh which might also have been a gush of rapture at the picture I presented. Then she observed, "We don't know you—we don't know you."

"You know me as much as I know you; that is, much more, because you know my name. And if you are English I am almost a countryman."

"We are not English," said my companion, watching me helplessly while I threw open the shutters of one of the divisions of the wide high window.

"You speak the language so beautifully: might I ask what you are?" Seen from above the garden was certainly shabby; but I perceived at a glance that it had great capabilities. She made no rejoinder, she was so lost in staring at me, and I exclaimed, "You don't mean to say you are also by chance American?"

"I don't know; we used to be."

"Used to be? Surely you haven't changed?"

"It's so many years ago—we are nothing."

"So many years that you have been living here? Well, I don't wonder at that; it's a grand old house. I suppose you all use the garden," I went on, "but I assure you I shouldn't be in your way. I would be very quiet and stay in one corner."

"We all use it?" she repeated after me, vaguely, not coming close to the window but looking at my shoes. She appeared to think me capable of throwing her out.

"I mean all your family, as many as you are."

"There is only one other; she is very old—she never goes down."

"Only one other, in all this great house!" I feigned to be not only amazed but almost scandalised. "Dear lady, you must have space then to spare!"

"To spare?" she repeated, in the same dazed way.

"Why, you surely don't live (two quiet women—I see *you* are quiet, at any rate) in fifty rooms!" Then with a burst of hope and cheer I demanded: "Couldn't you let me two or three? That would set me up!"

I had now struck the note that translated my purpose and I need not reproduce the whole of the tune I played. I ended by making my interlocutress believe that I was an honourable person, though of course I did not even attempt to persuade her that I was not an eccentric one. I repeated that I had studies to pursue; that I wanted quiet; that I delighted in a garden and had vainly sought one up and down the city; that I would undertake that before another month was over the dear old house should be smothered in flowers. I think it was the flowers that won my suit, for I afterwards found that Miss Tita (for such the name of this high tremulous spinster proved somewhat incongruously to be) had an insatiable appetite for them. When I speak of my suit as won I mean that before I left her she had promised that she would refer the question to her aunt. I inquired who her aunt might be and she answered, "Why, Miss Bordereau!" with an air of surprise, as if I might have been expected to know. There were contradictions like this in Tita Bordereau which, as I observed later, contributed to make her an odd and affecting person. It was the study of the two ladies to live so that the world should not touch them, and yet they had never altogether accepted the idea that it never heard of them. In Tita at any rate a grateful susceptibility to human contact had not died out, and contact of a limited order there would be if I should come to live in the house.

"We have never done anything of the sort; we have never had a lodger or any kind of inmate." So much as this she made a point of saying to me. "We are very poor, we live very badly. The rooms are very bare— that you might take; they have nothing in them. I don't know how you would sleep, how you would eat."

"With your permission, I could easily put in a bed and a few tables and chairs. *C'est la moindre des choses* and the affair of an hour or two. I know a little man from whom I can hire what I should want for a few months, for

a trifle, and my gondolier can bring the things round in
his boat. Of course in this great house you must have a
second kitchen, and my servant, who is a wonderfully
handy fellow" (this personage was an evocation of the
moment), "can easily cook me a chop there. My tastes
and habits are of the simplest; I live on flowers!" And then
I ventured to add that if they were very poor it was all
the more reason they should let their rooms. They were
bad economists—I had never heard of such a waste of
material.

I saw in a moment that the good lady had never before
been spoken to in that way, with a kind of humorous firmness which did not exclude sympathy but was on the contrary founded on it. She might easily have told me that my
sympathy was impertinent, but this by good fortune did not
occur to her. I left her with the understanding that she
would consider the matter with her aunt and that I might
come back the next day for their decision.

"The aunt will refuse; she will think the whole proceeding very *louche!*" Mrs. Prest declared shortly after this,
when I had resumed my place in her gondola. She had put
the idea into my head and now (so little are women to be
counted on) she appeared to take a despondent view of it.
Her pessimism provoked me and I pretended to have the
best hopes; I went so far as to say that I had a distinct
presentiment that I should succeed. Upon this Mrs. Prest
broke out, "Oh, I see what's in your head! You fancy
you have made such an impression in a quarter of an
hour that she is dying for you to come and can be depended upon to bring the old one round. If you do get in
you'll count it as a triumph."

I did count it as a triumph, but only for the editor (in
the last analysis), not for the man, who had not the tradition of personal conquest. When I went back on the morrow the little maid-servant conducted me straight through
the long sala (it opened there as before in perfect perspec-
tive and was lighter now, which I thought a good omen)
into the apartment from which the recipient of my former
visit had emerged on that occasion. It was a large shabby
parlour, with a fine old painted ceiling and a strange figure

sitting alone at one of the windows. They come back to me now almost with the palpitation they caused, the successive feelings that accompanied my consciousness that as the door of the room closed behind me I was really face to face with the Juliana of some of Aspern's most exquisite and most renowned lyrics. I grew used to her afterwards, though never completely; but as she sat there before me my heart beat as fast as if the miracle of resurrection had taken place for my benefit. Her presence seemed somehow to contain his, and I felt nearer to him at that first moment of seeing her than I ever had been before or ever have been since. Yes, I remember my emotions in their order, even including a curious little tremor that took me when I saw that the niece was not there. With her, the day before, I had become sufficiently familiar, but it almost exceeded my courage (much as I had longed for the event) to be left alone with such a terrible relic as the aunt. She was too strange, too literally resurgent. Then came a check, with the perception that we were not really face to face, inasmuch as she had over her eyes a horrible green shade which for her, served almost as a mask. I believed for the instant that she had put it on expressly, so that from underneath it she might scrutinise me without being scrutinised herself. At the same time it increased the presumption that there was a ghastly death's-head lurking behind it. The divine Juliana as a grinning skull—the vision hung there until it passed. Then it came to me that she *was* tremendously old—so old that death might take her at any moment, before I had time to get what I wanted from her. The next thought was a correction to that; it lighted up the situation. She would die next week, she would die to-morrow—then I could seize her papers. Meanwhile she sat there neither moving nor speaking. She was very small and shrunken, bent forward, with her hands in her lap. She was dressed in black and her head was wrapped in a piece of old black lace which showed no hair.

My emotion keeping me silent she spoke first, and the remark she made was exactly the most unexpected.

CHAPTER III

"OUR HOUSE is very far from the centre, but the little canal is very *comme il faut*."

"It's the sweetest corner of Venice and I can imagine nothing more charming," I hastened to reply. The old lady's voice was very thin and weak, but it had an agreeable, cultivated murmur and there was wonder in the thought that that individual note had been in Jeffrey Aspern's ear.

"Please to sit down there. I hear very well," she said quietly, as if perhaps I had been shouting at her; and the chair she pointed to was at a certain distance. I took possession of it, telling her that I was perfectly aware that I had intruded, that I had not been properly introduced and could only throw myself upon her indulgence. Perhaps the other lady, the one I had had the honour of seeing the day before, would have explained to her about the garden. That was literally what had given me courage to take a step so unconventional. I had fallen in love at sight with the whole place (she herself probably was so used to it that she did not know the impression it was capable of making on a stranger), and I had felt it was really a case to risk something. Was her own kindness in receiving me a sign that I was not wholly out in my calculation? It would render me extremely happy to think so. I could give her my word of honour that I was a most respectable, inoffensive person and that as an inmate they would be barely conscious of my existence. I would conform to any regulations, any restrictions if they would only let me enjoy the garden. Moreover I should be delighted to give her references, guarantees; they would be of the very best, both in Venice and in England as well as in America.

She listened to me in perfect stillness and I felt that she was looking at me with great attention, though I could see only the lower part of her bleached and shrivelled face. Independently of the refining process of old age it had a delicacy which once must have been great. She had been very fair, she had had a wonderful complexion. She was silent a little after I had ceased speaking; then she inquired, "If you are so fond of a garden why don't you go to *terra firma*, where there are so many far better than this?"

"Oh, it's the combination!" I answered, smiling; and then, with rather a flight of fancy, "It's the idea of a garden in the middle of the sea."

"It's not in the middle of the sea; you can't see the water."

I stared a moment, wondering whether she wished to convict me of fraud. "Can't see the water? Why, dear madam, I can come up to the very gate in my boat."

She appeared inconsequent, for she said vaguely in reply to this, "Yes, if you have got a boat. I haven't any; it's many years since I have been in one of the gondolas." She uttered these words as if the gondolas were a curious faraway craft which she knew only by hearsay.

"Let me assure you of the pleasure with which I would put mine at your service!" I exclaimed. I had scarcely said this however before I became aware that the speech was in questionable taste and might also do me the injury of making me appear too eager, too possessed of a hidden motive. But the old woman remained impenetrable and her attitude bothered me by suggesting that she had a fuller vision of me than I had of her. She gave me no thanks for my somewhat extravagant offer but remarked that the lady I had seen the day before was her niece; she would presently come in. She had asked her to stay away a little on purpose, because she herself wished to see me at first alone. She relapsed into silence and I asked myself why she had judged this necessary and what was coming yet; also whether I might venture on some judicious remark in praise of her companion. I went so far as to say that I should be delighted to see her again: she had been so very courteous to me, considering how odd she must have thought me—a declaration which drew from Miss Bordereau another of her whimsical speeches.

"She has very good manners; I bred her up myself!" I was on the point of saying that that accounted for the easy grace of the niece, but I arrested myself in time, and the next moment the old woman went on: "I don't care who you may be—I don't want to know; it signifies very little to-day." This had all the air of being a formula of dismissal, as if her next words would be that I might take myself off now that she had had the amusement of looking on the face of such a monster of indiscretion. Therefore I was all the more surprised when she added, with her soft, venerable quaver, "You may have as many rooms as you like—if you will pay a good deal of money."

I hesitated but for a single instant, long enough to ask myself what she meant in particular by this condition. First it struck me that she must have really a large sum in her mind; then I reasoned quickly that her idea of a large sum would probably not correspond to my own. My deliberation, I think, was not so visible as to diminish the promptitude with which I replied, "I will pay with pleasure and of course in advance whatever you may think it proper to ask me."

"Well then, a thousand francs a month," she rejoined instantly, while her baffling green shade continued to cover her attitude.

The figure, as they say, was startling and my logic had been at fault. The sum she had mentioned was, by the Venetian measure of such matters, exceedingly large; there was many an old palace in an out-of-the-way corner that I might on such terms have enjoyed by the year. But so far as my small means allowed I was prepared to spend money, and my decision was quickly taken. I would pay her with a smiling face what she asked, but in that case I would give myself the compensation of extracting the papers from her for nothing. Moreover if she had asked five times as much I should have risen to the occasion; so odious would it have appeared to me to stand chaffering with Aspern's Juliana. It was queer enough to have a question of money with her at all. I assured her that her views perfectly met my own and that on the morrow I should have the pleasure of putting three months' rent into her hand. She received this announcement with serenity and with no apparent sense that after all it would be becoming of her to say that I ought to see the rooms first. This did not occur to her and indeed her serenity was mainly what I wanted. Our little bargain was just concluded when the door opened and the younger lady appeared on the threshold. As soon as Miss Bordereau saw her niece she cried out almost gaily, "He will give three thousand—three thousand to-morrow!"

Miss Tita stood still, with her patient eyes turning from one of us to the other; then she inquired, scarcely above her breath, "Do you mean francs?"

"Did you mean francs or dollars?" the old woman asked of me at this.

"I think francs were what you said," I answered, smiling.

"That is very good," said Miss Tita, as if she had become conscious that her own question might have looked over-reaching.

"What do *you* know? You are ignorant," Miss Bordereau remarked; not with acerbity but with a strange, soft coldness.

"Yes, of money—certainly of money!" Miss Tita hastened to exclaim.

"I am sure you have your own branches of knowledge," I took the liberty of saying, genially. There was something painful to me, somehow, in the turn the conversation had taken, in the discussion of the rent.

"She had a very good education when she was young. I looked into that myself," said Miss Bordereau. Then she added, "But she has learned nothing since."

"I have always been with you," Miss Tita rejoined very mildly, and evidently with no intention of making an epigram.

"Yes, but for that!" her aunt declared, with more satirical force. She evidently meant that but for this her niece would never have got on at all; the point of the observa-

tion however being lost on Miss Tita, though she blushed
at hearing her history revealed to a stranger. Miss Bordereau went on, addressing herself to me: "And what time
will you come to-morrow with the money?"

"The sooner the better. If it suits you I will come at
noon."

"I am always here but I have my hours," said the old
woman, as if her convenience were not to be taken for
granted.

"You mean the times when you receive?"

"I never receive. But I will see you at noon, when you
come with the money."

"Very good, I shall be punctual;" and I added, "May
I shake hands with you, on our contract?" I thought there
ought to be some little form, it would make me really feel
easier, for I foresaw that there would be no other. Besides,
though Miss Bordereau could not to-day be called personally attractive and there was something even in her wasted
antiquity that bade one stand at one's distance, I felt an irresistible desire to hold in my own for a moment the hand
that Jeffrey Aspern had pressed.

For a minute she made no answer and I saw that my
proposal failed to meet with her approbation. She indulged
in no movement of withdrawal, which I half expected; she
only said coldly, "I belong to a time when that was not the
custom."

I felt rather snubbed but I exclaimed good-humouredly
to Miss Tita, "Oh, you will do as well!" I shook hands
with her while she replied, with a small flutter, "Yes, yes,
to show it's all arranged!"

"Shall you bring the money in gold?" Miss Bordereau
demanded, as I was turning to the door.

I looked at her a moment. "Aren't you a little afraid,
after all, of keeping such a sum as that in the house?" It
was not that I was annoyed at her avidity but I was really
struck with the disparity between such a treasure and such
scanty means of guarding it.

"Whom should I be afraid of if I am not afraid of you?"
she asked with her shrunken grimness.

"Ah well," said I, laughing, "I shall be in point of fact a protector and I will bring gold if you prefer."

"Thank you," the old woman returned with dignity and with an inclination of her head which evidently signified that I might depart. I passed out of the room, reflecting that it would not be easy to circumvent her. As I stood in the sala again I saw that Miss Tita had followed me and I supposed that as her aunt had neglected to suggest that I should take a look at my quarters it was her purpose to repair the omission. But she made no such suggestion; she only stood there with a dim, though not a languid smile, and with an effect of irresponsible, incompetent youth which was almost comically at variance with the faded facts of her person. She was not infirm, like her aunt, but she struck me as still more helpless, because her inefficiency was spiritual, which was not the case with Miss Bordereau's. I waited to see if she would offer to show me the rest of the house, but I did not precipitate the question, inasmuch as my plan was from this moment to spend as much of my time as possible in her society. I only observed at the end of a minute:

"I have had better fortune than I hoped. It was very kind of her to see me. Perhaps you said a good word for me."

"It was the idea of the money," said Miss Tita.

"And did you suggest that?"

"I told her that you would perhaps give a good deal."

"What made you think that?"

"I told her I thought you were rich."

"And what put that idea into your head?"

"I don't know; the way you talked."

"Dear me, I must talk differently now," I declared. "I'm sorry to say it's not the case."

"Well," said Miss Tita, "I think that in Venice the *forestieri*, in general, often give a great deal for something that after all isn't much." She appeared to make this remark with a comforting intention, to wish to remind me that if I had been extravagant I was not really foolishly singular. We walked together along the sala, and as I took its magnificent measure I said to her that I was afraid it would not form a part of my *quartiere*. Were my rooms by chance to be among those that opened into it? "Not if you go above, on the second floor," she answered with a little startled air, as if she had rather taken for granted I would know my proper place.

"And I infer that that's where your aunt would like me to be."

"She said your apartments ought to be very distinct."

"That certainly would be best." And I listened with respect while she told me that up above I was free to take whatever I liked; that there was another staircase, but only from the floor on which we stood, and that to pass from it to the garden-story or to come up to my lodging I should have in effect to cross the great hall. This was an immense point gained; I foresaw that it would constitute my whole leverage in my relations with the two ladies. When I asked Miss Tita how I was to manage at present to find my way up she replied with an access of that sociable shyness which constantly marked her manner.

"Perhaps you can't. I don't see—unless I should go with you." She evidently had not thought of this before.

We ascended to the upper floor and visited a long succession of empty rooms. The best of them looked over the garden; some of the others had a view of the blue lagoon, above the opposite rough-tiled housetops. They were all dusty and even a little disfigured with long neglect, but I saw that by spending a few hundred francs I should be able to convert three or four of them into a convenient habitation. My experiment was turning out costly, yet now that I had all but taken possession I ceased to allow this to trouble me. I mentioned to my companion a few of the things that I should put in, but she replied rather more precipitately than usual that I might do exactly what I liked; she seemed to wish to notify me that the Misses Bordereau would take no overt interest in my proceedings. I guessed that her aunt had instructed her to adopt this tone, and I may as well say now that I came afterwards to distinguish perfectly (as I believed) between the speeches she made on her own responsibility and those the old lady imposed upon her. She took no notice of the unswept con-

dition of the rooms and indulged in no explanations nor
apologies. I said to myself that this was a sign that Juliana
and her niece (disenchanting idea!) were untidy persons,
with a low Italian standard; but I afterwards recognized
that a lodger who had forced an entrance had no *locus
standi* as a critic. We looked out of a good many windows,
for there was nothing within the rooms to look at, and
still I wanted to linger. I asked her what several different
objects in the prospect might be, but in no case did she
appear to know. She was evidently not familiar with the
view—it was as if she had not looked at it for years—and I
presently saw that she was too preoccupied with something else to pretend to care for it. Suddenly she said—the
remark was not suggested:

"I don't know whether it will make any difference to
you, but the money is for me."

"The money?"

"The money you are going to bring."

"Why, you'll make me wish to stay here two or three
years." I spoke as benevolently as possible, though it had
begun to act on my nerves that with these women so associated with Aspern the pecuniary question should constantly come back.

"That would be very good for me," she replied, smiling.

"You put me on my honour!"

She looked as if she failed to understand this, but went
on: "She wants me to have more. She thinks she is going
to die."

"Ah, not soon, I hope!" I exclaimed, with genuine
feeling. I had perfectly considered the possibility that she
would destroy her papers on the day she should feel her
end really approach. I believed that she would cling to
them till then and I think I had an idea that she read
Aspern's letters over every night or at least pressed them
to her withered lips. I would have given a good deal to
have a glimpse of the latter spectacle. I asked Miss Tita
if the old lady were seriously ill and she replied that she
was only very tired—she had lived so very, very long. That
was what she said herself—she wanted to die for a change.
Besides, all her friends were dead long ago; either they

ought to have remained or she ought to have gone. That was another thing her aunt often said—she was not at all content.

"But people don't die when they like, do they?" Miss Tita inquired. I took the liberty of asking why, if there was actually enough money to maintain both of them, there would not be more than enough in case of her being left alone. She considered this difficult problem a moment and then she said, "Oh, well, you know, she takes care of me. She thinks that when I'm alone I shall be a great fool, I shall not know how to manage."

"I should have supposed rather that you took care of her. I'm afraid she is very proud."

"Why, have you discovered that already?" Miss Tita cried, with the glimmer of an illumination in her face.

"I was shut up with her there for a considerable time, and she struck me, she interested me extremely. It didn't take me long to make my discovery. She won't have much to say to me while I'm here."

"No, I don't think she will," my companion averred.

"Do you suppose she has some suspicion of me?"

Miss Tita's honest eyes gave me no sign that I had touched a mark. "I shouldn't think so—letting you in after all so easily."

"Oh, so easily! she has covered her risk. But where is it that one could take an advantage of her?"

"I oughtn't to tell you if I knew, ought I?" And Miss Tita added, before I had time to reply to this, smiling dolefully, "Do you think we have any weak points?"

"That's exactly what I'm asking. You would only have to mention them for me to respect them religiously."

She looked at me, at this, with that air of timid but candid and even gratified curiosity with which she had confronted me from the first; and then she said, "There is nothing to tell. We are terribly quiet. I don't know how the days pass. We have no life."

"I wish I might think that I should bring you a little."

"Oh, we know what we want," she went on. "It's all right."

There were various things I desired to ask her: how in

the world they did live; whether they had any friends or visitors, any relations in America or in other countries. But I judged such an inquiry would be premature; I must leave it to a later chance. "Well, don't *you* be proud," I contented myself with saying. "Don't hide from me altogether."

"Oh, I must stay with my aunt," she returned, without looking at me. And at the same moment, abruptly, without any ceremony of parting, she quitted me and disappeared, leaving me to make my own way downstairs. I remained a while longer, wandering about the bright desert (the sun was pouring in) of the old house, thinking the situation over on the spot. Not even the pattering little *serva* came to look after me and I reflected that after all this treatment showed confidence.

CHAPTER IV

PERHAPS IT DID, but all the same, six weeks later, towards the middle of June, the moment when Mrs. Prest undertook her annual migration, I had made no measureable advance. I was obliged to confess to her that I had no results to speak of. My first step had been unexpectedly rapid, but there was no appearance that it would be followed by a second. I was a thousand miles from taking tea with my hostesses—that privilege of which, as I reminded Mrs. Prest, we both had had a vision. She reproached me with wanting boldness and I answered that even to be bold you must have an opportunity: you may push on through a breach but you can't batter down a dead wall. She answered that the breach I had already made was big enough to admit an army and accused me of wasting precious hours in whimpering in her salon when I ought to have been carrying on the struggle in the field. It is true that I went to see her very often, on the theory that it would console me (I freely expressed my discouragement) for my want of success on my own premises. But I began to perceive that it did not console me to be perpetually chaffed for my scruples, especially when I was really so vigilant; and I was rather glad when my derisive friend closed her house for the summer. She had expected to gather amusement from the drama of my intercourse with the Misses Bordereau and she was disappointed that the intercourse, and consequently the drama, had not come off. "They'll lead you on to your ruin," she said before she left Venice. "They'll get all your money without showing you a scrap." I think I settled down to my business with more concentration after she had gone away.

It was a fact that up to that time I had not, save on a single brief occasion, had even a moment's contact with my queer hostesses. The exception had occurred when I carried them according to my promise the terrible three thousand francs. Then I found Miss Tita waiting for me in the hall, and she took the money from my hand so that I did not see her aunt. The old lady had promised to receive me, but she apparently thought nothing of breaking that vow. The money was contained in a bag of chamois leather, of respectable dimensions, which my banker had given me, and Miss Tita had to make a big fist to receive it. This she did with extreme solemnity, though I tried to treat the affair a little as a joke. It was in no jocular strain, yet it was with simplicity, that she inquired, weighing the money in her two palms: "Don't you think it's too much?" To which I replied that that would depend upon the amount of pleasure I should get for it. Hereupon she turned away from me quickly, as she had done the day before, murmuring in a tone different from any she had used hitherto: "Oh, pleasure, pleasure—there's no pleasure in this house!"

After this, for a long time, I never saw her, and I wondered that the common chances of the day should not have helped us to meet. It could only be evident that she was immensely on her guard against them; and in addition to this the house was so big that for each other we were lost in it. I used to look out for her hopefully as I crossed the sala in my comings and goings, but I was not rewarded with a glimpse of the tail of her dress. It was as if she never peeped out of her aunt's apartment. I used to wonder what she did there week after week and year after year. I had never encountered such a violent *parti pris* of seclusion; it was more than keeping quiet—it was like hunted creatures feigning death. The two ladies appeared to have no visitors whatever and no sort of contact with the world. I judged at least that people could not have come to the house and that Miss Tita could not have gone out without my having some observation of it. I did what I disliked myself for doing (reflecting that it was only once in a way): I questioned my servant about their habits and let him divine that I should be interested in any information he could pick up. But he picked up amazingly little for a knowing Venetian: it must be added that where there is a perpetual fast there are very few crumbs on the floor. His cleverness in other ways was sufficient, if it was not quite all that I had attributed to him on the occasion of my first interview with Miss Tita. He had helped my gondolier to bring me round a boat-load of furniture; and when these articles had been carried to the top of the palace and distributed according to our associated wisdom he organised my household with such promptitude as was consistent with the fact that it was composed exclusively of himself. He made me in short as comfortable as I could be with my indifferent prospects. I should have been glad if he had fallen in love with Miss Bordereau's maid or, failing this, had taken her in aversion; either event might have brought about some kind of catastrophe and a catastrophe might have led to some parley. It was my idea that she would have been sociable, and I myself on various occasions saw her flit to and fro on domestic errands, so that I was sure she was accessible. But I tasted of no gossip from that fountain, and I afterwards learned that Pasquale's affections were fixed upon an object that made him heedless of other women. This was a young lady with a powdered face, a yellow cotton gown and much leisure, who used often to come to see him. She practised, at her convenience, the art of a stringer of beads (these ornaments are made in Venice, in profusion; she had her pocket full of them and I used to find them on the floor of my apartment), and kept an eye on the maiden in the house. It was not for me of course to make the domestics tattle, and I never said a word to Miss Bordereau's cook.

It seemed to me a proof of the old lady's determination to have nothing to do with me that she should never have sent me a receipt for my three months' rent. For some days I looked out for it and then, when I had given it up, I wasted a good deal of time in wondering what her reason had been for neglecting so indispensable and familiar a form. At first I was tempted to send her a reminder, after which I relinquished the idea (against my judgment as to what was right in the particular case), on the general ground of wishing to keep quiet. If Miss Bordereau suspected me of ulterior aims she would suspect me less if I should be businesslike, and yet I consented not to be so. It was possible she intended her omission as an impertinence, a visible irony, to show how she could overreach people who attempted to overreach her. On that hypothesis it was well to let her see that one did not notice her little tricks. The real reading of the matter, I afterwards perceived, was simply the poor old woman's desire to emphasise the fact that I was in the enjoyment of a favour as rigidly limited as it had been liberally bestowed. She had given me part of her house and now she would not give me even a morsel of paper with her name on it. Let me say that even at first this did not make me too miserable, for the whole episode was essentially delightful to me. I foresaw that I should have a summer after my own literary heart, and the sense of holding my opportunity was much greater than the sense of losing it. There could be no Venetian business without patience, and since I adored the place I was much more in the spirit of it for having laid in a large provision. That spirit kept me perpetual company and seemed to look out at me from the revived immortal face—in which all his genius shone—of the great poet who was my prompter. I had invoked him and he had come; he hovered before me half the time; it was as if his bright ghost had returned to earth to tell me that he regarded the affair as his own no less than mine and that we should see it fraternally, cheerfully to a conclusion. It was as if he had said, "Poor dear, be easy with her; she has some natural prejudices; only give her time. Strange as it may appear to you she was very attractive in 1820. Meanwhile are we not in Venice together, and what better place is there for the meeting of dear friends? See how it glows with the advancing summer; how the sky and the sea and the rosy air and the marble of the palaces all shimmer and melt together." My eccentric private errand became a part of the general romance and the general glory—I felt even a mystic companionship, a moral fraternity with all those who in the past had been in the service of art. They had worked for beauty, for a devotion; and what else was I doing? That element was in everything that Jeffery Aspern had written and I was only bringing it to the light.

I lingered in the sala when I went to and fro; I used to watch—as long as I thought decent—the door that led to Miss Bordereau's part of the house. A person observing me might have supposed I was trying to cast a spell upon it or attempting some odd experiment in hypnotism. But I was only praying it would open or thinking what treasure probably lurked behind it. I hold it singular, as I look back, that I should never have doubted for a moment that the sacred relics were there; never have failed to feel a certain joy at being under the same roof with them. After all they were under my hand—they had not escaped me yet; and they made my life continuous, in a fashion, with the illustrious life they had touched at the other end. I lost myself in this satisfaction to the point of assuming—in my quiet extravagance—that poor Miss Tita also went back, went back, as I used to phrase it. She did indeed, the gentle spinster, but not quite so far as Jeffrey Aspern, who was simple hearsay to her, quite as he was to me. Only she had lived for years with Juliana, she had seen and handled the papers and (even though she was stupid) some esoteric knowledge had rubbed off on her. That was what the old woman represented—esoteric knowledge; and this was the idea with which my editorial heart used to thrill. It literally beat faster often, of an evening, when I had been out, as I stopped with my candle in the re-echoing hall on my way up to bed. It was as if at such a moment as that, in the stillness, after the long contradiction of the day, Miss Bordereau's secrets were in the air, the wonder of her survival more palpable. These were the acute impressions. I had them in another form, with more of a certain sort of reciprocity, during the hours that I sat in the garden looking up over the top of my book at the closed windows of my hostess. In these windows no sign of life ever appeared; it was as if, for fear of my catching a glimpse of them, the two ladies passed their days in the dark. But this only proved to me that they had something to conceal; which was what I had wished to demonstrate. Their motionless shutters became as expressive as eyes consciously closed, and I took comfort in thinking that at all events though invisible themselves they saw me between the lashes.

I made a point of spending as much time as possible in the garden, to justify the picture I had originally given of my horticultural passion. And I not only spent time, but (hang it! as I said) I spent money. As soon as I had got my rooms arranged and could give the proper thought to the matter I surveyed the place with a clever expert and made terms for having it put in order. I was sorry to do this, for personally I liked it better as it was, with its weeds and its wild, rough tangle, its sweet, characteristic Venetian shabbiness. I had to be consistent, to keep my promise that I would smother the house in flowers. Moreover I formed this graceful project that by flowers I would make my way—I would succeed by big nosegays. I would batter the old woman with lilies—I would bombard their citadel with roses. Their door would have to yield to the pressure when a mountain of carnations should be piled up against it. The place in truth had been brutally neglected. The Venetian capacity for dawdling is of the largest, and for a good many days unlimited litter was all my gardener had to show for his ministrations. There was a great digging of holes and carting about of earth, and after a while I grew so impatient that I had thoughts of sending for my bouquets to the nearest stand. But I reflected that the ladies would see through the chinks of their shutters that they must have been bought and might make up their minds from this that I was a humbug. So I composed myself and finally, though the delay was long, perceived some appearances of bloom. This encouraged me and I waited serenely enough till they multiplied. Meanwhile the real summer days arrived and began to pass, and as I look back upon them they seem to me almost the happiest of my life. I took more and more care to be in the garden whenever it was not too hot. I had an arbour arranged and a low table and an armchair put into it; and I carried out books and portfolios (I had always some business of writing in hand), and worked and waited and mused and hoped, while the golden hours elapsed and the plants drank in the light and the inscrutable old palace turned pale and then, as the day waned, began to flush in it and my papers rustled in the wandering breeze of the Adriatic.

Considering how little satisfaction I got from it at first it is remarkable that I should not have grown more tired of wondering what mystic rites of ennui the Misses Bordereau celebrated in their darkened rooms; whether this had always been the tenor of their life and how in previous years they had escaped elbowing their neighbours. It was clear that they must have had other habits and other circumstances; that they must once have been young or at least middle-aged. There was no end to the questions it was possible to ask about them and no end to the answers it was not possible to frame. I had known many of my country-people in Europe and was familiar with the strange ways they were liable to take up there; but the Misses Bordereau formed altogether a new type of the American absentee. Indeed it was plain that the American name had ceased to have any application to them—I had seen this in the ten minutes I spent in the old woman's room. You could never have said whence they came, from the appearance of either of them; wherever it was they had long ago dropped the local accent and fashion. There was nothing in them that one recognised, and putting the question of speech aside they might have been Norwegians or Spaniards. Miss Bordereau, after all, had been in Europe nearly three-quarters of a century; it appeared by some verses addressed to her by Aspern on the occasion of his own second absence from America—verses of which Cumnor and I had after infinite conjecture established solidly enough the date—that she was even then, as a girl of twenty, on the foreign side of the sea. There was an implication in the poem (I hope not just for the phrase) that he had come back for her sake. We had no real light upon her circumstances at that moment, any more than we had upon her origin, which we believed to be of the sort usually spoken of as modest. Cumnor had a theory that she had been a governess in some family in which the poet visited and that, in consequence of her position, there was from the first something unavowed, or rather something positively clandestine, in their relations. I on the other hand had hatched a little romance according to which she was the daughter of an artist, a painter or a sculptor, who had left the western world when the century was fresh, to study in the ancient schools. It was essential to my hypothesis that this amiable man should have lost his wife, should have been poor and unsuccessful and should have had a second daughter, of a disposition quite different from Juliana's. It was also indispensable that he should have been accompanied to Europe by these young ladies and should have established himself there for the remainder of a struggling, saddened life. There was a further implication that Miss Bordereau had had in her youth a perverse and adventurous, albeit a generous and fascinating character, and that she had passed through some singular vicissitudes. By what passions had she been ravaged, by what sufferings had she been blanched, what store of memories had she laid away for the monotonous future?

I asked myself these things as I sat spinning theories about her in my arbour and the bees droned in the flowers. It was incontestable that, whether for right or for wrong, most readers of certain of Aspern's poems (poems not as ambiguous as the sonnets—scarcely more divine, I think—of Shakespeare) had taken for granted that Juliana had not always adhered to the steep footway of renunciation. There hovered about her name a perfume of reckless passion, an intimation that she had not been exactly as the respectable young person in general. Was this a sign that her singer had betrayed her, had given her away, as we say nowadays, to posterity? Certain it is that it would have been difficult to put one's finger on the passage in which her fair fame suffered an imputation. Moreover was not any fame fair enough that was so sure of duration and was associated with works immortal through their beauty? It was a part of my idea that the young lady had had a foreign lover (and an unedifying tragical rupture) before her meeting with Jeffrey Aspern. She had lived with her father and sister in a queer old-fashioned, expatriated, artistic Bohemia, in the days when the æsthetic was only the academic and the painters who knew the best models for a *contadina* and *pifferaro* wore peaked hats and long hair. It was a society less furnished than the coteries of to-day (in its ignorance of the wonderful chances, the opportunities of the early bird, with which its path was strewn), with tatters of old stuff and fragments of old crockery; so that Miss Bordereau appeared not to have picked up or have inherited many objects of importance. There was no enviable *bric-à-brac*, with its provoking legend of cheapness, in the room in which I had seen her. Such a fact as that suggested bareness, but none the less it worked happily into the sentimental interest I had always taken in the early movements of my countrymen as visitors to Europe. When Americans went abroad in 1820 there was something romantic, almost heroic in it, as compared with the perpetual ferryings of the present hour, when photography and other conveniences have annihilated surprise. Miss Bordereau sailed with her family on a tossing brig, in the days of long voyages and sharp differences; she had her emotions on the top of yellow diligences, passed the night at inns where she dreamed of travellers' tales, and was struck, on reaching the eternal city, with the elegance of Roman pearls and scarfs. There was something touching to me in all that and my imagination frequently went back to the period. If Miss Bordereau carried it there of course Jeffrey Aspern at other times had done so a great deal more. It was a much more important fact, if one were looking at his genius critically, that he had lived in the days before the general transfusion. It had happened to me to regret that he had known Europe at all; I should have liked to see what he would have written without that experience, by which he had incontestably been enriched. But as his fate had ordered otherwise I went with him—I tried to judge how the old world would have struck him. It was not only there, however, that I watched him; the relations he had entertained with the new had even a livelier interest. His own country after all had had most of his life, and his muse, as they said at that time, was essentially American. That was originally what I had loved him for: that at a period when our native land was nude and crude and provincial, when the famous "atmosphere" it is supposed to lack was not even missed, when literature was lonely there and art and form almost impossible, he had found means to live and write like one of the first; to be free and general and not at all afraid; to feel, understand and express everything.

CHAPTER V

I WAS SELDOM AT HOME in the evening, for when I attempted to occupy myself in my apartments the lamplight brought in a swarm of noxious insects, and it was too hot for closed windows. Accordingly I spent the late hours either on the water (the moonlight of Venice is famous), or in the splendid square which serves as a vast forecourt to the strange old basilica of Saint Mark. I sat in front of Florian's *café*, eating ices, listening to music, talking with acquaintances: the traveller will remember how the immense cluster of tables and little chairs stretches like a promontory into the smooth lake of the Piazza. The whole place, of a summer's evening, under the stars and with all the lamps, all the voices and light footsteps on marble (the only sounds of the arcades that enclose it), is like an open-air saloon dedicated to cooling drinks and to a still finer degustation—that of the exquisite impressions received during the day. When I did not prefer to keep mine to myself there was always a stray tourist, disencumbered of his Bädeker, to discuss them with, or some domesticated painter rejoicing in the return of the season of strong effects. The wonderful church, with its low domes and bristling embroideries, the mystery of its mosaic and sculpture, looked ghostly in the tempered gloom, and the sea-breeze passed between the twin columns of the Piazzetta, the lintels of a door no longer guarded, as gently as if a rich curtain were swaying there. I used sometimes on these occasions to think of the Misses Bordereau and of the pity of their being shut up in apartments which in the Venetian July even Venetian vastness did not prevent from being stuffy. Their life seemed miles away from the life of the Piazza, and no doubt it was really too late to make the austere Juliana change her habits. But poor Miss Tita would have enjoyed one of Florian's ices, I was sure; sometimes I even had thoughts of carrying one home to her. Fortunately my patience bore fruit and I was not obliged to do anything so ridiculous.

One evening about the middle of July I came in earlier than usual—I forget what chance had led to this—and instead of going up to my quarters made my way into the garden. The temperature was very high; it was such a night as one would gladly have spent in the open air and I was in no hurry to go to bed. I had floated home in my gondola, listening to the slow splash of the oar in the narrow dark canals, and now the only thought that solicited me was the vague reflection that it would be pleasant to recline at one's length in the fragrant darkness on a garden bench. The odour of the canal was doubtless at the bottom of that aspiration and the breath of the garden, as I entered it, gave consistency to my purpose. It was delicious—just such an air as must have trembled with Romeo's vows when he stood among the flowers and raised his arms to his mistress's balcony. I looked at the windows of the palace to see if by chance the example of Verona (Verona being not far off) had been followed; but everything was dim, as usual, and everything was still. Juliana, on summer nights in her youth, might have murmured down from open windows at Jeffrey Aspern, but Miss Tita was not a poet's mistress any more than I was a poet. This however did not prevent my gratification from being great as I became aware on reaching the end of the garden that Miss Tita was seated in my little bower. At first I only made out an indistinct figure, not in the least counting on such an overture from one of my hostesses; it even occurred to me that some sentimental maidservant had stolen in to keep a tryst with her sweetheart. I was going to turn away, not to frighten her, when the figure rose to its height and I recognised Miss Bordereau's niece. I must do myself the justice to say that I did not wish to frighten her either, and much as I had longed for some such accident I should have been capable of retreating. It was as if I had laid a trap for her by coming home earlier than usual and adding to that eccentricity by creeping into the garden. As she rose she spoke to me, and then I reflected that perhaps, secure in my almost inveterate absence, it was her nightly practice to take a lonely airing. There was no trap, in truth, because I had had no suspicion. At first I took for granted that the words she uttered expressed discomfiture at my arrival; but as she repeated them —I had not caught them clearly—I had the surprise of hearing her say, "Oh, dear, I'm so very glad you've come!" She and her aunt had in common the property of unexpected speeches. She came out of the arbour almost as if she were going to throw herself into my arms.

I hasten to add that she did nothing of the kind; she did not even shake hands with me. It was a gratification to her to see me and presently she told me why—because she was nervous when she was out-of-doors at night alone. The plants and bushes looked so strange in the dark, and there were all sorts of queer sounds—she could not tell what they were—like the noises of animals. She stood close to me, looking about her with an air of greater security but without any demonstration of interest in me as an individual. Then I guessed that nocturnal prowlings were not in the least her habit, and I was also reminded (I had been struck with the circumstance in talking with her before I took possession) that it was impossible to over-estimate her simplicity.

"You speak as if you were lost in the backwoods," I said, laughing. "How you manage to keep out of this charming place when you have only three steps to take to get into it, is more than I have yet been able to discover. You hide away mighty well so long as I am on the premises, I know; but I had a hope that you peeped out a little at other times. You and your poor aunt are worse off than Carmelite nuns in their cells. Should you mind telling me how you exist without air, without exercise, without any sort of human contact? I don't see how you carry on the common business of life."

She looked at me as if I were talking some strange tongue and her answer was so little of an answer that I was considerably irritated.

"We go to bed very early—earlier than you would be-lieve." I was on the point of saying that this only deepened the mystery when she gave me some relief by adding, "Be-fore you came we were not so private. But I never have been out at night."

"Never in these fragrant alleys, blooming here under your nose?"

"Ah," said Miss Tita, "they were never nice till now!" There was an unmistakable reference in this and a flattering comparison, so that it seemed to me I had gained a small advantage. As it would help me to follow it up to establish a sort of grievance I asked her why, since she thought my garden nice, she had never thanked me in any way for the flowers I had been sending up in such quantities for the previous three weeks. I had not been discouraged—there had been, as she would have observed, a daily armful; but I had been brought up in the common forms and a word of recognition now and then would have touched me in the right place.

"Why I didn't know they were for me!"

"They were for both of you. Why should I make a dif-ference?"

Miss Tita reflected as if she might be thinking of a rea-son for that, but she failed to produce one. Instead of this she asked abruptly, "Why in the world do you want to know us?"

"I ought after all to make a difference," I replied. "That question is your aunt's; it isn't yours. You wouldn't ask it if you hadn't been put up to it."

"She didn't tell me to ask you," Miss Tita replied, with-out confusion; she was the oddest mixture of the shrinking and the direct.

"Well, she has often wondered about it herself and ex-pressed her wonder to you. She has insisted on it, so that she put the idea into your head that I am insufferably push-ing. Upon my word I think I have been very discreet. And how completely your aunt must have lost every tradition of sociability, to see anything out of the way in the idea that respectable intelligent people, living as we do under the same roof, should occasionally exchange a remark! What could be more natural? We are of the same country and we have at least some of the same tastes, since, like you, I am intensely fond of Venice."

My interlocutress appeared incapable of grasping more than one clause in any proposition, and she declared quickly, eagerly, as if she were answering my whole speech: "I am not in the least fond of Venice. I should like to go far away!"

"Has she always kept you back so?" I went on, to show her that I could be as irrelevant as herself.

"She told me to come out to-night; she has told me very often," said Miss Tita. "It is I who wouldn't come. I don't like to leave her."

"Is she too weak, is she failing?" I demanded, with more emotion, I think, than I intended to show. I judged this by the way her eyes rested upon me in the darkness. It embarrassed me a little, and to turn the matter off I continued genially: "Do let us sit down together comfortably somewhere and you will tell me all about her."

Miss Tita made no resistance to this. We found a bench less secluded, less confidential, as it were, than the one in the arbour; and we were still sitting there when I heard midnight ring out from those clear bells of Venice which vibrate with a solemnity of their own over the lagoon and hold the air so much more than the chimes of other places. We were together more than an hour and our interview gave, as it struck me, a great lift to my undertaking. Miss Tita accepted the situation without a protest; she had avoided me for three months, yet now she treated me almost as if these three months had made me an old friend. If I had chosen I might have inferred from this that though she had avoided me she had given a good deal of consideration to doing so. She paid no attention to the flight of time —never worried at my keeping her so long away from her aunt. She talked freely, answering questions and asking them and not even taking advantage of certain longish pauses with which they inevitably alternated to say she thought she had better go in. It was almost as if she were waiting for something—something I might say to her—and intended to give me my opportunity. I was the more struck by this as

she told me that her aunt had been less well for a good
many days and in a way that was rather new. She was
weaker; at moments it seemed as if she had no strength at
all; yet more than ever before she wished to be left alone.
That was why she had told her to come out—not even to
remain in her own room, which was alongside; she said her
niece irritated her, made her nervous. She sat still for hours
together, as if she were asleep; she had always done that,
musing and dozing; but at such times formerly she gave at
intervals some small sign of life, of interest, liking her companion to be near her with her work. Miss Tita confided to
me that at present her aunt was so motionless that she
sometimes feared she was dead; moreover she took hardly
any food—one couldn't see what she lived on. The great
thing was that she still on most days got up; the serious job
was to dress her, to wheel her out of her bedroom. She
clung to as many of her old habits as possible and she had
always, little company as they had received for years, made
a point of sitting in the parlour.

I scarcely knew what to think of all this—of Miss Tita's
sudden conversion to sociability and of the strange circumstance that the more the old lady appeared to decline toward her end the less she should desire to be looked after.
The story did not hang together, and I even asked myself
whether it were not a trap laid for me, the result of a design
to make me show my hand. I could not have told why my
companions (as they could only by courtesy be called)
should have this purpose—why they should try to trip up
so lucrative a lodger. At any rate I kept on my guard, so
that Miss Tita should not have occasion again to ask me if
I had an *arrière-pensée*. Poor woman, before we parted for
the night my mind was at rest as to *her* capacity for enter-
taining one.

She told me more about their affairs than I had hoped;
there was no need to be prying, for it evidently drew her
out simply to feel that I listened, that I cared. She ceased
wondering why I cared, and at last, as she spoke of the brilliant life they had led years before, she almost chattered. It
was Miss Tita who judged it brilliant; she said that when
they first came to live in Venice, years and years before (I

saw that her mind was essentially vague about dates and
the order in which events had occurred), there was scarcely
a week that they had not some visitor or did not make some
delightful *passeggio* in the city. They had seen all the curiosities; they had even been to the Lido in a boat (she spoke
as if I might think there was a way on foot); they had had
a collation there, brought in three baskets and spread out
on the grass. I asked her what people they had known and
she said, Oh! very nice ones—the Cavaliere Bombicci and
the Contessa Altemura, with whom they had had a great
friendship. Also English people—the Churtons and the
Goldies and Mrs. Stock-Stock, whom they had loved dearly;
she was dead and gone, poor dear. That was the case with
most of their pleasant circle (this expression was Miss Tita's
own), though a few were left, which was a wonder considering how they had neglected them. She mentioned the
names of two or three Venetian old women; of a certain
doctor, very clever, who was so kind—he came as a friend,
he had really given up practice; of the *avvocato* Pochin-
testa, who wrote beautiful poems and had addressed one to
her aunt. These people came to see them without fail every
year, usually at the *capo d'anno,* and of old her aunt used to
make them some little present—her aunt and she together:
small things that she, Miss Tita, made herself, like paper
lamp-shades or mats for the decanters of wine at dinner or
those woollen things that in cold weather were worn on the
wrists. The last few years there had not been many presents;
she could not think what to make and her aunt had lost her
interest and never suggested. But the people came all the
same; if the Venetians liked you once they liked you for
ever.

There was something affecting in the good faith of this
sketch of former social glories; the picnic at the Lido had
remained vivid through the ages and poor Miss Tita evidently was of the impression that she had had a brilliant
youth. She had in fact had a glimpse of the Venetian world
in its gossiping, home-keeping, parsimonious, professional
walks; for I observed for the first time that she had acquired
by contact something of the trick of the familiar, soft-
sounding, almost infantile speech of the place. I judged that

she had imbibed this invertebrate dialect, from the natural way the names of things and people—mostly purely local— rose to her lips. If she knew little of what they represented she knew still less of anything else. Her aunt had drawn in —her failing interest in the table-mats and lamp-shades was a sign of that—and she had not been able to mingle in society or to entertain it alone; so that the matter of her reminiscences struck one as an old world altogether. If she had not been so decent her references would have seemed to carry one back to the queer rococo Venice of Casanova. I found myself falling into the error of thinking of her too as one of Jeffrey Aspern's contemporaries; this came from her having so little in common with my own. It was possible, I said to myself, that she had not even heard of him; it might very well be that Juliana had not cared to lift even for her the veil that covered the temple of her youth. In this case she perhaps would not know of the existence of the papers, and I welcomed that presumption—it made me feel more safe with her—until I remembered that we had believed the letter of disavowal received by Cumnor to be in the handwriting of the niece. If it had been dictated to her she had of course to know what it was about; yet after all the effect of it was to repudiate the idea of any connection with the poet. I held it probable at all events that Miss Tita had not read a word of his poetry. Moreover if, with her companion, she had always escaped the interviewer there was little occasion for her having got it into her head that people were "after" the letters. People had not been after them, inasmuch as they had not heard of them; and Cumnor's fruitless feeler would have been a solitary accident.

When midnight sounded Miss Tita got up; but she stopped at the door of the house only after she had wandered two or three times with me round the garden. "When shall I see you again?" I asked, before she went in; to which she replied with promptness that she should like to come out the next night. She added however that she should not come—she was so far from doing everything she liked.

"You might do a few things that *I* like," I said with a sigh.

"Oh, you—I don't believe you!" she murmured, at this, looking at me with her simple solemnity.

"Why don't you believe me?"

"Because I don't understand you."

"That is just the sort of occasion to have faith." I could not say more, though I should have liked to, as I saw that I only mystified her; for I had no wish to have it on my conscience that I might pass for having made love to her. Nothing less should I have seemed to do had I continued to beg a lady to "believe in me" in an Italian garden on a mid-summer night. There was some merit in my scruples, for Miss Tita lingered and lingered: I perceived that she felt that she should not really soon come down again and wished therefore to protract the present. She insisted too on making the talk between us personal to ourselves; and altogether her behavior was such as would have been possible only to a completely innocent woman.

"I shall like the flowers better now that I know they are also meant for me."

"How could you have doubted it? If you will tell me the kind you like best I will send a double lot of them."

"Oh, I like them all best!" Then she went on, familiarly: "Shall you study—shall you read and write—when you go up to your rooms?"

"I don't do that at night, at this season. The lamplight brings in the animals."

"You might have known that when you came."

"I did know it!"

"And in winter do you work at night?"

"I read a good deal, but I don't often write." She listened as if these details had a rare interest, and suddenly a temptation quite at variance with the prudence I had been teaching myself associated itself with her plain, mild face. Ah yes, she was safe and I could make her safer! It seemed to me from one moment to another that I could not wait longer —that I really must take a sounding. So I went on: "In general before I go to sleep—very often in bed (it's a bad habit, but I confess to it), I read some great poet. In nine cases out of ten it's a volume of Jeffrey Aspern."

I watched her well as I pronounced that name but I saw nothing wonderful. Why should I indeed—was not Jeffrey Aspern the property of the human race?

"Oh, we read him—we *have* read him," she quietly replied.

"He is my poet of poets—I know him almost by heart."

For an instant Miss Tita hesitated; then her sociability was too much for her.

"Oh, by heart—that's nothing!" she murmured, smiling. "My aunt used to know him—to know him"—she paused an instant and I wondered what she was going to say—"to know him as a visitor."

"As a visitor?" I repeated, staring.

"He used to call on her and take her out."

I continued to stare. "My dear lady, he died a hundred years ago!"

"Well," she said, mirthfully, "my aunt is a hundred and fifty."

"Mercy on us!" I exclaimed; "why didn't you tell me before? I should like so to ask her about him."

"She wouldn't care for that—she wouldn't tell you," Miss Tita replied.

"I don't care what she cares for! She *must* tell me—it's not a chance to be lost."

"Oh, you should have come twenty years ago: then she still talked about him."

"And what did she say?" I asked, eagerly.

"I don't know—that he liked her immensely."

"And she—didn't she like him?"

"She said he was a god." Miss Tita gave me this information flatly, without expression; her tone might have made it a piece of trivial gossip. But it stirred me deeply as she dropped the words into the summer night; it seemed such a direct testimony.

"Fancy, fancy!" I murmured. And then, "Tell me this, please—has she got a portrait of him? They are distressingly rare."

"A portrait? I don't know," said Miss Tita; and now there was discomfiture in her face. "Well, good-night!" she added; and she turned into the house.

I accompanied her into the wide, dusky, stone-paved passage which on the ground floor corresponded with our grand sala. It opened at one end into the garden, at the other upon the canal, and was lighted now only by the small lamp that was always left for me to take up as I went to bed. An extinguished candle which Miss Tita apparently had brought down with her stood on the same table with it. "Good-night, good-night!" I replied, keeping beside her as she went to get her light. "Surely you would know, shouldn't you, if she had one?"

"If she had what?" the poor lady asked, looking at me queerly over the flame of her candle.

"A portrait of the god. I don't know what I wouldn't give to see it."

"I don't know what she has got. She keeps her things locked up." And Miss Tita went away, toward the staircase, with the sense evidently that she had said too much.

I let her go—I wished not to frighten her—and I contented myself with remarking that Miss Bordereau would not have locked up such a glorious possession as that—a thing a person would be proud of and hang up in a prominent place on the parlour-wall. Therefore of course she had not any portrait. Miss Tita made no direct answer to this and candle in hand, with her back to me, ascended two or three stairs. Then she stopped short and turned round looking at me across the dusky space.

"Do you write—do you write?" There was a shake in her voice—she could scarcely bring out what she wanted to ask.

"Do I write? Oh, don't speak of my writing on the same day with Aspern's!"

"Do you write about *him*—do you pry into his life?"

"Ah, that's your aunt's question; it can't be yours!" I said, in a tone of slightly wounded sensibility.

"All the more reason then that you should answer it. Do you, please?"

I thought I had allowed for the falsehoods I should have to tell; but I found that in fact when it came to the point I had not. Besides, now that I had an opening there was a kind of relief in being frank. Lastly (it was perhaps fanciful, even fatuous), I guessed that Miss Tita personally would not in the last resort be less my friend. So after a moment's hesitation I answered, "Yes, I have written about him and I am looking for more material. In heaven's name have you got any?"

"*Santo Dio!*" she exclaimed, without heeding my question; and she hurried upstairs and out of sight. I might count upon her in the last resort, but for the present she was visibly alarmed. The proof of it was that she began to hide again, so that for a fortnight I never beheld her. I found my patience ebbing and after four or five days of this I told the gardener to stop the flowers.

CHAPTER VI

ONE AFTERNOON, as I came down from my quarters to go out, I found Miss Tita in the sala: it was our first encounter on that ground since I had come to the house. She put on no air of being there by accident; there was an ignorance of such arts in her angular, diffident directness. That I might be quite sure she was waiting for me she informed me of the fact and told me that Miss Bordereau wished to see me: she would take me into the room at that moment if I had time. If I had been late for a love-tryst I would have stayed for this, and I quickly signified that I should be delighted to wait upon the old lady. "She wants to talk with you—to know you," Miss Tita said, smiling as if she herself appreciated that idea; and she led me to the door of her aunt's apartment. I stopped her a moment before she had opened it, looking at her with some curiosity. I told her that this was a great satisfaction to me and a great honour; but all the same I should like to ask what had made Miss Bordereau change so suddenly. It was only the other day that she wouldn't suffer me near her. Miss Tita was not embarrassed by my question; she had as many little unexpected serenities as if she told fibs, but the odd part of them was that they had on the contrary their source in her truthfulness. "Oh, my aunt changes," she answered; "it's so terribly dull—I suppose she's tired."

"But you told me that she wanted more and more to be alone."

Poor Miss Tita coloured, as if she found me over-insistent. "Well, if you don't believe she wants to see you—I haven't invented it! I think people often are capricious when they are very old."

"That's perfectly true. I only wanted to be clear as to

whether you have repeated to her what I told you the other night."

"What you told me?"

"About Jeffrey Aspern—that I am looking for materials."

"If I had told her do you think she would have sent for you?"

"That's exactly what I want to know. If she wants to keep him to herself she might have sent for me to tell me so."

"She won't speak of him," said Miss Tita. Then as she opened the door she added in a lower tone, "I have told her nothing."

The old woman was sitting in the same place in which I had seen her last, in the same position, with the same mystifying bandage over her eyes. Her welcome was to turn her almost invisible face to me and show me that while she sat silent she saw me clearly. I made no motion to shake hands with her; I felt too well on this occasion that that was out of place for ever. It had been sufficiently enjoined upon me that she was too sacred for that sort of reciprocity—too venerable to touch. There was something so grim in her aspect (it was partly the accident of her green shade), as I stood there to be measured, that I ceased on the spot to feel any doubt as to her knowing my secret, though I did not in the least suspect that Miss Tita had not just spoken the truth. She had not betrayed me, but the old woman's brooding instinct had served her; she had turned me over and over in the long, still hours and she had guessed. The worst of it was that she looked terribly like an old woman who at a pinch would burn her papers. Miss Tita pushed a chair forward, saying to me, "This will be a good place for you to sit." As I took possession of it I asked after Miss Bordereau's health; expressed the hope that in spite of the very hot weather it was satisfactory. She replied that it was good enough—good enough; that it was a great thing to be alive.

"Oh, as to that, it depends upon what you compare it with!" I exclaimed, laughing.

"I don't compare—I don't compare. If I did that I should have given everything up long ago."

I liked to think that this was a subtle allusion to the rapture she had known in the society of Jeffrey Aspern—

though it was true that such an allusion would have accorded ill with the wish I imputed to her to keep him buried in her soul. What it accorded with was my constant conviction that no human being had ever had a more delightful social gift than his, and what it seemed to convey was that nothing in the world was worth speaking of if one pretended to speak of that. But one did not! Miss Tita sat down beside her aunt, looking as if she had reason to believe some very remarkable conversation would come off between us.

"It's about the beautiful flowers," said the old lady; "you sent us so many—I ought to have thanked you for them before. But I don't write letters and I receive only at long intervals."

She had not thanked me while the flowers continued to come, but she departed from her custom so far as to send for me as soon as she began to fear that they would not come any more. I noted this; I remembered what an acquisitive propensity she had shown when it was a question of extracting gold from me, and I privately rejoiced at the happy thought I had had in suspending my tribute. She had missed it and she was willing to make a concession to bring it back. At the first sign of this concession I could only go to meet her. "I am afraid you have not had many, of late, but they shall begin again immediately—to-morrow, to-night."

"Oh, do send us some to-night!" Miss Tita cried, as if it were an immense circumstance.

"What else should you do with them? It isn't a manly taste to make a bower of your room," the old woman remarked.

"I don't make a bower of my room, but I am exceedingly fond of growing flowers, of watching their ways. There is nothing unmanly in that: it has been the amusement of philosophers, of statesmen in retirement; even I think of great captains."

"I suppose you know you can sell them—those you don't use," Miss Bordereau went on. "I daresay they wouldn't give you much for them; still, you could make a bargain"

"Oh, I have never made a bargain, as you ought to know My gardener disposes of them and I ask no questions."

"I would ask a few, I can promise you!" said Miss Bordereau; and it was the first time I had heard her laugh. I could not get used to the idea that this vision of pecuniary profit was what drew out the divine Juliana most.

"Come into the garden yourself and pick them; come as often as you like; come every day. They are all for you," I pursued, addressing Miss Tita and carrying off this veracious statement by treating it as an innocent joke. "I can't imagine why she doesn't come down," I added, for Miss Bordereau's benefit.

"You must make her come; you must come up and fetch her," said the old woman, to my stupefaction. "That odd thing you have made in the corner would be a capital place for her to sit."

The allusion to my arbour was irreverent; it confirmed the impression I had already received that there was a flicker of impertinence in Miss Bordereau's talk, a strange mocking lambency which must have been a part of her adventurous youth and which had outlived passions and faculties. None the less I asked, "Wouldn't it be possible for you to come down there yourself? Wouldn't it do you good to sit there in the shade, in the sweet air?"

"Oh, sir, when I move out of this it won't be to sit in the air, and I'm afraid that any that may be stirring around me won't be particularly sweet! It will be a very dark shade indeed. But that won't be just yet," Miss Bordereau continued, cannily, as if to correct any hopes that this courageous allusion to the last receptacle of her mortality might lead me to entertain. "I have sat here many a day and I have had enough of arbours in my time. But I'm not afraid to wait till I'm called."

Miss Tita had expected some interesting talk, but perhaps she found it less genial on her aunt's side (considering that I had been sent for with a civil intention) than she had hoped. As if to give the conversation a turn that would put our companion in a light more favourable she said to me, "Didn't I tell you the other night that she had sent me out? You see that I can do what I like!"

"Do you pity her—do you teach her to pity herself?" Miss Bordereau demanded, before I had time to answer this appeal. "She has a much easier life than I had when I was her age."

"You must remember that it has been quite open to me to think you rather inhuman."

"Inhuman? That's what the poets used to call the women a hundred years ago. Don't try that; you won't do as well as they!" Juliana declared. "There is no more poetry in the world—that I know of at least. But I won't bandy words with you," she pursued, and I well remember the old-fashioned, artificial sound she gave to the speech. "You have made me talk, talk! It isn't good for me at all." I got up at this and told her I would take no more of her time; but she detained me to ask, "Do you remember, the day I saw you about the rooms, that you offered us the use of your gondola?" And when I assented, promptly, struck again with her disposition to make a "good thing" of my being there and wondering what she now had in her eye, she broke out, "Why don't you take that girl out in it and show her the place?"

"Oh dear aunt, what do you want to do with me?" cried the "girl," with a piteous quaver. "I know all about the place!"

"Well then, go with him as a cicerone!" said Miss Bordereau, with an effect of something like cruelty in her implacable power of retort—an incongruous suggestion that she was a sarcastic, profane, cynical old woman. "Haven't we heard that there have been all sorts of changes in all these years? You ought to see them and at your age (I don't mean because you're so young), you ought to take the chances that come. You're old enough, my dear, and this gentleman won't hurt you. He will show you the famous sunsets, if they still go on—*do* they go on? The sun set for me so long ago. But that's not a reason. Besides, I shall never miss you; you think you are too important. Take her to the Piazza; it used to be very pretty," Miss Bordereau continued, addressing herself to me. "What have they done with the funny old church? I hope it hasn't tumbled down. Let her look at the shops; she may take some money, she may buy what she likes."

Poor Miss Tita had got up, discountenanced and helpless,

and as we stood there before her aunt it would certainly
have seemed to a spectator of the scene that the old woman
was amusing herself at our expense. Miss Tita protested, in
a confusion of exclamations and murmurs; but I lost no
time in saying that if she would do me the honour to accept
the hospitality of my boat I would engage that she should
not be bored. Or if she did not want so much of my company the boat itself, with the gondolier, was at her service;
he was a capital oar and she might have every confidence.
Miss Tita, without definitely answering this speech, looked
away from me, out of the window, as if she were going to
cry; and I remarked that once we had Miss Bordereau's approval we could easily come to an understanding. We would
take an hour, whichever she liked, one of the very next
days. As I made my obeisance to the old lady I asked her if
she would kindly permit me to see her again.

For a moment she said nothing; then she inquired, "Is it
very necessary to your happiness?"

"It diverts me more than I can say."

"You are wonderfully civil. Don't you know it almost
kills *me?*"

"How can I believe that when I see you more animated,
more brilliant than when I came in?"

"That is very true, aunt," said Miss Tita. "I think it does
you good."

"Isn't it touching, the solicitude we each have that the
other shall enjoy herself?" sneered Miss Bordereau. "If you
think me brilliant to-day you don't know what you are talking about; you have never seen an agreeable woman. Don't
try to pay me a compliment; I have been spoiled," she went
on. "My door is shut, but you may sometimes knock."

With this she dismissed me and I left the room. The latch
closed behind me, but Miss Tita, contrary to my hope, had
remained within. I passed slowly across the hall and before
taking my way down-stairs I waited a little. My hope was
answered; after a minute Miss Tita followed me. "That's a
delightful idea about the Piazza," I said. "When will you go
—to-night, to-morrow?"

She had been disconcerted, as I have mentioned, but I
had already perceived and I was to observe again that when

Miss Tita was embarrassed she did not (as most women would have done) turn away from you and try to escape, but came closer, as it were, with a deprecating, clinging appeal to be spared, to be protected. Her attitude was perpetually a sort of prayer for assistance, for explanation; and yet no woman in the world could have been less of a comedian. From the moment you were kind to her she depended on you absolutely; her self-consciousness dropped from her and she took the greatest intimacy, the innocent intimacy which was the only thing she could conceive, for granted. She told me she did not know what had got into her aunt; she had changed so quickly, she had got some idea. I replied that she must find out what the idea was and then let me know; we would go and have an ice together at Florian's and she should tell me while we listened to the band.

"Oh, it will take me a long time to find out!" she said, rather ruefully; and she could promise me this satisfaction neither for that night nor for the next. I was patient now, however, for I felt that I had only to wait; and in fact at the end of the week, one lovely evening after dinner, she stepped into my gondola, to which in honour of the occasion I had attached a second oar.

We swept in the course of five minutes into the Grand Canal; whereupon she uttered a murmur of ecstasy as fresh as if she had been a tourist just arrived. She had forgotten how splendid the great waterway looked on a clear, hot summer evening, and how the sense of floating between marble palaces and reflected lights disposed the mind to sympathetic talk. We floated long and far, and though Miss Tita gave no high-pitched voice to her satisfaction I felt that she surrendered herself. She was more than pleased, she was transported; the whole thing was an immense liberation. The gondola moved with slow strokes, to give her time to enjoy it, and she listened to the plash of the oars, which grew louder and more musically liquid as we passed into narrow canals, as if it were a revelation of Venice. When I asked her how long it was since she had been in a boat she answered, "Oh, I don't know; a long time—not since my aunt began to be ill." This was not the only example she gave me of her extreme vagueness about the previous years and the line which marked off the period when Miss Bordereau flourished. I was not at liberty to keep her out too long, but we took a considerable *giro* before going to the Piazza. I asked her no questions, keeping the conversation on purpose away from her domestic situation and the things I wanted to know; I poured treasures of information about Venice into her ears, described Florence and Rome, discoursed to her on the charms and advantages of travel. She reclined, receptive, on the deep leather cushions, turned her eyes conscientiously to everything I pointed out to her, and never mentioned to me till some time afterwards that she might be supposed to know Florence better than I, as she had lived there for years with Miss Bordereau. At last she asked, with the shy impatience of a child, "Are we not really going to the Piazza? That's what I want to see!" I immediately gave the order that we should go straight; and then we sat silent with the expectation of arrival. As some time still passed, however, she said suddenly, of her own movement, "I have found out what is the matter with my aunt: she is afraid you will go!"

"What has put that into her head?"

"She has had an idea you have not been happy. That is why she is different now."

"You mean she wants to make me happier?"

"Well, she wants you not to go; she wants you to stay."

"I suppose you mean on account of the rent," I remarked candidly.

Miss Tita's candour showed itself a match for my own. "Yes, you know; so that I shall have more."

"How much does she want you to have?" I asked, laughing. "She ought to fix the sum, so that I may stay till it's made up."

"Oh, that wouldn't please me," said Miss Tita. "It would be unheard of, your taking that trouble."

"But suppose I should have my own reasons for staying in Venice?"

"Then it would be better for you to stay in some other house."

"And what would your aunt say to that?"

"She wouldn't like it at all. But I should think you would do well to give up your reasons and go away altogether."

"Dear Miss Tita," I said, "it's not so easy to give them up!"

She made no immediate answer to this, but after a moment she broke out: "I think I know what your reasons are!"

"I daresay, because the other night I almost told you how I wish you would help me to make them good."

"I can't do that without being false to my aunt."

"What do you mean, being false to her?"

"Why, she would never consent to what you want. She has been asked, she has been written to. It made her fearfully angry."

"Then she *has* got papers of value?" I demanded, quickly.

"Oh, she has got everything!" sighed Miss Tita, with a curious weariness, a sudden lapse into gloom.

These words caused all my pulses to throb, for I regarded them as precious evidence. For some minutes I was too agitated to speak, and in the interval the gondola approached the Piazzetta. After we had disembarked I asked my companion whether she would rather walk round the square or go and sit at the door of the café; to which she replied that she would do whichever I liked best—I must only remember again how little time she had. I assured her there was plenty to do both, and we made the circuit of the long arcades. Her spirits revived at the sight of the bright shop-windows, and she lingered and stopped, admiring or disapproving of their contents, asking me what I thought of things, theorising about prices. My attention wandered from her; her words of a while before, "Oh, she has got everything!" echoed so in my consciousness. We sat down at last in the crowded circle at Florian's, finding an unoccupied table among those that were ranged in the square. It was a splendid night and all the world was out-of-doors; Miss Tita could not have wished the elements more auspicious for her return to society. I saw that she enjoyed it even more than she told; she was agitated with the multitude of her impressions. She had forgotten what an attractive thing the world

is, and it was coming over her that somehow she had for
the best years of her life been cheated of it. This did not
make her angry; but as she looked all over the charming
scene her face had, in spite of its smile of appreciation, the
flush of a sort of wounded surprise. She became silent, as if
she were thinking with a secret sadness of opportunities, for
ever lost, which ought to have been easy; and this gave me
a chance to say to her, "Did you mean a while ago that your
aunt has a plan of keeping me on by admitting me occasionally to her presence?"

"She thinks it will make a difference with you if you
sometimes see her. She wants you so much to stay that she
is willing to make that concession."

"And what good does she consider that I think it will do
me to see her?"

"I don't know; she thinks it's interesting," said Miss Tita,
simply. "You told her you found it so."

"So I did; but every one doesn't think so."

"No, of course not, or more people would try."

"Well, if she is capable of making that reflection she is
capable also of making this further one," I went on: "that
I must have a particular reason for not doing as others do,
in spite of the interest she offers—for not leaving her
alone." Miss Tita looked as if she failed to grasp this rather
complicated proposition; so I continued, "If you have not
told her what I said to you the other night may she not at
least have guessed it?"

"I don't know; she is very suspicious."

"But she has not been made so by indiscreet curiosity, by
persecution?"

"No, no; it isn't that," said Miss Tita, turning on me a
somewhat troubled face. "I don't know how to say it: it's on
account of something—ages ago, before I was born—in her
life."

"Something? What sort of thing?" I asked, as if I myself
could have no idea.

"Oh, she has never told me," Miss Tita answered; and I
was sure she was speaking the truth.

Her extreme limpidity was almost provoking, and I felt
for the moment that she would have been more satisfactory

if she had been less ingenuous. "Do you suppose it's something to which Jeffrey Aspern's letters and papers—I mean the things in her possession—have reference?"

"I daresay it is!" my companion exclaimed, as if this were a very happy suggestion. "I have never looked at any of those things."

"None of them? Then how do you know what they are?"

"I don't," said Miss Tita, placidly. "I have never had them in my hands. But I have seen them when she has had them out."

"Does she have them out often?"

"Not now, but she used to. She is very fond of them."

"In spite of their being compromising?"

"Compromising?" Miss Tita repeated, as if she was ignorant of the meaning of the word. I felt almost as one who corrupts the innocence of youth.

"I mean their containing painful memories."

"Oh, I don't think they are painful."

"You mean you don't think they affect her reputation?"

At this a singular look came into the face of Miss Bordereau's niece—a kind of confession of helplessness, an appeal to me to deal fairly, generously with her. I had brought her to the Piazza, placed her among charming influences, paid her an attention she appreciated, and now I seemed to let her perceive that all this had been a bribe—a bribe to make her turn in some way against her aunt. She was of a yielding nature and capable of doing almost anything to please a person who was kind to her; but the greatest kindness of all would be not to presume too much on this. It was strange enough, as I afterwards thought, that she had not the least air of resenting my want of consideration for her aunt's character, which would have been in the worst possible taste if anything less vital (from my point of view) had been at stake. I don't think she really measured it. "Do you mean that she did something bad?" she asked in a moment

"Heaven forbid I should say so, and it's none of my business. Besides, if she did," I added, laughing, "it was in other ages, in another world. But why should she not destroy her papers?"

"Oh, she loves them too much."

"Even now, when she may be near her end?"

"Perhaps when she's sure of that she will."

"Well, Miss Tita," I said, "it's just what I should like you to prevent."

"How can I prevent it?"

"Couldn't you get them away from her?"

"And give them to you?"

This put the case very crudely, though I am sure there was no irony in her intention. "Oh, I mean that you might let me see them and look them over. It isn't for myself; there is no personal avidity in my desire. It is simply that they would be of such immense interest to the public, such immeasurable importance as a contribution to Jeffrey Aspern's history."

She listened to me in her usual manner, as if my speech were full of reference to things she had never heard of, and I felt particularly like the reporter of a newspaper who forces his way into a house of mourning. This was especially the case when after a moment she said, "There was a gentleman who some time ago wrote to her in very much those words. He also wanted her papers."

"And did she answer him?" I asked, rather ashamed of myself for not having her rectitude.

"Only when he had written two or three times. He made her very angry."

"And what did she say?"

"She said he was a devil," Miss Tita replied, simply.

"She used that expression in her letter?"

"Oh no; she said it to me. She made me write to him."

"And what did you say?"

"I told him there were no papers at all."

"Ah, poor gentleman!" I exclaimed.

"I knew there were, but I wrote what she bade me."

"Of course you had to do that. But I hope I shall not pass for a devil."

"It will depend upon what you ask me to do for you," said Miss Tita, smiling.

"Oh, if there is a chance of *your* thinking so my affair is in a bad way! I sha'n't ask you to steal for me, nor even to fib—for you can't fib, unless on paper. But the principal thing is this—to prevent her from destroying the papers."

"Why, I have no control of her," said Miss Tita. "It's she who controls me."

"But she doesn't control her own arms and legs, does she? The way she would naturally destroy her letters would be to burn them. Now she can't burn them without fire, and she can't get fire unless you give it to her."

"I have always done everything she has asked," my companion rejoined. "Besides, there's Olimpia."

I was on the point of saying that Olimpia was probably corruptible, but I thought it best not to sound that note. So I simply inquired if that faithful domestic could not be managed.

"Every one can be managed by my aunt," said Miss Tita. And then she observed that her holiday was over; she must go home.

I laid my hand on her arm, across the table, to stay her a moment. "What I want of you is a general promise to help me."

"Oh, how can I—how can I?" she asked, wondering and troubled. She was half surprised, half frightened at my wishing to make her play an active part.

"This is the main thing: to watch her carefully and warn me in time, before she commits that horrible sacrilege."

"I can't watch her when she makes me go out."

"That's very true."

"And when you do too."

"Mercy on us; do you think she will have done anything to-night?"

"I don't know; she is very cunning."

"Are you trying to frighten me?" I asked.

I felt this inquiry sufficiently answered when my companion murmured in a musing, almost envious way, "Oh, but she loves them—she loves them!"

This reflection, repeated with such emphasis, gave me great comfort; but to obtain more of that balm I said, "If she shouldn't intend to destroy the objects we speak of before her death she will probably have made some disposition by will."

"By will?"

"Hasn't she made a will for your benefit?"

"Why, she has so little to leave. That's why she likes money," said Miss Tita.

"Might I ask, since we are really talking things over, what you and she live on?"

"On some money that comes from America, from a lawyer. He sends it every quarter. It isn't much!"

"And won't she have disposed of that?"

My companion hesitated—I saw she was blushing. "I believe it's mine," she said; and the look and tone which accompanied these words betrayed so the absence of the habit of thinking of herself that I almost thought her charming. The next instant she added, "But she had a lawyer once, ever so long ago. And some people came and signed something."

"They were probably witnesses. And you were not asked to sign? Well then," I argued, rapidly and hopefully, "it is because you are the legatee; she has left all her documents to you!"

"If she has it's with very strict conditions," Miss Tita responded, rising quickly, while the movement gave the words a little character of decision. They seemed to imply that the bequest would be accompanied with a command that the articles bequeathed should remain concealed from every inquisitive eye and that I was very much mistaken if I thought she was the person to depart from an injunction so solemn.

"Oh, of course you will have to abide by the terms," I said; and she uttered nothing to mitigate the severity of this conclusion. None the less, later, just before we disembarked at her own door, on our return, which had taken place almost in silence, she said to me abruptly, "I will do what I can to help you." I was grateful for this—it was very well so far as it went; but it did not keep me from remembering that night in a worried waking hour that I now had her word for it to reinforce my own impression that the old woman was very cunning.

CHAPTER VII

THE FEAR of what this side of her character might have led her to do made me nervous for days afterwards. I waited for an intimation from Miss Tita; I almost figured to myself that it was her duty to keep me informed, to let me know definitely whether or no Miss Bordereau had sacrificed her treasures. But as she gave no sign I lost patience and determined to judge so far as was possible with my own senses. I sent late one afternoon to ask if I might pay the ladies a visit, and my servant came back with surprising news. Miss Bordereau could be approached without the least difficulty; she had been moved out into the sala and was sitting by the window that overlooked the garden. I descended and found this picture correct; the old lady had been wheeled forth into the world and had a certain air, which came mainly perhaps from some brighter element in her dress, of being prepared again to have converse with it. It had not yet, however, begun to flock about her; she was perfectly alone and, though the door leading to her own quarters stood open, I had at first no glimpse of Miss Tita. The window at which she sat had the afternoon shade and, one of the shutters having been pushed back, she could see the pleasant garden, where the summer sun had by this time dried up too many of the plants—she could see the yellow light and the long shadows.

"Have you come to tell me that you will take the rooms for six months more?" she asked, as I approached her, startling me by something coarse in her cupidity almost as much as if she had not already given me a specimen of it. Juliana's desire to make our acquaintance lucrative had been, as I have sufficiently indicated, a false note in my image of the woman who had inspired a great poet with immortal lines; but I may say here definitely that I recognised after all that it behoved me to make a large allowance for her. It was I who had kindled the unholy flame; it was I who had put into her head that she had the means of making money. She appeared never to have thought of that; she had been living wastefully for years, in a house five times too big for her, on a footing that I could explain only by the presumption that, excessive as it was, the space she enjoyed cost her next to nothing and that small as were her revenues they left her, for Venice, an appreciable margin. I had descended on her one day and taught her to calculate, and my almost extravagant comedy on the subject of the garden had presented me irresistibly in the light of a victim. Like all persons who achieve the miracle of changing their point of view when they are old she had been intensely converted; she had seized my hint with a desperate, tremulous clutch.

I invited myself to go and get one of the chairs that stood, at a distance, against the wall (she had given herself no concern as to whether I should sit or stand); and while I placed it near her I began, gaily, "Oh, dear madam, what an imagination you have, what an intellectual sweep! I am a poor devil of a man of letters who lives from day to day. How can I take palaces by the year? My existence is precarious. I don't know whether six months hence I shall have bread to put in my mouth. I have treated myself for once; it has been an immense luxury. But when it comes to going on—!"

"Are your rooms too dear? if they are you can have more for the same money," Juliana responded. "We can arrange, we can *combinare*, as they say here."

"Well yes, since you ask me, they are too dear," I said. "Evidently you suppose me richer than I am."

She looked at me in her barricaded way. "If you write books don't you sell them?"

"Do you mean don't people buy them? A little—not so much as I could wish. Writing books, unless one be a great genius—and even then!—is the last road to fortune. I think there is no more money to be made by literature."

"Perhaps you don't choose good subjects. What do you write about?" Miss Bordereau inquired.

"About the books of other people. I'm a critic, an historian, in a small way." I wondered what she was coming to.

"And what other people, now?"

"Oh, better ones than myself: the great writers mainly—the great philosophers and poets of the past; those who are dead and gone and can't speak for themselves."

"And what do you say about them?"

"I say they sometimes attached themselves to very clever women!" I answered, laughing. I spoke with great deliberation, but as my words fell upon the air they struck me as imprudent. However, I risked them and I was not sorry, for perhaps after all the old woman would be willing to treat. It seemed to be tolerably obvious that she knew my secret: why therefore drag the matter out? But she did not take what I had said as a confession; she only asked:

"Do you think it's right to rake up the past?"

"I don't know that I know what you mean by raking it up; but how can we get at it unless we dig a little? The present has such a rough way of treading it down."

"Oh, I like the past, but I don't like critics," the old woman declared, with her fine tranquillity.

"Neither do I, but I like their discoveries."

"Aren't they mostly lies?"

"The lies are what they sometimes discover," I said, smiling at the quiet impertinence of this. "They often lay bare the truth."

"The truth is God's, it isn't man's; we had better leave it alone. Who can judge of it—who can say?"

"We are terribly in the dark, I know," I admitted; "but if we give up trying what becomes of all the fine things? What becomes of the work I just mentioned, that of the great philosophers and poets? It is all vain words if there is nothing to measure it by!"

"You talk as if you were a tailor," said Miss Bordereau, whimsically; and then she added quickly, in a different manner, "This house is very fine; the proportions are magnificent. To-day I wanted to look at this place again. I made them bring me out here. When your man came, just now, to learn if I would see you, I was on the point of sending for you, to ask if you didn't mean to go on. I wanted to judge what I'm letting you have. This sala is very grand," she pursued, like an auctioneer, moving a little, as I guessed, her invisible eyes. "I don't believe you often have lived in such a house, eh?"

"I can't often afford to!" I said.

"Well then, how much will you give for six months?"

I was on the point of exclaiming—and the air of excruciation in my face would have denoted a moral fact— "Don't, Juliana; for *his* sake, don't!" But I controlled myself and asked less passionately: "Why should I remain so long as that?"

"I thought you liked it," said Miss Bordereau, with her shrivelled dignity.

"So I thought I should."

For a moment she said nothing more, and I left my own words to suggest to her what they might. I half expected her to say, coldly enough, that if I had been disappointed we need not continue the discussion, and this in spite of the fact that I believed her now to have in her mind (however it had come there), what would have told her that my disappointment was natural. But to my extreme surprise she ended by observing: "If you don't think we have treated you well enough perhaps we can discover some way of treating you better." This speech was somehow so incongruous that it made me laugh again, and I excused myself by saying that she talked as if I were a sulky boy, pouting in the corner, to be "brought round." I had not a grain of complaint to make; and could anything have exceeded Miss Tita's graciousness in accompanying me a few nights before to the Piazza? At this the old woman went on: "Well, you brought it on yourself!" And then in a different tone, "She is a very nice girl." I assented cordially to this proposition, and she expressed the hope that I did so not merely to be obliging, but that I really liked her. Meanwhile I wondered still more what Miss Bordereau was coming to. "Except for me, to-day," she said, "she has not a relation in the world." Did she by describing her niece as amiable and unencumbered wish to represent her as a *parti*?

It was perfectly true that I could not afford to go on with my rooms at a fancy price and that I had already devoted

to my undertaking almost all the hard cash I had set apart
for it. My patience and my time were by no means exhausted, but I should be able to draw upon them only on
a more usual Venetian basis. I was willing to pay the venerable woman with whom my pecuniary dealings were such
a discord twice as much as any other *padrona di casa*
would have asked, but I was not willing to pay her twenty
times as much. I told her so plainly, and my plainness appeared to have some success, for she exclaimed, "Very
good; you have done what I asked—you have made an
offer!"

"Yes, but not for half a year. Only by the month."

"Oh, I must think of that then. She seemed disappointed
that I would not tie myself to a period, and I guessed that
she wished both to secure me and to discourage me; to say,
severely, "Do you dream that you can get off with less than
six months? Do you dream that even by the end of that time
you will be appreciably nearer your victory?" What was
more in my mind was that she had a fancy to play me the
trick of making me engage myself when in fact she had
annihilated the papers. There was a moment when my
suspense on this point was so acute that I all but broke out
with the question, and what kept it back was but a kind of
instinctive recoil (lest it should be a mistake), from the
last violence of self-exposure. She was such a subtle old
witch that one could never tell where one stood with her.
You may imagine whether it cleared up the puzzle when,
just after she had said she would think of my proposal
and without any formal transition, she drew out of her
pocket with an embarrassed hand a small object wrapped
in crumpled white paper. She held it there a moment and
then she asked, "Do you know much about curiosities?"

"About curiosities?"

"About antiquities, the old gimcracks that people pay so
much for to-day. Do you know the kind of price they
bring?"

I thought I saw what was coming, but I said ingenuously, "Do you want to buy something?"

"No, I want to sell. What would an amateur give me
for that?" She unfolded the white paper and made a mo-

tion for me to take from her a small oval portrait. I possessed myself of it with a hand of which I could only hope
that she did not perceive the tremor, and she added, "I
would part with it only for a good price."

At the first glance I recognised Jeffrey Aspern, and I
was well aware that I flushed with the act. As she was
watching me however I had the consistency to exclaim,
"What a striking face! Do tell me who it is."

"It's an old friend of mine, a very distinguished man in
his day. He gave it to me himself, but I'm afraid to mention his name, lest you never should have heard of him,
critic and historian as you are. I know the world goes fast
and one generation forgets another. He was all the fashion
when I was young."

She was perhaps amazed at my assurance, but I was surprised at hers; at her having the energy, in her state of
health and at her time of life, to wish to sport with me
that way simply for her private entertainment—the humour
to test me and practice on me. This, at least, was the interpretation that I put upon her production of the portrait, for
I could not believe that she really desired to sell it or cared
for any information I might give her. What she wished was
to dangle it before my eyes and put a prohibitive price on
it. "The face comes back to me, it torments me," I said,
turning the object this way and that and looking at it very
critically. It was a careful but not a supreme work of art,
larger than the ordinary miniature and representing a young
man with a remarkably handsome face, in a high-collared
green coat and a buff waistcoat. I judged the picture to have
a valuable quality of resemblance and to have been painted
when the model was about twenty-five years old. There are,
as all the world knows, three other portraits of the poet in
existence, but none of them is of so early a date as this
elegant production. "I have never seen the original but I
have seen other likenesses," I went on. "You expressed
doubt of this generation having heard of the gentleman,
but he strikes me for all the world as a celebrity. Now who
is he? I can't put my finger on him—I can't give him a
label. Wasn't he a writer? Surely he's a poet." I was de-

termined that it should be she, not I, who should first pronounce Jeffrey Aspern's name.

My resolution was taken in ignorance of Miss Bordereau's extremely resolute character, and her lips never
formed in my hearing the syllables that meant so much for
her. She neglected to answer my question but raised her
hand to take back the picture, with a gesture which though
ineffectual was in a high degree peremptory. "It's only a
person who should know for himself that would give me
my price," she said with a certain dryness.

"Oh, then, you have a price?" I did not restore the
precious thing; not from any vindictive purpose but because I instinctively clung to it. We looked at each other
hard while I retained it.

"I know the least I would take. What it occurred to me
to ask you about is the most I shall be able to get."

She made a movement, drawing herself together as if,
in a spasm of dread at having lost her treasure, she were
going to attempt the immense effort of rising to snatch it
from me. I instantly placed it in her hand again, saying as
I did so, "I should like to have it myself, but with your
ideas I could never afford it."

She turned the small oval plate over in her lap, with
its face down, and I thought I saw her catch her breath
a little, as if she had had a strain or an escape. This however did not prevent her saying in a moment, "You would
buy a likeness of a person you don't know, by an artist who
has no reputation?"

"The artist may have no reputation, but that thing is
wonderfully well painted," I replied, to give myself a reason.

"It's lucky you thought of saying that, because the
painter was my father."

"That makes the picture indeed precious!" I exclaimed,
laughing; and I may add that a part of my laughter came
from my satisfaction in finding that I had been right in my
theory of Miss Bordereau's origin. Aspern had of course
met the young lady when he went to her father's studio as
a sitter. I observed to Miss Bordereau that if she would

entrust me with her property for twenty-four hours I should be happy to take advice upon it; but she made no answer to this save to slip it in silence into her pocket. This convinced me still more that she had no sincere intention of selling it during her lifetime, though she may have desired to satisfy herself as to the sum her niece, should she leave it to her, might expect eventually to obtain for it. "Well, at any rate I hope you will not offer it without giving me notice," I said, as she remained irresponsive. "Remember that I am a possible purchaser."

"I should want your money first!" she returned, with unexpected rudeness; and then, as if she bethought herself that I had just cause to complain of such an insinuation and wished to turn the matter off, asked abruptly what I talked about with her niece when I went out with her that way in the evening.

"You speak as if we had set up the habit," I replied. "Certainly I should be very glad if it were to become a habit. But in that case I should feel a still greater scruple at betraying a lady's confidence."

"Her confidence? Has she got confidence?"

"Here she is—she can tell you herself," I said; for Miss Tita now appeared on the threshold of the old woman's parlour. "Have you got confidence, Miss Tita? Your aunt wants very much to know."

"Not in her, not in her!" the younger lady declared, shaking her head with a dolefulness that was neither jocular nor affected. "I don't know what to do with her; she has fits of horrid imprudence. She is so easily tired—and yet she has begun to roam—to drag herself about the house." And she stood looking down at her immemorial companion with a sort of helpless wonder, as if all their years of familiarity had not made her perversities, on occasion, any more easy to follow.

"I know what I'm about. I'm not losing my mind. I daresay you would like to think so," said Miss Bordereau, with a cynical little sigh.

"I don't suppose you came out here yourself. Miss Tita must have had to lend you a hand," I interposed, with a pacifying intention.

"Oh, she insisted that we should push her; and when she insists!" said Miss Tita, in the same tone of apprehension; as if there were no knowing what service that she disapproved of her aunt might force her next to render.

"I have always got most things done I wanted, thank God! The people I have lived with have humoured me," the old woman continued, speaking out of the gray ashes of her vanity.

"I suppose you mean that they have obeyed you."

"Well, whatever it is, when they like you."

"It's just because I like you that I want to resist," said Miss Tita, with a nervous laugh.

"Oh, I suspect you'll bring Miss Bordereau upstairs next, to pay me a visit," I went on; to which the old lady replied:

"Oh no; I can keep an eye on you from here!"

"You are very tired; you will certainly be ill tonight!" cried Miss Tita.

"Nonsense, my dear; I feel better at this moment than I have done for a month. To-morrow I shall come out again. I want to be where I can see this clever gentleman."

"Shouldn't you perhaps see me better in your sitting-room?" I inquired.

"Don't you mean shouldn't you have a better chance at me?" she returned, fixing me a moment with her green shade.

"Ah, I haven't that anywhere! I look at you but I don't see you."

"You excite her dreadfully—and that is not good," said Miss Tita, giving me a reproachful, appealing look.

"I want to watch you—I want to watch you!" the old lady went on.

"Well then, let us spend as much of our time together as possible—I don't care where—and that will give you every facility."

"Oh, I've seen you enough for to-day. I'm satisfied. Now I'll go home." Miss Tita laid her hands on the back of her aunt's chair and began to push, but I begged her to let me take her place. "Oh yes, you may move me this way—you sha'n't in any other!" Miss Bordereau exclaimed, as she felt herself propelled firmly and easily over the smooth, hard floor. Before we reached the door of her own apartment she commanded me to stop, and she took a long, last look up and down the noble sala. "Oh, it's a magnificent house!" she murmured; after which I pushed her forward. When we had entered the parlour Miss Tita told me that she should now be able to manage, and at the same moment the little red-haired *donna* came to meet her mistress. Miss Tita's idea was evidently to get her aunt immediately back to bed. I confess that in spite of this urgency I was guilty of the indiscretion of lingering; it held me there to think that I was nearer the documents I coveted—that they were probably put away somewhere in the faded, unsociable room. The place had indeed a bareness which did not suggest hidden treasures; there were no dusky nooks nor curtained corners, no massive cabinets nor chests with iron bands. Moreover it was possible, it was perhaps even probable that the old lady had consigned her relics to her bedroom, to some battered box that was shoved under the bed, to the drawer of some lame dressing-table, where they would be in the range of vision by the dim night-lamp. None the less I scrutinised every article of furniture, every conceivable cover for a hoard, and noticed that there were half a dozen things with drawers, and in particular a tall old secretary, with brass ornaments of the style of the Empire—a receptacle somewhat rickety but still capable of keeping a great many secrets. I don't know why this article fascinated me so, inasmuch as I certainly had no definite purpose of breaking into it; but I stared at it so hard that Miss Tita noticed me and changed colour. Her doing this made me think I was right and that wherever they might have been before, the Aspern papers at that moment languished behind the peevish little lock of the secretary. It was hard to remove my eyes from the dull mahogany front when I reflected that a simple panel divided me from the goal of my hopes; but I remembered my prudence and with an effort took leave of Miss Bordereau. To make the effort graceful I said to her that I should certainly bring her an opinion about the little picture.

"The little picture?" Miss Tita asked, surprised.

"What do *you* know about it, my dear?" the old woman demanded. "You needn't mind. I have fixed my price."

"And what may that be?"

"A thousand pounds."

"Oh Lord!" cried poor Miss Tita, irrepressibly.

"Is that what she talks to you about?" said Miss Bordereau.

"Imagine your aunt's wanting to know!" I had to separate from Miss Tita with only those words, though I should have liked immensely to add, "For heaven's sake meet me to-night in the garden!"

CHAPTER VIII

As IT TURNED OUT the precaution had not been needed, for three hours later, just as I had finished my dinner, Miss Bordereau's niece appeared, unannounced, in the open doorway of the room in which my simple repasts were served. I remember well that I felt no surprise at seeing her; which is not a proof that I did not believe in her timidity. It was immense, but in a case in which there was a particular reason for boldness it never would have prevented her from running up to my rooms. I saw that she was now quite full of a particular reason; it threw her forward—made her seize me, as I rose to meet her, by the arm.

"My aunt is very ill; I think she is dying!"

"Never in the world," I answered, bitterly. "Don't you be afraid!"

"Do go for a doctor—do, do! Olimpia is gone for the one we always have, but she doesn't come back; I don't know what has happened to her. I told her that if he was not at home she was to follow him where he had gone; but apparently she is following him all over Venice. I don't know what to do—she looks so as if she were sinking."

"May I see her, may I judge?" I asked. "Of course I shall be delighted to bring some one; but hadn't we better send my man instead, so that I may stay with you?"

Miss Tita assented to this and I despatched my servant for the best doctor in the neighbourhood. I hurried downstairs with her, and on the way she told me than an hour after I quitted them in the afternoon Miss Bordereau had had an attack of "oppression," a terrible difficulty in breathing. This had subsided but had left her so exhausted that she did not come up: she seemed all gone. I repeated that she was not gone, that she would not go yet; whereupon Miss Tita gave me a sharper sidelong glance than she had ever directed at me and said, "Really, what do you mean? I suppose you don't accuse her of making-believe!" I forget what reply I made to this, but I grant that in my heart I thought the old woman capable of any weird manœuvre. Miss Tita wanted to know what I had done to her; her aunt had told her that I had made her so angry. I declared I had done nothing—I had been exceedingly careful; to which my companion rejoined that Miss Bordereau had assured her she had had a scene with me—a scene that had upset her. I answered with some resentment that it was a scene of her own making—that I couldn't think what she was angry with me for unless for not seeing my way to give a thousand pounds for the portrait of Jeffrey Aspern. "And did she show you that? Oh gracious—oh deary me!" groaned Miss Tita, who appeared to feel that the situation was passing out of her control and that the elements of her fate were thickening around her. I said that I would give anything to possess it, yet that I had not a thousand pounds; but I stopped when we came to the door of Miss Bordereau's room. I had an immense curiosity to pass it, but I thought it my duty to represent to Miss Tita that if I made the invalid angry she ought perhaps to be spared the sight of me. "The sight of you? Do you think she can *see?*" my companion demanded, almost with indignation. I did think so but forbore to say it, and I softly followed my conductress.

I remember that what I said to her as I stood for a moment beside the old woman's bed was, "Does she never show you her eyes then? Have you never seen them?" Miss Bordereau had been divested of her green shade, but (it was not my fortune to behold Juliana in her nightcap) the upper half of her face was covered by the fall of a piece of dingy lacelike muslin, a sort of extemporised hood which, wound round her head, descended to the end of her nose, leaving nothing visible but her white withered cheeks and puckered mouth, closed tightly and, as it were, consciously. Miss Tita gave me a glance of surprise, evidently not seeing a reason for my impatience. "You mean that she always wears something? She does it to preserve them."

"Because they are so fine?"

"Oh, to-day, to-day!" And Miss Tita shook her head, speaking low. "But they used to be magnificent!"

"Yes indeed, we have Aspern's word for that." And as I looked again at the old woman's wrappings I could imagine that she had not wished to allow people a reason to say that the great poet had overdone it. But I did not waste my time in considering Miss Bordereau, in whom the appearance of respiration was so slight as to suggest that no human attention could ever help her more. I turned my eyes all over the room, rummaging with them the closets, the chests of drawers, the tables. Miss Tita met them quickly and read, I think, what was in them; but she did not answer it, turning away restlessly, anxiously, so that I felt rebuked, with reason, for a preoccupation that was almost profane in the presence of our dying companion. All the same I took another look, endeavouring to pick out mentally the place to try first, for a person who should wish to put his hand on Miss Bordereau's papers directly after her death. The room was a dire confusion; it looked like the room of an old actress. There were clothes hanging over chairs, odd-looking, shabby bundles here and there, and various pasteboard boxes piled together, battered, bulging and discoloured, which might have been fifty years old. Miss Tita after a moment noticed the direction of my eyes again and, as if she guessed how I judged the air of the place (forgetting I had no business to judge it at all), said, perhaps to defend herself from the imputation of complicity in such untidiness:

"She likes it this way; we can't move things. There are old bandboxes she has had most of her life." Then she added, half taking pity on my real thought, "Those things were *there*." And she pointed to a small, low trunk which stood under a sofa where there was just room for it. It appeared to be a queer, superannuated coffer, of painted wood, with elaborate handles and shrivelled straps and with the colour (it had last been endued with a coat of light green) much rubbed off. It evidently had travelled with

Juliana in the olden time—in the days of her adventures, which it had shared. It would have made a strange figure arriving at a modern hotel.

"*Were* there—they aren't now?" I asked, startled by Miss Tita's implication.

She was going to answer, but at that moment the doctor came in—the doctor whom the little maid had been sent to fetch and whom she had at last overtaken. My servant, going on his own errand, had met her with her companion in tow, and in the sociable Venetian spirit, retracing his steps with them, had also come up to the threshold of Miss Bordereau's room, where I saw him peeping over the doctor's shoulder. I motioned him away the more instantly that the sight of his prying face reminded me that I myself had almost as little to do there—an admonition confirmed by the sharp way the little doctor looked at me, appearing to take me for a rival who had the field before him. He was a short, fat, brisk gentleman who wore the tall hat of his profession and seemed to look at everything but his patient. He looked particularly at me, as if it struck him that I should be better for a dose, so that I bowed to him and left him with the women, going down to smoke a cigar in the garden. I was nervous; I could not go further; I could not leave the place. I don't know exactly what I thought might happen, but it seemed to me important to be there. I wandered about in the alleys—the warm night had come on—smoking cigar after cigar and looking at the light in Miss Bordereau's windows. They were open now, I could see; the situation was different. Sometimes the light moved, but not quickly; it did not suggest the hurry of a crisis. Was the old woman dying or was she already dead? Had the doctor said that there was nothing to be done at her tremendous age but to let her quietly pass away; or had he simply announced with a look a little more conventional that the end of the end had come? Were the other two women moving about to perform the offices that follow in such a case? It made me uneasy not to be nearer, as if I thought the doctor himself might carry away the papers with him. I bit my cigar hard as it came over me again that perhaps there were now no papers to carry!

I wandered about for an hour—for an hour and a half. I looked out for Miss Tita at one of the windows, having a vague idea that she might come there to give me some sign. Would she not see the red tip of my cigar moving about in the dark and feel that I wanted eminently to know what the doctor had said? I am afraid it is a proof my anxieties had made me gross that I should have taken in some degree for granted that at such an hour, in the midst of the greatest change that could take place in her life, they were uppermost also in poor Miss Tita's mind. My servant came down and spoke to me; he knew nothing save that the doctor had gone after a visit of half an hour. If he had stayed half an hour then Miss Bordereau was still alive: it could not have taken so much time as that to enunciate the contrary. I sent the man out of the house; there were moments when the sense of his curiosity annoyed me and this was one of them. *He* had been watching my cigar-tip from an upper window, if Miss Tita had not; he could not know what I was after and I could not tell him, though I was conscious he had fantastic private theories about me which he thought fine and which I, had I known them, should have thought offensive.

I went upstairs at last but I ascended no higher than the sala. The door of Miss Bordereau's apartment was open, showing from the parlour the dimness of a poor candle. I went toward it with a light tread and at the same moment Miss Tita appeared and stood looking at me as I approached. "She's better—she's better," she said, even before I had asked. "The doctor has given her something; she woke up, came back to life while he was there. He says there is no immediate danger."

"No immediate danger? Surely he thinks her condition strange!"

"Yes, because she had been excited. That affects her dreadfully."

"It will do so again then, because she excites herself. She did so this afternoon."

"Yes; she mustn't come out any more," said Miss Tita, with one of her lapses into a deeper placidity.

"What is the use of making such a remark as that if you

begin to rattle her about again the first time she bids you?"

"I won't—I won't do it any more."

"You must learn to resist her," I went on.

"Oh yes, I shall; I shall do so better if you tell me it's right."

"You mustn't do it for me; you must do it for yourself. It all comes back to you, if you are frightened."

"Well, I am not frightened now," said Miss Tita cheerfully. "She is very quiet."

"Is she conscious again—does she speak?"

"No, she doesn't speak, but she takes my hand. She holds it fast."

"Yes," I rejoined, "I can see what force she still has by the way she grabbed that picture this afternoon. But if she holds you fast how comes it that you are here?"

Miss Tita hesitated a moment; though her face was in deep shadow (she had her back to the light in the parlour and I had put down my own candle far off, near the door of the sala), I thought I saw her smile ingenuously. "I came on purpose—I heard your step."

"Why, I came on tiptoe, as inaudibly as possible."

"Well, I heard you," said Miss Tita.

"And is your aunt alone now?"

"Oh no; Olimpia is sitting there."

On my side I hesitated. "Shall we then step in there?" And I nodded at the parlour; I wanted more and more to be on the spot.

"We can't talk there—she will hear us."

I was on the point of replying that in that case we would sit silent, but I was too conscious that this would not do, as there was something I desired immensely to ask her. So I proposed that we should walk a little in the sala, keeping more at the other end, where we should not disturb the old lady. Miss Tita assented unconditionally; the doctor was coming again, she said, and she would be there to meet him at the door. We strolled through the fine super-fluous hall, where on the marble floor—particularly as at first we said nothing—our footsteps were more audible than I had expected. When we reached the other end—the wide window, inveterately closed, connecting with the balcony that overhung the canal—I suggested that we should remain there, as she would see the doctor arrive still better. I opened the window and we passed out on the balcony. The air of the canal seemed even heavier, hotter, than that of the sala. The place was hushed and void; the quiet neighbourhood had gone to sleep. A lamp, here and there, over the narrow black water, glimmered in double; the voice of a man going homeward singing, with his jacket on his shoulder and his hat on his ear, came to us from a distance. This did not prevent the scene from being very *comme il faut,* as Miss Bordereau had called it the first time I saw her. Presently a gondola passed along the canal with its slow rhythmical plash, and as we listened we watched it in silence. It did not stop, it did not carry the doctor; and after it had gone on I said to Miss Tita:

"And where are they now—the things that were in the trunk?"

"In the trunk?"

"That green box you pointed out to me in her room. You said her papers had been there; you seemed to imply that she had transferred them."

"Oh yes; they are not in the trunk," said Miss Tita.

"May I ask if you have looked?"

"Yes, I have looked—for you."

"How for me, dear Miss Tita? Do you mean you would have given them to me if you had found them?" I asked, almost trembling.

She delayed to reply and I waited. Suddenly she broke out, "I don't know what I would do—what I wouldn't!"

"Would you look again—somewhere else?"

She had spoken with a strange, unexpected emotion, and she went on in the same tone: "I can't—I can't—while she lies there. It isn't decent."

"No, it isn't decent," I replied, gravely. "Let the poor lady rest in peace." And the words, on my lips, were not hypocritical, for I felt reprimanded and shamed.

Miss Tita added in a moment, as if she had guessed this and were sorry for me, but at the same time wished to explain that I did drive her on or at least did insist too much:

"I can't deceive her that way. I can't deceive her—perhaps on her deathbed."

"Heaven forbid I should ask you, though I have been guilty myself!"

"You have been guilty?"

"I have sailed under false colours." I felt now as if I must tell her that I had given her an invented name, on account of my fear that her aunt would have heard of me and would refuse to take me in. I explained this and also that I had really been a party to the letter written to them by John Cumnor months before.

She listened with great attention, looking at me with parted lips, and when I had made my confession she said, "Then your real name—what is it?" She repeated it over twice when I had told her, accompanying it with the exclamation "Gracious, gracious!" Then she added, "I like your own best."

"So do I," I said, laughing. "Ouf! it's a relief to get rid of the other."

"So it was a regular plot—a kind of conspiracy?"

"Oh, a conspiracy—we were only two," I replied, leaving out Mrs. Prest of course.

She hesitated; I thought she was perhaps going to say that we had been very base. But she remarked after a moment, in a candid, wondering way, "How much you must want them!"

"Oh, I do, passionately!" I conceded, smiling. And this chance made me go on, forgetting my compunction of a moment before. "How can she possibly have changed their place herself? How can she walk? How can she arrive at that sort of muscular exertion? How can she lift and carry things?"

"Oh, when one wants and when one has so much will!" said Miss Tita, as if she had thought over my question already herself and had simply had no choice but that answer—the idea that in the dead of night, or at some moment when the coast was clear, the old woman had been capable of a miraculous effort.

"Have you questioned Olimpia? Hasn't she helped her

—hasn't she done it for her?" I asked; to which Miss Tita replied promptly and positively that their servant had had nothing to do with the matter, though without admitting definitely that she had spoken to her. It was as if she were a little shy, a little ashamed now of letting me see how much she had entered into my uneasiness and had me on her mind. Suddenly she said to me, without any immediate relevance:

"I feel as if you were a new person, now that you have got a new name."

"It isn't a new one; it is a very good old one, thank heaven!"

She looked at me a moment. "I do like it better."

"Oh, if you didn't I would almost go on with the other!"

"Would you really?"

I laughed again, but for all answer to this inquiry I said, "Of course if she can rummage about that way she can perfectly have burnt them."

"You must wait—you must wait," Miss Tita moralised mournfully; and her tone ministered little to my patience, for it seemed after all to accept that wretched possibility. I would teach myself to wait, I declared nevertheless; because in the first place I could not do otherwise and in the second I had her promise, given me the other night, that she would help me.

"Of course if the papers are gone that's no use," she said; not as if she wished to recede, but only to be conscientious.

"Naturally. But if you could only find out!" I groaned, quivering again.

"I thought you said you would wait."

"Oh, you mean wait even for that?"

"For what then?"

"Oh, nothing," I replied, rather foolishly, being ashamed to tell her what had been implied in my submission to delay —the idea that she would do more than merely find out. I know not whether she guessed this; at all events she appeared to become aware of the necessity for being a little more rigid.

"I didn't promise to deceive, did I? I don't think I did."

"It doesn't much matter whether you did or not, for you couldn't!"

I don't think Miss Tita would have contested this even had she not been diverted by our seeing the doctor's gondola shoot into the little canal and approach the house. I noted that he came as fast as if he belived that Miss Bordereau was still in danger. We looked down at him while he disembarked and then went back into the sala to meet him. When he came up however I naturally left Miss Tita to go off with him alone, only asking her leave to come back later for news.

I went out of the house and took a long walk, as far as the Piazza, where my restlessness declined to quit me. I was unable to sit down (it was very late now but there were people still at the little tables in front of the cafés); I could only walk round and round, and I did so half a dozen times. I was uncomfortable, but it gave me a certain pleasure to have told Miss Tita who I really was. At last I took my way home again, slowly getting all but inextricably lost, as I did whenever I went out in Venice: so that it was considerably past midnight when I reached my door. The sala, upstairs, was as dark as usual and my lamp as I crossed it found nothing satisfactory to show me. I was disappointed, for I had notified Miss Tita that I would come back for a report, and I thought she might have left a light there as a sign. The door of the ladies' apartment was closed; which seemed an intimation that my faltering friend had gone to bed, tired of waiting for me. I stood in the middle of the place, considering, hoping she would hear me and perhaps peep out, saying to myself too that she would never go to bed with her aunt in a state so critical; she would sit up and watch—she would be in a chair, in her dressing-gown. I went nearer the door; I stopped there and listened. I heard nothing at all and at last I tapped gently. No answer came and after another minute I turned the handle. There was no light in the room; this ought to have prevented me from going in, but it had no such effect. If I have candidly narrated the importunities, the indelicacies, of which my desire to possess myself of Jeffrey Aspern's papers had rendered me capable I need not

shrink from confessing this last indiscretion. I think it was
the worst thing I did; yet there were extenuating circumstances. I was deeply though doubtless not disinterestedly
anxious for more news of the old lady, and Miss Tita had
accepted from me, as it were, a rendezvous which it might
have been a point of honour with me to keep. It may be
said that her leaving the place dark was a positive sign
that she released me, and to this I can only reply that I
desired not to be released.

The door of Miss Bordereau's room was open and I
could see beyond it the faintness of a taper. There was no
sound—my footstep caused no one to stir. I came further
into the room; I lingered there with my lamp in my hand.
I wanted to give Miss Tita a chance to come to me if she
were with her aunt, as she must be. I made no noise to
call her; I only waited to see if she would not notice my
light. She did not, and I explained this (I found afterwards I was right) by the idea that she had fallen asleep.
If she had fallen asleep her aunt was not on her mind, and
by explanation ought to have led me to go out as I had
come. I must repeat again that it did not, for I found myself at the same moment thinking of something else. I had
no definite purpose, no bad intention, but I felt myself
held to the spot by an acute, though absurd, sense of opportunity. For what I could not have said, inasmuch as it was
not in my mind that I might commit a theft. Even if it
had been I was confronted with the evident fact that Miss
Bordereau did not leave her secretary, her cupboard and
the drawers of her tables gaping. I had no keys, no tools
and no ambition to smash her furniture. None the less it
came to me that I was now, perhaps alone, unmolested, at
the hour of temptation and secrecy, nearer to the torment-
ing treasure than I had ever been. I held up my lamp, let
the light play on the different objects as if it could tell me
something. Still there came no movement from the other
room. If Miss Tita was sleeping she was sleeping sound.
Was she doing so—generous creature—on purpose to leave
me the field? Did she know I was there and was she just
keeping quiet to see what I would do—what I *could* do?

But what could I do, when it came to that? She herself knew even better than I how little.

I stopped in front of the secretary, looking at it very idiotically; for what had it to say to me after all? In the first place it was locked, and in the second it almost surely contained nothing in which I was interested. Ten to one the papers had been destroyed; and even if they had not been destroyed the old woman would not have put them in such a place as that after removing them from the green trunk—would not have transferred them, if she had the idea of their safety on her brain, from the better hiding-place to the worse. The secretary was more conspicuous, more accessible in a room in which she could no longer mount guard. It opened with a key, but there was a little brass handle, like a button, as well; I saw this as I played my lamp over it. I did something more than this at that moment: I caught a glimpse of the possibility that Miss Tita wished me really to understand. If she did not wish me to understand, if she wished me to keep away, why had she not locked the door of communication between the sitting-room and the sala? That would have been a definite sign that I was to leave them alone. If I did not leave them alone she meant me to come for a purpose—a purpose now indicated by the quick, fantastic idea that to oblige me she had unlocked the secretary. She had not left the key, but the lid would probably move if I touched the button. This theory fascinated me, and I bent over very close to judge. I did not propose to do anything, not even—not in the least—to let down the lid; I only wanted to test my theory, to see if the cover *would* move. I touched the button with my hand—a mere touch would tell me; and as I did so (it is embarrassing for me to relate it), I looked over my shoulder. It was a chance, an instinct, for I had not heard anything. I almost let my luminary drop and certainly I stepped back, straightening myself up at what I saw. Miss Bordereau stood there in her night-dress, in the doorway of her room, watching me; her hands were raised, she had lifted the everlasting curtain that covered half her face, and for the first, the last, the only time I beheld her extraordinary eyes. They glared at me, they made me horribly ashamed. I never shall forget her strange little bent white tottering figure, with its lifted head, her attitude, her expression; neither shall I forget the tone in which as I turned, looking at her, she hissed out passionately, furiously:

"Ah, you publishing scoundrel!"

I know not what I stammered, to excuse myself, to explain; but I went towards her, to tell her I meant no harm. She waved me off with her old hands, retreating before me in horror; and the next thing I knew she had fallen back with a quick spasm, as if death had descended on her, into Miss Tita's arms.

CHAPTER IX

I LEFT VENICE the next morning, as soon as I learnt that the old lady had not succumbed, as I feared at the moment, to the shock I had given her—the shock I may also say she had given me. How in the world could I have supposed her capable of getting out of bed by herself? I failed to see Miss Tita before going; I only saw the *donna*, whom I entrusted with a note for her younger mistress. In this note I mentioned that I should be absent but for a few days. I went to Treviso, to Bassano, to Castelfranco; I took walks and drives and looked at musty old churches with ill-lighted pictures and spent hours seated smoking at the doors of cafés, where there were flies and yellow curtains, on the shady side of sleepy little squares. In spite of these pastimes, which were mechanical and perfunctory, I scantily enjoyed my journey: there was too strong a taste of the disagreeable in my life. It had been devilish awkward, as the young men say, to be found by Miss Bordereau in the dead of night examining the attachment of her bureau; and it had not been less so to have to believe for a good many hours afterward that it was highly probable I had killed her. In writing to Miss Tita I attempted to minimise these irregularities; but as she gave me no word of answer I could not know what impression I made upon her. It rankled in my mind that I had been called a publishing scoundrel, for certainly I did publish and certainly I had not been very delicate. There was a moment when I stood convinced that the only way to make up for this latter fault was to take myself away altogether on the instant; to sacrifice my hopes and relieve the two poor women for ever of the oppression of my intercourse. Then I reflected that I had better try a short absence first, for I must already have had a sense (unexpressed and dim) that in disappearing completely it would not be merely my own hopes that I should condemn to extinction. It would perhaps be sufficient if I stayed away long enough to give the elder lady time to think she was rid of me. That she would wish to be rid of me after this (if I was not rid of her) was now not to be doubted: that nocturnal scene would have cured her of the disposition to put up with my company for the sake of my dollars. I said to myself that after all I could not abandon Miss Tita, and I continued to say this even while I observed that she quite failed to comply with my earnest request (I had given her two or three addresses, at little towns, *poste restante*) that she would let me know how she was getting on. I would have made my servant write to me but that he was unable to manage a pen. It struck me there was a kind of scorn in Miss Tita's silence (little disdainful as she had ever been), so that I was uncomfortable and sore. I had scruples about going back and yet I had others about not doing so, for I wanted to put myself on a better footing. The end of it was that I did return to Venice on the twelfth day; and as my gondola gently bumped against Miss Bordereau's steps a certain palpitation of suspense told me that I had done myself a violence in holding off so long.

I had faced about so abruptly that I had not telegraphed to my servant. He was therefore not at the station to meet me, but he poked out his head from an upper window when I reached the house. "They have put her into the earth, *la vecchia*," he said to me in the lower hall, while he shouldered my valise; and he grinned and almost winked, as if he knew I should be pleased at the news.

"She's dead!" I exclaimed, giving him a very different look.

"So it appears, since they have buried her."

"It's all over? When was the funeral?"

"The other yesterday. But a funeral you could scarcely call it, signore; it was a dull little passeggio of two gondolas. Poveretta!" the man continued, referring apparently to Miss Tita. His conception of funerals was apparently that they were mainly to amuse the living.

I wanted to know about Miss Tita—how she was and where she was—but I asked him no more questions till we had got upstairs. Now that the fact had met me I took a bad view of it, especially of the idea that poor Miss Tita had had to manage by herself after the end. What did she know about arrangements, about the steps to take in such a case? Poveretta indeed! I could only hope that the doctor had given her assistance and that she had not been neglected by the old friends of whom she had told me, the little band of the faithful whose fidelity consisted in coming to the house once a year. I elicited from my servant that two old ladies and an old gentleman had in fact rallied round Miss Tita and had supported her (they had come for her in a gondola of their own) during the journey to the cemetery, the little red-walled island of tombs which lies to the north of the town, on the way to Murano. It appeared from these circumstances that the Misses Bordereau were Catholics, a discovery I had never made, as the old woman could not go to church and her niece, so far as I perceived, either did not or went only to early mass in the parish, before I was stirring. Certainly even the priests respected their seclusion; I had never caught the whisk of the curato's skirt. That evening, an hour later, I sent my servant down with five words written on a card, to ask Miss Tita if she would see me for a few moments. She was not in the house, where he had sought her, he told me when he came back, but in the garden walking about to refresh herself and gathering flowers. He had found her there and she would be very happy to see me.

I went down and passed half an hour with poor Miss Tita. She had always had a look of musty mourning (as if she were wearing out old robes of sorrow that would not come to an end), and in this respect there was no appreciable change in her appearance. But she evidently had been crying, crying a great deal—simply, satisfyingly, refreshingly, with a sort of primitive, retarded sense of loneliness and violence. But she had none of the formalism or the self-consciousness of grief, and I was almost surprised to see her standing there in the first dusk with her hands full of flowers, smiling at me with her reddened eyes. Her white face, in the frame of her mantilla, looked longer, leaner than usual. I had had an idea that she would be a good deal disgusted with me—would consider that I ought to have been on the spot to advise her, to help her; and, though I was sure there was no rancour in her composition and no great conviction of the importance of her affairs, I had prepared myself for a difference in her manner, for some little injured look, half familiar, half estranged, which should say to my conscience, "Well, you are a nice person to have professed things!" But historic truth compels me to declare that Tita Bordereau's countenance expressed unqualified pleasure in seeing her late aunt's lodger. That touched him extremely and he thought it simplified his situation until he found it did not. I was as kind to her that evening as I knew how to be, and I walked about the garden with her for half an hour. There was no explanation of any sort between us; I did not ask her why she had not answered my letter. Still less did I repeat what I had said to her in that communication; if she chose to let me suppose that she had forgotten the position in which Miss Bordereau surprised me that night and the effect of the discovery on the old woman I was quite willing to take it that way: I was grateful to her for not treating me as if I had killed her aunt.

We strolled and strolled and really not much passed between us save the recognition of her bereavement, conveyed in my manner and in a visible air that she had of depending on me now, since I let her see that I took an interest in her. Miss Tita had none of the pride that makes a person wish to preserve the look of independence; she did not in the least pretend that she knew at present what would become of her. I forbore to touch particularly on that however, for I certainly was not prepared to say that I would take charge of her. I was cautious; not ignobly, I think, for I felt that her knowledge of life was so small that in her unsophisticated vision there would be no reason why—since I seemed to pity her—I should not look after her. She told me how her aunt had died, very peacefully at the last, and how everything had been done afterwards by the care of her good friends (fortunately, thanks

to me, she said, smiling, there was money in the house; and
she repeated that when once the Italians like you they are
your friends for life); and when we had gone into this she
asked me about my *giro*, my impressions, the places I had
seen. I told her what I could, making it up partly, I am
afraid, as in my depression I had not seen much; and
after she had heard me she exclaimed, quite as if she had
forgotten her aunt and her sorrow, "Dear, dear, how much
I should like to do such things—to take a little journey!"
It came over me for the moment that I ought to propose
some tour, say I would take her anywhere she liked; and I
remarked at any rate that some excursion—to give her a
change—might be managed: we would think of it, talk it
over. I said never a word to her about the Aspern documents; asked no questions as to what she had ascertained
or what had otherwise happened with regard to them before Miss Bordereau's death. It was not that I was not on
pins and needles to know, but that I thought it more decent not to betray my anxiety so soon after the catastrophe.
I hoped she herself would say something, but she never
glanced that way, and I thought this natural at the time.
Later however, that night, it occurred to me that her silence was somewhat strange; for if she had talked of my
movements, of anything so detached as the Giorgione at
Castelfranco, she might have alluded to what she could
easily remember was in my mind. It was not to be supposed that the emotion produced by her aunt's death had
blotted out the recollection that I was interested in that
lady's relics, and I fidgeted afterwards as it came to me
that her reticence might very possibly mean simply that
nothing had been found. We separated in the garden (it
was she who said she must go in); now that she was alone
in the rooms I felt that (judged, at any rate, by Venetian
ideas) I was on rather a different footing in regard to visit-
ing her there. As I shook hands with her for good-night I
asked her if she had any general plan—had thought over
what she had better do. "Oh, yes, oh yes, but I haven't settled anything yet," she replied, quite cheerfully. Was her
cheerfulness explained by the impression that I would
settle for her?

I was glad the next morning that we had neglected practical questions, for this gave me a pretext for seeing her again immediately. There was a very practical question to be touched upon. I owed it to her to let her know formally that of course I did not expect her to keep me on as a lodger, and also to show some interest in her own tenure, what she might have on her hands in the way of a lease. But I was not destined, as it happened, to converse with her for more than an instant on either of these points. I sent her no message; I simply went down to the sala and walked to and fro there. I knew she would come out; she would very soon discover I was there. Somehow I preferred not to be shut up with her; gardens and big halls seemed better places to talk. It was a splendid morning, with something in the air that told of the waning of the long Venetian summer; a freshness from the sea which stirred the flowers in the garden and made a pleasant draught in the house, less shuttered and darkened now than when the old woman was alive. It was the beginning of autumn, of the end of the golden months. With this it was the end of my experiment—or would be in the course of half an hour, when I should really have learned that the papers had been reduced to ashes. After that there would be nothing left for me but to go to the station; for seriously (and as it struck me in the morning light) I could not linger there to act as guardian to a piece of middle-aged female helplessness. If she had not saved the papers wherein should I be indebted to her? I think I winced a little as I asked myself how much, if she *had* saved them, I should have to recognise and, as it were, to reward such a courtesy. Might not that circumstance after all saddle me with a guardianship? If this idea did not make me more uncomfortable as I walked up and down it was because I was convinced I had nothing to look to. If the old woman had not destroyed everything before she pounced upon me in the parlour she had done so afterwards.

It took Miss Tita rather longer than I had expected to guess that I was there; but when at last she came out she looked at me without surprise. I said to her that I had been waiting for her and she asked why I had not let her know. I was glad the next day that I had checked myself before remarking that I had wished to see if a friendly intuition would not tell her: it became a satisfaction to me that I had not indulged in that rather tender joke. What I did say was virtually the truth—that I was too nervous, since I expected her now to settle my fate.

"Your fate?" said Miss Tita, giving me a queer look; and as she spoke I noticed a rare change in her. She was different from what she had been the evening before—less natural, less quiet. She had been crying the day before and she was not crying now, and yet she struck me as less confident. It was as if something had happened to her during the night, or at least as if she had thought of something that troubled her—something in particular that affected her relations with me, made them more embarrassing and complicated. Had she simply perceived that her aunt's not being there now altered my position?

"I mean about our papers. *Are* there any? You must know now."

"Yes, there are a great many; more than I supposed." I was struck with the way her voice trembled as she told me this.

"Do you mean that you have got them in there—and that I may see them?"

"I don't think you can see them," said Miss Tita, with an extraordinary expression of entreaty in her eyes, as if the dearest hope she had in the world now was that I would not take them from her. But how could she expect me to make such a sacrifice as that after all that had passed between us? What had I come back to Venice for but to see them, to take them? My delight at learning they were still in existence was such that if the poor woman had gone down on her knees to beseech me never to mention them again I would have treated the proceeding as a bad joke. "I have got them but I can't show them," she added.

"Not even to me? Ah, Miss Tita!" I groaned, with a voice of infinite remonstrance and reproach.

She coloured and the tears came back to her eyes; I saw

that it cost her a kind of anguish to take such a stand but that a dreadful sense of duty had descended upon her. It made me quite sick to find myself confronted with that particular obstacle; all the more had it appeared to me I had been extremely encouraged to leave it out of account. I almost considered that Miss Tita had assured me that if she had no greater hindrance than that—! "You don't mean to say you made her a deathbed promise? It was precisely against your doing anything of that sort that I thought I was safe. Oh, I would rather she had burned the papers outright than that!"

"No, it isn't a promise," said Miss Tita.

"Pray what is it then?"

She hesitated and then she said, "She tried to burn them, but I prevented it. She had hid them in her bed."

"In her bed?"

"Between the mattresses. That's where she put them when she took them out of the trunk. I can't understand how she did it, because Olimpia didn't help her. She tells me so and I believe her. My aunt only told her afterwards so that she shouldn't touch the bed—anything but the sheets. So it was badly made," added Miss Tita, simply.

"I should think so! And how did she try to burn them?"

"She didn't try much; she was too weak, those last days. But she told me—she charged me. Oh, it was terrible! She couldn't speak after that night; she could only make signs."

"And what did you do?"

"I took them away. I locked them up."

"In the secretary?"

"Yes, in the secretary," said Miss Tita, reddening again.

"Did you tell her you would burn them?"

"No, I didn't—on purpose."

"On purpose to gratify me?"

"Yes, only for that."

"And what good will you have done me if after all you won't show them?"

"Oh, none; I know that—I know that."

"And did she believe you had destroyed them?"

"I don't know what she believed at the last. I couldn't tell—she was too far gone."

"Then if there was no promise and no assurance I can't see what ties you."

"Oh, she hated it so—she hated it so! She was so jealous. But here's the portrait—you may have that," Miss Tita announced, taking the little picture, wrapped up in the same manner in which her aunt had wrapped it, out of her pocket.

"I may have it—do you mean you give it to me?" I questioned, staring, as it passed into my hand.

"Oh yes."

"But it's worth money—a large sum."

"Well!" said Miss Tita, still with her strange look.

I did not know what to make of it, for it could scarcely mean that she wanted to bargain like her aunt. She spoke as if she wished to make me a present. "I can't take it from you as a gift," I said, "and yet I can't afford to pay you for it according to the ideas Miss Bordereau had of its value. She rated it at a thousand pounds."

"Couldn't we sell it?" asked Miss Tita.

"God forbid! I prefer the picture to the money."

"Well then keep it."

"You are very generous."

"So are you."

"I don't know why you should think so," I replied; and this was a truthful speech, for the singular creature appeared to have some very fine reference in her mind, which I did not in the least seize.

"Well, you have made a great difference for me," said Miss Tita.

I looked at Jeffrey Aspern's face in the little picture, partly in order not to look at that of my interlocutress, which had begun to trouble me, even to frighten me a little—it was so self-conscious, so unnatural. I made no answer to this last declaration; I only privately consulted Jeffrey Aspern's delightful eyes with my own (they were so young and brilliant, and yet so wise, so full of vision); I asked him what on earth was the matter with Miss Tita. He seemed to smile at me with friendly mockery, as if he were amused at my case. I had got into a pickle for him—as if he needed it! He was unsatisfactory, for the only moment since I had known him. Nevertheless, now that I held the little picture in my hand I felt that it would be a precious possession. "Is this a bribe to make me give up the papers?" I demanded in a moment, perversely. "Much as I value it, if I were to be obliged to choose, the papers are what I should prefer. Ah, but ever so much!"

"How can you choose—how can you choose?" Miss Tita asked, slowly, lamentably.

"I see! Of course there is nothing to be said, if you regard the interdiction that rests upon you as quite insurmountable. In this case it must seem to you that to part with them would be an impiety of the worst kind, a simple sacrilege!"

Miss Tita shook her head, full of her dolefulness. "You would understand if you had known her. I'm afraid," she quavered suddenly—"I'm afraid! She was terrible when she was angry."

"Yes, I saw something of that, that night. She was terrible. Then I saw her eyes. Lord, they were fine!"

"I see them—they stare at me in the dark!" said Miss Tita.

"You are nervous, with all you have been through."

"Oh yes, very—very!"

"You mustn't mind; that will pass away," I said, kindly. Then I added, resignedly, for it really seemed to me that I must accept the situation, "Well, so it is, and it can't be helped. I must renounce." Miss Tita, at this, looking at me, gave a low, soft moan, and I went on: "I only wish to heaven she had destroyed them; then there would be nothing more to say. And I can't understand why, with her ideas, she didn't."

"Oh, she lived on them!" said Miss Tita.

"You can imagine whether that makes me want less to see them," I answered, smiling. "But don't let me stand here as if I had it in my soul to tempt you to do anything base. Naturally you will understand I give up my rooms. I leave Venice immediately." And I took up my hat, which I had placed on a chair. We were still there rather awkwardly, on our feet, in the middle of the sala. She had left the door of the apartments open behind her but she had not led me that way.

A kind of spasm came into her face as she saw me take my hat. "Immediately—do you mean to-day?" The tone of the words was tragical—they were a cry of desolation.

"Oh no; not so long as I can be of the least service to you."

"Well, just a day or two more—just two or three days," she panted. Then controlling herself she added in another manner, "She wanted to say something to me—the last day—something very particular, but she couldn't."

"Something very particular?"

"Something more about the papers."

"And did you guess—have you any idea?"

"No, I have thought—but I don't know. I have thought all kinds of things."

"And for instance?"

"Well, that if you were a relation it would be different."

"If I were a relation?"

"If you were not a stranger. Then it would be the same for you as for me. Anything that is mine—would be yours, and you could do what you like. I couldn't prevent you—and you would have no responsibility."

She brought out this droll explanation with a little nervous rush, as if she were speaking words she had got by heart. They gave me an impression of subtlety and at first I failed to follow. But after a moment her face helped me to see further, and then a light came into my mind. It was embarrassing, and I bent my head over Jeffrey Aspern's portrait. What an odd expression was in his face! "Get out of it as you can, my dear fellow!" I put the picture into the pocket of my coat and said to Miss Tita, "Yes, I'll sell it for you. I sha'n't get a thousand pounds by any means, but I shall get something good."

She looked at me with tears in her eyes, but she seemed to try to smile as she remarked, "We can divide the money."

"No, no, it shall be all yours." Then I went on, "I think I know what your poor aunt wanted to say. She wanted to give directions that her papers should be buried with her."

Miss Tita appeared to consider this suggestion for a moment; after which she declared, with striking decision, "Oh no, she wouldn't have thought that safe!"

"It seems to me nothing could be safer."

"She had an idea that when people want to publish they are capable—" And she paused, blushing.

"Of violating a tomb? Mercy on us, what must she have thought of me!"

"She was not just, she was not generous!" Miss Tita cried with sudden passion.

The light that had come into my mind a moment before increased. "Ah, don't say that, for we *are* a dreadful race." Then I pursued, "If she left a will, that may give you some idea."

"I have found nothing of the sort—she destroyed it. She was very fond of me," Miss Tita added, incongruously. "She wanted me to be happy. And if any person should be kind to me—she wanted to speak of that."

I was almost awestricken at the astuteness with which the good lady found herself inspired, transparent astuteness as it was and sewn, as the phrase is, with white thread. "Depend upon it she didn't want to make any provision that would be agreeable to me."

"No, not to you but to me. She knew I should like it if you could carry out your idea. Not because she cared for you but because she did think of me," Miss Tita went on, with her unexpected, persuasive volubility. "You could see them—you could use them." She stopped, seeing that I perceived the sense of that conditional—stopped long enough for me to give some sign which I did not give. She must have been conscious however that though my face showed the greatest embarrassment that was ever painted on a human countenance it was not set as a stone, it was also full of compassion. It was a comfort to me a long time afterwards to consider that she could not have seen in me the smallest symptom of disrespect. "I don't know what to do; I'm too tormented, I'm too ashamed!" she continued, with vehemence. Then turning away from me and burying her face in her hands she burst into a flood of tears. If she did not know what to do it may be imagined whether I did any better. I stood there dumb, watching her while her sobs resounded in the great empty hall. In a moment she was facing me again, with her streaming eyes. "I would give you everything—and she would understand, where she is—she would forgive me!"

"Ah, Miss Tita—ah, Miss Tita," I stammered, for all reply. I did not know what to do, as I say, but at a venture I made a wild, vague movement, in consequence of which I found myself at the door. I remember standing there and staying, "It wouldn't do—it wouldn't do!" pensively, awkwardly, grotesquely, while I looked away to the opposite end of the sala as if there were a beautiful view there. The next thing I remember is that I was downstairs and out of the house. My gondola was there and my gondolier, reclining on the cushions, sprang up as soon as he saw me. I jumped in and to his usual *"Dove commanda?"* I replied, in a tone that made him stare, "Anywhere, anywhere; out into the lagoon!"

He rowed me away and I sat there prostrate, groaning softly to myself, with my hat pulled over my face. What in the name of the preposterous did she mean if she did not mean to offer me her hand? That was the price—that was the price! And did she think I wanted it, poor deluded, infatuated, extravagant lady? My gondolier, behind me, must have seen my ears red as I wondered, sitting there under the fluttering *tenda*, with my hidden face, noticing nothing as we passed—wondered whether her delusion, her infatuation had been my own reckless work. Did she think I had made love to her, even to get the papers? I had not, I had not; I repeated that over to myself for an hour, for two hours, till I was wearied if not convinced. I don't know where my gondolier took me; we floated aimlessly about on the lagoon, with slow, rare strokes. At last I became conscious that we were near the Lido, far up, on the right hand, as you turn your back to Venice, and I made him put me ashore. I wanted to walk, to move, to shed some of my bewilderment. I crossed the narrow strip and got to the sea-beach—I took my way toward Malamocco. But presently I flung myself down again on the warm sand, in the breeze, on the coarse dry grass. It took it out of me to think I had been so much at fault, that I had unwittingly but none the less deplorably trifled. But I had not given her cause—distinctly I had not. I had said to Mrs. Prest that I would make love to her; but it had been a joke without consequences and I had never said it to Tita Bordereau. I had been as kind as possible, because I really liked her; but since when had that become a crime where a woman of such an age and such an appearance was concerned? I am far from remembering clearly the succession of events and feelings during this long day of confusion, which I spent entirely in wandering about, without going home, until late at night; it only comes back to me that there were moments when I pacified my conscience and others when I lashed it into pain. I did not laugh all day—that I do recollect; the case, however it might have struck others, seemed to me so little amusing. It would have been better perhaps for me to feel the comic side of it. At any rate, whether I had given cause or not it went without saying that I could not pay the price. I could not accept. I could not, for a bundle of tattered papers, marry a ridiculous, pathetic, provincial old woman. It was a proof that she did not think the idea would come to me, her having determined to suggest it herself in that practical, argumentative, heroic way, in which the timidity however had been so much more striking than the boldness that her reasons appeared to come first and her feelings afterward.

As the day went on I grew to wish that I had never heard of Aspern's relics, and I cursed the extravagant curiosity that had put John Cumnor on the scent of them. We had more than enough material without them and my predicament was the just punishment of that most fatal of human follies, our not having known when to stop. It was very well to say it was no predicament, that the way out was simple, that I had only to leave Venice by the first train in the morning, after writing a note to Miss Tita, to be placed in her hand as soon as I got clear of the house; for it was a strong sign that I was embarrassed that when I tried to make up the note in my mind in advance (I would put it on paper as soon as I got home, before going to bed), I could not think of anything but "How can I thank you for the rare confidence you have placed in me?" That would never do; it sounded exactly as if an acceptance were to follow. Of course I might go away without writing a word, but that would be brutal and my idea was still to exclude brutal solutions. As my confusion cooled I was lost in wonder at the importance I had attached to Miss Bordereau's crumpled scraps; the thought of them became odious to me and I was as vexed with the old witch for the superstition that had prevented her from destroying them as I was with myself for having already spent more money than I could afford in attempting to control their fate. I forget what I did, where I went after leaving the Lido and at what hour or with what recovery of composure I made my way back to my boat. I only know that in the afternoon, when the air was aglow with the sunset, I was standing before the church of Saints John and Paul and looking up at the small square-jawed face of Bartolommeo Colleoni, the terrible *condottiere* who sits so sturdily astride of his huge bronze horse, on the high pedestal on which Venetian gratitude maintains him. The statue is incomparable, the finest of all mounted figures, unless that of Marcus Aurelius, who rides benignant before the Roman Capitol, be finer: but I was not thinking of that; I only found myself staring at the triumphant captain as if he had an oracle on his lips. The western light shines into all his grimness at that hour and makes it wonderfully personal. But he continued to look far over my head, at the red immersion of another day—he had seen so many go down into the lagoon through the centuries—and if he were thinking of battles and stratagems they were of a different quality from any I had to tell him of. He could not direct me what to do, gaze up at him as I might. Was it before this or after that I wandered about for an hour in the small canals, to the continued stupefaction of my gondolier, who had never seen me so restless and yet so void of a purpose and could extract from me no order but "Go anywhere—everywhere—all over the place"? He reminded me that I had not lunched and expressed therefore respectfully the hope that I would dine earlier. He had had long periods of leisure during the day, when I had left the boat and rambled, so that I was not obliged to consider him, and I told him that that day, for a change, I would touch no meat. It was an effect of poor Miss Tita's proposal, not altogether auspicious, that I had quite lost my appetite. I don't know why it happened that on this occasion I was more than ever struck with that queer air of sociability, of cousinship and family life, which makes up half the expression of Venice. Without streets and vehicles, the uproar of wheels, the brutality of horses, and with its little winding ways where people crowd together, where voices sound as in the corridors of a house, where the human step circulates as if it skirted the angles of furniture and shoes never wear out, the place has the character of an immense collective apartment, in which Piazza San Marco is the most ornamented corner and palaces and churches, for the rest, play the part of great divans of repose, tables of entertainment, expanses of decoration. And somehow the splendid common domicile, familiar, domestic and resonant, also resembles a theatre, with actors clicking over bridges and, in straggling processions, tripping along fondamentas. As you sit in your gondola the footways that in certain parts edge the canals assume to the eye the importance of a stage, meeting it at the same angle, and the Venetian figures, moving to and fro against the battered scenery of their little houses of comedy, strike you as members of an endless dramatic troupe.

I went to bed that night very tired, without being able to compose a letter to Miss Tita. Was this failure the reason why I became conscious the next morning as soon as I awoke of a determination to see the poor lady again the first moment she would receive me? That had something to do with it, but what had still more was the fact that during my sleep a very odd revulsion had taken place in my spirit. I found myself aware of this almost as soon as I opened my eyes; it made me jump out of my bed with the movement of a man who remembers that he has left the house door ajar or a candle burning under a shelf. Was I still in time to save my goods? That question was in my heart; for what had now come to pass was that in the unconscious cerebration of sleep I had swung back to a passionate appreciation of Miss Bordereau's papers. They were now more precious than ever and a kind of ferocity had come into my desire to possess them. The condition Miss Tita had attached to the possession of them no longer appeared an obstacle worth thinking of, and for an hour, that morning, my repentant imagination brushed it aside. It was absurd that I should be able to invent nothing; absurd to renounce so easily and turn away helpless from the idea that the only way to get hold of the papers was to unite myself to her for life. I would not unite myself and yet I would have them. I must add that by the time I sent down to ask if she would see me I had invented no alternative, though to do so I had had all the time that I was dressing. This failure was humiliating, yet what could the alternative be? Miss Tita sent back word that I might come; and as I descended the stairs and crossed the sala to her door—this time she received me in her aunt's forlorn parlour—I hoped she would not think my errand was to tell her I accepted her hand. She certainly would have made the day before the reflection that I declined it.

As soon as I came into the room I saw that she had drawn this inference, but I also saw something which had not been in my forecast. Poor Miss Tita's sense of her failure had produced an extraordinary alteration in her, but I had been too full of my literary concupiscence to think of that. Now I perceived it; I can scarcely tell how it startled me. She stood in the middle of the room with a face of mildness bent upon me, and her look of forgiveness, of absolution made her angelic. It beautified her; she was younger; she was not a ridiculous old woman. This optical trick gave her a sort of phantasmagoric brightness, and while I was still the victim of it I heard a whisper somewhere in the depths of my conscience: "Why not, after all —why not?" It seemed to me I was ready to pay the price. Still more distinctly however than the whisper I heard Miss Tita's own voice. I was so struck with the different effect she made upon me that at first I was not clearly aware of what she was saying; then I perceived she had bade me good-bye—she said something about hoping I should be very happy.

"Good-bye—good-bye?" I repeated, with an inflection interrogative and probably foolish.

I saw she did not feel the interrogation, she only heard the words; she had strung herself up to accepting our separation and they fell upon her ear as a proof. "Are you going to-day?" she asked. "But it doesn't matter, for whenever you go I shall not see you again. I don't want to." And she smiled strangely, with an infinite gentleness. She had never doubted that I had left her the day before in horror. How could she, since I had not come back before night to contradict, even as a simple form, such an idea? And now she had the force of soul—Miss Tita with force of soul was a new conception—to smile at me in her humiliation.

"What shall you do—where shall you go?" I asked.

"Oh, I don't know. I have done the great thing. I have destroyed the papers."

"Destroyed them?" I faltered.

"Yes; what was I to keep them for? I burnt them last night, one by one, in the kitchen."

"One by one?" I repeated, mechanically.

"It took a long time—there were so many." The room seemed to go round me as she said this and a real darkness for a moment descended upon my eyes. When it passed Miss Tita was there still, but the transfiguration was over and she had changed back to a plain, dingy, elderly person. It was in this character she spoke as she said, "I can't stay with you longer, I can't;" and it was in this character that she turned her back upon me, as I had turned mine upon her twenty-four hours before, and moved to the door of her room. Here she did what I had not done when I quitted her—she paused long enough to give me one look. I have never forgotten it and I sometimes still suffer from it, though it was not resentful. No, there was no resentment, nothing hard or vindictive in poor Miss Tita; for when, later, I sent her in exchange for the portrait of Jeffrey Aspern a larger sum of money than I had hoped to be able to gather for her, writing to her that I had sold the picture, she kept it with thanks; she never sent it back. I wrote to her that I had sold the picture, but I admitted to Mrs. Prest at the time (I met her in London, in the autumn), that it hangs above my writing-table. When I look at it my chagrin at the loss of the letters becomes almost intolerable.

The Spoils of Poynton

CHAPTER I

MRS. GERETH had said she would go with the rest to church, but suddenly it seemed to her that she should not be able to wait even till church-time for relief: breakfast, at Waterbath, was a punctual meal, and she had still nearly an hour on her hands. Knowing the church to be near, she prepared in her room for the little rural walk, and on her way down again, passing through corridors and observing imbecilities of decoration, the æsthetic misery of the big commodious house, she felt a return of the tide of last night's irritation, a renewal of everything she could secretly suffer from ugliness and stupidity. Why did she consent to such contacts, why did she so rashly expose herself? She had had, heaven knew, her reasons, but the whole experience was to be sharper than she had feared. To get away from it and out into the air, into the presence of sky and trees, flowers and birds was a necessity of every nerve. The flowers at Waterbath would probably go wrong in color and the nightingales sing out of tune; but she remembered to have heard the place described as possessing those advantages that are usually spoken of as natural. There were advantages enough it clearly didn't possess. It was hard for her to believe that a woman could look presentable who had been kept awake for hours by the wall-paper in her room; yet none the less, as in her fresh widow's weeds she rustled across the hall, she was sustained by the consciousness, which always added to the unction of her social Sundays, that she was, as usual, the only person in the house incapable of wearing in her preparation the horrible stamp of the same exceptional smartness that would be conspicuous in a grocer's wife. She would rather have perished than have looked *endimanchée*.

She was fortunately not challenged, the hall being empty of the other women, who were engaged precisely in array-ing themselves to that dire end. Once in the grounds, she recognized that, with a site, a view that struck the note, set an example to its inmates, Waterbath ought to have been charming. How she herself, with such elements to handle, would have taken the fine hint of nature! Suddenly, at the turn of a walk, she came on a member of the party, a young lady seated on a bench in deep and lonely meditation. She had observed the girl at dinner and afterwards: she was always looking at girls with an apprehensive or speculative reference to her son. Deep in her heart was a conviction that Owen would, in spite of all her spells, marry at last a frump; and this from no evidence that she could have repre-sented as adequate, but simply from her deep uneasiness, her belief that such a special sensibility as her own could have been inflicted on a woman only as a source of anguish. It would be her fate, her discipline, her cross, to have a frump brought hideously home to her. This girl, one of the two Vetches, had no beauty, but Mrs. Gereth, scanning the dullness for a sign of life, had been straightway able to classify such a figure as the least, for the moment, of her afflictions. Fleda Vetch was dressed with an idea, though perhaps with not much else; and that made a bond when there was none other, especially as in this case the idea was real, not imitation. Mrs. Gereth had long ago generalized the truth that the temperament of the frump is amply con-sistent with a certain usual prettiness. There were five girls in the party, and the prettiness of this one, slim, pale, and black-haired, was less likely than that of the others ever to occasion an exchange of platitudes. The two less de-veloped Brigstocks, daughters of the house, were in par-ticular tiresomely "lovely." A second glance, this morning, at the young lady before her conveyed to Mrs. Gereth the soothing assurance that she also was guiltless of looking hot and fine. They had had no talk as yet, but this was a note that would effectually introduce them if the girl should show herself in the least conscious of their community. She got up from her seat with a smile that but partly dissipated the prostration Mrs. Gereth had recognized in her attitude.

The elder woman drew her down again, and for a minute, as they sat together, their eyes met and sent out mutual soundings. "Are you safe? Can I utter it?" each of them said to the other, quickly recognizing, almost proclaiming, their common need to escape. The tremendous fancy, as it came to be called, that Mrs. Gereth was destined to take to Fleda Vetch virtually began with this discovery that the poor child had been moved to flight even more promptly than herself. That the poor child no less quickly perceived how far she could now go was proved by the immense friendliness with which she instantly broke out: "Isn't it too dreadful?"

"Horrible—horrible!" cried Mrs. Gereth, with a laugh, "and it's really a comfort to be able to say it." She had an idea, for it was her ambition, that she successfully made a secret of that awkward oddity, her proneness to be rendered unhappy by the presence of the dreadful. Her passion for the exquisite was the cause of this, but it was a passion she considered that she never advertised nor gloried in, contenting herself with letting it regulate her steps and show quietly in her life, remembering at all times that there are few things more soundless than a deep devotion. She was therefore struck with the acuteness of the little girl who had already put a finger on her hidden spring. What was dreadful now, what was horrible, was the intimate ugliness of Waterbath, and it was of that phenomenon these ladies talked while they sat in the shade and drew refreshment from the great tranquil sky, from which no blue saucers were suspended. It was an ugliness fundamental and systematic, the result of the abnormal nature of the Brigstocks, from whose composition the principle of taste had been extravagantly omitted. In the arrangement of their home some other principle, remarkably active, but uncanny and obscure, had operated instead, with consequences depressing to behold, consequences that took the form of a universal futility. The house was bad in all conscience, but it might have passed if they had only let it alone. This saving mercy was beyond them; they had smothered it with trumpery ornament and scrapbook art, with strange excrescences and bunchy draperies, with gimcracks that might have been keepsakes for maid-servants and nondescript conveniences that might have been prizes for the blind. They had gone wildly astray over carpets and curtains; they had an infallible instinct for disaster, and were so cruelly doom-ridden that it rendered them almost tragic. Their drawing-room, Mrs. Gereth lowered her voice to mention, caused her face to burn, and each of the new friends confided to the other that in her own apartment she had given way to tears. There was in the elder lady's a set of comic water-colors, a family joke by a family genius, and in the younger's a souvenir from some centennial or other Exhibition, that they shudderingly alluded to. The house was perversely full of souvenirs of places even more ugly than itself and of things it would have been a pious duty to forget. The worst horror was the acres of varnish, something advertised and smelly, with which everything was smeared; it was Fleda Vetch's conviction that the application of it, by their own hands and hilariously shoving each other, was the amusement of the Brigstocks on rainy days.

When, as criticism deepened, Fleda dropped the suggestion that some people would perhaps see something in Mona, Mrs. Gereth caught her up with a groan of protest, a smothered familiar cry of "Oh, my dear!" Mona was the eldest of the three, the one Mrs. Gereth most suspected. She confided to her young friend that it was her suspicion that had brought her to Waterbath; and this was going very far, for on the spot, as a refuge, a remedy, she had clutched at the idea that something might be done with the girl before her. It was her fancied exposure at any rate that had sharpened the shock; made her ask herself with a terrible chill if fate could really be plotting to saddle her with a daughter-in-law brought up in such a place. She had seen Mona in her appropriate setting and she had seen Owen, handsome and heavy, dangle beside her; but the effect of these first hours had happily not been to darken the prospect. It was clearer to her that she could never accept Mona, but it was after all by no means certain that Owen would ask her to. He had sat by somebody else at dinner, and afterwards he had talked to Mrs. Firmin, who was as dreadful as all the rest, but redeemingly married. His

heaviness, which in her need of expansion she freely
named, had two aspects: one of them his monstrous lack of
taste, the other his exaggerated prudence. If it should come
to a question of carrying Mona with a high hand there
would be no need to worry, for that was rarely his manner
of proceeding.

Invited by her companion, who had asked if it weren't
wonderful, Mrs. Gereth had begun to say a word about
Poynton; but she heard a sound of voices that made her
stop short. The next moment she rose to her feet, and
Fleda could see that her alarm was by no means quenched.
Behind the place where they had been sitting the ground
dropped with a certain steepness, forming a long grassy
bank, up which Owen Gereth and Mona Brigstock, dressed
for church but making a familiar joke of it, were in the
act of scrambling and helping each other. When they had
reached the even ground Fleda was able to read the meaning
of the exclamation in which Mrs. Gereth had expressed
her reserves on the subject of Miss Brigstock's personality.
Miss Brigstock had been laughing and even romping, but
the circumstance hadn't contributed the ghost of an expression to her countenance. Tall, straight and fair, long-
limbed and strangely festooned, she stood there without
a look in her eye or any perceptible intention of any sort in
any other feature. She belonged to the type in which speech
is an unaided emission of sound and the secret of being is
impenetrably and incorruptibly kept. Her expression would
probably have been beautiful if she had had one, but
whatever she communicated she communicated, in a manner best known to herself, without signs. This was not the
case with Owen Gereth, who had plenty of them, and all
very simple and immediate. Robust and artless, eminently
natural, yet perfectly correct, he looked pointlessly active
and pleasantly dull. Like his mother and like Fleda Vetch,
but not for the same reason, this young pair had come out
to take a turn before church.

The meeting of the two couples was sensibly awkward,
and Fleda, who was sagacious, took the measure of the
shock inflicted on Mrs. Gereth. There had been intimacy—
oh yes, intimacy as well as puerility—in the horse-play of

which they had just had a glimpse. The party began to
stroll together to the house, and Fleda had again a sense of
Mrs. Gereth's quick management in the way the lovers, or
whatever they were, found themselves separated. She
strolled behind with Mona, the mother possessing herself of
her son, her exchange of remarks with whom, however,
remained, as they went, suggestively inaudible. That member of the party in whose intenser consciousness we shall
most profitably seek a reflection of the little drama with
which we are concerned received an even livelier impression of Mrs. Gereth's intervention from the fact that ten
minutes later, on the way to church, still another pairing
had been effected. Owen walked with Fleda, and it was
an amusement to the girl to feel sure that this was by his
mother's direction. Fleda had other amusements as well:
such as noting that Mrs. Gereth was now with Mona Brigstock; such as observing that she was all affability to that
young woman; such as reflecting that, masterful and clever,
with a great bright spirit, she was one of those who impose
themselves as an influence; such as feeling finally that Owen
Gereth was absolutely beautiful and delightfully dense.
This young person had even from herself wonderful secrets
of delicacy and pride; but she came as near distinctness as
in the consideration of such matters she had ever come at
all in now surrendering herself to the idea that it was of a
pleasant effect and rather remarkable to be stupid without
offense—of a pleasanter effect and more remarkable indeed than to be clever and horrid. Owen Gereth at any
rate, with his inches, his features, and his lapses, was neither
of these latter things. She herself was prepared, if she
should ever marry, to contribute all the cleverness, and she
liked to think that her husband would be a force grateful
for direction. She was in her small way a spirit of the
same family as Mrs. Gereth. On that flushed and huddled
Sunday a great matter occurred; her little life became
aware of a singular quickening. Her meagre past fell away
from her like a garment of the wrong fashion, and as she
came up to town on the Monday what she stared at in the
surburban fields from the train was a future full of the
things she particularly loved.

CHAPTER II

THESE WERE neither more nor less than the things with which she had had time to learn from Mrs. Gereth that Poynton overflowed. Poynton, in the south of England, was this lady's established, or rather her disestablished home, having recently passed into the possession of her son. The father of the boy, an only child, had died two years before, and in London, with his mother, Owen was occupying for May and June a house good-naturedly lent them by Colonel Gereth, their uncle and brother-in-law. His mother had laid her hand so engagingly on Fleda Vetch that in a very few days the girl knew it was possible they should suffer together in Cadogan Place almost as much as they had suffered together at Waterbath. The kind colonel's house was also an ordeal, but the two women, for the ensuing month, had at least the relief of their confessions. The great drawback of Mrs. Gereth's situation was that, thanks to the rare perfection of Poynton, she was condemned to wince wherever she turned. She had lived for a quarter of a century in such warm closeness with the beautiful that, as she frankly admitted, life had become for her a kind of fool's paradise. She couldn't leave her own house without peril of exposure. She didn't say it in so many words, but Fleda could see she held that there was nothing in England really to compare to Poynton. There were places much grander and richer, but there was no such complete work of art, nothing that would appeal so to those who were really informed. In putting such elements into her hand fortune had given her an inestimable chance; she knew how rarely well things had gone with her and that she had tasted a happiness altogether rare.

There had been in the first place the exquisite old house itself, early Jacobean, supreme in every part: it was a provocation, an inspiration, a matchless canvas for the picture. Then there had been her husband's sympathy and generosity, his knowledge and love, their perfect accord and beautiful life together, twenty-six years of planning and seeking, a long, sunny harvest of taste and curiosity. Lastly, she never denied, there had been her personal gift, the genius, the passion, the patience of the collector—a patience, an almost infernal cunning, that had enabled her to do it all with a limited command of money. There wouldn't have been money enough for any one else, she said with pride, but there had been money enough for her. They had saved on lots of things in life, and there were lots of things they hadn't had, but they had had in every corner of Europe their swing among the Jews. It was fascinating to poor Fleda, who hadn't a penny in the world nor anything nice at home, and whose only treasure was her subtle mind, to hear this genuine English lady, fresh and fair, young in the fifties, declare with gayety and conviction that she was herself the greatest Jew who had ever tracked a victim. Fleda, with her mother dead, hadn't so much even as a home, and her nearest chance of one was that there was some appearance her sister would become engaged to a curate whose eldest brother was supposed to have property and would perhaps allow him something. Her father paid some of her bills, but he didn't like her to live with him; and she had lately, in Paris, with several hundred other young women, spent a year in a studio, arming herself for the battle of life by a course with an impressionist painter. She was determined to work, but her impressions, or somebody's else, were as yet her only material. Mrs. Gereth had told her she liked her because she had an extraordinary *flair;* but under the circumstances a *flair* was a questionable boon: in the dry places in which she had mainly moved she could have borne a chronic catarrh. She was constantly summoned to Cadogan Place, and before the month was out was kept to stay, to pay a visit of which the end, it was agreed, should have nothing to do with the beginning. She had a sense, partly exultant and partly

alarmed, of having quickly become necessary to her imperious friend, who indeed gave a reason quite sufficient for
it in telling her there was nobody else who understood.
From Mrs. Gereth there was in these days an immense
deal to understand, though it might be freely summed up in
the circumstance that she was wretched. She told Fleda that
she couldn't completely know why till she should have seen
the things at Poynton. Fleda could perfectly grasp this
connection, which was exactly one of the matters that, in
their inner mystery, were a blank to everybody else.

The girl had a promise that the wonderful house should
be shown her early in July, when Mrs. Gereth would return to it as to her home; but even before this initiation
she put her finger on the spot that in the poor lady's
troubled soul ached hardest. This was the misery that
haunted her, the dread of the inevitable surrender. What
Fleda had to sit up to was the confirmed appearance that
Owen Gereth would marry Mona Brigstock, marry her in
his mother's teeth, and that such an act would have incal-
culable bearings. They were present to Mrs. Gereth, her
companion could see, with a vividness that at moments
almost ceased to be that of sanity. She would have to give
up Poynton, and give it up to a product of Waterbath—
that was the wrong that rankled, the humiliation at which
Fleda would be able adequately to shudder only when she
should know the place. She did know Waterbath, and she
despised it—she had that qualification for sympathy. Her
sympathy was intelligent, for she read deep into the matter;
she stared, aghast, as it came home to her for the first
time, at the cruel English custom of the expropriation of
the lonely mother. Mr. Gereth had apparently been a very
amiable man, but Mr. Gereth had left things in a way that
made the girl marvel. The house and its contents had been
treated as a single splendid object; everything was to go
straight to his son, and his widow was to have a maintenance
and a cottage in another county. No account whatever had
been taken of her relation to her treasures, of the passion
with which she had waited for them, worked for them,
picked them over, made them worthy of each other and
the house, watched them, loved them, lived with them. He

appeared to have assumed that she would settle questions with her son, that he could depend upon Owen's affection. And in truth, as poor Mrs. Gereth inquired, how could he possibly have had a prevision—he who turned his eyes instinctively from everything repulsive—of anything so abnormal as a Waterbath Brigstock? He had been in ugly houses enough, but had escaped that particular nightmare. Nothing so perverse could have been expected to happen as that the heir to the loveliest thing in England should be inspired to hand it over to a girl so exceptionally tainted. Mrs. Gereth spoke of poor Mona's taint as if to mention it were almost a violation of decency, and a person who had listened without enlightenment would have wondered of what fault the girl had been or had indeed not been guilty. But Owen had from a boy never cared, had never had the least pride or pleasure in his home.

"Well, then, if he doesn't care!"—Fleda exclaimed, with some impetuosity; stopping short, however, before she completed her sentence.

Mrs. Gereth looked at her rather hard. "If he doesn't care?"

Fleda hesitated; she had not quite had a definite idea. "Well—he'll give them up."

"Give what up?"

"Why, those beautiful things."

"Give them up to whom?" Mrs. Gereth more boldly stared.

"To you, of course—to enjoy, to keep for yourself."

"And leave his house as bare as your hand? There's nothing in it that isn't precious."

Fleda considered; her friend had taken her up with a smothered ferocity by which she was slightly disconcerted. "I don't mean of course that he should surrender everything; but he might let you pick out the things to which you're most attached."

"I think he would if he were free," said Mrs. Gereth.

"And do you mean, as it is, that *she*'ll prevent him?" Mona Brigstock, between these ladies, was now nothing but "she."

"By every means in her power."

"But surely not because she understands and appreciates them?"

"No," Mrs Gereth replied, "but because they belong to the house and the house belongs to Owen. If I should wish to take anything, she would simply say, with that motionless mask: 'It goes with the house.' And day after day, in the face of every argument, of every consideration of generosity, she would repeat, without winking, in that voice like the squeeze of a doll's stomach: 'It goes with the house—it goes with the house.' In that attitude they'll shut themselves up."

Fleda was struck, was even a little startled with the way Mrs. Gereth had turned this over—had faced, if indeed only to recognize its futility, the notion of a battle with her only son. These words led her to make an inquiry which she had not thought it discreet to make before; she brought out the idea of the possibility, after all, of her friend's continuing to live at Poynton. Would they really wish to proceed to extremities? Was no good-humored, graceful compromise to be imagined or brought about? Couldn't the same roof cover them? Was it so very inconceivable that a married son should, for the rest of her days, share with so charming a mother the home she had devoted more than a score of years to making beautiful for him? Mrs. Gereth hailed this question with a wan, compassionate smile; she replied that a common household, in such a case, was exactly so inconceivable that Fleda had only to glance over the fair face of the English land to see how few people had ever conceived it. It was always thought a wonder, a "mistake," a piece of overstrained sentiment; and she confessed that she was as little capable of a flight of that sort as Owen himself. Even if they both had been capable, they would still have Mona's hatred to reckon with. Fleda's breath was sometimes taken away by the great bounds and elisions which, on Mrs. Gereth's lips, the course of discussion could take. This was the first she had heard of Mona's hatred, though she certainly had not needed Mrs. Gereth to tell her that in close quarters that young lady would prove secretly mulish. Later Fleda perceived indeed that perhaps almost any girl would hate

a person who should be so markedly averse to having anything to do with her. Before this, however, in conversation
with her young friend, Mrs. Gereth furnished a more vivid
motive for her despair by asking how she could possibly be
expected to sit there with the new proprietors and accept—
or call it, for a day, endure—the horrors they would perpetrate in the house. Fleda reasoned that they wouldn't after
all smash things nor burn them up; and Mrs. Gereth admitted when pushed that she didn't quite suppose they
would. What she meant was that they would neglect them,
ignore them, leave them to clumsy servants (there wasn't
an object of them all but should be handled with perfect
love), and in many cases probably wish to replace them by
pieces answerable to some vulgar modern notion of the
convenient. Above all, she saw in advance, with dilated
eyes, the abominations they would inevitably mix up with
them—the maddening relics of Waterbath, the little
brackets and pink vases, the sweepings of bazaars, the
family photographs and illuminated texts, the "household
art" and household piety of Mona's hideous home. Wasn't
it enough simply to contend that Mona would approach
Poynton in the spirit of a Brigstock, and that in the spirit
of a Brigstock she would deal with her acquisition? Did
Fleda really see *her*, Mrs. Gereth demanded, spending the
remainder of her days with such a creature's elbow in her
eye?

Fleda had to declare that she certainly didn't, and that
Waterbath had been a warning it would be frivolous to
overlook. At the same time she privately reflected that
they were taking a great deal for granted, and that, inasmuch as to her knowledge Owen Gereth had positively
denied his betrothal, the ground of their speculations was
by no means firm. It seemed to our young lady that in a
difficult position Owen conducted himself with some natural
art; treating this domesticated confidant of his mother's
wrongs with a simple civility that almost troubled her conscience, so deeply she felt that she might have had for him
the air of siding with that lady against him. She wondered
if he would ever know how little really she did this, and that
she was there, since Mrs. Gereth had insisted, not to betray,

but essentially to confirm and protect. The fact that his mother disliked Mona Brigstock might have made him dislike the object of her preference, and it was detestable to Fleda to remember that she might have appeared to him to offer herself as an exemplary contrast. It was clear enough, however, that the happy youth had no more sense for a motive than a deaf man for a tune, a limitation by which, after all, she could gain as well as lose. He came and went very freely on the business with which London abundantly furnished him, but he found time more than once to say to her, "It's awfuly nice of you to look after poor Mummy." As well as his quick speech, which shyness made obscure—it was usually as desperate as a "rush" at some violent game—his child's eyes in his man's face put it to her that, you know, this really meant a good deal for him and that he hoped she would stay on. With a person in the house who, like herself, was clever, poor Mummy was conveniently occupied; and Fleda found a beauty in the candor and even in the modesty which apparently kept him from suspecting that two such wiseheads could possibly be occupied with Owen Gereth.

CHAPTER III

THEY WENT AT LAST, the wiseheads, down to Poynton, where the palpitating girl had the full revelation. *"Now do you know how I feel?"* Mrs. Gereth asked when in the wonderful hall, three minutes after their arrival, her pretty associate dropped on a seat with a soft gasp and a roll of dilated eyes. The answer came clearly enough, and in the rapture of that first walk through the house Fleda took a prodigious span. She perfectly understood how Mrs. Gereth felt—she had understood but meagerly before; and the two women embraced with tears over the tightening of their bond—tears which on the younger one's part were the natural and usual sign of her submission to perfect beauty. It was not the first time she had cried for the joy of admiration, but it was the first time the mistress of Poynton, often as she had shown her house, had been present at such an exhibition. She exulted in it; it quickened her own tears; she assured her companion that such an occasion made the poor old place fresh to her again and more precious than ever. Yes, nobody had ever, that way, felt what she had achieved: people were so grossly ignorant, and everybody, even the knowing ones, as they thought themselves, more or less dense. What Mrs. Gereth had achieved was indeed an exquisite work; and in such an art of the treasure-hunter, in selection and comparison refined to that point, there was an element of creation, of personality. She had commended Fleda's *flair,* and Fleda now gave herself up to satiety. Preoccupations and scruples fell away from her; she had never known a greater happiness than the week she passed in this initiation.

Wandering through clear chambers where the general

effect made preferences almost as impossible as if they had
been shocks, pausing at open doors where vistas were long
and bland, she would, even if she had not already known,
have discovered for herself that Poynton was the record of
a life. It was written in great syllables of color and form,
the tongues of other countries and the hands of rare artists.
It was all France and Italy, with their ages composed to
rest. For England you looked out of old windows—it was
England that was the wide embrace. While outside, on the
low terraces, she contradicted gardeners and refined on
nature, Mrs. Gereth left her guest to finger fondly the
brasses that Louis Quinze might have thumbed, to sit with
Venetian velvets just held in a loving palm, to hang over
cases of enamels and pass and repass before cabinets. There
were not many pictures—the panels and the stuffs were
themselves the picture; and in all the great wainscoted
house there was not an inch of pasted paper. What struck
Fleda most in it was the high pride of her friend's taste,
a fine arrogance, a sense of style which, however amused
and amusing, never compromised nor stooped. She felt
indeed, as this lady had intimated to her that she would,
both a respect and a compassion that she had not known
before; the vision of the coming surrender filled her with
an equal pain. To give it all up, to die to it—that thought
ached in her breast. She herself could imagine clinging there
with a closeness separate from dignity. To have created
such a place was to have had dignity enough; when there
was a question of defending it the fiercest attitude was the
right one. After so intense a taking of possession she too
was to give it up; for she reflected that if Mrs. Gereth's
remaining there would have offered her a sort of future—
stretching away in safe years on the other side of a gulf—
the advent of the others could only be, by the same law, a
great vague menace, the ruffling of a still water. Such were
the emotions of a hungry girl whose sensibility was almost
as great as her opportunities for comparison had been
small. The museums had done something for her, but
nature had done more.

If Owen had not come down with them nor joined them
later, it was because he still found London jolly; yet the

question remained of whether the jollity of London was
not merely the only name his small vocabulary yielded for
the jollity of Mona Brigstock. There was indeed in his
conduct another ambiguity—something that required ex-
plaining so long as his motive didn't come to the surface.
If he was in love, what was the matter? And what was the
matter still more if he wasn't? The mystery was at last
cleared up: this Fleda gathered from the tone in which,
one morning at breakfast, a letter just opened made Mrs.
Gereth cry out. Her dismay was almost a shriek: "Why,
he's bringing her down—he wants her to see the house!"
They flew, the two women, into each other's arms and,
with their heads together, soon made out that the reason,
the baffling reason why nothing had yet happened, was that
Mona didn't know, or Owen didn't, whether Poynton
would really please her. She was coming down to judge; and
could anything in the world be more like poor Owen than
the ponderous probity which had kept him from pressing
her for a reply till she should have learned whether she
approved what he had to offer her? That was a scruple
it had naturally been impossible to impute. If only they
might fondly hope, Mrs. Gereth wailed, that the girl's ex-
pectations would be dashed! There was a fine consistency,
a sincerity quite affecting, in her arguing that the better the
place should happen to look and to express the conceptions
to which it owed its origin, the less it would speak to an
intelligence so primitive. How could a Brigstock possibly
understand what it was all about? How, really, could a
Brigstock logically do anything but hate it? Mrs. Gereth,
even as she whisked away linen shrouds, persuaded herself
of the possibility on Mona's part of some bewildered blankness, some collapse of admiration that would prove disconcerting to her swain—a hope of which Fleda at least
could see the absurdity and which gave the measure of the
poor lady's strange, almost maniacal disposition to thrust
in everywhere the question of "things," to read all behavior in the light of some fancied relation to them.
"Things" were of course the sum of the world; only, for
Mrs. Gereth, the sum of the world was rare French furniture and Oriental china. She could at a stretch imagine

people's not having, but she couldn't imagine their not
wanting and not missing.

The young couple were to be accompanied by Mrs.
Brigstock, and with a prevision of how fiercely they would
be watched Fleda became conscious, before the party
arrived, of an amused, diplomatic pity for them. Almost
as much as Mrs. Gereth's her taste was her life, but her
life was somehow the larger for it. Besides, she had another
care now: there was some one she wouldn't have liked to
see humiliated even in the form of a young lady who
would contribute to his never suspecting so much delicacy.
When this young lady appeared Fleda tried, so far as the
wish to efface herself allowed, to be mainly the person to
take her about, show her the house, and cover up her ignorance. Owen's announcement had been that, as trains
made it convenient, they would present themselves for
luncheon and depart before dinner; but Mrs. Gereth, true
to her system of glaring civility, proposed and obtained an
extension, a dining and spending of the night. She made her
young friend wonder against what rebellion of fact she was
sacrificing in advance so profusely to form. Fleda was
appalled, after the first hour, by the rash innocence with
which Mona had accepted the responsibility of observation,
and indeed by the large levity with which, sitting there like
a bored tourist in fine scenery, she exercised it. She felt in
her nerves the effect of such a manner on her companion's,
and it was this that made her want to entice the girl away,
give her some merciful warning or some jocular cue. Mona
met intense looks, however, with eyes that might have been
blue beads, the only ones she had—eyes into which Fleda
thought it strange Owen Gereth should have to plunge for
his fate and his mother for a confession of whether Poynton
was a success. She made no remark that helped to supply
this light; her impression at any rate had nothing in common
with the feeling that, as the beauty of the place throbbed
out like music, had caused Fleda Vetch to burst into tears.
She was as content to say nothing as if, Mrs. Gereth afterwards exclaimed, she had been keeping her mouth shut in
a railway tunnel. Mrs. Gereth contrived at the end of an
hour to convey to Fleda that it was plain she was brutally

ignorant; but Fleda more subtly discovered that her ignorance was obscurely active.

She was not so stupid as not to see that something,
though she scarcely knew what, was expected of her that
she couldn't give; and the only mode her intelligence suggested of meeting the expectation was to plant her big feet
and pull another way. Mrs. Gereth wanted her to rise,
somehow or somewhere, and was prepared to hate her if
she didn't: very well, she couldn't, she wouldn't rise; she
already moved at the altitude that suited her, and was able
to see that, since she was exposed to the hatred, she might
at least enjoy the calm. The smallest trouble, for a girl with
no nonsense about her, was to earn what she incurred; so
that, a dim instinct teaching her she would earn it best by
not being effusive, and combining with the conviction that
she now held Owen, and therefore the place, she had the
pleasure of her honesty as well as of her security. Didn't
her very honesty lead her to be belligerently blank about
Poynton inasmuch as it was just Poynton that was forced
upon her as a subject for effusiveness? Such subjects, to
Mona Brigstock, had an air almost of indecency, and the
house became uncanny to her through such an appeal—
an appeal that, somewhere in the twilight of her being, as
Fleda was sure, she thanked heaven she *was* the girl stiffly
to draw back from. She was a person whom pressure at a
given point infallibly caused to expand in the wrong place
instead of, as it is usually administered in the hope of
doing, the right one. Her mother, to make up for this, broke
out universally, pronounced everything "most striking,"
and was visibly happy that Owen's captor should be so
far on the way to strike: but she jarred upon Mrs. Gereth
by her formula of admiration, which was that anything
she looked at was "in the style" of something else. This
was to show how much she had seen, but it only showed
she had seen nothing; everything at Poynton was in the
style of Poynton, and poor Mrs. Brigstock, who at least
was determined to rise, and had brought with her a trophy
of her journey, a "lady's magazine" purchased at the station,
a horrible thing with patterns for antimacassars, which,
as it was quite new, the first number, and seemed so clever,

she kindly offered to leave for the house, was in the style of a vulgar old woman who wore silver jewelry and tried to pass off a gross avidity as a sense of the beautiful.

By the day's end it was clear to Fleda Vetch that, however Mona judged, the day had been determinant; whether or no she felt the charm, she felt the challenge: at an early moment Owen Gereth would be able to tell his mother the worst. Nevertheless, when the elder lady, at bedtime, coming in a dressing-gown and a high fever to the younger one's room, cried out, "She hates it; but what will she do?" Fleda pretended vagueness, played at obscurity and assented disingenuously to the proposition that they at least had a respite. The future was dark to her, but there was a silken thread she could clutch in the gloom —she would never give Owen away. He might give himself—he even certainly would; but that was his own affair, and his blunders, his innocence, only added to the appeal he made to her. She would cover him, she would protect him, and beyond thinking her a cheerful inmate he would never guess her intention, any more than, beyond thinking her clever enough for anything, his acute mother would discover it. From this hour, with Mrs. Gereth, there was a flaw in her frankness: her admirable friend continued to know everything she did; what was to remain unknown was the general motive.

From the window of her room, the next morning before breakfast, the girl saw Owen in the garden with Mona, who strolled beside him with a listening parasol, but without a visible look for the great florid picture that had been hung there by Mrs. Gereth's hand. Mona kept dropping her eyes, as she walked, to catch the sheen of her patent-leather shoes, which resembled a man's and which she kicked forward a little—it gave her an odd movement—to help her see what she thought of them. When Fleda came down Mrs. Gereth was in the breakfast-room; and at that moment Owen, through a long window, passed in alone from the terrace and very endearingly kissed his mother. It immediately struck the girl that she was in their way, for hadn't he been borne on a wave of joy exactly to announce, before the Brigstocks departed, that Mona had at last faltered out the sweet word he had been waiting for? He shook hands with his friendly violence, but Fleda contrived not to look into his face: what she liked most to see in it was not the reflection of Mona's big boot-toes. She could bear well enough that young lady herself, but she couldn't bear Owen's opinion of her. She was on the point of slipping into the garden when the movement was checked by Mrs. Gereth's suddenly drawing her close, as if for the morning embrace, and then, while she kept her there with the bravery of the night's repose, breaking out: "Well, my dear boy, what *does* your young friend there make of our odds and ends?"

"Oh, she thinks they're all right!"

Fleda immediately guessed from his tone that he had not come in to say what she supposed; there was even something in it to confirm Mrs. Gereth's belief that their danger had dropped. She was sure, moreover, that his tribute to Mona's taste was a repetition of the eloquent words in which the girl had herself recorded it; she could indeed hear, with all vividness, the pretty passage between the pair. "Don't you think it's rather jolly, the old shop?" "Oh, it's all right!" Mona had graciously remarked; and then they had probably, with a slap on a back, run another race up or down a green bank. Fleda knew Mrs. Gereth had not yet uttered a word to her son that would have shown him how much she feared; but it was impossible to feel her friend's arm round her and not become aware that this friend was now throbbing with a strange intention. Owen's reply had scarcely been of a nature to usher in a discussion of Mona's sensibilities; but Mrs. Gereth went on, in a moment, with an innocence of which Fleda could measure the cold hypocrisy: "Has she any sort of feeling for nice old things?" The question was as fresh as the morning light.

"Oh, of course she likes everything that's nice." And Owen, who constitutionally disliked questions—an answer was almost as hateful to him as a "trick" to a big dog—smiled kindly at Fleda and conveyed that she would understand what he meant even if his mother didn't. Fleda, however, mainly understood that Mrs. Gereth, with an odd, wild laugh, held her so hard that she hurt her.

"I could give up everything without a pang, I think, to a person I could trust, I could respect." The girl heard her voice tremble under the effort to show nothing but what she wanted to show, and felt the sincerity of her implication that the piety most real to her was to be on one's knees before one's high standard. "The best things here, as you know, are the things your father and I collected, things all that we worked for and waited for and suffered for. Yes," cried Mrs. Gereth, with a fine freedom of fancy, "there are things in the house that we almost starved for! They were our religion, they were our life, they were *us!* And now they're only *me*—except that they're also *you,* thank God, a little, you dear!" she continued, suddenly inflicting on Fleda a kiss apparently intended to knock her into position. "There isn't one of them I don't know and love—yes, as one remembers and cherishes the happiest moments of one's life. Blindfold, in the dark, with the brush of a finger, I could tell one from another. They're living things to me; they know me, they return the touch of my hand. But I could let them all go, since I have to, so strangely, to another affection, another conscience. There's a care they want, there's a sympathy that draws out their beauty. Rather than make them over to a woman ignorant and vulgar, I think I'd deface them with my own hands. Can't you see me, Fleda, and wouldn't you do it yourself?"— she appealed to her companion with glittering eyes. "I couldn't bear the thought of such a woman here—I *couldn't.* I don't know what she'd do; she'd be sure to invent some deviltry, if it should be only to bring in her own little belongings and horrors. The world is full of cheap gimcracks, in this awful age, and they're thrust in at one at every turn. They'd be thrust in here, on top of my treasures, my own. Who would save *them* for me—I ask you who *would?*" and she turned again to Fleda with a dry, strained smile. Her handsome, high-nosed, excited face might have been that of Don Quixote tilting at a windmill. Drawn into the eddy of this outpouring, the girl, scared and embarrassed, laughed off her exposure; but only to feel herself more passionately caught up and, as it seemed to her, thrust down the fine open mouth (it showed such perfect

teeth) with which poor Owen's slow cerebration gaped.
"*You* would, of course—only you, in all the world, because you know, you feel, as I do myself, what's good
and true and pure." No severity of the moral law could
have taken a higher tone in this implication of the young
lady who had not the only virtue Mrs. Gereth actively
esteemed. "*You* would replace me, *you* would watch over
them, *you* would keep the place right," she austerely pursued, "and with you here—yes, with you, I believe I might
rest, at last, in my grave!" She threw herself on Fleda's
neck, and before Fleda, horribly shamed, could shake her
off, had burst into tears which couldn't have been explained,
but which might perhaps have been understood.

CHAPTER IV

A WEEK LATER Owen Gereth came down to inform his
mother that he had settled with Mona Brigstock; but it was
not at all a joy to Fleda, conscious how much to himself it
would be a surprise, that he should find her still in the
house. That dreadful scene before breakfast had made her
position false and odious; it had been followed, after they
were left alone, by a scene of her own making with her
extravagant friend. She notified Mrs. Gereth of her instant
departure: she couldn't possibly remain after being offered
to Owen, that way, before her very face, as his mother's
candidate for the honor of his hand. That was all he could
have seen in such an outbreak and in the indecency of her
standing there to enjoy it. Fleda had on the prior occasion
dashed out of the room by the shortest course and in her
confusion had fallen upon Mona in the garden. She had
taken an aimless turn with her, and they had had some
talk, rendered at first difficult and almost disagreeable by
Mona's apparent suspicion that she had been sent out to
spy, as Mrs. Gereth had tried to spy, into her opinions.
Fleda was sagacious enough to treat these opinions as a
mystery almost awful; which had an effect so much more
than reassuring that at the end of five minutes the young
lady from Waterbath suddenly and perversely said: "Why
has she never had a winter garden thrown out? If ever I
have a place of my own I mean to have one." Fleda, dismayed, could see the thing—something glazed and piped,
on iron pillars, with untidy plants and cane sofas; a shiny
excrescence on the noble face of Poynton. She remembered
at Waterbath a conservatory where she had caught a bad
cold in the company of a stuffed cockatoo fastened to a

tropical bough and a waterless fountain composed of shells stuck into some hardened paste. She asked Mona if her idea would be to make something like this conservatory; to which Mona replied: "Oh no, much finer; we haven't got a winter garden at Waterbath." Fleda wondered if she meant to convey that it was the only grandeur they lacked, and in a moment Mona went on: "But we have got a billiard-room—that I will say for us!" There was no billiard-room at Poynton, but there would evidently be one, and it would have, hung on its walls, framed at the "Stores," caricature-portraits of celebrities, taken from a "society-paper."

When the two girls had gone in to breakfast it was for Fleda to see at a glance that there had been a further passage, of some high color, between Owen and his mother; and she had turned pale in guessing to what extremity, at her expense, Mrs. Gereth had found occasion to proceed. Hadn't she, after her clumsy flight, been pressed upon Owen in still clearer terms? Mrs. Gereth would practically have said to him: "If you'll take *her,* I'll move away without a sound. But if you take any one else, any one I'm not sure of, as I am of her—heaven help me, I'll fight to the death!" Breakfast, this morning, at Poynton, had been a meal singularly silent, in spite of the vague little cries with which Mrs. Brigstock turned up the underside of plates and the knowing but alarming raps administered by her big knuckles to porcelain cups. Some one had to respond to her, and the duty assigned itself to Fleda, who, while pretending to meet her on the ground of explanation, wondered what Owen thought of a girl still indelicately anxious, after she had been grossly hurled at him, to prove by exhibitions of her fine taste that she was really what his mother pretended. This time, at any rate, their fate was sealed: Owen, as soon as he should get out of the house, would describe to Mona that lady's extraordinary conduct, and if anything more had been wanted to "fetch" Mona, as he would call it, the deficiency was now made up. Mrs. Gereth in fact took care of that—took care of it by the way, at the last, on the threshold, she said to the younger of her departing guests, with an irony of which the sting was wholly in the sense, not at all in the sound: "We haven't had the talk we might have had, have we? You'll feel that I've neglected you, and you'll treasure it up against me. *Don't,* because really, you know, it has been quite an accident, and I've all sorts of information at your disposal. If you should come down again (only you won't, ever,—I feel that!) I should give you plenty of time to worry it out of me. Indeed there are some things I should quite insist on your learning; not permit you at all, in any settled way, *not* to learn. Yes indeed, you'd put me through, and I should put you, my dear! We should have each other to reckon with, and you would see me as I really am. I'm not a bit the vague, mooning, easy creature I dare say you think. However, if you won't come, you won't; *n'en parlons plus.* It *is* stupid here after what you're accustomed to. We can only, all round, do what we can, eh? For heaven's sake, don't let your mother forget her precious publication, the female magazine, with the what-do-you-call-'em?—the grease-catchers. There!"

Mrs. Gereth, delivering herself from the doorstep, had tossed the periodical higher in air than was absolutely needful—tossed it toward the carriage the retreating party was about to enter. Mona, from the force of habit, the reflex action of the custom of sport, had popped out, with a little spring, a long arm and intercepted the missile as easily as she would have caused a tennis-ball to rebound from a racket. "Good catch!" Owen had cried, so genuinely pleased that practically no notice was taken of his mother's impressive remarks. It was to the accompaniment of romping laughter, as Mrs. Gereth afterwards said, that the carriage had rolled away; but it was while that laughter was still in the air that Fleda Vetch, white and terrible, had turned upon her hostess with her scorching "How *could* you? Great God, how *could* you?" This lady's perfect blankness was from the first a sign of her serene conscience, and the fact that till indoctrinated she didn't even know what Fleda meant by resenting her late offense to every susceptibility gave our young woman a sore, scared perception that her own value in the house was just the value, as one might say, of a good agent. Mrs. Gereth was generously sorry,

but she was still more surprised—surprised at Fleda's not
having liked to be shown off to Owen as the right sort of
wife for him. Why not, in the name of wonder, if she
absolutely *was* the right sort? She had admitted on explanation that she could see what her young friend meant
by having been laid, as Fleda called it, at his feet; but it
struck the girl that the admission was only made to please
her, and that Mrs. Gereth was secretly surprised at her not
being as happy to be sacrificed to the supremacy of a high
standard as she was happy to sacrifice her. She had taken a
tremendous fancy to her, but that was on account of the
fancy—to Poynton of course—Fleda herself had taken.
Wasn't this latter fancy then so great after all? Fleda felt
that she could declare it to be great indeed when really for
the sake of it she could forgive what she had suffered and,
after reproaches and tears, asseverations and kisses, after
learning that she was cared for only as a priestess of the
altar and a view of her bruised dignity which left no alternative to flight, could accept the shame with the balm, consent not to depart, take refuge in the thin comfort of at
least knowing the truth. The truth was simply that all Mrs.
Gereth's scruples were on one side and that her ruling passion had in a manner despoiled her of her humanity. On
the second day, after the tide of emotion had somewhat
ebbed, she said soothingly to her companion: "But you
would, after all, marry him, you know, darling, wouldn't
you, if that girl were not there? I mean of course if he
were to ask you," Mrs. Gereth had thoughtfully added.

"Marry him if he were to ask me? Most distinctly not!"

The question had not come up with this definiteness before, and Mrs. Gereth was clearly more surprised than ever.
She marveled a moment. "Not even to have Poynton?"

"Not even to have Poynton."

"But why on earth?" Mrs. Gereth's sad eyes were fixed
on her.

Fleda colored; she hesitated. "Because he's too stupid!"
Save on one other occasion, at which we shall in time arrive,
little as the reader may believe it, she never came nearer
to betraying to Mrs. Gereth that she was in love with Owen.
She found a dim amusement in reflecting that if Mona had

not been there and he had not been too stupid and he verily
had asked her, she might, should she have wished to keep
her secret, have found it possible to pass off the motive of
her action as a mere passion for Poynton.

Mrs. Gereth evidently thought in these days of little but
things hymeneal; for she broke out with sudden rapture, in
the middle of the week: "I know what they'll do: they *will*
marry, but they'll go and live at Waterbath!" There was
positive joy in that form of the idea, which she embroidered
and developed: it seemed so much the safest thing that
could happen. "Yes, I'll have you, but I won't go *there!*"
Mona would have said with a vicious nod at the southern
horizon: "we'll leave your horrid mother alone there for
life." It would be an ideal solution, this ingress the lively
pair, with their spiritual need of a warmer medium, would
playfully punch in the ribs of her ancestral home; for it
would not only prevent recurring panic at Poynton—it
would offer them, as in one of their gimcrack baskets or
other vessels of ugliness, a definite daily felicity that Poynton could never give. Owen might manage his estate just
as he managed it now, and Mrs. Gereth would manage
everything else. When, in the hall, on the unforgettable
day of his return, she had heard his voice ring out like a
call to a terrier, she had still, as Fleda afterwards learned,
clutched frantically at the conceit that he had come, at the
worst, to announce some compromise; to tell her she would
have to put up with the girl, yes, but that some way would
be arrived at of leaving her in personal possession. Fleda
Vetch, whom from the first hour no illusion had brushed
with its wing, now held her breath, went on tiptoe,
wandered in outlying parts of the house and through
delicate, muffled rooms, while the mother and son faced
each other below. From time to time she stopped to listen;
but all was so quiet she was almost frightened: she had
vaguely expected a sound of contention. It lasted longer
than she would have supposed, whatever it was they were
doing; and when finally, from a window, she saw Owen
stroll out of the house, stop and light a cigarette and then
pensively lose himself in the plantations, she found other
matter for trepidation in the fact that Mrs. Gereth didn't

immediately come rushing up into her arms. She wondered whether she oughtn't to go down to her, and measured the gravity of what had occurred by the circumstance, which she presently ascertained, that the poor lady had retired to her room and wished not to be disturbed. This admonition had been for her maid, with whom Fleda conferred as at the door of a death-chamber; but the girl, without either fatuity or resentment, judged that, since it could render Mrs. Gereth indifferent even to the ministrations of disinterested attachment, the scene had been tremendous.

She was absent from luncheon, where indeed Fleda had enough to do to look Owen in the face; there would be so much to make that hateful in their common memory of the passage in which his last visit had terminated. This had been her apprehension at least; but as soon as he stood there she was constrained to wonder at the practical simplicity of the ordeal—a simplicity which was really just his own simplicity, the particular thing that, for Fleda Vetch, some other things of course aiding, made almost any direct relation with him pleasant. He had neither wit, nor tact, nor inspiration: all she could say was that when they were together the alienation these charms were usually depended on to allay didn't occur. On this occasion, for instance, he did so much better than "carry off" an awkward remembrance: he simply didn't have it. He had clean forgotten that she was the girl his mother would have fobbed off on him; he was conscious only that she was there in a manner for service—conscious of the dumb instinct that from the first had made him regard her not as complicating his intercourse with that personage, but as simplifying it. Fleda found beautiful that this theory should have survived the incident of the other day; found exquisite that whereas she was conscious, through faint reverberations, that for her kind little circle at large, whom it didn't concern, her tendency had begun to define itself as parasitical, this strong young man, who had a right to judge and even a reason to loathe her, didn't judge and didn't loathe, let her down gently, treated her as if she pleased him, and in fact evidently liked her to be just where she was. She asked herself what he did when Mona denounced her, and the only answer to the question was that perhaps Mona didn't denounce her. If Mona was inarticulate he wasn't such a fool, then, to marry her. That he was glad Fleda was there was at any rate sufficiently shown by the domestic familiarity with which he said to her: "I must tell you I've been having an awful row with my mother. I'm engaged to be married to Miss Brigstock."

"Ah, really?" cried Fleda, achieving a radiance of which she was secretly proud. "How very exciting!"

"Too exciting for poor Mummy. She won't hear of it. She has been slating her fearfully. She says she's a 'barbarian.'"

"Why, she's lovely!" Fleda exclaimed.

"Oh, she's all right. Mother must come round."

"Only give her time," said Fleda. She had advanced to the threshold of the door thus thrown open to her and, without exactly crossing it, she threw in an appreciative glance. She asked Owen when his marriage would take place, and in the light of his reply read that Mrs. Gereth's wretched attitude would have no influence at all on the event, absolutely fixed when he came down, and distant by only three months. He liked Fleda's seeming to be on his side, though that was a secondary matter, for what really most concerned him now was the line his mother took about Poynton, her declared unwillingness to give it up.

"Naturally I want my own house, you know," he said, "and my father made every arrangement for me to have it. But she may make it devilish awkward. What in the world's a fellow to do?" This it was that Owen wanted to know, and there could be no better proof of his friendliness than his air of depending on Fleda Vetch to tell him. She questioned him, they spent an hour together, and, as he gave her the scale of the concussion from which he had rebounded, she found herself saddened and frightened by the material he seemed to offer her to deal with. It *was* devilish awkward, and it was so in part because Owen had no imagination. It had lodged itself in that empty chamber that his mother hated the surrender because she hated Mona. He didn't of course understand why she hated Mona, but this belonged to an order of mysteries that never troubled him: there were lots of things, especially in people's minds, that a fellow didn't understand. Poor Owen went through life with a frank dread of people's minds: there were explanations he would have been almost as shy of receiving as of giving. There was therefore nothing that accounted for anything, though in its way it was vivid enough, in his picture to Fleda of his mother's virtual refusal to move. That was simply what it was; for didn't she refuse to move when she as good as declared that she would move only with the furniture? It was the furniture she wouldn't give up; and what was the good of Poynton without the furniture? Besides, the furniture happened to be his, just as everything else happened to be. The furniture—the word, on his lips, had somehow, for Fleda, the sound of washing-stands and copious bedding, and she could well imagine the note it might have struck for Mrs. Gereth. The girl, in this interview with him, spoke of the contents of the house only as "the works of art." It didn't, however, in the least matter to Owen what they were called; what did matter, she easily guessed, was that it had been laid upon him by Mona, been made in effect a condition of her consent, that he should hold his mother to the strictest accountability for them. Mona had already entered upon the enjoyment of her rights. She had made him feel that Mrs. Gereth had been liberally provided for, and had asked him cogently what room there would be at Ricks for the innumerable treasures of the big house. Ricks, the sweet little place offered to the mistress of Poynton as the refuge of her declining years, had been left to the late Mr. Gereth, a considerable time before his death, by an old maternal aunt, a good lady who had spent most of her life there. The house had in recent times been let, but it was amply furnished, it contained all the defunct aunt's possessions. Owen had lately inspected it, and he communicated to Fleda that he had quietly taken Mona to see it. It wasn't a place like Poynton—what dower-house ever was?—but it was an awfully jolly little place, and Mona had taken a tremendous fancy to it. If there were a few things at Poynton that were Mrs. Gereth's peculiar property, of course she must take them away with her; but one of the matters that became clear to Fleda was that this transfer would be immediately subject to Miss Brigstock's approval. The special business that she herself now became aware of being charged with was that of seeing Mrs. Gereth safely and singly off the premises.

Her heart failed her, after Owen had returned to London, with the ugliness of this duty—with the ugliness, indeed, of the whole close conflict. She saw nothing of Mrs. Gereth that day; she spent it in roaming with sick sighs, in feeling, as she passed from room to room, that what was expected of her companion was really dreadful. It would have been better never to have had such a place than to have had it and lose it. It was odious to *her* to have to look for solutions: what a strange relation between mother and son when there was no fundamental tenderness out of which a solution would irrepressibly spring! Was it Owen who was mainly responsible for that poverty? Fleda couldn't think so when she remembered that, so far as he was concerned, Mrs. Gereth would still have been welcome to have her seat by the Poynton fire. The fact that from the moment one accepted his marrying one saw no very different course for Owen to take made her all the rest of that aching day find her best relief in the mercy of not having yet to face her hostess. She dodged and dreamed and romanced away the time; instead of inventing a remedy or a compromise, instead of preparing a plan by which a scandal might be averted, she gave herself, in her sentient solitude, up to a mere fairy tale, up to the very taste of the beautiful peace with which she would have filled the air if only something might have been that could never have been.

CHAPTER V

"I'LL GIVE UP THE HOUSE if they'll let me take what I require!" That, on the morrow, was what Mrs. Gereth's stifled night had qualified her to say, with a tragic face, at breakfast. Fleda reflected that what she "required" was simply every object that surrounded them. The poor woman would have admitted this truth and accepted the conclusion to be drawn from it, the reduction to the absurd of her attitude, the exaltation of her revolt. The girl's dread of scandal, of spectators and critics, diminished the more she saw how little vulgar avidity had to do with this rigor. It was not the crude love of possession; it was the need to be faithful to a trust and loyal to an idea. The idea was surely noble: it was that of the beauty Mrs. Gereth had so patiently and consummately wrought. Pale but radiant, with her back to the wall, she rose there like a heroine guarding a treasure. To give up the ship was to flinch from her duty; there was something in her eyes that declared she would die at her post. If their difference should become public the shame would be all for the others. If Waterbath thought it could afford to expose itself, then Waterbath was welcome to the folly. Her fanaticism gave her a new distinction, and Fleda perceived almost with awe that she had never carried herself so well. She trod the place like a reigning queen or a proud usurper; full as it was of splendid pieces, it could show in these days no ornament so effective as its menaced mistress.

Our young lady's spirit was strangely divided; she had a tenderness for Owen which she deeply concealed, yet it left her occasion to marvel at the way a man was made who could care in any relation for a creature like Mona Brig-

stock when he had known in any relation a creature like
Adela Gereth. With such a mother to give him the pitch,
how could he take it so low? She wondered that she didn't
despise him for this, but there was something that kept her
from it. If there had been nothing else it would have
sufficed that she really found herself from this moment
the medium of communication with him.

"He'll come back to assert himself," Mrs. Gereth had
said; and the following week Owen in fact reappeared. He
might merely have written, Fleda could see, but he had
come in person because it was at once "nicer" for his
mother and stronger for his cause. He didn't like the
row, though Mona probably did; if he hadn't a sense of
beauty he had after all a sense of justice; but it was inevitable he should clearly announce at Poynton the date
at which he must look to find the house vacant. "You don't
think I'm rough or hard, do you?" he asked of Fleda, his
impatience shining in his idle eyes as the dining-hour shines
in club-windows. "The place at Ricks stands there with open
arms. And then I give her lots of time. Tell her she can
remove everything that belongs to her." Fleda recognized
the elements of what the newspapers call a deadlock in the
circumstance that nothing at Poynton belonged to Mrs.
Gereth either more or less than anything else. She must
either take everything or nothing, and the girl's suggestion
was that it might perhaps be an inspiration to do the latter
and begin again on a clean page. What, however, was the
poor woman, in that case, to begin with? What was she to
do at all, on her meagre income, but make the best of the
objets d'art of Ricks, the treasures collected by Mr.
Gereth's maiden aunt? She had never been near the place:
for long years it had been let to strangers, and after that
the foreboding that it would be her doom had kept her
from the abasement of it. She had felt that she should see it
soon enough, but Fleda (who was careful not to betray to
her that Mona had seen it and had been gratified) knew
her reasons for believing that the maiden aunt's principles
had had much in common with the principles of Waterbath.
The only thing, in short, that she would ever have to do with
the objets d'art of Ricks would be to turn them out into the

road. What belonged to her at Poynton, as Owen said, would conveniently mitigate the void resulting from that demonstration.

The exchange of observations between the friends had grown very direct by the time Fleda asked Mrs. Gereth whether she literally meant to shut herself up and stand a siege, or whether it was her idea to expose herself, more informally, to be dragged out of the house by constables. "Oh, I prefer the constables and the dragging!" the heroine of Poynton had answered. "I want to make Owen and Mona do everything that will be most publicly odious." She gave it out that it was her one thought now to force them to a line that would dishonor them and dishonor the tradition they embodied, though Fleda was privately sure that she had visions of an alternative policy. The strange thing was that, proud and fastidious all her life, she now showed so little distaste for the world's hearing of the squabble. What had taken place in her above all was that a long resentment had ripened. She hated the effacement to which English usage reduced the widowed mother: she had discoursed of it passionately to Fleda; contrasted it with the beautiful homage paid in other countries to women in that position, women no better than herself, whom she had seen acclaimed and enthroned, whom she had known and envied; made in short as little as possible a secret of the injury, the bitterness she found in it. The great wrong Owen had done her was not his "taking up" with Mona—that was disgusting, but it was a detail, an accidental form; it was his failure from the first to understand what it was to have a mother at all, to appreciate the beauty and sanctity of the character. She was just his mother as his nose was just his nose, and he had never had the least imagination or tenderness or gallantry about her. One's mother, gracious heaven, if one were the kind of fine young man one ought to be, the only kind Mrs. Gereth cared for, was a subject for poetry, for idolatry. Hadn't she often told Fleda of her friend Madame de Jaume, the wittiest of women, but a small, black, crooked person, each of whose three boys, when absent, wrote to her every day of their lives? She had the house in Paris, she had the house in Poitou, she had more than in

the lifetime of her husband (to whom, in spite of her appearance, she had afforded repeated cause for jealousy),
because she had to the end of her days the supreme word
about everything. It was easy to see that Mrs. Gereth
would have given again and again her complexion, her
figure, and even perhaps the spotless virtue she had still
more successfully retained, to have been the consecrated
Madame de Jaume. She wasn't, alas, and this was what she
had at present a magnificent occasion to protest against.
She was of course fully aware of Owen's concession, his
willingness to let her take away with her the few things she
liked best; but as yet she only declared that to meet him on
this ground would be to give him a triumph, to put him
impossibly in the right. "Liked best"? There wasn't a thing
in the house that she didn't like best, and what she liked
better still was to be left where she was. How could Owen
use such an expression without being conscious of his
hypocrisy? Mrs. Gereth, whose criticism was often gay,
dilated with sardonic humor on the happy look a dozen
objects from Poynton would wear and the charming effect
they would conduce to when interspersed with the peculiar
features of Ricks. What had her whole life been but an
effort toward completeness and perfection? Better Waterbath at once, in its cynical unity, than the ignominy of
such a mixure!

All this was of no great help to Fleda, in so far as
Fleda tried to rise to her mission of finding a way out.
When at the end of a fortnight Owen came down once
more, it was ostensibly to tackle a farmer whose proceedings
had been irregular; the girl was sure, however, that he had
really come, on the instance of Mona, to see what his
mother was doing. He wished to satisfy himself that she
was preparing her departure, and he wished to perform a
duty, distinct but not less imperative, in regard to the
question of the perquisites with which she would retreat.
The tension between them was now such that he had to
perpetrate these offenses without meeting his adversary.
Mrs. Gereth was as willing as himself that he should address to Fleda Vetch whatever cruel remarks he might
have to make: she only pitied her poor young friend for

repeated encounters with a person as to whom she perfectly understood the girl's repulsion. Fleda thought it nice
of Owen not to have expected her to write to him; he
wouldn't have wished any more than herself that she should
have the air of spying on his mother in his interest. What
made it comfortable to deal with him in this more familiar
way was the sense that she understood so perfectly how
poor Mrs. Gereth suffered, and that she measured so adequately the sacrifice the other side did take rather mon-
strously for granted. She understood equally how Owen
himself suffered, now that Mona had already begun to
make him do things he didn't like. Vividly Fleda ap-
prehended how *she* would have first made him like anything
she would have made him do; anything even as disagreeable
as this appearing there to state, virtually on Mona's behalf,
that of course there must be a definite limit to the number
of articles appropriated. She took a longish stroll with
him in order to talk the matter over; to say if she didn't
think a dozen pieces, chosen absolutely at will, would be a
handsome allowance; and above all to consider the very
delicate question of whether the advantage enjoyed by
Mrs. Gereth mightn't be left to her honor. To leave it so
was what Owen wished; but there was plainly a young lady
at Waterbath to whom, on his side, he already had to
render an account. He was as touching in his offhand an-
noyance as his mother was tragic in her intensity; for if he
couldn't help having a sense of propriety about the whole
matter, so he could as little help hating it. It was for his
hating it, Fleda reasoned, that she liked him so, and her
insistence to his mother on the hatred perilously resembled,
on one or two occasions, a revelation of the liking. There
were moments when, in conscience, that revelation pressed
her; inasmuch as it was just on the ground of her not
liking him that Mrs. Gereth trusted her so much. Mrs.
Gereth herself didn't in these days like him at all, and she
was of course and always on Mrs. Gereth's side. He ended
really, while the preparations for his marriage went on,
by quite a little custom of coming and going; but on no
one of these occasions would his mother receive him. He
talked only with Fleda and strolled with Fleda; and when

he asked her, in regard to the great matter, if Mrs. Gereth were really doing nothing, the girl usually replied: "She pretends not to be, if I may say so; but I think she's really thinking over what she'll take." When her friend asked her what Owen was doing, she could have but one answer: "He's waiting, dear lady, to see what *you* do!"

Mrs. Gereth, a month after she had received her great shock, did something abrupt and extraordinary: she caught up her companion and went to have a look at Ricks. They had come to London first and taken a train from Liverpool Street, and the least of the sufferings they were armed against was that of passing the night. Fleda's admirable dressing-bag had been given her by her friend. "Why, it's charming!" she exclaimed a few hours later, turning back again into the small prim parlor from a friendly advance to the single plate of the window. Mrs. Gereth hated such windows, the one flat glass, sliding up and down, especially when they enjoyed a view of four iron pots on pedestals, painted white and containing ugly geraniums, ranged on the edge of a gravel-path and doing their best to give it the air of a terrace. Fleda had instantly averted her eyes from these ornaments, but Mrs. Gereth grimly gazed, wondering of course how a place in the deepest depths of Essex and three miles from a small station could contrive to look so suburban. The room was practically a shallow box, with the junction of the walls and ceiling guiltless of curve or cornice and marked merely by the little band of crimson paper glued round the top of the other paper, a turbid gray sprigged with silver flowers. This decoration was rather new and quite fresh; and there was in the centre of the ceiling a big square beam papered over in white, as to which Fleda hesitated about venturing to remark that it was rather picturesque. She recognized in time that this remark would be weak and that, throughout, she should be able to say nothing either for the mantelpieces or for the doors, of which she saw her companion become sensible with a soundless moan. On the subject of doors especially Mrs. Gereth had the finest views: the thing in the world she most despised was the meanness of the single flap. From end to end, at Poynton, there were high double leaves. At

Ricks the entrances to the rooms were like the holes of rabbit-hutches.

It was all, none the less, not so bad as Fleda had feared; it was faded and melancholy, whereas there had been a danger that it would be contradictious and positive, cheerful and loud. The house was crowded with objects of which the aggregation somehow made a thinness and the futility a grace; things that told her they had been gathered as slowly and as lovingly as the golden flowers of Poynton. She too, for a home, could have lived with them: they made her fond of the old maiden-aunt; they made her even wonder if it didn't work more for happiness not to have tasted, as she herself had done, of knowledge. Without resources, without a stick, as she said, of her own, Fleda was moved, after all, to some secret surprise at the pretensions of a shipwrecked woman who could hold such an asylum cheap. The more she looked about the surer she felt of the character of the maiden-aunt, the sense of whose dim presence urged her to pacification: the maiden-aunt had been a dear; she would have adored the maiden-aunt. The poor lady had had some tender little story; she had been sensitive and ignorant and exquisite: that too was a sort of origin, a sort of atmosphere for relics and rarities, though different from the sorts most prized at Poynton. Mrs. Gereth had of course more than once said that one of the deepest mysteries of life was the way that, by certain natures, hideous objects could be loved; but it wasn't a question of love, now, for these: it was only a question of a certain practical patience. Perhaps some thought of that kind had stolen over Mrs. Gereth when, at the end of a brooding hour, she exclaimed, taking in the house with a strenuous sigh: "Well, something can be done with it!" Fleda had repeated to her more than once the indulgent fancy about the maiden-aunt—she was so sure she had deeply suffered. "I'm sure I hope she did!" was, however, all that Mrs. Gereth had replied.

CHAPTER VI

IT WAS A GREAT RELIEF to the girl at last to perceive that
the dreadful move would really be made. What might
happen if it shouldn't had been from the first indefinite.
It was absurd to pretend that any violence was probable—
a tussel, dishevelment, shrieks; yet Fleda had an imagination
of a drama, a "great scene," a thing, somehow, of indignity
and misery, of wounds inflicted and received, in which indeed, though Mrs. Gereth's presence, with movements and
sounds, loomed large to her, Owen remained indistinct
and on the whole unaggressive. He wouldn't be there with
a cigarette in his teeth, very handsome and insolently
quiet: that was only the way he would be in a novel, across
whose interesting page some such figure, as she half closed
her eyes, seemed to her to walk. Fleda had rather, and indeed with shame, a confused, pitying vision of Mrs. Gereth
with her great scene left in a manner on her hands, Mrs.
Gereth missing her effect and having to appear merely hot
and injured and in the wrong. The symptoms that she would
be spared even that spectacle resided not so much, through
the chambers of Poynton, in an air of concentration as in
the hum of buzzing alternatives. There was no common
preparation, but one day, at the turn of a corridor, she
found her hostess standing very still, with the hanging
hands of an invalid and the active eyes of an adventurer.
These eyes appeared to Fleda to meet her own with a
strange, dim bravado, and there was a silence, almost
awkward, before either of the friends spoke. The girl
afterwards thought of the moment as one in which her
hostess mutely accused her of an accusation, meeting it,
however, at the same time, by a kind of defiant acceptance.

Yet it was with mere melancholy candor that Mrs. Gereth at last sighingly exclaimed: "I'm thinking over what I had better take!" Fleda could have embraced her for this virtual promise of a concession, the announcement that she had finally accepted the problem of knocking together a shelter with the small salvage of the wreck.

It was true that when after their return from Ricks they tried to lighten the ship, the great embarrassment was still immutably there, the odiousness of sacrificing the exquisite things one wouldn't take to the exquisite things one would. This immediately made the things one wouldn't take the very things one ought to, and, as Mrs. Gereth said, condemned one, in the whole business, to an eternal vicious circle. In such a circle, for days, she had been tormentedly moving, prowling up and down, comparing incomparables. It was for that one had to cling to them and their faces of supplication. Fleda herself could judge of these faces, so conscious of their race and their danger, and she had little enough to say when her companion asked her if the whole place, perversely fair on October afternoons, looked like a place to give up. It looked, to begin with, through some effect of season and light, larger than ever, immense, and it was filled with the hush of sorrow, which in turn was all charged with memories. Everything was in the air—every history of every find, every circumstance of every struggle. Mrs. Gereth had drawn back every curtain and removed every cover; she prolonged the vistas, opened wide the whole house, gave it an appearance of awaiting a royal visit. The shimmer of wrought substances spent itself in the brightness; the old golds and brasses, old ivories and bronzes, the fresh old tapestries and deep old damasks threw out a radiance in which the poor woman saw in solution all her old loves and patiences, all her old tricks and triumphs.

Fleda had a depressed sense of not, after all, helping her much: this was lightened indeed by the fact that Mrs. Gereth, letting her off easily, didn't now seem to expect it. Her sympathy, her interest, her feeling for everything for which Mrs. Gereth felt, were a force that really worked to prolong the deadlock. "I only wish I bored you and my possessions bored you," that lady, with some humor, declared; "then you'd make short work with me, bundle me off, tell me just to pile certain things into a cart and have done." Fleda's sharpest difficulty in having to act up to the character of thinking Owen a brute, or at least to carry off the inconsistency of seeing him when he came down. By good fortune it was her duty, her function, as well as a protection to Mrs. Gereth. She thought of him perpetually, and her eyes had come to rejoice in his manly magnificence more even than they rejoiced in the royal cabinets of the red saloon. She wondered, very faintly at first, why he came so often; but of course she knew nothing about the business he had in hand, over which, with men red-faced and leather-legged, he was sometimes closeted for an hour in a room of his own that was the one monstrosity of Poynton: all tobacco-pots and bootjacks, his mother had said—such an array of arms of aggression and castigation that he himself had confessed to eighteen rifles and forty whips. He was arranging for settlements on his wife, he was doing things that would meet the views of the Brigstocks. Considering the house was his own, Fleda thought it nice of him to keep himself in the background while his mother remained; making his visits, at some cost of ingenuity about trains from town, only between meals, doing everything to let it press lightly upon her that he was there. This was rather a stoppage to her meeting Mrs. Gereth on the ground of his being a brute; the most she really at last could do was not to contradict her when she repeated that he was watching—just insultingly watching. He *was* watching, no doubt; but he watched somehow with his head turned away. He knew that Fleda knew at present what he wanted of her, so that it would be gross of him to say it over and over. It existed as a confidence between them, and made him sometimes, with his wandering stare, meet her eyes as if a silence so pleasant could only unite them the more. He had no great flow of speech, certainly, and at first the girl took for granted that this was all there was to be said about the matter. Little by little she speculated as to whether, with a person who, like herself, could put him, after all, at a sort of domestic ease, it was not supposable that he would have more conversation if he were not keeping some of it back for Mona.

From the moment she suspected he might be thinking what Mona would say to his chattering so to an underhand "companion," who was all but paid, this young lady's repressed emotion began to require still more repression. She grew impatient of her situation at Poynton; she privately pronounced it false and horrid. She said to herself that she had let Owen know that she had, to the best of her power, directed his mother in the general sense he desired; that he quite understood it and that he also understood how unworthy it was of either of them to stand over the good lady with a notebook and a lash. Wasn't this practical unanimity just practical success? Fleda became aware of a sudden desire, as well as of pressing reasons, to bring her stay at Poynton to a close. She had not, on the one hand, like a minion of the law, undertaken to see Mrs. Gereth down to the train and locked, in sign of her abdication, into a compartment; neither had she on the other committed herself to hold Owen indefinitely in dalliance while his mother gained time or dug a countermine. Besides, people *were* saying that she fastened like a leech on other people—people who had houses where something was to be picked up: this revelation was frankly made by her sister, now distinctly doomed to the curate and in view of whose nuptials she had almost finished, as a present, a wonderful piece of embroidery, suggested, at Poynton, by an old Spanish altar-cloth. She would have to exert herself still further for the intended recipient of this offering, turn her out for her marriage with more than that drapery. She would go up to town, in short, to dress Maggie; and their father, in lodgings at West Kensington, would stretch a point and take them in. He, to do him justice, never reproached her with profitable devotions; so far as they existed he consciously profited by them. Mrs. Gereth gave her up as heroically as if she had been a great bargain, and Fleda knew that she wouldn't at present miss any visit of Owen's, for Owen was shooting at Waterbath. Owen shooting was Owen lost, and there was scant sport at Poynton.

The first news she had from Mrs. Gereth was news of that lady's having accomplished, in form at least, her migration. The letter was dated from Ricks, to which place she had been transported by an impulse apparently as sudden as the inspiration she had obeyed before. "Yes, I've literally come," she wrote, "with a bandbox and a kitchen-maid; I've crossed the Rubicon, I've taken possession. It has been like plumping into cold water: I saw the only thing was to do it, not to stand shivering. I shall have warmed the place a little by simply being here for a week; when I come back the ice will have been broken. I didn't write to you to meet me on my way through town, because I know how busy you are and because, besides, I'm too savage and odious to be fit company even for you. You'd say I really go too far, and there's no doubt whatever I do. I'm here, at any rate, just to look round once more, to see that certain things are done before I enter in force. I shall probably be at Poynton all next week. There's more room than I quite measured the other day, and a rather good set of old Worcester. But what are space and time, what's even old Worcester, to your wretched and affectionate A. G.?"

The day after Fleda received this letter she had occasion to go into a big shop in Oxford Street—a journey that she achieved circuitously, first on foot and then by the aid of two omnibuses. The second of these vehicles put her down on the side of the street opposite her shop, and while, on the curbstone, she humbly waited, with a parcel, an umbrella, and a tucked-up frock, to cross in security, she became aware that, close beside her, a hansom had pulled up short, in obedience to the brandished stick of a demonstrative occupant. This occupant was Owen Gereth, who had caught sight of her as he rattled along and who, with an exhibition of white teeth that, from under the hood of the cab, had almost flashed through the fog, now alighted to ask her if he couldn't give her a lift. On finding that her destination was only over the way he dismissed his vehicle and joined her, not only piloting her to the shop, but taking her in; with the assurance that his errands didn't matter, that it amused him to be concerned with hers. She told him she had come to buy a trimming for her sister's frock,

and he expressed an hilarious interest in the purchase. His
hilarity was almost always out of proportion to the case,
but it struck her at present as more so than ever; especially
when she had suggested that he might find it a good time to
buy a garnishment of some sort for Mona. After wondering an instant whether he gave the full satiric meaning, such
as it was, to this remark, Fleda dismissed the possibility as
inconceivable. He stammered out that it was for *her* he
would like to buy something, something "ripping," and that
she must give him the pleasure of telling him what would
best please her: he couldn't have a better opportunity for
making her a present—the present, in recognition of all she
had done for Mummy, that he had had in his head for
weeks.

Fleda had more than one small errand in the big bazaar,
and he went up and down with her, pointedly patient, pretending to be interested in questions of tape and of change.
She had now not the least hesitation in wondering what
Mona would think of such proceedings. But they were not
her doing—they were Owen's; and Owen, inconsequent
and even extravagant, was unlike anything she had ever
seen him before. He broke off, he came back, he repeated
questions without heeding answers, he made vague, abrupt
remarks about the resemblances of shopgirls and the uses
of chiffon. He unduly prolonged their business together,
giving Fleda a sense that he was putting off something
particular that he had to face. If she had ever dreamed
of Owen Gereth as nervous she would have seen him with
some such manner as this. But why should he be nervous?
Even at the height of the crisis his mother hadn't made him
so, and at present he was satisfied about his mother. The
one idea he stuck to was that Fleda should mention something she would let him give her: there was everything in
the wonderful place, and he made her incongruous offers—a traveling-rug, a massive clock, a table for
breakfast in bed, and above all, in a resplendent binding, a
set of somebody's "works." His notion was a testimonial, a
tribute, and the "works" would be a graceful intimation
that it was her cleverness he wished above all to com-
memorate. He was immensely in earnest, but the articles he

pressed upon her betrayed a delicacy that went to her heart: what he would really have liked, as he saw them tumbled about, was one of the splendid stuffs for a gown— a choice proscribed by his fear of seeming to patronize her, to refer to her small means and her deficiencies. Fleda found it easy to chaff him about his exaggeration of her deserts; she gave the just measure of them in consenting to accept a small pin-cushion, costing sixpence, in which the letter F was marked out with pins. A sense of loyalty to Mona was not needed to enforce this discretion, and after that first allusion to her she never sounded her name. She noticed on this occasion more things in Owen Gereth than she had ever noticed before, but what she noticed most was that he said no word of his intended. She asked herself what he had done, in so long a parenthesis, with his loyalty or at least his "form;" and then reflected that even if he had done something very good with them the situation in which such a question could come up was already a little strange. Of course he wasn't doing anything so vulgar as making love to her; but there was a kind of punctilio for a man who was engaged.

That punctilio didn't prevent Owen from remaining with her after they had left the shop, from hoping she had a lot more to do, and from pressing her to look with him, for a possible glimpse of something she might really let him give her, into the windows of other establishments. There was a moment when, under this pressure, she made up her mind that his tribute would be, if analyzed, a tribute to her insignificance. But all the same he wanted her to come somewhere and have luncheon with him: what was that a tribute to? She must have counted very little if she didn't count too much for a romp in a restaurant. She had to get home with her trimming, and the most, in his company, she was amenable to was a retracing of her steps to the Marble Arch and then, after a discussion when they had reached it, a walk with him across the Park. She knew Mona would have considered that she ought to take the omnibus again; but she had now to think for Owen as well as for herself—she couldn't think for Mona. Even in the Park the autumn air was thick, and as they moved westward

over the grass, which was what Owen preferred, the cool
grayness made their words soft, made them at last rare and
everything else dim. He wanted to stay with her—he wanted
not to leave her: he had dropped into complete silence, but
that was what his silence said. What was it he had post-
poned? What was it he wanted still to postpone? She grew
a little scared as they strolled together and she thought. It
was too confused to be believed, but it was as if somehow
he felt differently. Fleda Vetch didn't suspect him at first of
feeling differently to *her,* but only of feeling differently to
Mona; yet she was not unconscious that this latter difference would have had something to do with his being on the
grass beside her. She had read in novels about gentlemen
who on the eve of marriage, winding up the past, had surrendered themselves for the occasion to the influence of a
former tie; and there was something in Owen's behavior
now, something in his very face, that suggested a resemblance to one of those gentlemen. But whom and what, in
that case, would Fleda herself resemble? She wasn't a
former tie, she wasn't any tie at all; she was only a deep
little person for whom happiness was a kind of pearl-diving
plunge. It was down at the very bottom of all that had lately
happened; for all that had lately happened was that Owen
Gereth had come and gone at Poynton. That was the small
sum of her experience, and what it had made for her was
her own affair, quite consistent with her not having dreamed
it had made a tie—at least what *she* called one—for Owen.
The old one, at any rate, was Mona—Mona whom he had
known so very much longer.

They walked far, to the southwest corner of the great
Gardens, where, by the old round pond and the old red
palace, when she had put out her hand to him in farewell,
declaring that from the gate she must positively take a
conveyance, it seemed suddenly to rise between them that
this was a real separation. She was on his mother's side,
she belonged to his mother's life, and his mother, in the
future, would never come to Poynton. After what had
passed she wouldn't even be at his wedding, and it was not
possible now that Mrs. Gereth should mention that cere-

mony to the girl, much less express a wish that the girl should be present at it. Mona, from decorum and with reference less to the bridegroom than to the bridegroom's mother, would of course not invite any such girl as Fleda. Everything therefore was ended; they would go their different ways; this was the last time they would stand face to face. They looked at each other with the fuller sense of it and, on Owen's part, with an expression of dumb trouble, the intensification of his usual appeal to any interlocutor to add the right thing to what he said. To Fleda, at this moment, it appeared that the right thing might easily be the wrong. He only said, at any rate: "I want you to understand, you know—I want you to understand."

What did he want her to understand? He seemed unable to bring it out, and this understanding was moreover exactly what she wished not to arrive at. Bewildered as she was, she had already taken in as much as she should know what to do with; the blood also was rushing into her face. He liked her—it was stupefying—more than he really ought: that was what was the matter with him and what he desired her to assimilate; so that she was suddenly as frightened as some thoughtless girl who finds herself the object of an overture from a married man.

"Good-bye, Mr. Gereth—I *must* get on!" she declared with a cheerfulness that she felt to be an unnatural grimace. She broke away from him sharply, smiling, backing across the grass and then turning altogether and moving as fast as she could. "Good-bye, good-bye!" she threw off again as she went, wondering if he would overtake her before she reached the gate; conscious with a red disgust that her movement was almost a run; conscious too of just the confused, handsome face with which he would look after her. She felt as if she had answered a kindness with a great flouncing snub, but at any rate she had got away, though the distance to the gate, her ugly gallop down the Broad Walk, every graceless jerk of which hurt her, seemed endless. She signed from afar to a cab on the stand in the Kensington Road and scrambled into it, glad of the encompassment of the four-wheeler that had officiously obeyed her summons and that, at the end of twenty yards, when she had violently pulled up a glass, permitted her to recognize the fact that she was on the point of bursting into tears.

CHAPTER VII

As soon as her sister was married she went down to Mrs. Gereth at Ricks—a promise to this effect having been promptly exacted and given; and her inner vision was much more fixed on the alterations there, complete now, as she understood, than on the success of her plotting and pinching for Maggie's happiness. Her imagination, in the interval, had indeed had plenty to do and numerous scenes to visit; for when on the summons just mentioned it had taken a flight from West Kensington to Ricks, it had hung but an hour over the terrace of painted pots and then yielded to a current of the upper air that swept it straight off to Poynton and to Waterbath. Not a sound had reached her of any supreme clash, and Mrs. Gereth had communicated next to nothing; giving out that, as was easily conceivable, she was too busy, too bitter, and too tired for vain civilities. All she had written was that she had got the new place well in hand and that Fleda would be surprised at the way it was turning out. Everything was even yet upside down; nevertheless, in the sense of having passed the threshold of Poynton for the last time, the amputation, as she called it, had been performed. Her leg had come off—she had now begun to stump along with the lovely wooden substitute; she would stump for life, and what her young friend was to come and admire was the beauty of her movement and the noise she made about the house. The reserve of Poynton and Waterbath had been matched by the austerity of Fleda's own secret, under the discipline of which she had repeated to herself a hundred times a day that she rejoiced at having cares that excluded all thought of it. She had lavished herself, in act, on Maggie and the curate, and had opposed to her father's selfishness a sweetness quite ecstatic. The young couple wondered why they had waited so long, since everything was after all so easy. She had thought of everything, even to how the "quietness" of the wedding should be relieved by champagne and her father kept brilliant on a single bottle. Fleda knew, in short, and liked the knowledge, that for several weeks she had appeared exemplary in every relation of life.

She had been perfectly prepared to be surprised at Ricks, for Mrs. Gereth was a wonder-working wizard, with a command, when all was said, of good material; but the impression in wait for her on the threshold made her catch her breath and falter. Dusk had fallen when she arrived, and in the plain square hall, one of the few good features, the glow of a Venetian lamp just showed, on either wall, the richness of an admirable tapestry. This instant perception that the place had been dressed at the expense of Poynton was a shock: it was as if she had abruptly seen herself in the light of an accomplice. The next moment, folded in Mrs. Gereth's arms, her eyes were diverted; but she had already had, in a flash, the vision of the great gaps in the other house. The two tapestries, not the largest, but those most splendidly toned by time, had been on the whole its most uplifted pride. When she could really see again she was on a sofa in the drawing-room, staring with intensity at an object soon distinct as the great Italian cabinet that, at Poynton, had been in the red saloon. Without looking, she was sure the room was occupied with other objects like it, stuffed with as many as it could hold of the trophies of her friend's struggle. By this time the very fingers of her glove, resting on the seat of the sofa, had thrilled at the touch of an old velvet brocade, a wonderous texture that she could recognize, would have recognized among a thousand, without dropping her eyes on it. They stuck to the cabinet with a kind of dissimulated dread, while she painfully asked herself whether she should notice it, notice everything, or just pretend not to be affected. How could she pretend not to be affected, with the very pendants of the lustres tinkling at her and with Mrs. Gereth, beside her and staring at her even as she herself stared at the cabinet, hunching up a back like Atlas under his globe? She was appalled at this image of what Mrs. Gereth had on her shoulders. That lady was waiting and watching her, bracing herself, and preparing the same face of confession and defiance she had shown the day, at Poynton, she had been surprised in the corridor. It was farcical not to speak; and yet to exclaim, to participate, would give one a bad sense of being mixed up with a theft. This ugly word sounded, for herself, in Fleda's silence, and the very violence of it jarred her into a scared glance, as of a creature detected, to right and left. But what again the full picture most showed her was the far-away empty sockets, a scandal of nakedness in high, bare walls. She at last uttered something formal and incoherent—she didn't know what: it had no relation to either house. Then she felt Mrs. Gereth's hand once more on her arm. "I've arranged a charming room for you—it's really lovely. You'll be very happy there." This was spoken with extraordinary sweetness and with a smile that meant, "Oh, I know what you're thinking; but what does it matter when you're so loyally on my side?" It had come indeed to a question of "sides," Fleda thought, for the whole place was in battle array. In the soft lamplight, with one fine feature after another looming up into sombre richness, it defied her not to pronounce it a triumph of taste. Her passion for beauty leaped back into life; and was not what now most appealed to it a certain gorgeous audacity? Mrs. Gereth's high hand was, as mere great effect, the climax of the impression.

"It's too wonderful, what you've done with the house!"— the visitor met her friend's eyes. They lighted up with joy— that friend herself so pleased with what she had done. This was not at all, in its accidental air of enthusiasm, what Fleda wanted to have said: it offered her as stupidly announcing from the first minute on whose side she was. Such was clearly the way Mrs. Gereth took it: she threw herself upon the delightful girl and tenderly embraced her again; so that Fleda soon went on, with a studied difference and a cooler inspection: "Why, you brought away absolutely everything!"

"Oh no, not everything; I saw how little I could get into this scrap of a house. I only brought away what I required."

Fleda had got up; she took a turn round the room. "You 'required' the very best pieces—the *morceaux de musée,* the individual gems!"

"I certainly didn't want the rubbish, if that's what you mean." Mrs. Gereth, on the sofa, followed the direction of her companion's eyes; with the light of her satisfaction still in her face, she slowly rubbed her large, handsome hands. Wherever she was, she was herself the great piece in the gallery. It was the first Fleda had heard of there being "rubbish" at Poynton, but she didn't for the moment take up this insincerity; she only, from where she stood in the room, called out, one after the other, as if she had had a list in her hand, the pieces that in the great house had been scattered and that now, if they had a fault, were too much like a minuet danced on a hearth-rug. She knew them each, in every chink and charm—knew them by the personal name their distinctive sign or story had given them; and a second time she felt how, against her intention, this uttered knowledge struck her hostess as so much free approval. Mrs. Gereth was never indifferent to approval, and there was nothing she could so love you for as for doing justice to her deep morality. There was a particular gleam in her eyes when Fleda exclaimed at last, dazzled by the display: "And even the Maltese cross!" That description, though technically incorrect, had always been applied, at Poynton, to a small but marvelous crucifix of ivory, a masterpiece of delicacy, of expression, and of the great Spanish period, the existence and precarious accessibility of which she had heard of at Malta, years before, by an odd and romantic chance—a clue followed through mazes of secrecy till the treasure was at last unearthed.

" 'Even' the Maltese cross?" Mrs. Gereth rose as she sharply echoed the words. "My dear child, you don't suppose I'd have sacrificed *that!* For what in the world would you have taken me?"

"A *bibelot* the more or the less," Fleda said, "could have made little difference in this grand general view of you. I take you simply for the greatest of all conjurers. You've operated with a quickness—and with a quietness!" Her voice trembled a little as she spoke, for the plain meaning of her words was that what her friend had achieved belonged to the class of operation essentially involving the protection of darkness. Fleda felt she really could say nothing at all if she couldn't say that she knew what the danger had been. She completed her thought by a resolute and perfectly candid question: "How in the world did you get off with them?"

Mrs. Gereth confessed to the fact of danger with a cynicism that surprised the girl. "By calculating, by choosing my time. I *was* quiet, and I *was* quick. I manœuvred; then at the last rushed!" Fleda drew a long breath: she saw in the poor woman something much better than sophistical ease, a crude elation that was a comparatively simple state to deal with. Her elation, it was true, was not so much from what she had done as from the way she had done it— by as brilliant a stroke as any commemorated in the annals of crime. "I succeeded because I had thought it all out and left nothing to chance: the whole process was organized in advance, so that the mere carrying it into effect took but a few hours. It was largely a matter of money: oh, I was horribly extravagant—I had to turn on so many people. But they were all to be had—a little army of workers, the packers, the porters, the helpers of every sort, the men with the mighty vans. It was a question of arranging in Tottenham Court Road and of paying the price. I haven't paid it yet; there'll be a horrid bill; but at least the thing's done! Expedition pure and simple was the essence of the bargain. 'I can give you two days,' I said; 'I can't give you another second.' They undertook the job, and the two days saw them through. The people came down on a Tuesday morning; they were off on the Thursday. I admit that some of them worked all Wednesday night. I had thought it all out; I stood over them; I showed them how. Yes, I coaxed them, I made love to them. Oh, I was inspired—they found me wonderful. I neither ate nor slept, but I was as calm as I am now. I didn't know what was in me; it was worth finding out. I'm very remarkable, my dear: I lifted tons with my own arms. I'm tired, very, very tired; but there's neither a scratch nor a nick, there isn't a teacup missing." Magnificent both in her exhaustion and in her triumph, Mrs. Gereth sank on the sofa again, the sweep of her eyes a rich synthesis and the restless friction of her hands a clear betrayal. "Upon my word," she laughed, "they really look better here!"

Fleda had listened in awe. "And no one at Poynton said anything? There was no alarm?"

"What alarm should there have been? Owen left me almost defiantly alone: I had taken a time that I had reason to believe was safe from a descent." Fleda had another wonder, which she hesitated to express: it would scarcely do to ask Mrs. Gereth if she hadn't stood in fear of her servants. She knew, moreover, some of the secrets of her humorous household rule, all made up of shocks to shyness and provocations to curiosity—a diplomacy so artful that several of the maids quite yearned to accompany her to Ricks. Mrs. Gereth, reading sharply the whole of her visitor's thought, caught it up with fine frankness. "You mean that I was watched—that he had his myrmidons, pledged to wire him if they should see what I was 'up to'? Precisely. I know the three persons you have in mind: I had them in mind myself. Well, I took a line with them— I settled them."

Fleda had had no one in particular in mind; she had never believed in the myrmidons; but the tone in which Mrs. Gereth spoke added to her suspense. "What did you do to them?"

"I took hold of them hard—I put them in the forefront. I made them work."

"To move the furniture?"

"To help, and to help so as to please me. That was the way to take them; it was what they had least expected. I marched up to them and looked each straight in the eye, giving him the chance to choose if he'd gratify me or gratify my son. He gratified *me*. They were too stupid!"

Mrs. Gereth massed herself there more and more as an immoral woman, but Fleda had to recognize that she too would have been stupid and she too would have gratified her. "And when did all this take place?"

"Only last week; it seems a hundred years. We've worked here as fast as we worked there, but I'm not settled yet: you'll see in the rest of the house. However, the worst is over."

"Do you really think so?" Fleda presently inquired. "I mean, does he, after the fact, as it were, accept it?"

"Owen—what I've done? I haven't the least idea," said Mrs. Gereth.

"Does Mona?"

"You mean that she'll be the soul of the row?"

"I hardly see Mona as the 'soul' of anything," the girl replied. "But have they made no sound? Have you heard nothing at all?"

"Not a whisper, not a step, in all the eight days. Perhaps they don't know. Perhaps they're crouching for a leap."

"But wouldn't they have gone down as soon as you left?"

"They may not have known of my leaving." Fleda wondered afresh; it struck her as scarcely supposable that some sign shouldn't have flashed from Poynton to London. If the storm was taking this term of silence to gather, even in Mona's breast, it would probably discharge itself in some startling form. The great hush of every one concerned was strange; but when she pressed Mrs. Gereth for some explanation of it, that lady only replied, with her brave irony: "Oh, I took their breath away!" She had no illusions, however; she was still prepared to fight. What indeed was her spoliation of Poynton but the first engagement of a campaign?

All this was exciting, but Fleda's spirit dropped, at bedtime, in the chamber embellished for her pleasure, where she found several of the objects that in her earlier room she had most admired. These had been reinforced by other pieces from other rooms, so that the quiet air of it was a harmony without a break, the finished picture of a maiden's bower. It was the sweetest Louis Seize, all assorted and combined—old chastened, figured, faded France. Fleda was impressed anew with her friend's genius for composition. She could say to herself that no girl in England, that night, went to rest with so picked a guard; but there was no joy for her in her privilege, no sleep even for the tired hours that made the place, in the embers of the fire and the winter dawn, look gray, somehow, and loveless. She couldn't care for such things when they came to her in such ways; there was a wrong about them all that turned them to ugliness. In the watches of the night she saw Poynton dishonored; she had cared for it as a happy whole, she reasoned, and the parts of it now around her seemed to suffer like chopped limbs. Before going to bed she had walked about with Mrs. Gereth and seen at whose expense the whole house had been furnished. At poor Owen's, from top to bottom—there wasn't a chair he hadn't sat upon. The maiden aunt had been exterminated—no trace of her to tell her tale. Fleda tried to think of some of the things at Poynton still unappropriated, but her memory was a blank about them, and in trying to focus the old combinations she saw again nothing but gaps and scars, a vacancy that gathered at moments into something worse. This concrete image was her greatest trouble, for it was Owen Gereth's face, his sad, strange eyes, fixed upon her now as they had never been. They stared at her out of the darkness, and their expression was more than she could bear: it seemed to say that he was in pain and that it was somehow her fault. He had looked to her to help him, and this was what her help had been. He had done her the honor to ask her to exert herself in his interest, confiding to her a task of difficulty, but of the highest delicacy. Hadn't that been exactly the sort of service she longed to render him? Well, her way of rendering it had been simply to betray him and hand him over to his enemy. Shame, pity, resentment oppressed her in turn; in the last of these feelings the others were quickly submerged. Mrs. Gereth had imprisoned her in that torment of taste; but it was clear to her for an hour at least that she might hate Mrs. Gereth.

Something else, however, when morning came, was even more intensely definite: the most odious thing in the world for her would be ever again to meet Owen. She took on the spot a resolve to neglect no precaution that could lead to her going through life without that accident. After this, while she dressed, she took still another. Her position had become, in a few hours, intolerably false; in as few more hours as possible she would therefore put an end to it. The way to put an end to it would be to inform Mrs.

Gereth that, to her great regret, she couldn't be with her now, couldn't cleave to her to the point that everything about her so plainly urged. She dressed with a sort of violence, a symbol of the manner in which this purpose was precipitated. The more they parted company the less likely she was to come across Owen; for Owen would be drawn closer to his mother now by the very necessity of bringing her down. Fleda, in the inconsequence of distress, wished to have nothing to do with her fall; she had had too much to do with everything. She was well aware of the importance, before breakfast and in view of any light they might shed on the question of motive, of not suffering her invidious expression of a difference to be accompanied by the traces of tears; but it none the less came to pass, downstairs, that after she had subtly put her back to the window, to make a mystery of the state of her eyes, she stupidly let a rich sob escape her before she could properly meet the consequences of being asked if she wasn't delighted with her room. This accident struck her on the spot as so grave that she felt the only refuge to be instant hypocrisy, some graceful impulse that would charge her emotion to the quickened sense of her friend's generosity—a demonstration entailing a flutter round the table and a renewed embrace, and not so successfully improvised but that Fleda fancied Mrs. Gereth to have been only half reassured. She had been startled, at any rate, and she might remain suspicious: this reflection interposed by the time, after breakfast, the girl had recovered sufficiently to say what was in her heart. She accordingly didn't say it that morning at all: she had absurdly veered about; she had encountered the shock of the fear that Mrs. Gereth, with sharpened eyes, might wonder why the deuce (she often wondered in that phrase) she had grown so warm about Owen's rights. She would doubtless, at a pinch, be able to defend them on abstract grounds, but that would involve a discussion, and the idea of a discussion made her nervous for her secret. Until in some way Poynton should return the blow and give her a cue, she must keep nervousness down; and she called herself a fool for having forgotten, however briefly, that her one safety was in silence.

Directly after luncheon Mrs. Gereth took her into the garden for a glimpse of the revolution—or at least, said the mistress of Ricks, of the great row—that had been decreed there; but the ladies had scarcely placed themselves for this view before the younger one found herself embracing a prospect that opened in quite another quarter. Her attention was called to it, oddly, by the streamers of the parlor-maid's cap, which, flying straight behind the neat young woman who unexpectedly burst from the house and showed a long red face as she ambled over the grass, seemed to articulate in their flutter the name that Fleda lived at present only to catch. "Poynton—Poynton!" said the morsels of muslin; so that the parlor-maid became on the instant an actress in the drama, and Fleda, assuming pusillanimously that she herself was only a spectator, looked across the footlights at the exponent of the principal part. The manner in which this artist returned her look showed that she was equally preoccupied. Both were haunted alike by possibilities, but the apprehension of neither, before the announcement was made, took the form of the arrival at Ricks, in the flesh, of Mrs. Gereth's victim. When the messenger informed them that Mr. Gereth was in the drawing-room, the blank "Oh!" emitted by Fleda was quite as precipitate as the sound on her hostess's lips, besides being, as she felt, much less pertinent. "I thought it would be somebody," that lady afterwards said; "but I expected on the whole a solicitor's clerk." Fleda didn't mention that she herself had expected on the whole a pair of constables. She was surprised by Mrs. Gereth's question to the parlor-maid.

"For whom did he ask?"

"Why, for *you*, of course, dearest friend!" Fleda interjected, falling instinctively into the address that embodied the intensest pressure. She wanted to put Mrs. Gereth between her and her danger.

"He asked for Miss Vetch, mum," the girl replied, with a face that brought startlingly to Fleda's ear the muffled chorus of the kitchen.

"Quite proper," said Mrs. Gereth austerely. Then to Fleda: "Please go to him."

"But what to do?"

"What you always do—to see what he wants." Mrs. Gereth dismissed the maid. "Tell him Miss Vetch will come." Fleda saw that nothing was in the mother's imagination at this moment but the desire not to meet her son. She had completely broken with him, and there was little in what had just happened to repair the rupture. It would now take more to do so than his presenting himself uninvited at her door. "He's right in asking for you—he's aware that you're still our communicator; nothing has occurred to alter that. To what he wishes to transmit through you I'm ready, as I've been ready before, to listen. As far as *I*'m concerned, if I couldn't meet him a month ago, how am I to meet him to-day? If he has come to say, 'My dear mother, you're here, in the hovel into which I've flung you, with consolations that give me pleasure,' I'll listen to him; but on no other footing. That's what you're to ascertain, please. You'll oblige me as you've obliged me before. There!" Mrs. Gereth turned her back and, with a fine imitation of superiority, began to redress the miseries immediately before her. Fleda meanwhile hesitated, lingered for some minutes where she had been left, feeling secretly that her fate still had her in hand. It had put her face to face with Owen Gereth, and it evidently meant to keep her so. She was reminded afresh of two things: one of which was that, though she judged her friend's rigor, she had never really had the story of the scene enacted in the great awestricken house between the mother and the son weeks before—the day the former took to her bed in her overthrow; the other was, that at Ricks as at Poynton, it was before all things her place to accept thankfully a usefulness not, she must remember, universally acknowledged. What determined her at the last, while Mrs. Gereth disappeared in the shrubbery, was that, though she was at a distance from the house and the drawing-room was turned the other way, she could absolutely see the young man alone there with the sources of his pain. She saw his simple stare at his tapestries, heard his heavy tread on his carpets and the hard breath of his sense of unfairness. At this she went to him fast.

CHAPTER VIII

"I ASKED FOR YOU," he said when she stood there, "because I heard from the flyman who drove me from the station to the inn that he had brought you here yesterday. We had some talk, and he mentioned it."

"You didn't know I was here?"

"No. I knew only that you had had, in London, all that you told me, that day, to do; and it was Mona's idea that after your sister's marriage you were staying on with your father. So I thought you were with him still."

"I am," Fleda replied, idealizing a little the fact. "I'm here only for a moment. But do you mean," she went on, "that if you had known I was with your mother you wouldn't have come down?"

The way Owen hung fire at this question made it sound more playful than she had intended. She had, in fact, no consciousness of any intention but that of confining herself rigidly to her function. She could already see that, in whatever he had now braced himself for, she was an element he had not reckoned with. His preparation had been of a different sort—the sort congruous with his having been careful to go first and lunch solidly at the inn. He had not been forced to ask for her, but she became aware, in his presence, of a particular desire to make him feel that no harm could really come to him. She might upset him, as people called it, but she would take no advantage of having done so. She had never seen a person with whom she wished more to be light and easy, to be exceptionally human. The account he presently gave of the matter was that he indeed wouldn't have come if he had known she was on the spot; because then, didn't she see? he could have written to her. He would have had her there to let fly at his mother.

"That would have saved me—well, it would have saved me a lot. Of course I would rather see you than her," he somewhat awkwardly added. "When the fellow spoke of you, I assure you I quite jumped at you. In fact I've no real desire to see Mummy at all. If she thinks I *like* it—!" He sighed disgustedly. "I only came down because it seemed better than any other way. I didn't want her to be able to say I hadn't been all right. I dare say you know she has taken everything; or if not quite everything, why, a lot more than one ever dreamed. You can see for yourself— she has got half the place down. She has got them crammed —you can see for yourself!" He had his old trick of artless repetition, his helpless iteration of the obvious; but he was sensibly different, for Fleda, if only by the difference of his clear face, mottled over and almost disfigured by little points of pain. He might have been a fine young man with a bad toothache; with the first even of his life. What ailed him above all, she felt, was that trouble was new to him: he had never known a difficulty; he had taken all his fences, his world wholly the world of the personally possible, rounded indeed by a gray suburb into which he had never had occasion to stray. In this vulgar and ill-lighted region he had evidently now lost himself. "We left it quite to her honor, you know," he said ruefully.

"Perhaps you've a right to say that you left it a little to mine." Mixed up with the spoils there, rising before him as if she were in a manner their keeper, she felt that she must absolutely dissociate herself. Mrs. Gereth had made it impossible to do anything but give her away. "I can only tell you that, on my side, I left it to her. I never dreamed either that she would pick out so many things.

"And you don't really think it's fair, do you? You *don't!*" He spoke very quickly; he really seemed to plead.

Fleda faltered a moment. "I think she has gone too far." Then she added: "I shall immediately tell her that I've said that to you."

He appeared puzzled by this statement, but he presently

rejoined: "You haven't then said to mamma what you think?"

"Not yet; remember that I only got here last night." She appeared to herself ignobly weak. "I had had no idea what she was doing; I was taken completely by surprise. She managed it wonderfully."

"It's the sharpest thing I ever saw in *my* life!" They looked at each other with intelligence, in appreciation of the sharpness, and Owen quickly broke into a loud laugh. The laugh was in itself natural, but the occasion of it strange; and stranger still, to Fleda, so that she too almost laughed, the inconsequent charity with which he added: "Poor dear old Mummy! That's one of the reasons I asked for you," he went on—"to see if you'd back her up."

Whatever he said or did, she somehow liked him the better for it. "How can I back her up, Mr. Gereth, when I think, as I tell you, that she has made a great mistake?"

"A great mistake! That's all right." He spoke—it wasn't clear to her why—as if this declaration were a great point gained.

"Of course there are many things she hasn't taken," Fleda continued.

"Oh yes, a lot of things. But you wouldn't know the place, all the same." He looked about the room with his discolored, swindled face, which deepened Fleda's compassion for him, conjuring away any smile at so candid an image of the dupe. "You'd know this one soon enough, wouldn't you? These are just the things she ought to have left. Is the whole house full of them?"

"The whole house," said Fleda uncompromisingly. She thought of her lovely room.

"I never knew how much I cared for them. They're awfully valuable, aren't they?" Owen's manner mystified her; she was conscious of a return of the agitation he had produced in her on that last bewildering day, and she reminded herself that, now she was warned, it would be inexcusable of her to allow him to justify the fear that had dropped on her. "Mother thinks I never took any notice, but I assure you I was awfully proud of everything. Upon my honor, I *was* proud, Miss Vetch."

There was an oddity in his helplessness; he appeared to wish to persuade her and to satisfy himself that she sincerely felt how worthy he really was to treat what had happened as an injury. She could only exclaim, almost as helplessly as himself: "Of course you did justice! It's all most painful. I shall instantly let your mother know," she again declared, "the way I've spoken of her to you." She clung to that idea as to the sign of her straightness.

"You'll tell her what you think she ought to do?" he asked with some eagerness.

"What she ought to do?"

"*Don't* you think it—I mean that she ought to give them up?"

"To give them up?" Fleda hesitated again.

"To send them back—to keep it quiet." The girl had not felt the impulse to ask him to sit down among the monuments of his wrong, so that, nervously, awkwardly, he fidgeted about the room with his hands in his pockets and an effect of returning a little into possession through the formulation of his view. "To have them packed and dispatched again, since she knows so well how. She does it beautifully"—he looked close at two or three precious pieces. "What's sauce for the goose is sauce for the gander!"

He had laughed at his way of putting it, but Fleda remained grave. "Is that what you came to say to her?"

"Not exactly those words. But I did come to say"—he stammered, then brought it out—"I did come to say we must have them right back."

"And did you think your mother would see you?"

"I wasn't sure, but I thought it right to try—to put it to her kindly, don't you see? If she won't see me, then she has herself to thank. The only other way would have been to set the lawyers at her."

"I'm glad you didn't do that."

"I'm dashed if I want to!" Owen honestly declared. "But what's a fellow to do if she won't meet a fellow?"

"What do you call meeting a fellow?" Fleda asked, with a smile.

"Why, letting *me* tell her a dozen things she can have."

This was a transaction that Fleda, after a moment, had

to give up trying to represent to herself. "If she won't do that—?" she went on.

"I'll leave it all to my solicitor. *He* won't let her off: by Jove, I know the fellow!"

"That's horrible!" said Fleda, looking at him in woe. "It's utterly beastly!"

His want of logic as well as his vehemence startled her; and with her eyes still on his she considered before asking him the question these things suggested. At last she asked it. "Is Mona very angry?"

"Oh dear, yes!" said Owen.

She had perceived that he wouldn't speak of Mona without her beginning. After waiting fruitlessly now for him to say more, she continued: "She has been there again? She has seen the state of the house?"

"Oh dear, yes!" Owen repeated.

Fleda disliked to appear not to take account of his brevity, but it was just because she was struck by it that she felt the pressure of the desire to know more. What it suggested was simply what her intelligence supplied, for he was incapable of any art of insinuation. Wasn't it at all events the rule of communication with him to say for him what he couldn't say? This truth was present to the girl as she inquired if Mona greatly resented what Mrs. Gereth had done. He satisfied her promptly; he was standing before the fire, his back to it, his long legs apart, his hands, behind him, rather violently jiggling his gloves. "She hates it awfully. In fact, she refuses to put up with it at all. Don't you see?—she saw the place with all the things."

"So that of course she misses them."

"Misses them—rather! She was awfully sweet on them." Fleda remembered how sweet Mona had been, and reflected that if that was the sort of plea he had prepared it was indeed as well he shouldn't see his mother. This was not all she wanted to know, but it came over her that it was all she needed. "You see it puts me in the position of not carrying out what I promised," Owen said. "As she says herself"—he hesitated an instant—"it's just as if I had obtained her under false pretenses." Just before, when he spoke with more drollery than he knew, it had left Fleda serious; but now his own clear gravity had the effect of exciting her mirth. She laughed out, and he looked surprised, but went on: "She regards it as a regular sell."

Fleda was silent; but finally, as he added nothing, she exclaimed: "Of course it makes a great difference!" She knew all she needed, but none the less she risked, after another pause, an interrogative remark. "I forget when it is that your marriage takes place?"

Owen came away from the fire and, apparently at a loss where to turn, ended by directing himself to one of the windows. "It's a little uncertain; the date isn't quite fixed."

"Oh, I thought I remembered that at Poynton you had told me a day, and that it was near at hand."

"I dare say I did; it was for the 19th. But we've altered that—she wants to shift it." He looked out of the window; then he said: "In fact, it won't come off till Mummy has come round."

"Come round?"

"Put the place as it was." In his offhand way he added: "You know what I mean!"

He spoke not impatiently, but with a kind of intimate familiarity, the sweetness of which made her feel a pang for having forced him to tell her what was embarrassing to him, what was even humiliating. Yes indeed, she knew all she needed: all she needed was that Mona had proved apt at putting down that wonderful patent-leather foot. Her type was misleading only to the superficial, and no one in the world was less superficial than Fleda. She had guessed the truth at Waterbath and she had suffered from it at Poynton; at Ricks the only thing she could do was to accept it with the dumb exaltation that she felt rising. Mona had been prompt with her exercise of the member in question, for it might be called prompt to do that sort of thing before marriage. That she had indeed been premature who should say save those who should have read the matter in the full light of results? Neither at Waterbath nor at Poynton had even Fleda's thoroughness discovered all that there was—or rather, all that there was not—in Owen Gereth. "Of course it makes all the difference!" she said in answer to his last words. She pursued, after considering:

"What you wish me to say from you then to your mother is that you demand immediate and practically complete restitution?"

"Yes, please. It's tremendously good of you."

"Very well, then. Will you wait?"

"For Mummy's answer?" Owen stared and looked perplexed; he was more and more fevered with so much vivid expression of his case. "Don't you think that if I'm here she may hate it worse—think I may want to make her reply bang off?"

Fleda thought. "You don't, then?"

"I want to take her in the right way, don't you know?— treat her as if I gave her more than just an hour or two."

"I see," said Fleda. "Then, if you don't wait—goodbye."

This again seemed not what he wanted. "Must *you* do it bang off?"

"I'm only thinking she'll be impatient—I mean, you know, to learn what will have passed between us."

"I see," said Owen, looking at his gloves. "I can give her a day or two, you know. Of course I didn't come down to sleep," he went on. "The inn seems a horrid hole. I know all about the trains—having no idea you were here." Almost as soon as his interlocutress he was struck with the absence of the visible, in this, as between effect and cause. "I mean because in that case I should have felt I could stop over. I should have felt I could talk with you a blessed sight longer than with Mummy."

"We've already talked a long time," smiled Fleda.

"Awfully, haven't we?" He spoke with the stupidity she didn't object to. Inarticulate as he was, he had more to say; he lingered perhaps because he was vaguely aware of the want of sincerity in her encouragement to him to go. "There's one thing, please," he mentioned, as if there might be a great many others too. "Please don't say anything about Mona."

She didn't understand. "About Mona?"

"About its being *her* that thinks she has gone too far." This was still slightly obscure, but now Fleda understood.

"It mustn't seem to come from *her* at all, don't you know? That would only make Mummy worse."

Fleda knew exactly how much worse, but she felt a delicacy about explicitly assenting: She was already immersed moreover in the deep consideration of what might make "Mummy" better. She couldn't see as yet at all; she could only clutch at the hope of some inspiration after he should go. Oh, there was a remedy, to be sure, but it was out of the question; in spite of which, in the strong light of Owen's troubled presence, of his anxious face and restless step, it hung there before her for some minutes. She felt that, remarkably, beneath the decent rigor of his errand, the poor young man, for reasons, for weariness, for disgust, would have been ready not to insist. His fitness to fight his mother had left him—he wasn't in fighting trim. He had no natural avidity and even no special wrath; he had none that had not been taught him, and it was doing his best to learn the lesson that had made him so sick. He had his delicacies, but he hid them away like presents before Christmas. He was hollow, perfunctory, pathetic; he had been girded by another hand. That hand had naturally been Mona's, and it was heavy even now on his strong, broad back. Why then had he originally rejoiced so in its touch? Fleda dashed aside this question, for it had nothing to do with her problem. Her problem was to help him to live as a gentleman and carry through what he had undertaken; her problem was to reinstate him in his rights. It was quite irrelevant that Mona had no intelligence of what she had lost—quite irrelevant that she was moved not by the privation, but by the insult: she had every reason to be moved, though she was so much more movable, in the vindictive way, at any rate, than one might have supposed—assuredly more than Owen himself had imagined.

"Certainly I shall not mention Mona," Fleda said, "and there won't be the slightest necessity for it. The wrong's quite sufficiently yours, and the demand you make is perfectly justified by it."

"I can't tell you what it is to me to feel you on my side!" Owen exclaimed.

"Up to this time," said Fleda, after a pause, "your mother has had no doubt of my being on hers."

"Then of course she won't like your changing."

"I dare say she won't like it at all."

"Do you mean to say you'll have a regular kick-up with her?"

"I don't exactly know what you mean by a regular kick-up. We shall naturally have a great deal of discussion—if she consents to discuss the matter at all. That's why you must decidedly give her two or three days."

"I see you think she *may* refuse to discuss it at all," said Owen.

"I'm only trying to be prepared for the worst. You must remember that to have to withdraw from the ground she has taken, to make a public surrender of what she has publicly appropriated, will go uncommonly hard with her pride."

Owen considered; his face seemed to broaden, but not into a smile. "I suppose she's tremendously proud, isn't she?" This might have been the first time it had occurred to him.

"You know better than I," said Fleda, speaking with high extravagance.

"I don't know anything in the world half so well as you. If I were as clever as you I might hope to get round her." Owen hesitated; then he went on: "In fact I don't quite see what even you can say or do that will really fetch her."

"Neither do I, as yet. I must think—I must pray!" the girl pursued, smiling. "I can only say to you that I'll try. I *want* to try, you know—I want to help you." He stood looking at her so long on this that she added with much distinctness: "So you must leave me, please, quite alone with her. You must go straight back."

"Back to the inn?"

"Oh no, back to town. I'll write to you tomorrow."

He turned about vaguely for his hat.

"There's the chance, of course, that she may be afraid."

"Afraid, you mean, of the legal steps you may take?"

"I've got a perfect case—I could have her up. The Brigstocks say it's simple stealing."

"I can easily fancy what the Brigstocks say!" Fleda permitted herself to remark without solemnity.

"It's none of their business, is it?" was Owen's unexpected rejoiner. Fleda had already noted that no one so slow could ever have had such rapid transitions.

She showed her amusement. "They've a much better right to say it's none of mine."

"Well, at any rate, you don't call her names."

Fleda wondered whether Mona did; and this made it all the finer of her to exclaim in a moment: "You don't know what I shall call her if she holds out!"

Owen gave her a gloomy glance; then he blew a speck off the crown of his hat. "But if you do have a set-to with her?"

He paused so long for a reply that Fleda said: "I don't think I know what you mean by a set-to."

"Well, if she calls *you* names."

"I don't think she'll do that."

"What I mean to say is, if she's angry at your backing me up—what will you do then? She can't possibly like it, you know."

"She may very well not like it; but everything depends. I must see what I shall do. You mustn't worry about me."

She spoke with decision, but Owen seemed still unsatisfied. "You won't go away, I hope?"

"Go away?"

"If she does take it ill of you."

Fleda moved to the door and opened it. "I'm not prepared to say. You must have patience and see."

"Of course I must," said Owen—"of course, of course." But he took no more advantage of the open door than to say: "You want me to be off, and I'm off in a minute. Only, before I go, please answer me a question. If you *should* leave my mother, where would you go?"

Fleda smiled again. "I haven't the least idea."

"I suppose you'd go back to London."

"I haven't the least idea," Fleda repeated.

"You don't—a—live anywhere in particular, do you?" the young man went on. He looked conscious as soon as he had spoken; she could see that he felt himself to have al-

luded more grossly than he meant to the circumstance of
her having, if one were plain about it, no home of her own.
He had meant it as an illusion of a tender sort to all that
she would sacrifice in the case of a quarrel with his mother;
but there was indeed no graceful way of touching on that.
One just couldn't be plain about it.

Fleda, wound up as she was, shrank from any treatment
at all of the matter, and she made no answer to his question. "I *won't* leave your mother," she said. "I'll produce
an effect on her; I'll convince her absolutely."

"I believe you will, if you look at her like that!"

She was wound up to such a height that there might well
be a light in her pale, fine little face—a light that, while,
for all return, at first, she simply shone back at him, was
intensely reflected in his own. "I'll make her see it—I'll
make her see it!" She rang out like a silver bell. She had at
that moment a perfect faith that she should succeed; but it
passed into something else when, the next instant, she became aware that Owen, quickly getting between her and the
door she had opened, was sharply closing it, as might be
said, in her face. He had done this before she could stop
him, and he stood there with his hand on the knob and
smiled at her strangely. Clearer than he could have spoken
it was the sense of those seconds of silence.

"When I got into this I didn't know you, and now that I
know you how can I tell you the difference? And *she*'s so
different, so ugly and vulgar, in the light of this squabble.
No, like *you* I've never known one. It's another thing,
it's a new thing altogether. Listen to me a little: can't
something be done?" It was what had been in the air in
those moments at Kensington, and it only wanted words to
be a committed act. The more reason, to the girl's excited
mind, why it shouldn't have words; her one thought was not
to hear, to keep the act uncommitted. She would do this if
she had to be horrid.

"Please let me out, Mr. Gereth," she said; on which he
opened the door with an hesitation so very brief that in
thinking of these things afterwards—for she was to think
of them forever—she wondered in what tone she could

have spoken. They went into the hall, where she encountered the parlor-maid, of whom she inquired whether Mrs. Gereth had come in.

"No, miss; and I think she has left the garden. She has gone up the back road." In other words, they had the whole place to themselves. It would have been a pleasure, in a different mood, to converse with that parlor-maid.

"Please open the house-door," said Fleda.

Owen, as if in quest of his umbrella, looked vaguely about the hall—looked even wistfully up the staircase—while the neat young woman complied with Fleda's request. Owen's eyes then wandered out of the open door. "I think it's awfully nice here," he observed; "I assure you I could do with it myself."

"I should think you might, with half your things here! It's Poynton itself—almost. Good-bye, Mr. Gereth," Fleda added. Her intention had naturally been that the neat young woman, opening the front door, should remain to close it on the departing guest. That functionary, however, had acutely vanished behind a stiff flap of green baize which Mrs. Gereth had not yet had time to abolish. Fleda put out her hand, but Owen turned away—he couldn't find his umbrella. She passed into the open air—she was determined to get him out; and in a moment he joined her in the little plastered portico which had small resemblance to any feature of Poynton. It was, as Mrs. Gereth had said, like the portico of a house in Brompton.

"Oh, I don't mean with all the things here," he explained in regard to the opinion he had just expressed. "I mean I could put up with it just as it was; it had a lot of good things, don't you think? I mean if everything was back at Poynton, if everything was all right." He brought out these last words with a sort of smothered sigh. Fleda didn't understand his explanation unless it had reference to another and more wonderful exchange—the restoration to the great house not only of its tables and chairs, but of its alienated mistress. This would imply the installation of his own life at Ricks, and obviously that of another person. Such another person could scarcely be Mona Brigstock. He put out his hand now; and once more she heard his unsounded words: "With everything patched up at the other place, I could live here with *you*. Don't you see what I mean?"

Fleda saw perfectly, and, with a face in which she flattered herself that nothing of this vision appeared, gave him her hand and said: "Good-bye, good-bye."

Owen held her hand very firmly and kept it even after an effort made by her to recover it—an effort not repeated, as she felt it best not to show she was flurried. That solution —of her living with him at Ricks—disposed of him beautifully, and disposed not less so of herself; it disposed admirably too of Mrs. Gereth. Fleda could only vainly wonder how it provided for poor Mona. While he looked at her, grasping her hand, she felt that now indeed she was paying for his mother's extravagance at Poynton—the vividness of that lady's public plea that little Fleda Vetch was the person to insure the general peace. It was to that vividness poor Owen had come back, and if Mrs. Gereth had had more discretion little Fleda Vetch wouldn't have been in a predicament. She saw that Owen had at this moment his sharpest necessity of speech, and so long as he didn't release her hand she could only submit to him. Her defense would be perhaps to look blank and hard; so she looked as blank and as hard as she could, with the reward of an immediate sense that this was not a bit what he wanted. It even made him hang fire, as if he were suddenly ashamed of himself, were recalled to some idea of duty and of honor. Yet he none the less brought it out. "There's one thing I dare say I ought to tell you, if you're going so kindly to act for me; though of course you'll see for yourself it's a thing it won't do to tell *her*." What was it? He made her wait for it again, and while she waited, under firm coercion, she had the extraordinary impression that Owen's simplicity was in eclipse. His natural honesty was like the scent of a flower, and she felt at this moment as if her nose had been brushed by the bloom without the odor. The allusion was undoubtedly to his mother; and was not what he meant about the matter in question the opposite of what he said—that it just *would* do to tell her? It would have been the first time he had said the opposite of what he meant, and there was certainly a fascination in the phenomenon, as well as a challenge to suspense in the ambiguity. "It's just that I understand from Mona, you know," he stammered; "it's just that she has made no bones about bringing home to me—" He tried to laugh, and in the effort he faltered again.

"About bringing home to you?"—Fleda encouraged him.

He was sensible of it, he achieved his performance. "Why, that if I don't get the things back—every blessed one of them except a few *she*'ll pick out—she won't have anything more to say to me."

Fleda, after an instant, encouraged him again. "To say to you?"

"Why, she simply won't marry me, don't you see?"

Owen's legs, not to mention his voice, had wavered while he spoke, and she felt his possession of her hand loosen so that she was free again. Her stare of perception broke into a lively laugh. "Oh, you're all right, for you *will* get them. You will; you're quite safe; don't worry!" She fell back into the house with her hand on the door. "Goodbye, good-bye." She repeated it several times, laughing bravely, quite waving him away and, as he didn't move and save that he was on the other side of it, closing the door in his face quite as he had closed that of the drawing-room in hers. Never had a face, never at least had such a handsome one, been so presented to that offense. She even held the door a minute, lest he should try to come in again. At last, as she heard nothing, she made a dash for the stairs and ran up.

CHAPTER IX

IN KNOWING A WHILE before all she needed, Fleda had
been far from knowing as much as that; so that once upstairs, where, in her room, with her sense of danger and
trouble, the age of Louis Seize suddenly struck her as
wanting in taste and point, she felt that she now for the
first time knew her temptation. Owen had put it before her
with an art beyond his own dream. Mona would cast him
off if he didn't proceed to extremities; if his negotiation with
his mother should fail he would be completely free. That
negotiation depended on a young lady to whom he had
pressingly suggested the condition of his freedom; and as if
to aggravate the young lady's predicament designing fate
had sent Mrs. Gereth, as the parlor-maid said, "up the back
road." This would give the young lady more time to make
up her mind that nothing should come of the negotiation.
There would be different ways of putting the question to
Mrs. Gereth, and Fleda might profitably devote the moments before her return to a selection of the way that would
most surely be tantamount to failure. This selection indeed
required no great adroitness; it was so conspicuous that
failure would be the reward of an effective introduction of
Mona. If that abhorred name should be properly invoked
Mrs. Gereth would resist to the death, and before enven-
omed resistance Owen would certainly retire. His retirement would be into single life, and Fleda reflected that he
had now gone away conscious of having practically told
her so. She could only say, as she waited for the back road
to disgorge, that she hoped it was a consciousness he enjoyed. There was something *she* enjoyed; but that was a
very different matter. To know that she had become to

him an object of desire gave her wings that she felt herself
flutter in the air: it was like the rush of a flood into her own
accumulations. These stored depths had been fathomless
and still, but now, for half an hour, in the empty house,
they spread till they overflowed. He seemed to have made it
right for her to confess to herself her secret. Strange then
there should be for him in return nothing that such a confession could make right! How could it make right that he
should give up Mona for another woman? His attitude was
a sorry appeal to Fleda to legitimate that. But he didn't
believe it himself, and he had none of the courage of his
suggestion. She could easily see how wrong everything
must be when a man so made to be manly was wanting in
courage. She had upset him, as people called it, and he
had spoken out from the force of the jar of finding her
there. He had upset her too, heaven knew, but she was one
of those who could pick themselves up. She had the real
advantage, she considered, of having kept him from seeing
that she had been overthrown.

She had moreover at present completely recovered her
feet, though there was in the intensity of the effort required
to do so a vibration which throbbed away into an immense
allowance for the young man. How could she after all know
what, in the disturbance wrought by his mother, Mona's
relations with him might have become? If he had been able
to keep his wits, such as they were, more about him he
would probably have felt—as sharply as she felt on his
behalf—that so long as those relations were not ended he
had no right to say even the little he had said. He had no
right to appear to wish to draw in another girl to help him
to an escape. If he was in a plight he must get out of the
plight himself, he must get out of it first, and anything he
should have to say to any one else must be deferred and
detached. She herself, at any rate—it was her own case
that was in question—couldn't dream of assisting him save
in the sense of their common honor. She could never be the
girl to be drawn in, she could never lift her finger against
Mona. There was something in her that would make it a
shame to her forever to have owed her happiness to an
interference. It would seem intolerably vulgar to her to

have "ousted" the daughter of the Brigstocks; and merely to have abstained even wouldn't assure her that she had been straight. Nothing was really straight but to justify her little pensioned presence by her use; and now, won over as she was to heroism, she could see her use only as some high and delicate deed. She couldn't do anything at all, in short, unless she could do it with a kind of pride, and there would be nothing to be proud of in having arranged for poor Owen to get off easily. Nobody had a right to get off easily from pledges so deep, so sacred. How could Fleda doubt they had been tremendous when she knew so well what any pledge of her own would be? If Mona was so formed that she could hold such vows light, that was Mona's peculiar business. To have loved Owen apparently, and yet to have loved him only so much, only to the extent of a few tables and chairs, was not a thing she could so much as try to grasp. Of a different way of loving him she was herself ready to give an instance, an instance of which the beauty indeed would not be generally known. It would not perhaps if revealed be generally understood, inasmuch as the effect of the particular pressure she proposed to exercise would be, should success attend it, to keep him tied to an affection that had died a sudden and violent death. Even in the ardor of her meditation Fleda remained in sight of the truth that it would be an odd result of her magnanimity to prevent her friend's shaking off a woman he disliked. If he didn't dislike Mona, what was the matter with him? And if he did, Fleda asked, what was the matter with her own silly self?

Our young lady met this branch of the temptation it pleased her frankly to recognize by declaring that to encourage any such cruelty would be tortuous and base. She had nothing to do with his dislikes; she had only to do with his good-nature and his good name. She had joy of him just as he was, but it was of these things she had the greatest. The worst aversion and the liveliest reaction moreover wouldn't alter the fact—since one was facing facts—that but the other day his strong arms must have clasped a remarkably handsome girl as close as she had permitted. Fleda's emotion at this time was a wondrous mixture, in which Mona's permissions and Mona's beauty figured powerfully as aids to reflection. She herself had no beauty, and *her* permissions were the stony stares she had just practiced in the drawing-room—a consciousness of a kind appreciably to add to the particular sense of triumph that made her generous. I may not perhaps too much diminish the merit of that generosity if I mention that it could take the flight we are considering just because really, with the telescope of her long thought, Fleda saw what might bring her out of the wood. Mona herself would bring her out; at the least Mona possibly might. Deep down plunged the idea that even should she achieve what she had promised Owen, there was still the contingency of Mona's independent action. She might by that time, under stress of temper or of whatever it was that was now moving her, have said or done the things there is no patching up. If the rupture should come from Waterbath they might all be happy yet. This was a calculation that Fleda wouldn't have committed to paper, but it affected the total of her sentiments. She was meanwhile so remarkably constituted that while she refused to profit by Owen's mistake, even while she judged it and hastened to cover it up, she could drink a sweetness from it that consorted little with her wishing it mightn't have been made. There was no harm done, because he had instinctively known, poor dear, with whom to make it, and it was a compensation for seeing him worried that he hadn't made it with some horrid mean girl who would immediately have dished him by making a still bigger one. Their protected error (for she indulged a fancy that it was hers too) was like some dangerous, lovely living thing that she had caught and could keep—keep vivid and helpless in the cage of her own passion and look at and talk to all day long. She had got it well locked up there by the time that, from an upper window, she saw Mrs. Gereth again in the garden. At this she went down to meet her.

CHAPTER X

FLEDA'S LINE had been taken, her word was quite ready; on the terrace of the painted pots she broke out before her interlocutress could put a question. "His errand was perfectly simple: he came to demand that you shall pack everything straight up again and send it back as fast as the railway will carry it."

The back road had apparently been fatiguing to Mrs. Gereth; she rose there rather white and wan with her walk. A certain sharp thinness was in her ejaculation of "Oh!"—after which she glanced about her for a place to sit down. The movement was a criticism of the order of events that offered such a piece of news to a lady coming in tired; but Fleda could see that in turning over the possibilities this particular peril was the one that during the last hour her friend had turned up oftenest. At the end of the short, gray day, which had been moist and mild, the sun was out; the terrace looked to the south, and a bench, formed as to legs and arms of iron representing knotted boughs, stood against the warmest wall of the house. The mistress of Ricks sank upon it and presented to her companion the handsome face she had composed to hear everything. Strangely enough, it was just this fine vessel of her attention that made the girl most nervous about what she must drop in. "Quite a 'demand,' dear, is it?" asked Mrs. Gereth, drawing in her cloak.

"Oh, that's what I should call it!" Fleda laughed, to her own surprise.

"I mean with the threat of enforcement and that sort of thing."

"Distinctly with the threat of enforcement—what would be called, I suppose, coercion."

"What sort of coercion?" said Mrs. Gereth.

"Why, legal, don't you know?—what he calls setting the lawyers at you."

"Is that what he calls it?" She seemed to speak with disinterested curiosity.

"That's what he calls it," said Fleda.

Mrs. Gereth considered an instant. "Oh, the lawyers!" she exclaimed lightly. Seated there almost cosily in the reddening winter sunset, only with her shoulders raised a little and her mantle tightened as if from a slight chill, she had never yet looked to Fleda so much in possession nor so far from meeting unsuspectedness halfway. "Is he going to send them down here?"

"I dare say he thinks it may come to that."

"The lawyers can scarcely do the packing," Mrs. Gereth humorously remarked.

"I suppose he means them—in the first place, at least—to try to talk you over."

"In the first place, eh? And what does he mean in the second?"

Fleda hesitated; she had not foreseen that so simple an inquiry could disconcert her. "I'm afraid I don't know."

"Didn't you ask?" Mrs. Gereth spoke as if she might have said, "What then were you doing all the while?"

"I didn't ask very much," said her companion. "He has been gone some time. The great thing seemed to be to understand clearly that he wouldn't be content with anything less than what he mentioned."

"My just giving everything back?"

"Your just giving everything back."

"Well, darling, what did you tell him?" Mrs. Gereth blandly inquired.

Fleda faltered again, wincing at the term of endearment, at what the words took for granted, charged with the confidence she had now committed herself to betray. "I told him I would tell you!" She smiled, but she felt that her smile was rather hollow and even that Mrs. Gereth had begun to look at her with some fixedness.

"Did he seem very angry?"

"He seemed very sad. He takes it very hard," Fleda added.

"And how does *she* take it?"

"Ah, that—that I felt a delicacy about asking."

"So you didn't ask?" The words had the note of surprise.

Fleda was embarrassed; she had not made up her mind definitely to lie. "I didn't think you'd care." That small untruth she would risk.

"Well—I don't!" Mrs. Gereth declared; and Fleda felt less guilty to hear her, for the statement was as inexact as her own. "Didn't you say anything in return?" Mrs. Gereth presently continued.

"Do you mean in the way of justifying you?"

"I didn't mean to trouble you to do that. My justification," said Mrs. Gereth, sitting there warmly and, in the lucidity of her thought, which nevertheless hung back a little, dropping her eyes on the gravel—"my justification was all the past. My justification was the cruelty—" But at this, with a short, sharp gesture, she checked herself. "It's too good of me to talk—now." She produced these sentences with a cold patience, as if addressing Fleda in the girl's virtual and actual character of Owen's representative. Our young lady crept to and fro before the bench, combating the sense that it was occupied by a judge, looking at her boot-toes, reminding herself in doing so of Mona, and lightly crunching the pebbles as she walked. She moved about because she was afraid, putting off from moment to moment the exercise of the courage she had been sure she possessed. That courage would all come to her if she could only be equally sure that what she should be called upon to do for Owen would be to suffer. She had wondered, while Mrs. Gereth spoke, how that lady would describe her justification. She had described it as if to be irreproachably fair, give her adversary the benefit of every doubt, and then dismiss the question forever. "Of course," Mrs. Gereth went on, "if we didn't succeed in showing him at Poynton the ground we took, it's simply that he shuts his

eyes. What I supposed was that you would have given him
your opinion that if I was the woman so signally to assert
myself, I'm also the woman to rest upon it imperturbably
enough."

Fleda stopped in front of her hostess. "I gave him my
opinion that you're very logical, very obstinate, and very
proud."

"Quite right, my dear: I'm a rank bigot—about that
sort of thing!" and Mrs. Gereth jerked her head at the
contents of the house. "I've never denied it. I'd kidnap—
to save them, to convert them—the children of heretics.
When I know I'm right I go to the stake. Oh, he may burn
me alive!" she cried with a happy face. "Did he abuse me?"
she then demanded.

Fleda had remained there, gathering in her purpose.
"How little you know him!"

Mrs. Gereth stared, then broke into a laugh that her
companion had not expected. "Ah, my dear, certainly not
so well as you!" The girl, at this, turned away again—she
felt she looked too conscious; and she was aware that,
during a pause, Mrs. Gereth's eyes watched her as she
went. She faced about afresh to meet them, but what she
met was a question that reinforced them. "Why had you a
'delicacy' as to speaking of Mona?"

She stopped again before the bench, and an inspiration
came to her. "I should think *you* would know," she said
with proper dignity.

Blankness was for a moment on Mrs. Gereth's brow;
then light broke—she visibly remembered the scene in the
breakfast-room after Mona's night at Poynton. "Because
I contrasted you—told him *you* were the one?" Her eyes
looked deep. "You were—you are still!"

Fleda gave a bold dramatic laugh. "Thank you, my
love—with all the best things at Ricks!"

Mrs. Gereth considered, trying to penetrate, as it seemed;
but at last she brought out roundly: "For you, you know,
I'd send them back!"

The girl's heart gave a tremendous bound; the right way
dawned upon her in a flash. Obscurity indeed the next
moment engulfed this course, but for a few thrilled seconds

she had understood. To send the things back "for her"
meant of course to send them back if there were even a
dim chance that she might become mistress of them. Fleda's
palpitation was not allayed as she asked herself what por-
tent Mrs. Gereth had suddenly perceived of such a chance:
that perception could come only from a sudden suspicion
of her secret. This suspicion, in turn, was a tolerably straight
consequence of that implied view of the propriety of surrender from which, she was well aware, she could say
nothing to dissociate herself. What she first felt was that if
she wished to rescue the spoils she wished also to rescue her
secret. So she looked as innocent as she could and said as
quickly as possible: "For me? Why in the world for me?"

"Because you're so awfully keen."

"Am I? Do I strike you so? You know I hate him,"
Fleda went on.

She had the sense for a while of Mrs. Gereth's regarding
her with the detachment of some stern, clever stranger.
"Then what's the matter with you? Why do you want me
to give in?"

Fleda hesitated; she felt herself reddening. "I've only
said your son wants it. I haven't said *I* do."

"Then say it and have done with it!"

This was more peremptory than any word her friend,
though often speaking in her presence with much point,
had ever yet directly addressed to her. It affected her like
the crack of a whip, but she confined herself, with an effort,
to taking it as a reminder that she must keep her head. "I
know he has his engagement to carry out."

"His engagement to marry? Why, it's just that engagement we loathe!"

"Why should *I* loathe it?" Fleda asked with a strained
smile. Then, before Mrs. Gereth could reply, she pursued:
"I'm thinking of his general undertaking—to give her the
house as she originally saw it."

"To give her the house!" Mrs. Gereth brought up the
words from the depth of the unspeakable. The effort was
like the moan of an autumn wind; it was in the power of
such an image to make her turn pale.

"I'm thinking," Fleda continued, "of the simple question

of his keeping faith on an important clause of his contract: it doesn't matter whether it's with a stupid girl or with a monster of cleverness. I'm thinking of his honor and his good name."

"The honor and good name of a man you hate?"

"Certainly," the girl resolutely answered. "I don't see why you should talk as if one had a petty mind. You don't think so. It's not on that assumption you've ever dealt with me. I can do your son justice, as he put his case to me."

"Ah, then he did put his case to you!" Mrs. Gereth exclaimed, with an accent of triumph. "You seemed to speak just now as if really nothing of any consequence had passed between you."

"Something always passes when one has a little imagination," our young lady declared.

"I take it you don't mean that Owen has any!" Mrs. Gereth cried with her large laugh.

Fleda was silent a moment. "No, I don't mean that Owen has any," she returned at last.

"Why is it you hate him so?" her hostess abruptly inquired.

"Should I love him for all he has made you suffer?"

Mrs. Gereth slowly rose at this and, coming across the walk, took her young friend in her arms and kissed her. She then passed into one of Fleda's an arm perversely and imperiously sociable. "Let us move a little," she said, holding her close and giving a slight shiver. They strolled along the terrace, and she brought out another question. "He *was* eloquent, then, poor dear—he poured forth the story of his wrongs?"

Fleda smiled down at her companion, who, cloaked and perceptibly bowed, leaned on her heavily and gave her an odd, unwonted sense of age and cunning. She took refuge in an evasion. "He couldn't tell me anything that I didn't know pretty well already."

"It's very true that you know everything. No, dear, you haven't a petty mind; you've a lovely imagination and you're the nicest creature in the world. If you were inane, like most girls—like every one, in fact—I would have insulted you, I would have outraged you, and then you would

have fled from me in terror. No, now that I think of it,"
Mrs. Gereth went on, "you wouldn't have fled from me;
nothing, on the contrary, would have made you budge.
You would have cuddled into your warm corner, but you
would have been wounded and weeping and martyrized,
and you would have taken every opportunity to tell people
I'm a brute—as indeed I should have been!" They went to
and fro, and she would not allow Fleda, who laughed and
protested, to attenuate with any light civility this spirited
picture. She praised her cleverness and her patience; then
she said it was getting cold and dark and they must go in
to tea. She delayed quitting the place, however, and reverted
instead to Owen's ultimatum, about which she asked another question or two; in particular whether it had struck
Fleda that he really believed she would comply with such
a summons.

"I think he really believes that if I try hard enough I
can make you:" after uttering which words our young
lady stopped short and emulated the embrace she had
received a few moments before.

"And you've promised to try: I see. You didn't tell me
that, either," Mrs. Gereth added as they went on. "But
you're rascal enough for anything!" While Fleda was occupied in thinking in what terms she could explain why she
had indeed been rascal enough for the reticence thus denounced, her companion broke out with an inquiry somewhat irrelevant and even in form somewhat profane. "Why
the devil, at any rate, doesn't it come off?"

Fleda hesitated. "You mean their marriage?"

"Of course I mean their marriage!"

Fleda hesitated again. "I haven't the least idea."

"You didn't ask him?"

"Oh, how in the world can you fancy?" She spoke in a
shocked tone.

"Fancy your putting a question so indelicate? *I* should
have put it—I mean in your place; but I'm quite coarse,
thank God!" Fleda felt privately that she herself was coarse,
or at any rate would presently have to be; and Mrs. Gereth,
with a purpose that struck the girl as increasing, continued:
"What, then, *was* the day to be? Wasn't it just one of these?"

"I'm sure I don't remember."

It was part of the great rupture and an effect of Mrs. Gereth's character that up to this moment she had been completely and haughtily indifferent to that detail. Now, however, she had a visible reason for being clear about it. She bethought herself and she broke out—"Isn't the day past?" Then, stopping short, she added: "Upon my word, they must have put it off!" As Fleda made no answer to this she sharply went on: "*Have* they put it off?"

"I haven't the least idea," said the girl.

Her hostess was looking at her hard again. "Didn't he tell you—didn't he say anything about it?"

Fleda, meanwhile, had had time to make her reflections, which were moreover the continued throb of those that had occupied the interval between Owen's departure and his mother's return. If she should now repeat his words, this wouldn't at all play the game of her definite vow; it would only play the game of her little gagged and blinded desire. She could calculate well enough the effect of telling Mrs. Gereth how she had had it from Owen's troubled lips that Mona was only waiting for the restitution and would do nothing without it. The thing was to obtain the restitution without imparting that knowledge. The only way, also, not to impart it was not to tell any truth at all about it; and the only way to meet this last condition was to reply to her companion, as she presently did: "He told me nothing whatever: he didn't touch on the subject."

"Not in any way?"

"Not in any way."

Mrs. Gereth watched Fleda and considered. "You haven't any idea if they are waiting for the things?"

"How should I have? I'm not in their counsels."

"I dare say they are—or that Mona is." Mrs. Gereth reflected again; she had a bright idea. "If I don't give in, I'll be hanged if she'll not break off."

"She'll never, never break off!" said Fleda.

"Are you sure?"

"I can't be sure, but it's my belief."

"Derived from *him?*"

The girl hung fire a few seconds. "Derived from him."

Mrs. Gereth gave her a long last look, then turned abruptly away. "It's an awful bore you didn't really get it out of him! Well, come to tea," she added rather dryly, passing straight into the house.

CHAPTER XI

THE SENSE of her adversary's dryness, which was ominous of something she couldn't read, made Fleda, before complying, linger a little on the terace; she felt the need moreover of taking breath after such a flight into the cold air of denial. When at last she rejoined Mrs. Gereth she found her erect before the drawing-room fire. Their tea had been set out in the same quarter, and the mistress of the house, for whom the preparation of it was in general a high and undelegated function, was in an attitude to which the hissing urn made no appeal. This omission, for Fleda, was such a further sign of something to come that, to disguise her apprehension, she immediately and without an apology took the duty in hand; only, however, to be promptly reminded that she was performing it confusedly and not counting the journeys of the little silver shovel she emptied into the pot. "Not *five,* my dear—the usual three," said her hostess, with the same dryness; watching her then in silence while she clumsily corrected her mistake. The tea took some minutes to draw, and Mrs. Gereth availed herself of them suddenly to exclaim: "You haven't yet told me, you know, how it is you propose to 'make' me!"

"Give everything back?" Fleda looked into the pot again and uttered her question with a briskness that she felt to be a little overdone. "Why, by putting the question well before you; by being so eloquent that I shall persuade you, shall act upon you; by making you sorry for having gone so far," she said boldly; "by simply and earnestly asking it of you, in short; and by reminding you at the same time that it's the first thing I ever have so asked. Oh, you've done things for me—endless and beautiful things," she exclaimed; "but you've done them all from your own generous impulse. I've never so much as hinted to you to lend me a postage-stamp."

"Give me a cup of tea," said Mrs. Gereth. A moment later, taking the cup, she replied: "No, you've never asked me for a postage-stamp."

"That gives me a pull!" Fleda returned, smiling.

"Puts you in the situation of expecting that I shall do this thing just simply to oblige you?"

The girl hesitated. "You said a while ago that for me you *would* do it."

"For you, but not for your eloquence. Do you understand what I mean by the difference?" Mrs. Gereth asked as she stood stirring her tea.

Fleda, to postpone answering, looked round, while she drank it, at the beautiful room. "I don't in the least like, you know, your having taken so much. It was a great shock to me, on my arrival here, to find you had done so."

"Give me some more tea," said Mrs. Gereth; and there was a moment's silence as Fleda poured out another cup. "If you were shocked, my dear, I'm bound to say you concealed your shock."

"I know I did. I was afraid to show it."

Mrs. Gereth drank off her second cup. "And you're not afraid now?"

"No, I'm not afraid now."

"What has made the difference?"

"I've pulled myself together." Fleda paused; then she added: "and I've seen Mr. Owen."

"You've seen Mr. Owen"—Mrs. Gereth concurred. She put down her cup and sank into a chair, in which she leaned back, resting her head and gazing at her young friend. "Yes, I did tell you a while ago that for you I'd do it. But you haven't told me yet what you'll do in return."

Fleda thought an instant. "Anything in the wide world you may require."

"Oh, 'anything' is nothing at all! That's too easily said." Mrs. Gereth, reclining more completely, closed her eyes with an air of disgust, an air indeed of inviting slumber.

Fleda looked at her quiet face, which the appearance of

slumber always made particularly handsome; she noted
how much the ordeal of the last few weeks had added to
its indications of age. "Well then, try me with something.
What is it you demand?"

At this, opening her eyes, Mrs. Gereth sprang straight
up. "Get him away from her!"

Fleda marveled: her companion had in an instant become young again. "Away from Mona? How in the
world—?"

"By not looking like a fool!" cried Mrs. Gereth very
sharply. She kissed her, however, on the spot, to make up
for this roughness, and summarily took off her hat, which,
on coming into the house, our young lady had not removed.
She applied a friendly touch to the girl's hair and gave a
businesslike pull to her jacket. "I say don't look like an
idiot, because you happen not to be one, not the least bit.
I'm idiotic; I've been so, I've just discovered, ever since our
first days together. I've been a precious donkey; but that's
another affair."

Fleda, as if she humbly assented, went through no form
of controverting this; she simply stood passive to her companion's sudden refreshment of her appearance. "How *can*
I get him away from her?" she presently demanded.

"By letting yourself go."

"By letting myself go?" She spoke mechanically, still more
like an idiot, and felt as if her face flamed out the insincerity of her question. It was vividly back again, the vision
of the real way to act upon Mrs. Gereth. This lady's movements were now rapid; she turned off from her as quickly
as she had seized her, and Fleda sat down to steady herself
for full responsibility.

Her hostess, without taking up her ejaculation, gave a
violent poke at the fire and then faced her again. "You've
done two things, then, to-day—haven't you?—that you've
never done before. One has been asking me the service, or
favor, or concession—whatever you call it—that you just
mentioned; the other has been telling me—certainly too for
the first time—an immense little fib."

"An immense little fib?" Fleda felt weak; she was glad of
the support of her seat.

"An immense big one, then!" said Mrs. Gereth irritatedly. "You don't in the least 'hate' Owen, my darling. You care for him very much. In fact, my own, you're in love with him—there! Don't tell me any more lies!" cried Mrs. Gereth with a voice and a face in the presence of which Fleda recognized that there was nothing for her but to hold herself and take them. When once the truth was out, it was out, and she could see more and more every instant that it would be the only way. She accepted therefore what had to come; she leaned back her head and closed her eyes as her companion had done just before. She would have covered her face with her hands but for the still greater shame. "Oh, you're a wonder, a wonder," said Mrs. Gereth; "you're magnificent, and I was right, as soon as I saw you, to pick you out and trust you!" Fleda closed her eyes tighter at this last word, but her friend kept it up. "I never dreamed of it till a while ago, when, after he had come and gone, we were face to face. Then something stuck out of you; it strongly impressed me, and I didn't know at first quite what to make of it. It was that you had just been with him and that you were not natural. Not natural to *me*," she added with a smile. "I pricked up my ears, and all that this might mean dawned upon me when you said you had asked nothing about Mona. It put me on the scent, but I didn't show you, did I? I felt it was *in* you, deep down, and that I must draw it out. Well, I *have* drawn it, and it's a blessing. Yesterday, when you shed tears at breakfast, I was awfully puzzled. What has been the matter with you all the while? Why, Fleda, it isn't a crime, don't you know that?" cried the delighted woman. "When I was a girl I was always in love, and not always with such nice people as Owen. I didn't behave as well as you; compared with you I think I must have been horrid. But if you're proud and reserved, it's your own affair; I'm proud too, though I'm not reserved—that's what spoils it. I'm stupid, above all—that's what I am; so dense that I really blush for it. However, no one but you could have deceived me. If I trusted you, moreover, it was exactly to be cleverer than myself. You must be so now more than ever!" Suddenly Fleda felt her hands grasped: Mrs. Gereth had plumped down at her feet and was leaning on her knees. "Save him—save him: you *can!*" she passionately pleaded. "How could you *not* like him, when he's such a dear? He *is* a dear, darling; there's no harm in my own boy! You can do what you will with him—you know you can! What else does he give us all this time for? Get him away from her; it's as if he besought you to, poor wretch! Don't abandon him to such a fate, and I'll never abandon *you*. Think of him with that creature, that future! If you'll take him I'll give up everything. There, it's a solemn promise, the most sacred of my life! Get the better of her, and he shall have every stick I removed. Give me your word, and I'll accept it. I'll write for the packers to-night!"

Fleda, before this, had fallen forward on her companion's neck, and the two women, clinging together, had got up while the younger wailed on the other's bosom. "You smooth it down because you see more in it than there can ever be; but after my hideous double game how will you be able to believe in me again?"

"I see in it simply what *must* be, if you've a single spark of pity. Where on earth was the double game, when you've behaved like such a saint? You've been beautiful, you've been exquisite, and all our trouble is over."

Fleda, drying her eyes, shook her head ever so sadly. "No, Mrs. Gereth, it isn't over. I can't do what you ask—I can't meet your condition."

Mrs. Gereth stared; the cloud gathered in her face again. "Why, in the name of goodness, when you adore him? I know what you see in him," she declared in another tone. "You're right!"

Fleda gave a faint, stubborn smile. "He cares for her too much."

"Then why doesn't he marry her? He's giving you an extraordinary chance."

"He doesn't dream I've ever thought of him," said Fleda. "Why should he, if you didn't?"

"It wasn't with me you were in love, my duck." Then Mrs. Gereth added: "I'll go and tell him."

"If you do any such thing, you shall never see me again,—absolutely, literally never!"

Mrs. Gereth looked hard at her young friend, showing she saw she must believe her. "Then you're perverse, you're wicked. Will you swear he doesn't know?"

"Of course he doesn't know!" cried Fleda indignantly.

Her interlocutress was silent a little. "And that he has no feeling on *his* side?"

"For me?" Fleda stared. "Before he has even married her?"

Mrs. Gereth gave a sharp laugh at this. "He ought at least to appreciate your wit. Oh, my dear, you *are* a treasure! Doesn't he appreciate anything? Has he given you absolutely no symptom—not looked a look, not breathed a sigh?"

"The case," said Fleda coldly, "is as I've had the honor to state it."

"Then he's as big a donkey as his mother! But you know you must account for their delay," Mrs. Gereth remarked.

"Why must I?" Fleda asked after a moment.

"Because you were closeted with him here so long. You can't pretend at present, you know, not to have any art."

The girl hesitated an instant; she was conscious that she must choose between two risks. She had had a secret and the secret was gone. Owen had one, which was still unbruised, and the greater risk now was that his mother should lay her formidable hand upon it. All Fleda's tenderness for him moved her to protect it; so she faced the smaller peril. "Their delay," she brought herself to reply, "may perhaps be Mona's doing. I mean because he has lost her the things."

Mrs. Gereth jumped at this. "So that she'll break altogether if I keep them?"

Fleda winced. "I've told you what I believe about that. She'll make scenes and conditions; she'll worry him. But she'll hold him fast; she'll never give him up."

Mrs. Gereth turned it over. "Well, I'll keep them, to try her," she finally pronounced; at which Fleda felt quite sick, as if she had given everything and got nothing.

CHAPTER XII

"I must in common decency let him know that I've talked of the matter with you," she said to her hostess that evening. "What answer do you wish me to write to him?"

"Write to him that you must see him again," said Mrs. Gereth.

Fleda looked very blank. "What on earth am I to see him for?"

"For anything you like."

The girl would have been struck with the levity of this had she not already, in an hour, felt the extent of the change suddenly wrought in her commerce with her friend —wrought above all, to that friend's view, in her relation to the great issue. The effect of what had followed Owen's visit was to make that relation the very key of the crisis. Pressed upon her, goodness knew, the crisis had been, but it now seemed to put forth big, encircling arms—arms that squeezed till they hurt and she must cry out. It was as if everything at Ricks had been poured into a common receptacle, a public ferment of emotion and zeal, out of which it was ladled up to be tasted and talked about; everything at least but the one little treasure of knowledge that she kept back. She ought to have liked this, she reflected, because it meant sympathy, meant a closer union with the source of so much in her life that had been beautiful and renovating; but there were fine instincts in her that stood off. She had had—and it was not merely at this time—to recognize that there were things for which Mrs. Gereth's *flair* was not so happy as for bargains and "marks." It wouldn't be happy now as to the best action on the knowledge she had just gained; yet as from this moment they were still more intimately together, so a person deeply in her debt would simply have to stand and meet what was to come. There were ways in which she could sharply incommode such a person, and not only with the best conscience in the world, but with a sort of brutality of good intentions. One of the straightest of these strokes, Fleda saw, would be the dance of delight over the mystery Mrs. Gereth had laid bare— the loud, lawful, tactless joy of the explorer leaping upon the strand. Like any other lucky discoverer, she would take possession of the fortunate island. She was nothing if not practical: almost the only thing she took account of in her young friend's soft secret was the excellent use she could make of it—a use so much to her taste that she refused to feel a hinderance in the quality of the material. Fleda put into Mrs. Gereth's answer to her question a good deal more meaning than it would have occurred to her a few hours before that she was prepared to put, but she had on the spot a foreboding that even so broad a hint would live to be bettered.

"Do you suggest that I shall propose to him to come down here again?" she presently inquired.

"Dear, no; say that you'll go up to town and meet him." It *was* bettered, the broad hint; and Fleda felt this to be still more the case when, returning to the subject before they went to bed, her companion said: "I make him over to you wholly, you know—to do what you please with. Deal with him in your own clever way—I ask no questions. All I ask is that you succeed."

"That's charming," Fleda replied, "but it doesn't tell me a bit; you'll be so good as to consider, in what terms to write to him. It's not an answer from you to the message I was to give you."

"The answer to his message is perfectly distinct: he shall have everything in the place the minute he'll say he'll marry you."

"You really pretend," Fleda asked, "to think me capable of transmitting him that news?"

"What else can I really pretend when you threaten so to cast me off if I speak the word myself?"

"Oh, if *you* speak the word!" the girl murmured very gravely, but happy at least to know that in this direction Mrs. Gereth confessed herself warned and helpless. Then she added: "How can I go on living with you on a footing of which I so deeply disapprove? Thinking as I do that you've despoiled him far more than is just or merciful—for if I expected you to take something, I didn't in the least expect you to take everything—how can I stay here without a sense that I'm backing you up in your cruelty and participating in your ill-gotten gains?" Fleda was determined that if she had the chill of her exposed and investigated state she would also have the convenience of it, and that if Mrs. Gereth popped in and out of the chamber of her soul she would at least return the freedom. "I shall quite hate, you know, in a day or two, every object that surrounds you—become blind to all the beauty and rarity that I formerly delighted in. Don't think me harsh; there's no use in my not being frank now. If I leave you, everything's at an end."

Mrs. Gereth, however, was imperturbable: Fleda had to recognize that her advantage had become too real. "It's too beautiful, the way you care for him; it's music in my ears. Nothing else but such a passion could make you say such things; that's the way I should have been too, my dear. Why didn't you tell me sooner? I'd have gone right in for you; I never would have moved a candlestick. Don't stay with me if it torments you; don't, if you suffer, be where you see the old rubbish. Go up to town—go back for a little to your father's. It need be only for a little; two or three weeks will see us through. Your father will take you and be glad, if you only will make him understand what it's a question of—of your getting yourself off his hands forever. *I'll* make him understand, you know, if you feel shy. I'd take you up myself, I'd go with you, to spare your being bored; we'd put up at an hotel and we might amuse ourselves a bit. We haven't had much pleasure since we met, have we? But of course that wouldn't suit our book. I should be a bugaboo to Owen—I should be fatally in the way. Your chance is there—your chance is to be alone; for God's sake, use it to the right end. If you're in want of money I've a little I can give you. But I ask no questions—not a question as small as your shoe!"

She asked no questions, but she took the most extraordinary things for granted. Fleda felt this still more at the end of a couple of days. On the second of these our young lady wrote to Owen; her emotion had to a certain degree cleared itself—there was something she could say briefly. If she had given everything to Mrs. Gereth and as yet got nothing, so she had on the other hand quickly reacted—it took but a night—against the discouragement of her first check. Her desire to serve him was too passionate, the sense that he counted upon her too sweet: these things caught her up again and gave her a new patience and a new subtlety. It shouldn't really be for nothing that she had given so much; deep within her burned again the resolve to get something back. So what she wrote to Owen was simply that she had had a great scene with his mother, but that he must be patient and give her time. It was difficult, as they both had expected, but she was working her hardest for him. She had made an impression—she would do everything to follow it up. Meanwhile he must keep intensely quiet and take no other steps; he must only trust her and pray for her and believe in her perfect loyalty. She made no allusion whatever to Mona's attitude, nor to his not being, as regarded that young lady, master of the situation; but she said in a postscript, in reference to his mother, "Of course she wonders a good deal why your marriage doesn't take place." After the letter had gone she regretted having used the word "loyalty;" there were two or three milder terms which she might as well have employed. The answer she immediately received from Owen was a little note of which she met all the deficiencies by describing it to herself as pathetically simple, but which, to prove that Mrs. Gereth might ask as many questions as she liked, she at once made his mother read. He had no art with his pen, he had not even a good hand, and his letter, a short profession of friendly confidence, consisted of but a few familiar and colorless words of acknowledgment and assent. The gist of it was that he would certainly, since Miss

Vetch recommended it, not hurry mamma too much. He would not for the present cause her to be approached by any one else, but he would nevertheless continue to hope that she would see she *must* come round. "Of course, you know," he added, "she can't keep me waiting indefinitely. Please give her my love and tell her that. If it can be done peaceably I know you're just the one to do it."

Fleda had awaited his rejoinder in deep suspense; such was her imagination of the possibility of his having, as she tacitly phrased it, let himself go on paper that when it arrived she was at first almost afraid to open it. There was indeed a distinct danger, for if he should take it into his head to write her love-letters the whole chance of aiding him would drop: she would have to return them, she would have to decline all further communication with him: it would be quite the end of the business. This imagination of Fleda's was a faculty that easily embraced all the heights and depths and extremities of things; that made a single mouthful, in particular, of any tragic or desperate necessity. She was perhaps at first just a trifle disappointed not to find in the note in question a syllable that strayed from the text; but the next moment she had risen to a point of view from which it presented itself as a production almost inspired in its simplicity. It was simple even for Owen, and she wondered what had given him the cue to be more so than usual. Then she saw how natures that are right just do the things that are right. He wasn't clever—his manner of writing showed it; but the cleverest man in England couldn't have had more the instinct that, under the circumstances, was the supremely happy one, the instinct of giving her something that would do beautifully to be shown to Mrs. Gereth. This was a kind of divination, for naturally he couldn't know the line Mrs. Gereth was taking. It was furthermore explained—and that was the most touching part of all—by his wish that she herself should notice how awfully well he was behaving. His very bareness called her attention to his virtue; and these were the exact fruits of her beautiful and terrible admonition. He was cleaving to Mona; he was doing his duty; he was making tremendously sure he should be without reproach.

If Fleda handed this communication to her friend as a triumphant gage of the innocence of the young man's heart, her elation lived but a moment after Mrs. Gereth had pounced upon the tell-tale spot in it. "Why in the world, then," that lady cried, "does he still not breathe a breath about the day, the *day*, the DAY?" She repeated the word with a crescendo of superior acuteness; she proclaimed that nothing could be more marked than its absence—an absence that simply spoke volumes. What did it prove in fine but that she was producing the effect she had toiled for—that she had settled or was rapidly settling Mona?

Such a challenge Fleda was obliged in some manner to take up. "You may be settling Mona," she returned with a smile, "but I can hardly regard it as sufficient evidence that you're settling Mona's lover."

"Why not, with such a studied omission on his part to gloss over in any manner the painful tension existing between them—the painful tension that, under providence, I've been the means of bringing about? He gives you by his silence clear notice that his marriage is practically off."

"He speaks to me of the only thing that concerns me. He gives me clear notice that he abates not one jot of his demand."

"Well, then, let him take the only way to get it satisfied."

Fleda had no need to ask again what such a way might be, nor was her support removed by the fine assurance with which Mrs. Gereth could make her argument wait upon her wish. These days, which dragged their length into a strange, uncomfortable fortnight, had already borne more testimony to that element than all the other time the two women had passed together. Our young lady had been at first far from measuring the whole of a feature that Owen himself would probably have described as her companion's "cheek." She lived now in a kind of bath of boldness, felt as if a fierce light poured in upon her from windows open wide; and the singular part of the ordeal was that she couldn't protest against it fully without incurring, even to her own mind, some reproach of ingratitude, some charge of smallness. If Mrs. Gereth's apparent determination to hustle her into Owen's arms was accompanied with an air of holding her

dignity rather cheap, this was after all only as a consequence
of her being held in respect to some other attributes rather
dear. It was a new version of the old story of being kicked
upstairs. The wonderful woman was the same woman who,
in the summer, at Poynton, had been so puzzled to conceive why a good-natured girl shouldn't have contributed
more to the personal rout of the Brigstocks—shouldn't
have been grateful even for the handsome puff of Fleda
Vetch. Only her passion was keener now and her scruple
more absent; the fight made a demand upon her, and her
pugnacity had become one with her constant habit of
using such weapons as she could pick up. She had no
imagination about anybody's life save on the side she
bumped against. Fleda was quite aware that she would have
otherwise been a rare creature; but a rare creature was
originally just what she had struck her as being. Mrs.
Gereth had really no perception of anybody's nature—had
only one question about persons: were they clever or
stupid? To be clever meant to know the marks. Fleda knew
them by direct inspiration, and a warm recognition of this
had been her friend's tribute to her character. The girl had
hours, now, of sombre wishing that she might never see
anything good again: that kind of experience was evidently
not an infallible source of peace. She would be more at
peace in some vulgar little place that should owe its *cachet*
to Tottenham Court Road. There were nice strong horrors
in West Kensington; it was as if they beckoned her and
wooed her back to them. She had a relaxed recollection of
Waterbath; and of her reasons for staying on at Ricks the
force was rapidly ebbing. One of these was her pledge to
Owen—her vow to press his mother close; the other was
the fact that of the two discomforts, that of being prodded
by Mrs. Gereth and that of appearing to run after somebody
else, the former remained for a while the more endurable.

As the days passed, however, it became plainer to Fleda
that her only chance of success would be in lending herself
to this low appearance. Then, moreover, at last, her nerves
settling the question, the choice was simply imposed by
the violence done to her taste—to whatever was left of
that high principle, at least, after the free and reckless

meeting, for months, of great drafts and appeals. It was all very well to try to evade discussion: Owen Gereth was looking to her for a struggle, and it wasn't a bit of a struggle to be disgusted and dumb. She was on too strange a footing—that of having presented an ultimatum and having had it torn up in her face. In such a case as that the envoy always departed; he never sat gaping and dawdling before the city. Mrs. Gereth, every morning, looked publicly into "The Morning Post," the only newspaper she received; and every morning she treated the blankness of that journal as fresh evidence that everything was "off." What did the Post exist for but to tell you your children were wretchedly married?—so that if such a source of misery was dry, what could you do but infer that for once you had miraculously escaped? She almost taunted Fleda with supineness in not getting something out of somebody— in the same breath indeed in which she drenched her with a kind of appreciation more onerous to the girl than blame. Mrs. Gereth herself had of course washed her hands of the matter; but Fleda knew people who knew Mona and would be sure to be in her confidence—inconceivable people who admired her and had the privilege of Waterbath. What was the use therefore of being the most natural and the easiest of letter-writers, if no sort of side-light— in some pretext for correspondence—was, by a brilliant creature, to be got out of such barbarians? Fleda was not only a brilliant creature, but she heard herself commended in these days for new and strange attractions; she figured suddenly, in the queer conversations of Ricks, as a distinguished, almost as a dangerous beauty. That retouching of her hair and dress in which her friend had impulsively indulged on a first glimpse of her secret was by implication very frequently repeated. She had the sense not only of being advertised and offered, but of being counseled and enlightened in ways that she scarcely understood—arts obscure even to a poor girl who had had, in good society and motherless poverty, to look straight at realities and fill out blanks.

These arts, when Mrs. Gereth's spirits were high, were handled with a brave and cynical humor with which Fleda's fancy could keep no step: they left our young lady wondering what on earth her companion wanted her to do. "I want you to cut in!"—that was Mrs. Gereth's familiar and comprehensive phrase for the course she prescribed. She challenged again and again Fleda's picture, as she called it (though the sketch was too slight to deserve the name), of the indifference to which a prior attachment had committed the proprietor of Poynton. "Do you mean to say that, Mona or no Mona, he could see you that way, day after day, and not have the ordinary feelings of a man?" This was the sort of interrogation to which Fleda was fitfully and irrelevantly treated. She had grown almost used to the refrain. "Do you mean to say that when, the other day, one had quite made you over to him, the great gawk, and he was, on this very spot, utterly alone with you——" The poor girl at this point never left any doubt of what she meant to say, but Mrs. Gereth could be trusted to break out in another place and at another time. At last Fleda wrote to her father that he must take her in for a while; and when, to her companion's delight, she returned to London, that lady went with her to the station and wafted her on her way. "The Morning Post" had been delivered as they left the house, and Mrs. Gereth had brought it with her for the traveler, who never spent a penny on a newspaper. On the platform, however, when this young person was ticketed, labeled, and seated, she opened it at the window of the carriage, exclaiming as usual, after looking into it a moment: "Nothing—nothing—nothing: don't tell *me!*" Every day that there was nothing was a nail in the coffin of the marriage. An instant later the train was off, but, moving quickly beside it, while Fleda leaned inscrutably forth, Mrs. Gereth grasped her friend's hand and looked up with wonderful eyes. "Only let yourself go, darling—only let yourself go!"

CHAPTER XIII

THAT SHE DESIRED to ask no questions Mrs. Gereth conscientiously proved by closing her lips tight after Fleda had gone to London. No letter from Ricks arrived at West Kensington, and Fleda, with nothing to communicate that could be to the taste of either party, forbore to open a correspondence. If her heart had been less heavy she might have been amused to perceive how much rope this reticence of Ricks seemed to signify to her that she could take. She had at all events no good news for her friend save in the sense that her silence was not bad news. She was not yet in a position to write that she had "cut in;" but neither, on the other hand, had she gathered material for announcing that Mona was undisseverable from her prey. She had made no use of the pen so glorified by Mrs. Gereth to wake up the echoes of Waterbath; she had sedulously abstained from inquiring what in any quarter, far or near, was said or suggested or supposed. She only spent a matutinal penny on "The Morning Post;" she only saw, on each occasion, that that inspired sheet had as little to say about the imminence as about the abandonment of certain nuptials. It was at the same time obvious that Mrs. Gereth triumphed on these occasions much more than she trembled, and that with a few such triumphs repeated she would cease to tremble at all. What was most manifest, however, was that she had had a rare preconception of the circumstances that would have ministered, had Fleda been disposed, to the girl's cutting in. It was brought home to Fleda that these circumstances would have particularly favored intervention; she was quickly forced to do them a secret justice. One of the effects of her intimacy with Mrs. Gereth was that she had

quite lost all sense of intimacy with any one else. The lady
of Ricks had made a desert around her, possessing and
absorbing her so utterly that other partakers had fallen
away. Hadn't she been admonished, months before, that
people considered they had lost her and were reconciled
on the whole to the privation? Her present position in the
great unconscious town defined itself as obscure: she regarded it at any rate with eyes suspicious of that lesson.
She neither wrote notes nor received them; she indulged
in no reminders nor knocked at any doors; she wandered
vaguely in the western wilderness or cultivated shy forms of
that "household art" for which she had had a respect before
tasting the bitter tree of knowledge. Her only plan was to
be as quiet as a mouse, and when she failed in the attempt
to lose herself in the flat suburb she felt like a lonely fly
crawling over a dusty chart.

How had Mrs. Gereth known in advance that if she had
chosen to be "vile" (that was what Fleda called it) everything would happen to help her?—especially the way her
poor father, after breakfast, doddered off to his club, showing seventy when he was really fifty-seven, and leaving her
richly alone for the day. He came back about midnight,
looking at her very hard and not risking long words—only
making her feel by inimitable touches that the presence of
his family compelled him to alter all his hours. She had in
their common sitting-room the company of the objects he
was fond of saying that he had collected—objects, shabby
and battered, of a sort that appealed little to his daughter:
old brandy-flasks and match-boxes, old calendars and
hand-books, intermixed with an assortment of pen-wipers
and ash-trays, a harvest he had gathered in from penny
bazaars. He was blandly unconscious of that side of Fleda's
nature which had endeared her to Mrs. Gereth, and she had
often heard him wish to goodness there was something
striking she cared for. Why didn't she try collecting something?—it didn't matter what. She would find it gave an
interest to life, and there was no end of little curiosities
one could easily pick up. He was conscious of having a
taste for fine things which his children had unfortunately
not inherited. This indicated the limits of their acquaintance

with him—limits which, as Fleda was now sharply aware, could only leave him to wonder what the mischief she was there for. As she herself echoed this question to the letter she was not in a position to clear up the mystery. She couldn't have given a name to her errand in town or explained it save by saying that she had had to get away from Ricks. It was intensely provisional, but what was to come next? Nothing could come next but a deeper anxiety. She had neither a home nor an outlook—nothing in all the wide world but a feeling of suspense.

Of course she had her duty—her duty to Owen—a definite undertaking, reaffirmed, after his visit to Ricks, under her hand and seal; but there was no sense of possession attached to that; there was only a horrible sense of privation. She had quite moved from under Mrs. Gereth's wide wing; and now that she was really among the pen-wipers and ash-trays she was swept, at the thought of all the beauty she had forsworn, by short, wild gusts of despair. If her friend should really keep the spoils she would never return to her. If that friend should on the other hand part with them, what on earth would there be to return to? The chill struck deep as Fleda thought of the mistress of Ricks reduced, in vulgar parlance, to what she had on her back: There was nothing to which she could compare such an image but her idea of Marie Antoinette in the Conciergerie, or perhaps the vision of some tropical bird, the creature of hot, dense forests, dropped on a frozen moor to pick up a living. The mind's eye could see Mrs. Gereth, indeed, only in her thick, colored air; it took all the light of her treasures to make her concrete and distinct. She loomed for a moment, in any mere house, gaunt and unnatural; then she vanished as if she had suddenly sunk into a quicksand. Fleda lost herself in the rich fancy of how, if *she* were mistress of Poynton, a whole province, as an abode, should be assigned there to the august queen-mother. She would have returned from her campaign with her baggage-train and her loot, and the palace would unbar its shutters and the morning flash back from its halls. In the event of a surrender the poor woman would never again be able to begin to collect: She was now too old and too moneyless, and

times were altered and good things impossibly dear. A
surrender, furthermore, to any daughter-in-law save an
oddity like Mona needn't at all be an abdication in fact; any
other fairly nice girl whom Owen should have taken it into
his head to marry would have been positively glad to have,
for the museum, a custodian who was a walking catalogue
and who understood beyond any one in England the hygiene
and temperament of rare pieces. A fairly nice girl would
somehow be away a good deal and would at such times
count it a blessing to feel Mrs. Gereth at her post.

Fleda had fully recognized, the first days, that, quite apart
from any question of letting Owen know where she was, it
would be a charity to give him some sign: it would be weak,
it would be ugly, to be diverted from that kindness by the
fact that Mrs. Gereth had attached a tinkling bell to it. A
frank relation with him was only superficially discredited:
she ought for his own sake to send him a word of cheer. So
she repeatedly reasoned, but she as repeatedly delayed
performance: if her general plan had been to be as still
as a mouse, an interview like the interview at Ricks would
be an odd contribution to that ideal. Therefore with a confused preference of practice to theory she let the days go
by; she felt that nothing was so imperative as the gain of
precious time. She shouldn't be able to stay with her father
forever, but she might now reap the benefit of having
married her sister. Maggie's union had been built up
round a small spare room. Concealed in this apartment
she might try to paint again, and abetted by the grateful
Maggie—for Maggie at least was grateful—she might try
to dispose of her work. She had not indeed struggled with
a brush since her visit to Waterbath, where the sight of the
family splotches had put her immensely on her guard.
Poynton moreover had been an impossible place for producing; no active art could flourish there but a Buddhis-
tic contemplation. It had stripped its mistress clean of all
feeble accomplishments; her hands were imbrued neither
with ink nor with water-color. Close to Fleda's present
abode was the little shop of a man who mounted and
framed pictures and desolately dealt in artists' materials.
She sometimes paused before it to look at a couple of shy

experiments for which its dull window constituted publicity, small studies placed there for sale and full of warning to a young lady without fortune and without talent. Some such young lady had brought them forth in sorrow; some such young lady, to see if they had been snapped up, had passed and repassed as helplessly as she herself was doing. They never had been, they never would be, snapped up; yet they were quite above the actual attainment of some other young ladies. It was a matter of discipline with Fleda to take an occasional lesson from them; besides which, when she now quitted the house, she had to look for reasons after she was out. The only place to find them was in the shop-windows. They made her feel like a servant-girl taking her "afternoon," but that didn't signify: perhaps some day she would resemble such a person still more closely. This continued a fortnight, at the end of which the feeling was suddenly dissipated. She had stopped as usual in the presence of the little pictures; then, as she turned away, she had found herself face to face with Owen Gereth.

At the sight of him two fresh waves passed quickly across her heart, one at the heels of the other. The first was an instant perception that this encounter was not an accident; the second a consciousness as prompt that the best place for it was the street. She knew before he told her that he had been to see her, and the next thing she knew was that he had had information from his mother. Her mind grasped these things while he said with a smile: "I saw only your back, but I was sure. I was over the way. I've been at your house."

"How came you to know my house?" Fleda asked.

"I like that!" he laughed. "How came you not to let me know that you were there?"

Fleda, at this, thought it best also to laugh. "Since I didn't let you know, why did you come?"

"Oh, I say!" cried Owen. "Don't add insult to injury. Why in the world didn't you let me know? I came because I want awfully to see you." He hesitated, then he added: "I got the tip from mother: she has written to me—fancy!"

They still stood where they had met. Fleda's instinct was

to keep him there; the more so that she could already see
him take for granted that they would immediately proceed
together to her door. He rose before her with a different air:
he looked less ruffled and bruised than he had done at
Ricks, he showed a recovered freshness. Perhaps, however,
this was only because she had scarcely seen him at all as
yet in London form, as he would have called it—"turned
out" as he was turned out in town. In the country, heated
with the chase and splashed with the mire, he had always
reminded her of a picturesque peasant in national costume.
This costume, as Owen wore it, varied from day to day; it
was as copious as the wardrobe of an actor; but it never
failed of suggestions of the earth and the weather, the
hedges and the ditches, the beasts and the birds. There had
been days when it struck her as all nature in one pair of
boots. It didn't make him now another person that he was
delicately dressed, shining and splendid—that he had a
higher hat and light gloves with black seams, and a spear-
like umbrella; but it made him, she soon decided, really
handsomer, and that in turn gave him—for she never
could think of him, or indeed of some other things, without the aid of his vocabulary—a tremendous pull. Yes,
this was for the moment, as he looked at her, the great
fact of their situation—his pull was tremendous. She tried
to keep the acknowledgement of it from trembling in her
voice as she said to him with more surprise than she
really felt: "You've then reopened relations with her?"

"It's she who has reopened them with me. I got her letter
this morning. She told me you were here and that she
wished me to know it. She didn't say much; she just gave
me your address. I wrote her back, you know, 'Thanks no
end. Shall go to-day.' So we *are* in correspondence again,
aren't we? She means of course that you've something to
tell me from her, eh? But if you have, why haven't you let
a fellow know?" He waited for no answer to this, he had so
much to say. "At your house, just now, they told me how
long you've been here. Haven't you known all the while
that I'm counting the hours? I left a word for you—that I
would be back at six; but I'm awfully glad to have caught

you so much sooner. You don't mean to say you're not going home!" he exclaimed in dismay. "The young woman there told me you went out early."

"I've been out a very short time," said Fleda, who had hung back with the general purpose of making things difficult for him. The street would make them difficult; she could trust the street. She reflected in time, however, that to betray to him she was afraid to admit him would give him more a feeling of facility than of anything else. She moved on with him after a moment, letting him direct their course to her door, which was only round a corner: she considered as they went that it might not prove such a stroke to have been in London so long and yet not to have called him. She desired he should feel she was perfectly simple with him, and there was no simplicity in that. None the less, on the steps of the house, though she had a key, she rang the bell; and while they waited together and she averted her face she looked straight into the depths of what Mrs. Gereth had meant by giving him the "tip." This had been perfidious, had been monstrous of Mrs. Gereth, and Fleda wondered if her letter had contained only what Owen repeated.

CHAPTER XIV

When Owen and Fleda were in her father's little place and, among the brandy-flasks and pen-wipers, still more disconcerted and divided, the girl—to do something, though it would make him stay—had ordered tea, he put the letter before her quite as if he had guessed her thought. "She's still a bit nasty—fancy!" He handed her the scrap of a note which he had pulled out of his pocket and from its envelope. "Fleda Vetch," it ran, "is at 10 Raphael Road, West Kensington. Go to see her, and try, for God's sake, to cultivate a glimmer of intelligence." When in handing it back to him she took in his face she saw that its heightened color was the effect of his watching her read such an allusion to his want of wit. Fleda knew what it was an allusion to, and his pathetic air of having received this buffet, tall and fine and kind as he stood there, made her conscious of not quite concealing her knowledge. For a minute she was kept silent by an angered sense of the trick that had been played her. It was a trick because Fleda considered there had been a covenant; and the trick consisted of Mrs. Gereth's having broken the spirit of their agreement while conforming in a fashion to the letter. Under the girl's menace of a complete rupture she had been afraid to make of her secret the use she itched to make; but in the course of these days of separation she had gathered pluck to hazard an indirect betrayal. Fleda measured her hesitations and the impulse which she had finally obeyed and which the continued procrastination of Waterbath had encouraged, had at last made irresistible. If in her high-handed manner of playing their game she had not named the thing hidden, she had named the hiding-place. It was over the sense of this wrong that Fleda's lips closed tight: she was afraid of aggravating her case by some ejaculation that would make Owen prick up his ears. A great, quick effort, however, helped her to avoid the danger; with her constant idea of keeping cool and repressing a visible flutter, she found herself able to choose her words. Meanwhile he had exclaimed with his uncomfortable laugh: "That's a good one for me, Miss Vetch, isn't it?"

"Of course you know by this time that your mother's very sharp," said Fleda.

"I think I can understand well enough when I know what's to be understood," the young man asserted. "But I hope you won't mind my saying that you've kept me pretty well in the dark about that. I've been waiting, waiting, waiting; so much has depended on your news. If you've been working for me I'm afraid it has been a thankless job. Can't she say what she'll do, one way or the other? I can't tell in the least where I am, you know. I haven't really learnt from you, since I saw you there, where *she* is. You wrote me to be patient, and upon my soul I have been. But I'm afraid you don't quite realize what I'm to be patient with. At Waterbath, don't you know? I've simply to account and answer for the damned things. Mona looks at me and waits, and I, hang it, I look at you and do the same." Fleda had gathered fuller confidence as he continued; so plain was it that she had succeeded in not dropping into his mind the spark that might produce the glimmer invoked by his mother. But even this fine assurance gave a start when, after an appealing pause, he went on: "I hope, you know, that after all you're not keeping anything back from me."

In the full face of what she was keeping back such a hope could only make her wince; but she was prompt with her explanations in proportion as she felt they failed to meet him. The smutty maid came in with tea-things, and Fleda, moving several objects, eagerly accepted the diversion of arranging a place for them on one of the tables. "I've been trying to break your mother down because it has seemed there may be some chance of it. That's why I've let you go on expecting it. She's too proud to veer round all at once, but I think I speak correctly in saying that I've made an impression."

In spite of ordering tea she had not invited him to sit down; she herself made a point of standing. He hovered by the window that looked into Raphael Road; she kept at the other side of the room; the stunted slavey, gazing wide-eyed at the beautiful gentleman and either stupidly or cunningly bringing but one thing at a time, came and went between the tea-tray and the open door.

"You pegged at her so hard?" Owen asked.

"I explained to her fully your position and put before her much more strongly than she liked what seemed to me her absolute duty."

Owen waited a little. "And having done that, you departed?"

Fleda felt the full need of giving a reason for her departure; but at first she only said with cheerful frankness: "I departed."

Her companion again looked at her in silence. "I thought you had gone to her for several months."

"Well," Fleda replied, "I couldn't stay. I didn't like it. I didn't like it at all—I couldn't bear it," she went on. "In the midst of those trophies of Poynton, living with them, touching them, using them, I felt as if I were backing her up. As I was not a bit of an accomplice, as I hate what she has done, I didn't want to be, even to the extent of the mere look of it—what is it you call such people?—an accessory after the fact." There was something she kept back so rigidly that the joy of uttering the rest was double. She felt the sharpest need of giving him all the other truth. There was a matter as to which she had deceived him, and there was a matter as to which she had deceived Mrs. Gereth, but her lack of pleasure in deception as such came home to her now. She busied herself with the tea and, to extend the occupation, cleared the table still more, spreading out the coarse cups and saucers and the vulgar little plates. She was aware that she produced more confusion than symmetry, but she was also aware that she was violently nervous. Owen tried to help her with something: this made rather for disorder. "My reason for not writing to you," she pursued, "was simply that I was hoping to hear more from Ricks. I've waited from day to day for that."

"But you've heard nothing?"

"Not a word."

"Then what I understand," said Owen, "is that, practically, you and Mummy have quarreled. And you've done it—I mean you personally—for *me*."

"Oh no, we haven't quarreled a bit!" Then with a smile: "We've only diverged."

"You've diverged uncommonly far!"—Owen laughed back. Fleda, with her hideous crockery and her father's collections, could conceive that these objects, to her visitor's perception even more strongly than to her own, measured the length of the swing from Poynton and Ricks; she was aware too that her high standards figured vividly enough even to Owen's simplicity to make him reflect that West Kensington was a tremendous fall. If she had fallen it was because she had acted for him. She was all the more content he should thus see she *had* acted, as the cost of it, in his eyes, was none of her own showing. "What seems to have happened," he exclaimed, "is that you've had a row with her and yet not moved her!"

Fleda considered a moment; she was full of the impression that, notwithstanding her scant help, he saw his way clearer than he had seen it at Ricks. He might mean many things; and what if the many should mean in their turn only one? "The difficulty is, you understand, that she doesn't really see into your situation." She hesitated. "She doesn't comprehend why your marriage hasn't yet taken place."

Owen stared. "Why, for the reason I told you: that Mona won't take another step till mother has given full satisfaction. Everything must be there. You see, everything *was* there the day of that fatal visit."

"Yes, that's what I understood from you at Ricks," said Fleda; "but I haven't repeated it to your mother." She had hated, at Ricks, to talk with him about Mona, but now that scruple was swept away. If he could speak of Mona's visit as fatal, she need at least not pretend not to notice it. It

made all the difference that she had tried to assist him and
had failed: to give him any faith in her service she must give
him all her reasons but one. She must give him, in other
words, with a corresponding omission, all Mrs. Gereth's.
"You can easily see that, as she dislikes your marriage,
anything that may seem to make it less certain works in her
favor. Without my telling her, she has suspicions and views
that are simply suggested by your delay. Therefore it
didn't seem to me right to make them worse. By holding
off long enough, she thinks she may put an end to your
engagement. If Mona's waiting, she believes she may at last
tire Mona out." That, in all conscience, Fleda felt was lucid
enough.

So the young man, following her attentively, appeared
equally to feel. "So far as that goes," he promptly declared,
"she *has* at last tired Mona out." He uttered the words with
a strange approach to hilarity.

Fleda's surprise at this aberration left her a moment
looking at him. "Do you mean your marriage is off?"

Owen answered with a kind of gay despair. "God knows,
Miss Vetch, where or when or what my marriage is! If it
isn't 'off,' it certainly, at the point things have reached,
isn't *on*. I haven't seen Mona for ten days, and for a week
I haven't heard from her. She used to write me every week,
don't you know? She won't budge from Waterbath, and I
haven't budged from town." Then he suddenly broke out:
"If she *does* chuck me, will mother come round?"

Fleda, at this, felt that her heroism had come to its real
test—felt that in telling him the truth she should effectively
raise a hand to push his impediment out of the way. Was
the knowledge that such a motion would probably dispose
forever of Mona capable of yielding to the conception of
still giving her every chance she was entitled to? That conception was heroic, but at the same moment it reminded
Fleda of the place it had held in her plan, she was also reminded of the not less urgent claim of the truth. Ah, the
truth—there was a limit to the impunity with which one
could juggle with it! Wasn't what she had most to remember
the fact that Owen had a right to his property and that he

had also her vow to stand by him in the effort to recover it? How did she stand by him if she hid from him the single way to recover it of which she was quite sure? For an instant that seemed to her the fullest of her life she debated. "Yes," she said at last, "if your marriage is really abandoned, she will give up everything she has taken."

"That's just what makes Mona hesitate!" Owen honestly exclaimed. "I mean the idea that I shall get back the things only if she gives me up."

Fleda thought an instant. "'You mean makes her hesitate to keep you—not hesitate to renounce you?"

Owen looked a trifle bewildered. "She doesn't see the use of hanging on, as I haven't even yet put the matter into legal hands. She's awfully keen about that, and awfully disgusted that I don't. She says it's the only real way, and she thinks I'm afraid to take it. She has given me time and then has given me again more. She says I give Mummy too much. She says I'm a muff to go pottering on. That's why she's drawing off so hard, don't you see?"

"I don't see very clearly. Of course you must give her what you offered her; of course you must keep your word. There must be no mistake about *that!*" the girl declared.

Owen's bewilderment visibly increased. "You think, then, as she does, that I *must* send down the police?"

The mixture of reluctance and dependence in this made her feel how much she was failing him. She had the sense of "chucking" him too. "No, no, not yet!" she said, though she had really no other and no better course to prescribe. "Doesn't it occur to you," she asked in a moment, "that if Mona is, as you say, drawing away, she may have, in doing so, a very high motive? She knows the immense value of all the objects detained by your mother, and to restore the spoils of Poynton she is ready—is that it!—to make a sacrifice. The sacrifice is that of an engagement she had entered upon with joy."

Owen had been blank a moment before, but he followed this argument with success—a success so immediate that it enabled him to produce with decision: "Ah, she's not that sort! She wants them herself," he added; "she wants to feel they're hers; she doesn't care whether I have them or not! And if she can't get them she doesn't want *me*. If she can't get them she doesn't want anything at all."

This was categoric; Fleda drank it in. "She takes such an interest in them?"

"So it appears."

"So much that they're *all*, and that she can let everything else absolutely depend upon them?"

Owen weighed her question as if he felt the responsibility of his answer. But that answer came in a moment, and, as Fleda could see, out of a wealth of memory. "She never wanted them particularly till they seemed to be in danger. Now she has an idea about them; and when she gets hold of an idea—Oh dear me!" He broke off, pausing and looking away as with a sense of the futility of expression: it was the first time Fleda had ever heard him explain a matter so pointedly or embark at all on a generalization. It was striking, it was touching to her, as he faltered, that he appeared but half capable of floating his generalization to the end. The girl, however, was so far competent to fill up his blank as that she had divined, on the occasion of Mona's visit to Poynton, what would happen in the event of the accident at which he glanced. She had there with her own eyes seen Owen's betrothed get hold of an idea. "I say, you know, *do* give me some tea!" he went on irrelevantly and familiarly.

Her profuse preparations had all this time had no sequel, and, with a laugh that she felt to be awkward, she hastily complied with his request. "It's sure to be horrid," she said; "we don't have at all good things." She offered him also bread and butter, of which he partook, holding his cup and saucer in his other hand and moving slowly about the room. She poured herself a cup, but not to take it; after which, without wanting it, she began to eat a small stale biscuit. She was struck with the extinction of the unwillingness she had felt at Ricks to contribute to the bandying between them of poor Mona's name; and under this influence she presently resumed: "Am I to understand that she engaged herself to marry you without caring for you?"

Owen looked out into Raphael Road. "She *did* care for me awfully. But she can't stand the strain."

"The strain of what?"

"Why, of the whole wretched thing."

"The whole thing has indeed been wretched, and I can easily conceive its effect upon her," Fleda said.

Her visitor turned sharp round. "You *can?*" There was a light in his strong stare. "You can understand it's spoiling her temper and making her come down on *me?* She behaves as if I were of no use to her at all!"

Fleda hesitated. "She's rankling under the sense of her wrong."

"Well, was it *I*, pray, who perpetrated the wrong? Ain't I doing what I can to get the thing arranged?"

The ring of his question made his anger at Mona almost resemble for a minute an anger at Fleda; and this resemblance in turn caused our young lady to observe how handsome he looked when he spoke, for the first time in her hearing, with that degree of heat, and used, also for the first time, such a term as "perpetrated." In addition, his challenge rendered still more vivid to her the mere flimsiness of her own aid. "Yes, you've been perfect," she said. "You've had a most difficult part. You've *had* to show tact and patience, as well as firmness, with your mother, and you've strikingly shown them. It's I who, quite unintentionally, have deceived you. I haven't helped you at all to your remedy."

"Well, you wouldn't at all events have ceased to like me, would you?" Owen demanded. It evidently mattered to him to know if she really justified Mona. "I mean of course if you *had* liked me—liked me as *she* liked me," he explained.

Fleda looked this inquiry in the face only long enough to recognize that, in her embarrassment, she must take instant refuge in a superior one. "I can answer that better if I know how kind to her you've been. *Have* you been kind to her?" she asked as simply as she could.

"Why, rather, Miss Vetch!" Owen declared. "I've done every blessed thing she wished. I rushed down to Ricks, as you saw, with fire and sword, and the day after that I went to see her at Waterbath." At this point he checked himself, though it was just the point at which her interest deepened. A different look had come into his face as he put down his empty teacup. "But why should I tell you such things, for any good it does me? I gather that you've no suggestion to make me now except that I shall request my solicitor to act. *Shall* I request him to act?"

Fleda scarcely heard his words; something new had suddenly come into her mind. "When you went to Waterbath after seeing me," she asked, "did you tell her all about that?"

Owen looked conscious. "All about it?"

"That you had had a long talk with me, without seeing your mother at all?"

"Oh yes, I told her exactly, and that you had been most awfully kind, and that I had placed the whole thing in your hands."

Fleda was silent a moment. "Perhaps that displeased her," she at last suggested.

"It displeased her fearfully," said Owen, looking very queer.

"Fearfully?" broke from the girl. Somehow, at the word, she was startled.

"She wanted to know what right you had to meddle. She said you were not honest."

"Oh!" Fleda cried, with a long wail. Then she controlled herself. "I see."

"She abused you, and I defended you. She denounced you—"

She checked him with a gesture. "Don't tell me what she did!" She had colored up to her eyes, where, as with the effect of a blow in the face, she quickly felt the tears gathering. It was a sudden drop in her great flight, a shock to her attempt to watch over what Mona was entitled to. While she had been straining her very soul in this attempt, the object of her magnanimity had been pronouncing her "not honest." She took it all in, however, and after an instant was able to speak with a smile. She would not have been surprised to learn, indeed, that her smile was strange. "You had said a while ago that your mother and I quarreled about you. It's much more true that you and Mona have quarreled about *me*."

Owen hesitated, but at last he brought it out. "What I mean to say is, don't you know, that Mona, if you don't mind my saying so, has taken it into her head to be jealous."

"I see," said Fleda. "Well, I dare say our conferences have looked very odd."

"They've looked very beautiful, and they've been very beautiful. Oh, I've told her the sort you are!" the young man pursued.

"That of course hasn't made her love me better."

"No, nor love me," said Owen. "Of course, you know, she says she loves me."

"And do you say you love her?"

"I say nothing else—I say it all the while. I said it the other day a dozen times." Fleda made no immediate rejoinder to this, and before she could choose one he repeated his question of a moment before. "*Am* I to tell my solicitor to act?"

She had at that moment turned away from this solution, precisely because she saw in it the great chance of her secret. If she should determine him to adopt it she might put out her hand and take him. It would shut in Mrs. Gereth's face the open door of surrender: she would flare up and fight, flying the flag of a passionate, an heroic defense. The case would obviously go against her, but the proceedings would last longer than Mona's patience or Owen's propriety. With a formal rupture he would be at large; and she had only to tighten her fingers round the string that would raise the curtain on that scene. "You tell me you 'say' you love her, but is there nothing more in it than your saying so? You wouldn't say so, would you, if it's not true? What in the world has become, in so short a time, of the affection that led to your engagement?"

"The deuce knows what has become of it, Miss Vetch!" Owen cried. "It seemed all to go to pot as this horrid struggle came on." He was close to her now, and, with his face lighted again by the relief of it, he looked all his helpless history into her eyes. "As I saw you and noticed you more, as I knew you better and better, I felt less and less—I couldn't help it—about anything or any one else. I wished I had known you sooner—I knew I should have liked you better than any one in the world. But it wasn't you who made the difference," he eagerly continued, "and I was

awfully determined to stick to Mona to the death. It was
she herself who made it, upon my soul, by the state she got
into, the way she sulked, the way she took things, and the
way she let me have it! She destroyed our prospects and
our happiness, upon my honor. She made just the same
smash of them as if she had kicked over that tea-table. She
wanted to know all the while what was passing between us,
between you and me; and she wouldn't take my solemn assurance that nothing was passing but what might have
directly passed between me and old Mummy. She said a
pretty girl like you was a nice old Mummy for me, and, if
you'll believe it, she never called you anything else but
that. I'll be hanged if I haven't been good, haven't I? I
haven't breathed a breath of any sort to you, have I?
You'd have been down on me hard if I had, wouldn't you?
You're down on me pretty hard as it is, I think, aren't
you? But I don't care what you say now, or what Mona
says, either, or a single rap what any one says: she has
given me at last, by her confounded behavior, a right to
speak out, to utter the way I feel about it. The way I feel
about it, don't you know, is that it had all better come to an
end. You ask me if I don't love her, and I suppose it's
natural enough you should. But you ask it at the very
moment I'm half mad to say to you that there's only one
person on the whole earth I *really* love, and that that person—" Here Owen pulled up short, and Fleda wondered
if it was from the effect of his perceiving, through the
closed door, the sound of steps and voices on the landing
of the stairs. She had caught this sound herself with surprise
and a vague uneasiness: it was not an hour at which her
father ever came in, and there was no present reason why
she should have a visitor. She had a fear, which after a few
seconds deepened: a visitor was at hand; the visitor would
be simply Mrs. Gereth. That lady wished for a near view of
the consequence of her note to Owen. Fleda straightened
herself with the instant thought that if this was what Mrs.
Gereth desired Mrs. Gereth should have it in a form not
to be mistaken. Owen's pause was the matter of a moment,
but during that moment our young couple stood with their
eyes holding each other's eyes and their ears catching the

suggestion, still through the door, of a murmured confer-
ence in the hall. Fleda had begun to make the movement to
cut it short when Owen stopped her with a grasp of her
arm. "You're surely able to guess," he said, with his voice
dropped and her arm pressed as she had never known such
a drop or such a pressure—"you're surely able to guess the
one person on earth I love?"

The handle of the door turned, and Fleda had only time
to jerk at him: "Your mother!"

The door opened, and the smutty maid, edging in, announced "Mrs. Brigstock!"

CHAPTER XV

MRS. BRIGSTOCK, in the doorway, stood looking from one of the occupants of the room to the other; then they saw her eyes attach themselves to a small object that had lain hitherto unnoticed on the carpet. This was the biscuit of which, on giving Owen his tea, Fleda had taken a perfunctory nibble: she had immediately laid it on the table, and that subsequently, in some precipitate movement, she should have brushed it off was doubtless a sign of the agitation that possessed her. For Mrs. Brigstock there was apparently more in it than met the eye. Owen at any rate picked it up, and Fleda felt as if he were removing the traces of some scene that the newspapers would have characterized as lively. Mrs. Brigstock clearly took in also the sprawling tea-things and the mark as of high water in the full faces of her young friends. These elements made the little place a vivid picture of intimacy. A minute was filled by Fleda's relief at finding her visitor not to be Mrs. Gereth, and a longer space by the ensuing sense of what was really more compromising in the actual apparition. It dimly occurred to her that the lady of Ricks had also written to Waterbath. Not only had Mrs. Brigstock never paid her a call, but Fleda would have been unable to figure her so employed. A year before the girl had spent a day under her roof, but never feeling that Mrs. Brigstock regarded this as constituting a bond. She had never stayed in any house but Poynton where the imagination of a bond, one way or the other, prevailed. After the first astonishment she dashed gayly at her guest, emphasizing her welcome and wondering how her whereabouts had become known at Waterbath. Had not Mrs. Brigstock quitted that residence for the very purpose of laying her hand on the associate of Mrs. Gereth's misconduct? The spirit in which this hand was to be laid our young lady was yet to ascertain; but she was a person who could think ten thoughts at once—a circumstance which, even putting her present plight at its worst, gave her a great advantage over a person who required easy conditions for dealing even with one. The very vibration of the air, however, told her that whatever Mrs. Brigstock's spirit might originally have been, it had been sharply affected by the sight of Owen. He was essentially a surprise: she had reckoned with everything that concerned him but his presence. With that, in awkward silence, she was reckoning now, as Fleda could see, while she effected with friendly aid an embarrassed transit to the sofa. Owen would be useless, would be deplorable: that aspect of the case Fleda had taken in as well. Another aspect was that he would admire her, adore her, exactly in proportion as she herself should rise gracefully superior. Fleda felt for the first time free to let herself "go," as Mrs. Gereth had said, and she was full of the sense that to "go" meant now to aim straight at the effect of moving Owen to rapture at her simplicity and tact. It was her impression that he had no positive dislike of Mona's mother; but she couldn't entertain that notion without a glimpse of the implication that he had a positive dislike of Mrs. Brigstock's daughter. Mona's mother declined tea, declined a better seat, declined a cushion, declined to remove her boa: Fleda guessed that she had not come on purpose to be dry, but that the voice of the invaded room had itself given her the hint.

"I just came on the mere chance," she said. "Mona found yesterday, somewhere, the card of invitation to your sister's marriage that you sent us, or your father sent us, some time ago. We couldn't be present—it was impossible; but as it had this address on it I said to myself that I might find you here."

"I'm very glad to be at home," Fleda responded.

"Yes, that doesn't happen very often, does it?" Mrs. Brigstock looked round afresh at Fleda's home.

"Oh, I came back from Ricks last week. I shall be here now till I don't know when."

"We thought it very likely you would have come back. We knew of course of your having been at Ricks. If I didn't find you I thought I might perhaps find Mr. Vetch," Mrs. Brigstock went on.

"I'm sorry he's out. He's always out—all day long."

Mrs. Brigstock's round eyes grew rounder. "All day long?"

"All day long," Fleda smiled.

"Leaving you quite to yourself?"

"A good deal to myself, but a little, to-day, as you see, to Mr. Gereth,—" and the girl looked at Owen to draw him into their sociability. For Mrs. Brigstock he had immediately sat down; but the movement had not corrected the sombre stiffness taking possession of him at the sight of her. Before he found a response to the appeal addressed to him Fleda turned again to her other visitor. "Is there any purpose for which you would like my father to call on you?"

Mrs. Brigstock received this question as if it were not to be unguardedly answered; upon which Owen intervened with pale irrelevance: "I wrote to Mona this morning of Miss Vetch's being in town; but of course the letter hadn't arrived when you left home."

"No, it hadn't arrived. I came up for the night—I've several matters to attend to." Then looking with an intention of fixedness from one of her companions to the other, "I'm afraid I've interrupted your conversation," Mrs. Brigstock said. She spoke without effectual point, had the air of merely announcing the fact. Fleda had not yet been confronted with the question of the sort of person Mrs. Brigstock was; she had only been confronted with the question of the sort of person Mrs. Gereth scorned her for being. She was really, somehow, no sort of person at all, and it came home to Fleda that if Mrs. Gereth could see her at this moment she would scorn her more than ever. She had a face of which it was impossible to say anything but that it was pink, and a mind that it would be possible to describe only if one had been able to mark it in a similar fashion. As nature had made this organ neither green nor blue nor yellow, there was nothing to know it by: it strayed and bleated like an unbranded sheep. Fleda felt for it at this moment much of the kindness of compassion, since Mrs. Brigstock had brought it with her to do something for her that she regarded as delicate. Fleda was quite prepared to help it to perform, if she should be able to gather what it wanted to do. What she gathered, however, more and more, was that it wanted to do something different from what it had wanted to do in leaving Waterbath. There was still nothing to enlighten her more specifically in the way her visitor continued: "You must be very much taken up. I believe you quite espouse his dreadful quarrel."

Fleda vaguely demurred. "His dreadful quarrel?"

"About the contents of the house. Aren't you looking after them for him?"

"She knows how awfully kind you've been to me," Owen said. He showed such discomfiture that he really gave away their situation; and Fleda found herself divided between the hope that he would take leave and the wish that he should see the whole of what the occasion might enable her to bring to pass for him.

She explained to Mrs. Brigstock. "Mrs. Gereth, at Ricks, the other day, asked me particularly to see him for her."

"And did she ask you also particularly to see him here in town?" Mrs. Brigstock's hideous bonnet seemed to argue for the unsophisticated truth; and it was on Fleda's lips to reply that such had indeed been Mrs. Gereth's request. But she checked herself, and before she could say anything else Owen had addressed their companion.

"I made a point of letting Mona know that I should be here, don't you see? That's exactly what I wrote her this morning."

"She would have had no doubt you would be here, if you had a chance," Mrs. Brigstock returned. "If your letter had arrived it might have prepared me for finding you here at tea. In that case I certainly wouldn't have come."

"I'm glad, then, it didn't arrive. Shouldn't you like him to go?" Fleda asked.

Mrs. Brigstock looked at Owen and considered: nothing showed in her face but that it turned a deeper pink. "I should like him to go with *me*." There was no menace in her tone, but she evidently knew what she wanted. As Owen made no response to this Fleda glanced at him to invite him to assent; then, for fear that he wouldn't, and would thereby make his case worse, she took upon herself to declare that she was sure he would be very glad to meet such a wish. She had no sooner spoken than she felt that the words had a bad effect of intimacy: she had answered for him as if she had been his wife. Mrs. Brigstock continued to regard him as if she had observed nothing, and she continued to address Fleda: "I've not seen him for a long time—I've particular things to say to him."

"So have I things to say to you, Mrs. Brigstock!" Owen interjected. With this he took up his hat as if for an immediate departure.

The other visitor meanwhile turned to Fleda. "What is Mrs. Gereth going to do?"

"Is that what you came to ask me?" Fleda demanded.

"That and several other things."

"Then you had much better let Mr. Gereth go, and stay by yourself and make me a pleasant visit. You can talk with him when you like, but it is the first time you've been to see me."

This appeal had evidently a certain effect; Mrs. Brigstock visibly wavered. "I can't talk with him whenever I like," she returned; "he hasn't been near us since I don't know when. But there are things that have brought me here."

"They are not things of any importance," Owen, to Fleda's surprise, suddenly asserted. He had not at first taken up Mrs. Brigstock's expression of a wish to carry him off: Fleda could see that the instinct at the bottom of this was that of standing by her, of seeming not to abandon her. But abruptly, all his soreness working within him, it had struck him that he should abandon her still more if he should leave her to be dealt with by her other visitor. "You must allow me to say, you know, Mrs. Brigstock, that I don't think you should come down on Miss Vetch about anything. It's very good of her to take the smallest interest in us and our horrid little squabble. If you want to talk about it, talk about it with *me*." He was flushed with the idea of protecting Fleda, of exhibiting his consideration for her. "I don't like your cross-questioning her, don't you see? She's as straight as a die: *I*'ll tell you all about her!" he declared with an excited laugh. "Please come off with me and let her alone."

Mrs. Brigstock, at this, became vivid at once; Fleda thought she looked most peculiar. She stood straight up, with a queer distention of her whole person and of everything in her face but her mouth, which she gathered into a small, tight orifice. Fleda was painfully divided; her joy was deep within, but it was more relevant to the situation that she should not appear to associate herself with the tone of familiarity in which Owen addressed a lady who had been, and was perhaps still, about to become his mother-in-law. She laid on Mrs. Brigstock's arm a repressive hand. Mrs. Brigstock, however, had already exclaimed on her having so wonderful a defender. "He speaks, upon my word, as if I had come here to be rude to you!"

At this, grasping her hard, Fleda laughed; then she achieved the exploit of delicately kissing her. "I'm not in the least afraid to be alone with you, or of your tearing me to pieces. I'll answer any question that you can possibly dream of putting to me."

"I'm the proper person to answer Mrs. Brigstock's questions," Owen broke in again, "and I'm not a bit less ready to meet them than you are." He was firmer than she had ever seen him: it was as if she had not known he could be so firm.

"But she'll only have been here a few minutes. What sort of a visit is that?" Fleda cried.

"It has lasted long enough for my purpose. There was something I wanted to know, but I think I know it now."

"Anything you don't know I dare say I can tell you!" Owen observed as he impatiently smoothed his hat with the cuff of his coat.

Fleda by this time desired immensely to keep his companion, but she saw she could do so only at the cost of provoking on his part a further exhibition of the sheltering attitude, which he exaggerated precisely because it was the first thing, since he had begun to "like" her, that he had been able frankly to do for her. It was not in her interest that Mrs. Brigstock should be more struck than she already was with that benevolence. "There may be things you know that I don't," she presently said to her, with a smile. "But I've a sort of sense that you're laboring under some great mistake."

Mrs. Brigstock, at this, looked into her eyes more deeply and yearningly than she had supposed Mrs. Brigstock could look; it was the flicker of a certain willingness to give her a chance. Owen, however, quickly spoiled everything. "Nothing is more probable than that Mrs. Brigstock is doing what you say; but there's no one in the world to whom you owe an explanation. I may owe somebody one—I dare say I do; but not you, no!"

"But what if there's one that it's no difficulty at all for me to give?" Fleda inquired. "I'm sure that's the only one Mrs. Brigstock came to ask, if she came to ask any at all."

Again the good lady looked hard at her young hostess. "I came, I believe, Fleda, just, you know, to plead with you."

Fleda, with a bright face, hesitated a moment. "As if I were one of those bad women in a play?"

The remark was disastrous. Mrs. Brigstock, on whom her brightness was lost, evidently thought it singularly free. She turned away, as from a presence that had really defined itself as objectionable, and Fleda had a vain sense that her good humor, in which there was an idea, was taken for impertinence, or at least for levity. Her allusion was improper, even if she herself wasn't; Mrs. Brigstock's emotion simplified: it came to the same thing. "I'm quite ready," that lady said to Owen rather mildly and woundedly. "I do want to speak to you very much."

"I'm completely at your service." Owen held out his hand to Fleda. "Good-bye, Miss Vetch. I hope to see you again to-morrow." He opened the door for Mrs. Brigstock, who passed before the girl with an oblique, averted salutation. Owen and Fleda, while he stood at the door, then faced each other darkly and without speaking. Their eyes met once more for a long moment, and she was conscious there was something in hers that the darkness didn't quench, that he had never seen before and that he was perhaps never to see again. He stayed long enough to take it—to take it with a sombre stare that just showed the dawn of wonder; then he followed Mrs. Brigstock out of the house.

CHAPTER XVI

HE HAD UTTERED THE HOPE that he should see her the next
day, but Fleda could easily reflect that he wouldn't see her
if she were not there to be seen. If there was a thing in the
world she desired at that moment, it was that the next day
should have no point of resemblance with the day that had
just elapsed. She accordingly aspired to an absence: she
would go immediately down to Maggie. She ran out that
evening and telegraphed to her sister, and in the morning
she quitted London by an early train. She required for this
step no reason but the sense of necessity. It was a strong
personal need; she wished to interpose something, and there
was nothing she could interpose but distance, but time. If
Mrs. Brigstock had to deal with Owen she would allow
Mrs. Brigstock the chance. To be there, to be in the midst
of it, was the reverse of what she craved: she had already
been more in the midst of it than had ever entered into her
plan. At any rate she had renounced her plan; she had no
plan now but the plan of separation. This was to abandon
Owen, to give up the fine office of helping him back to his
own; but when she had undertaken that office she had not
foreseen that Mrs. Gereth would defeat it by a manœuvre
so simple. The scene at her father's rooms had extinguished
all offices, and the scene at her father's rooms was of Mrs.
Gereth's producing. Owen, at all events, must now act for
himself: he had obligations to meet, he had satisfactions to
give, and Fleda fairly ached with the wish that he might be
equal to them. She never knew the extent of her tenderness
for him till she became conscious of the present force of her
desire that he should be superior, be perhaps even sublime.
She obscurely made out that superiority, that sublimity,

mightn't after all be fatal. She closed her eyes and lived for a day or two in the mere beauty of confidence. It was with her on the short journey; it was with her at Maggie's; it glorified the mean little house in the stupid little town. Owen had grown larger to her: he would do, like a man, whatever he should have to do. He wouldn't be weak—not as she was: she herself was weak exceedingly.

Arranging her few possessions in Maggie's fewer receptacles, she caught a glimpse of the bright side of the fact that her old things were not such a problem as Mrs. Gereth's. Picking her way with Maggie through the local puddles, diving with her into smelly cottages and supporting her, at smellier shops, in firmness over the weight of joints and the taste of cheese, it was still her own secret that was universally interwoven. In the puddles, the cottages, the shops she was comfortably alone with it; that comfort prevailed even while, at the evening meal, her brother-in-law invited her attention to a diagram, drawn with a fork on too soiled a tablecloth, of the scandalous drains of the Convalescent Home. To be alone with it she had come away from Ricks; and now she knew that to be alone with it she had come away from London. This advantage was of course menaced, but not immediately destroyed, by the arrival, on the second day, of the note she had been sure she should receive from Owen. He had gone to West Kensington and found her flown, but he had got her address from the little maid and then hurried to a club and written to her. "Why have you left me just when I want you most?" he demanded. The next words, it was true, were more reassuring on the question of his steadiness. "I don't know what your reason may be," they went on, "nor why you've not left a line for me; but I don't think you can feel that I did anything yesterday that it wasn't right for me to do. As regards Mrs. Brigstock, certainly, I just felt what was right and I did it. She had no business whatever to attack you that way, and I should have been ashamed if I had left her there to worry you. I won't have you worried by any one; no one shall be disagreeable to you but me. I didn't mean to be so yesterday, and I don't to-day; but I'm perfectly free now to want you, and I want you much more than you've allowed me to explain. You'll see if I'm not all right, if you'll let me come to you. Don't be afraid—I'll not hurt you nor trouble you. I give you my honor I'll not hurt any one. Only I *must* see you, on what I had to say to Mrs. B. She was nastier than I thought she could be, but I'm behaving like an angel. I assure you I'm all right—that's exactly what I want you to see. You owe me something, you know, for what you said you would do and haven't done; what your departure without a word gives me to understand—doesn't it?—that you definitely can't do. Don't simply forsake me. See me, if you only see me once. I sha'n't wait for any leave—I shall come down to-morrow. I've been looking into trains and find there's something that will bring me down just after lunch and something very good for getting me back. I won't stop long. For God's sake, be there."

This communication arrived in the morning, but Fleda would still have had time to wire a protest. She debated on that alternative; then she read the note over and found in one phrase an exact statement of her duty. Owen's simplicity had expressed it, and her subtlety had nothing to answer. She owed him something for her obvious failure, and what she owed him was to receive him. If indeed she had known he would make this attempt she might have been held to have gained nothing by her flight. Well, she had gained what she had gained—she had gained the interval. She had no compunction for the greater trouble she should give the young man; it was now doubtless right that he should have as much trouble as possible. Maggie, who thought she was in her confidence, but was immensely not, had reproached her for having left Mrs. Gereth, and Maggie was just in this proportion gratified to hear of the visitor with whom, early in the afternoon, she would have to ask to be left alone. Maggie liked to see far, and now she could sit upstairs and rake the whole future. She had known that, as she familiarly said, there was something the matter with Fleda, and the value of that knowledge was augmented by the fact that there was apparently also something the matter with Mr. Gereth.

Fleda, downstairs, learned soon enough what this was.

It was simply that, as he announced the moment he stood before her, he was now all right. When she asked him what he meant by that state he replied that he meant he could practically regard himself henceforth as a free man: he had had at West Kensington, as soon as they got into the street, such a horrid scene with Mrs. Brigstock.

"I knew what she wanted to say to me: that's why I was determined to get her off. I knew I shouldn't like it, but I was perfectly prepared," said Owen. "She brought it out as soon as we got round the corner; she asked me point-blank if I was in love with you."

"And what did you say to that?"

"That it was none of her business."

"Ah," said Fleda, "I'm not so sure!"

"Well, *I* am, and I'm the person most concerned. Of course I didn't use just those words: I was perfectly civil, quite as civil as she. But I told her I didn't consider she had a right to put me any such question. I said I wasn't sure that even Mona had, with the extraordinary line, you know, that Mona has taken. At any rate the whole thing, the way *I* put it, was between Mona and me; and between Mona and me, if she didn't mind, it would just have to remain."

Fleda was silent a little. "All that didn't answer her question."

"Then you think I ought to have told her?"

Again our young lady reflected. "I think I'm rather glad you didn't."

"I knew what I was about," said Owen. "It didn't strike me that she had the least right to come down on us that way and ask for explanations."

Fleda looked very grave, weighing the whole matter. "I dare say that when she started, when she arrived, she didn't mean to 'come down.'"

"What then did she mean to do?"

"What she said to me just before she went: she meant to plead with me."

"Oh, I heard her!" said Owen. "But plead with you for what?"

"For you, of course—to entreat me to give you up. She

thinks me awfully designing—that I've taken some sort of possession of you."

Owen stared. "You haven't lifted a finger! It's I who have taken possession."

"Very true, you've done it all yourself." Fleda spoke gravely and gently, without a breath of coquetry. "But those are shades between which she's probably not obliged to distinguish. It's enough for her that we're singularly intimate."

"I am, but you're not!" Owen exclaimed.

Fleda gave a dim smile. "You make me at least feel that I'm learning to know you very well when I hear you say such a thing as that. Mrs. Brigstock came to get round me, to supplicate me," she went on; "but to find you there, looking so much at home, paying me a friendly call and shoving the tea-things about—that was too much for her patience. She doesn't know, you see, that I'm after all a decent girl. She simply made up her mind on the spot that I'm a very bad case."

"I couldn't stand the way she treated you, and that was what I had to say to her," Owen returned.

"She's simple and slow, but she's not a fool: I think she treated me, on the whole, very well." Fleda remembered how Mrs. Gereth had treated Mona when the Brigstocks came down to Poynton.

Owen evidently thought her painfully perverse. "It was you who carried it off; you behaved like a brick. And so did I, I consider. If you only knew the difficulty I had! I told her you were the noblest and straightest of women."

"That can hardly have removed her impression that there are things I put you up to."

"It didn't," Owen replied with candor. "She said our relation, yours and mine, isn't innocent."

"What did she mean by that?"

"As you may suppose, I particularly inquired. Do you know what she had the cheek to tell me?" Owen asked. "She didn't better it much: she said she meant that it's excessively unnatural."

Fleda considered afresh. "Well, it is!" she brought out at last.

"Then, upon my honor, it's only you who make it so!" Her perversity was distinctly too much for him. "I mean you make it so by the way you keep me off."

"Have I kept you off to-day?" Fleda sadly shook her head, raising her arms a little and dropping them.

Her gesture of resignation gave him a pretext for catching at her hand, but before he could take it she had put it behind her. They had been seated together on Maggie's single sofa, and her movement brought her to her feet, while Owen, looking at her reproachfully, leaned back in discouragement. "What good does it do me to be here when I find you only a stone?"

She met his eyes with all the tenderness she had not yet uttered, and she had not known till this moment how great was the accumulation. "Perhaps, after all," she risked, "there may be even in a stone still some little help for you."

Owen sat there a minute staring at her. "Ah, you're beautiful, more beautiful than any one," he broke out, "but I'll be hanged if I can ever understand you! On Tuesday, at your father's, you were beautiful—as beautiful, just before I left, as you are at this instant. But the next day, when I went back, I found it had apparently meant nothing; and now, again, that you let me come here and you shine at me like an angel, it doesn't bring you an inch nearer to saying what I want you to say." He remained a moment longer in the same position; then he jerked himself up. "What I want you to say is that you like me—what I want you to say is that you pity me." He sprang up and came to her. "What I want you to say is that you'll *save* me!"

Fleda hesitated. "Why do you need saving, when you announced to me just now that you're a free man?"

He too hesitated, but he was not checked. "It's just for the reason that I'm free. Don't you know what I mean, Miss Vetch? I want you to marry me."

Fleda, at this, put out her hand in charity; she held his own, which quickly grasped it a moment, and if he had described her as shining at him it may be assumed that she shone all the more in her deep, still smile. "Let me hear a little more about your freedom first," she said. "I gather

that Mrs. Brigstock was not wholly satisfied with the way
you disposed of her question."

"I dare say she wasn't. But the less she's satisfied the
more I'm free."

"What bearing have *her* feelings, pray?" Fleda asked.

"Why, Mona's much worse than her mother. She wants
much more to give me up."

"Then why doesn't she do it?"

"She will, as soon as her mother gets home and tells her."

"Tells her what?" Fleda inquired.

"Why, that I'm in love with *you!*"

Fleda debated. "Are you so very sure she will?"

"Certainly I'm sure, with all the evidence I already have.
That will finish her!" Owen declared.

This made his companion thoughtful again. "Can you
take such pleasure in her being 'finished'—a poor girl
you've once loved?"

Owen waited long enough to take in the question; then
with a serenity startling even to her knowledge of his
nature, "I don't think I can have *really* loved her, you
know," he replied.

Fleda broke into a laugh which gave him a surprise as
visible as the emotion it testified to. "Then how am I to
know that you 'really' love—anybody else?"

"Oh, I'll show you that!" said Owen.

"I must take it on trust," the girl pursued. "And what if
Mona doesn't give you up?" she added.

Owen was baffled but a few seconds; he had thought of
everything. "Why, that's just where you come in."

"To save you? I see. You mean I must get rid of her for
you." His blankness showed for a little that he felt the chill
of her cold logic; but as she waited for his rejoinder she
knew to which of them it cost most. He gasped a minute,
and that gave her time time to say: "You see, Mr. Owen,
how impossible it is to talk of such things yet!"

Like lightning he had grasped her arm. "You mean you
will talk of them?" Then as he began to take the flood of
assent from her eyes: "You *will* listen to me? Oh, you dear,
you dear—when, when?"

"Ah, when it isn't mere misery!" The words had broken from her in a sudden loud cry, and what next happened was that the very sound of her pain upset her. She heard her own true note; she turned short away from him; in a moment she had burst into sobs; in another his arms were round her; the next she had let herself go so far that even Mrs. Gereth might have seen it. He clasped her, and she gave herself—she poured out her tears on his breast; something prisoned and pent throbbed and gushed; something deep and sweet surged up—something that came from far within and far off, that had begun with the sight of him in his indifference and had never had rest since then. The surrender was short, but the relief was long: she felt his lips upon her face and his arms tightened with his full divination. What she did, what she *had* done, she scarcely knew: she only was aware, as she broke from him again, of what had taken place in his own quick breast. What had taken place was that, with the click of a spring, he saw. He had cleared the high wall at a bound; they were together without a veil. She had not a shred of a secret left; it was as if a whirlwind had come and gone, laying low the great false front that she had built up stone by stone. The strangest thing of all was the momentary sense of desolation.

"Ah, all the while you *cared?*" Owen read the truth with a wonder so great that it was visibly almost a sadness, a terror caused by his sudden perception of where the impossibility was not. That made it all perhaps elsewhere.

"I cared, I cared, I cared!" Fleda moaned it as defiantly as if she were confessing a misdeed. "How couldn't I care? But you mustn't, you must never, never ask! It isn't for us to talk about!" she insisted. "Don't speak of it, don't speak!"

It was easy indeed not to speak when the difficulty was to find words. He clasped his hands before her as he might have clasped them at an altar; his pressed palms shook together while he held his breath and while she stilled herself in the effort to come round again to the real and the right. He helped this effort, soothing her into a seat with a touch as light as if she had really been something sacred. She sank into a chair and he dropped before her on his knees; she fell back with closed eyes and he buried his face in her

lap. There was no way to thank her but this act of prostration, which lasted, in silence, till she laid consenting hands
on him, touched his head and stroked it, held it in her
tenderness till he acknowledged his long density. He made
the avowal seem only his—made her, when she rose again,
raise him at last, softly, as if from the abasement of shame.
If in each other's eyes now, however, they saw the truth,
this truth, to Fleda, looked harder even than before—all
the harder that when, at the very moment she recognized
it, he murmured to her ecstatically, in fresh possession of
her hands, which he drew up to his breast, holding them
tight there with both his own: "I'm saved, I'm saved,—I
am! I'm ready for anything. I have your word. Come!" he
cried, as if from the sight of a response slower than he
needed, and in the tone he so often had of a great boy at a
great game.

She had once more disengaged herself, with the private
vow that he shouldn't yet touch her again. It was all too
horribly soon—her sense of this was rapidly surging back.
"We mustn't talk, we mustn't talk; we must *wait!*" she intensely insisted. "I don't know what you mean by your
freedom; I don't see it, I don't feel it. Where is it yet,
where, your freedom? If it's real there's plenty of time, and
if it isn't there's more than enough. I hate myself," she protested, "for having anything to say about her: it's like
waiting for dead men's shoes! What business is it of mine
what she does? She has her own trouble and her own plan.
It's too hideous to watch her and count on her!"

Owen's face, at this, showed a reviving dread, the fear of
some darksome process of her mind. "If you speak for
yourself I can understand, but why is it hideous for *me?*"

"Oh, I mean for myself!" Fleda said impatiently.

"*I* watch her, *I* count on her: how can I do anything else?
If I count on her to let me definitely know how we stand,
I do nothing in life but what she herself has led straight up
to. I never thought of asking you to 'get rid of her' for me,
and I never would have spoken to you if I hadn't held that
I *am* rid of her, that she has backed out of the whole thing.
Didn't she do so from the moment she began to put it off? I
had already applied for the license; the very invitations

were half addressed. Who but she, all of a sudden, demanded an unnatural wait? It was none of *my* doing; I had never dreamed of anything but coming up to the scratch." Owen grew more and more lucid, and more confident of the effect of his lucidity. "She called it 'taking a stand,' to see what mother would do. I told her mother would do what I would make her do; and to that she replied that she would like to see me make her first. I said I would arrange that everything should be all right, and she said she really preferred to arrange it herself. It was a flat refusal to trust me in the smallest degree. Why then had she pretended so tremendously to care for me? And of course, at present," said Owen, "she trusts me, if possible, still less."

Fleda paid this statement the homage of a minute's muteness. "As to that, naturally, she has reason."

"Why on earth has she reason?" Then, as his companion, moving away, simply threw up her hands, "I never looked at you—not to call looking—till she had regularly driven me to it," he went on. "I know what I'm about. I do assure you I'm all right!"

"You're not all right—you're all wrong?" Fleda cried in despair. "You mustn't stay here, you mustn't!" she repeated with clear decision. "You make me say dreadful things, and I feel as if I made *you* say them." But before he could reply she took it up in another tone. "Why in the world, if everything had changed, didn't you break off?"

"I?—" The inquiry seemed to have moved him to stupefaction. "Can you ask me that question when I only wanted to please you? Didn't you seem to show me, in your wonderful way, that that was exactly how? I didn't break off just on purpose to leave it to *her*. I didn't break off so that there shouldn't be a thing to be said against me."

The instant after her challenge Fleda had faced him again in self-reproof. "There *isn't* a thing to be said against you, and I don't know what nonsense you make me talk! You *have* pleased me, and you've been right and good, and it's the only comfort, and you must go. Everything must come from Mona, and if it doesn't come we've said entirely too much. You must leave me alone—forever."

"Forever?" Owen gasped.

"I mean unless everything is different."

"Everything *is* different—when I *know!*"

Fleda winced at what he knew; she made a wild gesture which seemed to whirl it out of the room. The mere allusion was like another embrace. "You know nothing—and you must go and wait! You mustn't break down at this point."

He looked about him and took up his hat: it was as if, in spite of frustration, he had got the essence of what he wanted and could afford to agree with her to the extent of keeping up the forms. He covered her with his fine, simple smile, but made no other approach. "Oh, I'm so awfully happy!" he exclaimed.

She hesitated: she would only be impeccable even though she should have to be sententious. "You'll be happy if you're perfect!" she risked.

He laughed out at this, and she wondered if, with a new-born acuteness, he saw the absurdity of her speech, and that no one was happy just because no one could be what she so lightly prescribed. "I don't pretend to be perfect, but I shall find a letter to-night!"

"So much the better, if it's the kind of one you desire." That was the most she could say, and having made it sound as dry as possible she lapsed into a silence so pointed as to deprive him of all pretext for not leaving her. Still, nevertheless, he stood there, playing with his hat and filling the long pause with a strained and anxious smile. He wished to obey her thoroughly, to appear not to presume on any advantage he had won from her; but there was clearly something he longed for beside. While he showed this by hanging on she thought of two other things. One of these was that his countenance, after all, failed to bear out his description of his bliss. As for the other, it had no sooner come into her head than she found it seated, in spite of her resolution, on her lips. It took the form of an inconsequent question. "When did you say Mrs. Brigstock was to have gone back?"

Owen stared. "To Waterbath? She was to have spent the night in town, don't you know? But when she left me, after our talk, I said to myself that she would take an evening train. I know I made her want to get home."

"Where did you separate?" Fleda asked.

"At the West Kensington station—she was going to Victoria. I had walked with her there, and our talk was all on the way."

Fleda pondered a moment. "If she did go back that night you would have heard from Waterbath by this time."

"I don't know," said Owen. "I thought I might hear this morning."

"She can't have gone back," Fleda declared. "Mona would have written on the spot."

"Oh yes, she *will* have written bang off!" Owen cheerfully conceded.

Fleda thought again. "Then, even in the event of her mother's not having got home till the morning, you would have had your letter at the latest to-day. You see she has had plenty of time."

Owen hesitated; then, "Oh, she's all right!" he laughed. "I go by Mrs. Brigstock's certain effect on her—the effect of the temper the old lady showed when we parted. Do you know what she asked me?" he sociably continued. "She asked me in a kind of nasty manner if I supposed you 'really' cared anything about me. Of course I told her I supposed you didn't—not a solitary rap. How could I suppose you *do*, with your extraordinary ways? It doesn't matter; I could see she thought I lied."

"You should have told her, you know, that I had seen you in town only that one time," Fleda observed.

"By Jove, I did—for *you!* It was only for you."

Something in this touched the girl so that for a moment she could not trust herself to speak. "You're an honest man," she said at last. She had gone to the door and opened it. "Good-bye."

Even yet, however, he hung back; and she remembered how, at the end of his hour at Ricks, she had been put to it to get him out of the house. He had in general a sort of cheerful slowness which helped him at such times, though she could now see his strong fist crumple his big, stiff gloves as if they had been paper. "But even if there's no letter—" he began. He began, but there he left it.

"You mean, even if she doesn't let you off? Ah, you ask me too much!" Fleda spoke from the tiny hall, where she had taken refuge between the old barometer and the old mackintosh. "There are things too utterly for yourselves alone. How can I tell? What do I know? Good-bye, good-bye! If she doesn't let you off, it will be because she *is* attached to you."

"She's not, she's not: there's nothing in it! Doesn't a fellow know?—except with *you!*" Owen ruefully added. With this he came out of the room, lowering his voice to secret supplication, pleading with her really to meet him on the ground of the negation of Mona. It was this betrayal of his need of support and sanction that made her retreat— harden herself in the effort to save what might remain of all she had given, given probably for nothing. The very vision of him as he thus morally clung to her was the vision of a weakness somewhere in the core of his bloom, a blessed manly weakness of which, if she had only the valid right, it would be all a sweetness to take care. She faintly sickened, however, with the sense that there was as yet no valid right poor Owen could give. "You can take it from my honor, you know," he whispered, "that she loathes me."

Fleda had stood clutching the knob of Maggie's little painted stair-rail; she took, on the stairs, a step backward. "Why then doesn't she prove it in the only clear way?"

"She *has* proved it. Will you believe it if you see the letter?"

"I don't want to see any letter," said Fleda. "You'll miss your train."

Facing him, waving him away, she had taken another upward step; but he sprang to the side of the stairs and brought his hand, above the banister, down hard on her wrist. "Do you mean to tell me that I must marry a woman I hate?"

From her step she looked down into his raised face. "Ah, you see it's not true that you're free!" She seemed almost to exult. "It's not true—it's not true!"

He only, at this, like a buffeting swimmer, gave a shake of his head and repeated his question. "Do you mean to tell me I must marry such a woman?"

Fleda hesitated; he held her fast. "No. Anything is better than that."

"Then, in God's name, what must I do?"

"You must settle that with her. You mustn't break faith. Anything is better than that. You must at any rate be utterly sure. She *must* love you—how can she help it? *I* wouldn't give you up!" said Fleda. She spoke in broken bits, panting out her words. "The great thing is to keep faith. Where *is* a man if he doesn't? If he doesn't he may be so cruel. So cruel, so cruel, so cruel!" Fleda repeated. "I couldn't have a hand in *that,* you know: that's my position—that's mine. You offered her marriage: it's a tremendous thing for her." Then looking at him another moment, "*I* wouldn't give you up!" she said again. He still had hold of her arm; she took in his blank alarm. With a quick dip of her face she reached his hand with her lips, pressing them to the back of it with a force that doubled the force of her words. "Never, never, never!" she cried; and before he could succeed in seizing her she had turned and, scrambling up the stairs, got away from him even faster than she had got away from him at Ricks.

CHAPTER XVII

TEN DAYS after his visit she received a communication from Mrs. Gereth—a telegram of eight words, exclusive of signature and date. "Come up immediately and stay with me here"—it was characteristically sharp, as Maggie said; but, as Maggie added, it was also characteristically kind. "Here" was an hotel in London, and Maggie had embraced a condition of life which already began to produce in her some yearning for hotels in London. She would have responded in an instant, and she was surprised that her sister seemed to hesitate. Fleda's hesitation, which lasted but an hour, was expressed in that young lady's own mind by the reflection that in obeying her friend's summons she shouldn't know what she should be "in for." Her friend's summons, however, was but another name for her friend's appeal; and Mrs. Gereth's bounty had laid her under obligations more sensible than any reluctance. In the event—that is at the end of her hour—she testified to her gratitude by taking the train and to her mistrust by leaving her luggage. She went as if she had gone up for the day. In the train, however, she had another thoughtful hour, during which it was her mistrust that mainly deepened. She felt as if for ten days she had sat in darkness, looking to the east for a dawn that had not yet glimmered. Her mind had lately been less occupied with Mrs. Gereth; it had been so exceptionally occupied with Mona. If the sequel was to justify Owen's prevision of Mrs. Brigstock's action upon her daughter, this action was at the end of a week as much a mystery as ever. The stillness, all round, had been exactly what Fleda desired, but it gave her for the time a deep sense of failure, the sense of a sudden drop from a height at which she had all things beneath her. She had nothing beneath her now; she herself was at the bottom of the heap. No sign had reached her from Owen—poor Owen, who had clearly no news to give about his precious letter from Waterbath. If Mrs. Brigstock had hurried back to obtain that this letter should be written, Mrs. Brigstock might then have spared herself so great an inconvenience. Owen had been silent for the best of all reasons—the reason that he had had nothing in life to say. If the letter had not been written he would simply have had to introduce some large qualification into his account of his freedom. He had left his young friend under her refusal to listen to him until he should be able, on the contrary, to extend that picture; and his present submission was all in keeping with the rigid honesty that his young friend had prescribed.

It was this that formed the element through which Mona loomed large; Fleda had enough imagination, a fine enough feeling for life, to be impressed with such an image of successful immobility. The massive maiden at Waterbath *was* successful from the moment she could entertain her resentments as if they had been poor relations who needn't put her to expense. She was a magnificent dead weight; there was something positive and portentous in her quietude. "What game are they all playing?" poor Fleda could only ask; for she had an intimate conviction that Owen was now under the roof of his betrothed. That was stupefying if he really hated Mona; and if he didn't really hate her what had brought him to Raphael Road and to Maggie's? Fleda had no real light, but she felt that to account for the absence of any result of their last meeting would take a supposition of the full sacrifice to charity that she had held up before him. If he had gone to Waterbath it had been simply because he had to go. She had as good as told him that he would have to go; that this was an inevitable incident of his keeping perfect faith—faith so literal that the smallest subterfuge would always be a reproach to him. When she tried to remember that it was for herself he was taking his risk, she felt how weak a way that was of expressing Mona's supremacy. There would be no need of keeping him up if there were nothing to keep him up to. Her eyes grew wan as she

discerned in the impenetrable air that Mona's thick outline
never wavered an inch. She wondered fitfully what Mrs.
Gereth had by this time made of it, and reflected with a
strange elation that the sand on which the mistress of
Ricks had built a momentary triumph was quaking beneath the surface. As The Morning Post still held its peace,
she would be, of course, more confident; but the hour was
at hand at which Owen would have absolutely to do either
one thing or the other. To keep perfect faith was to inform
against his mother, and to hear the police at her door would
be Mrs. Gereth's awakening. How much she was beguiled
Fleda could see from her having been for a whole month
quite as deep and dark as Mona. She had let her young
friend alone because of the certitude, cultivated at Ricks,
that Owen had done the opposite. He had done the opposite
indeed, but much good had that brought forth! To have
sent for her now, Fleda felt, was from this point of view
wholly natural: she had sent for her to show at last how
much she had scored. If, however, Owen was really at
Waterbath the refutation of that boast was easy.

Fleda found Mrs. Gereth in modest apartments and with
an air of fatigue in her distinguished face—a sign, as she
privately remarked, of the strain of that effort to be discreet
of which she herself had been having the benefit. It was a
constant feature of their relation that this lady could make
Fleda blench a little, and that the effect proceeded from the
intense pressure of her confidence. If the confidence had
been heavy even when the girl, in the early flush of devotion, had been able to feel herself most responsive, it drew
her heart into her mouth now that she had reserves and
conditions, now that she couldn't simplify with the same
bold hand as her protectress. In the very brightening of the
tired look, and at the moment of their embrace, Fleda felt
on her shoulders the return of the load, so that her spirit
frankly quailed as she asked herself what she had brought
up from her trusted seclusion to support it. Mrs. Gereth's
free manner always made a joke of weakness, and there
was in such a welcome a richness, a kind of familiar noble-
ness, that suggested shame to a harried conscience. Something had happened, she could see, and she could also see,

in the bravery that seemed to announce it had changed everything, a formidable assumption that what had happened was what a healthy young woman must like. The absence of luggage had made this young woman feel meagre even before her companion, taking in the bareness at a second glance, exclaimed upon it and roundly rebuked her. Of course she had expected her to stay.

Fleda thought best to show bravery too, and to show it from the first. "What you expected, dear Mrs. Gereth, is exactly what I came up to ascertain. It struck me as right to do that first. I mean to ascertain, without making preparations."

"Then you'll be so good as to make them on the spot!" Mrs. Gereth was most emphatic. "You're going abroad with me."

Fleda wondered, but she also smiled. "To-night—to-morrow?"

"In as few days as possible. That's all that's left for me now." Fleda's heart, at this, gave a bound; she wondered to what particular difference in Mrs. Gereth's situation as last known to her it was an allusion. "I've made my plan," her friend continued: "I go for at least a year. We shall go straight to Florence; we can manage there. I of course don't look to you, however," she added, "to stay with me all that time. That will require to be settled. Owen will have to join us as soon as possible; he may not be quite ready to get off with us. But I'm convinced it's quite the right thing to go. It will make a good change; it will put in a decent interval."

Fleda listened; she was deeply mystified. "How kind you are to me!" she presently said. The picture suggested so many questions that she scarcely knew which to ask first. She took one at a venture. "You really have it from Mr. Gereth that he'll give us his company?"

If Mr. Gereth's mother smiled in response to this, Fleda knew that her smile was a tacit criticism of such a form of reference to her son. Fleda habitually spoke of him as Mr. Owen, and it was a part of her present vigilance to appear to have relinquished that right. Mrs. Gereth's manner confirmed a certain impression of her pretending to more than she felt; her very first words had conveyed it, and it reminded Fleda of the conscious courage with which, weeks before, the lady had met her visitor's first startled stare at the clustered spoils of Poynton. It was her practice to take immensely for granted whatever she wished. "Oh, if you'll answer for him, it will do quite as well!" she said. Then she put her hands on the girl's shoulders and held them at arm's length, as if to shake them a little, while in the depths of her shining eyes Fleda discovered something obscure and unquiet. "You bad, false thing, why didn't you tell me?" Her tone softened her harshness, and her visitor had never had such a sense of her indulgence. Mrs. Gereth could show patience; it was a part of the general bribe, but it was also like the handing in of a heavy bill before which Fleda could only fumble in a penniless pocket. "You must perfectly have known at Ricks, and yet you practically denied it. That's why I call you bad and false!" It was apparently also why she again almost roughly kissed her.

"I think that before I answer you I had better know what you're talking about," Fleda said.

Mrs. Gereth looked at her with a slight increase of hardness. "You've done everything you need for modesty, my dear! If he's sick with love of you, you haven't had to wait for me to inform you."

Fleda hesitated. "Has he informed *you*, dear Mrs. Gereth?"

Dear Mrs. Gereth smiled sweetly. "How could he, when our situation is such that he communicates with me only through you, and that you are so tortuous you conceal everything?"

"Didn't he answer the note in which you let him know that I was in town?" Fleda asked.

"He answered it sufficiently by rushing off on the spot to see you."

Mrs. Gereth met that allusion with a prompt firmness that made almost insolently light of any ground of complaint, and Fleda's own sense of responsibility was now so vivid that all resentments turned comparatively pale. She had no heart to produce a grievance; she could only, left as she was with the little mystery on her hands, pro-

duce, after a moment, a question. "How then do you come
to know that your son has ever thought—"

"That he would give his ears to get you?" Mrs. Gereth
broke in. "I had a visit from Mrs. Brigstock."

Fleda opened her eyes. "She went down to Ricks?"

"The day after she had found Owen at your feet. She
knows everything."

Fleda shook her head sadly; she was more startled than
she cared to show. This odd journey of Mrs. Brigstock's,
which, with a simplicity equal for once to Owen's, she had
not divined, now struck her as having produced the hush
of the last ten days. "There are things she doesn't know!"
she presently exclaimed.

"She knows he would do anything to marry you."

"He hasn't told her so," Fleda said.

"No, but he has told you. That's better still!" laughed
Mrs. Gereth. "My dear child," she went on with an air that
affected the girl as a sort of blind profanity, "don't try to
make yourself out better than you are. I know what you
are. I haven't lived with you so much for nothing. You're
not quite a saint in heaven yet. Lord, what a creature
you'd have thought me in my good time! But you do like
it, fortunately, you idiot. You're pale with your passion,
you sweet thing. That's exactly what I wanted to see. I
can't for the life of me think where the shame comes in."
Then with a finer significance, a look that seemed to Fleda
strange, she added: "It's all right."

"I've seen him but twice," said Fleda.

"But twice?" Mrs. Gereth still smiled.

"On the occasion, at papa's, that Mrs. Brigstock told you
of, and one day, since then, down at Maggie's."

"Well, those things are between yourselves, and you
seem to me both poor creatures at best." Mrs. Gereth spoke
with a rich humor which tipped with light for an instant a
real conviction. "I don't know what you've got in your
veins: you absurdly exaggerated the difficulties. But
enough is as good as a feast, and when once I get you
abroad together—!" She checked herself as if from excess
of meaning; what might happen when she should get them

abroad together was to be gathered only from the way she slowly rubbed her hands.

The gesture, however, made the promise so definite that for a moment her companion was almost beguiled. But there was nothing to account, as yet, for the wealth of Mrs. Gereth's certitude: the visit of the lady of Waterbath appeared but half to explain it. "Is it permitted to be surprised," Fleda deferentially asked, "at Mrs. Brigstock's thinking it would help her to see you?"

"It's never permitted to be surprised at the aberrations of born fools," said Mrs. Gereth. "If a cow should try to calculate, that's the kind of happy thought she'd have. Mrs. Brigstock came down to plead with me."

Fleda mused a moment. "That's what she came to do with *me*," she then honestly returned. "But what did she expect to get of you, with your opposition so marked from the first?"

"She didn't know I want *you*, my dear. It's a wonder, with all my violence—the gross publicity I've given my desires. But she's as stupid as an owl—she doesn't feel your charm."

Fleda felt herself flush slightly, but she tried to smile. "Did you tell her all about it? Did you make her understand you want me?"

"For what do you take me? I wasn't such a donkey."

"So as not to aggravate Mona?" Fleda suggested.

"So as not to aggravate Mona, naturally. We've had a narrow course to steer, but thank God we're at last in the open!"

"What do you call the open, Mrs. Gereth?" Fleda demanded. Then as the other faltered: "Do you know where Mr. Owen is to-day?"

Mrs. Gereth stared. "Do you mean he's at Waterbath? Well, that's your own affair. I can bear it if *you* can."

"Wherever he is, I can bear it," Fleda said. "But I haven't the least idea where he is."

"Then you ought to be ashamed of yourself!" Mrs. Gereth broke out with a change of note that showed how deep a passion underlay everything she had said. The poor woman, catching her companion's hand, however, the next moment, as if to retract something of this harshness, spoke more patiently. "Don't you understand, Fleda, how immensely, how devotedly, I've trusted you?" Her tone was indeed a supplication.

Fleda was infinitely shaken; she was silent a little. "Yes, I understand. Did she go to you to complain of me?"

"She came to see what she could do. She had been tremendously upset, the day before, by what had taken place at your father's, and she had posted down to Ricks on the inspiration of the moment. She hadn't meant it on leaving home; it was the sight of you closeted there with Owen that had suddenly determined her. The whole story, she said, was written in your two faces: she spoke as if she had never seen such an exhibition. Owen was on the brink, but there might still be time to save him, and it was with this idea she had bearded me in my den. 'What won't a mother do, you know?'—that was one of the things she said. What wouldn't a mother do indeed? I thought I had sufficiently shown her what! She tried to break me down by an appeal to my good nature, as she called it, and from the moment she opened on *you*, from the moment she denounced Owen's falsity, I was as good-natured as she could wish. I understood that it was a plea for mere mercy, that you and he between you were killing her child. Of course I was delighted that Mona should be killed, but I was studiously kind to Mrs. Brigstock. At the same time I was honest, I didn't pretend to anything I couldn't feel. I asked her why the marriage hadn't taken place months ago, when Owen was perfectly ready; and I showed her how completely that fatuous mistake on Mona's part cleared his responsibility. It was she who had killed *him*—it was she who had destroyed his affection, his illusions. Did she want him now when he was estranged, when he was disgusted, when he had a sore grievance? She reminded me that Mona had a sore grievance too, but she admitted that she hadn't come to me to speak of that. What she had come to me for was not to get the old things back, but simply to get Owen. What she wanted was that I would, in simple pity, see fair play. Owen had been awfully bedeviled—she didn't call it that, she called it 'misled'—but it was simply you who had bedeviled him. He would be all right still if I would see that you were out of the way. She asked me point-blank if it was possible I could want him to marry you."

Fleda had listened in unbearable pain and growing terror, as if her interlocutress, stone by stone, were piling some fatal mass upon her breast. She had the sense of being buried alive, smothered in the mere expansion of another will; and now there was but one gap left to the air. A single word, she felt, might close it, and with the question that came to her lips as Mrs. Gereth paused she seemed to herself to ask, in cold dread, for her doom. "What did you say to that?" she inquired.

"I was embarrassed, for I saw my danger—the danger of her going home and saying to Mona that I was backing you up. It had been a bliss to learn that Owen had really turned to you, but my joy didn't put me off my guard. I reflected intensely for a few seconds; then I saw my issue."

"Your issue?" Fleda murmured.

"I remembered how you had tied my hands about saying a word to Owen."

Fleda wondered. "And did you remember the little letter that, with your hands tied, you still succeeded in writing to him?"

"Perfectly; my little letter was a model of reticence. What I remembered was all that in those few words I forbade myself to say. I had been an angel of delicacy—I had effaced myself like a saint. It was not for me to have done all that and then figure to such a woman as having done the opposite. Besides, it was none of her business."

"Is that what you said to her?" Fleda asked.

"I said to her that her question revealed a total misconception of the nature of my present relations with my son. I said to her that I had no relations with him at all, and that nothing had passed between us for months. I said to her that my hands were spotlessly clean of any attempt to make him make up to you. I said to her that I had taken from Poynton what I had a right to take, but had done nothing else in the world. I was determined that if I had bit my tongue off to oblige you I would at least have the righteousness that my sacrifice gave me."

"And was Mrs. Brigstock satisfied with your answer?"

"She was visibly relieved."

"It was fortunate for you," said Fleda "that she's apparently not aware of the manner in which, almost under her nose, you advertised me to him at Poynton."

Mrs. Gereth appeared to recall that scene; she smiled with a serenity remarkably effective as showing how cheerfully used she had grown to invidious allusions to it. "How should she be aware of it?"

"She would if Owen had described your outbreak to Mona."

"Yes, but he didn't describe it. All his instinct was to conceal it from Mona. He wasn't conscious, but he was already in love with you!" Mrs. Gereth declared.

Fleda shook her head wearily. "No—I was only in love with him!"

Here was a faint illumination with which Mrs. Gereth instantly mingled her fire. "You dear old wretch!" she exclaimed; and she again, with ferocity, embraced her young friend.

Fleda submitted like a sick animal: she would submit to everything now. "Then what further passed?"

"Only that she left me thinking she had got something."

"And what had she got?"

"Nothing but her luncheon. But *I* got everything!"

"Everything?" Fleda quavered.

Mrs. Gereth, struck apparently by something in her tone, looked at her from a tremendous height. "Don't fail me now!"

It sounded so like a menace that, with a full divination at last, the poor girl fell weakly into a chair. "What on earth have you done?"

Mrs. Gereth stood there in all the glory of a great stroke. "I've settled you." She filled the room, to Fleda's scared vision, with the glare of her magnificence. "I've sent everything back."

"Everything?" Fleda gasped.

"To the smallest snuff-box. The last load went yesterday. The same people did it. Poor little Ricks is empty." Then as if, for a crowning splendor, to check all deprecation, "They're yours, you goose!" Mrs. Gereth concluded, holding up her handsome head and rubbing her white hands. Fleda saw that there were tears in her deep eyes.

CHAPTER XVIII

She was slow to take in the announcement, but when she had done so she felt it to be more than her cup of bitterness would hold. Her bitterness was her anxiety, the taste of which suddenly sickened her. What had she become, on the spot, but a traitress to her friend? The treachery increased with the view of the friend's motive, a motive magnificent as a tribute to her value. Mrs. Gereth had wished to make sure of her and had reasoned that there would be no such way as by a large appeal to her honor. If it be true, as men have declared, that the sense of honor is weak in women, some of the bearings of this stroke might have thrown a light on the question. What was now, at all events, put before Fleda was that she had been made sure of, for the greatness of the surrender imposed an obligation as great. There was an expression she had heard used by young men with whom she danced: the only word to fit Mrs. Gereth's intention was that Mrs. Gereth had designed to "fetch" her. It was a calculated, it was a crushing bribe; it looked her in the eyes and said simply: "That's what I do for you!" What Fleda was to do in return required no pointing out. The sense, at present, of how little she had done made her almost cry aloud with pain; but her first endeavor, in the face of the fact, was to keep such a cry from reaching her companion. How little she had done Mrs. Gereth didn't yet know, and possibly there would be still some way of turning round before the discovery. On her own side too Fleda had almost made one: she had known she was wanted, but she had not after all conceived how magnificently much. She had been treated by her friend's act as a conscious prize, but what made her a conscious prize was only the power the act itself imputed to her. As high, bold diplomacy it dazzled and carried her off her feet. She admired the noble risk of it, a risk Mrs. Gereth had faced for the utterly poor creature that the girl now felt herself. The change it instantly wrought in her was, moreover, extraordinary: it transformed at a touch her emotion on the subject of concessions. A few weeks earlier she had jumped at the duty of pleading for them, practically quarreling with the lady of Ricks for her refusal to restore what she had taken. She had been sore with the wrong to Owen, she had bled with the wounds of Poynton; now however, as she heard of the replenishment of the void that had so haunted her, she came as near sounding an alarm as if from the deck of a ship she had seen a person she loved jump into the sea. Mrs. Gereth had become in a flash the victim; poor little Ricks had been laid bare in a night. If Fleda's feeling about the old things had taken precipitate form the form would have been a frantic command. It was indeed for mere want of breath that she didn't shout: "Oh, stop them—it's no use; bring them back—it's too late!" And what most kept her breathless was her companion's very grandeur. Fleda distinguished as never before the purity of such a passion; it made Mrs. Gereth august and almost sublime. It was absolutely unselfish—she cared nothing for mere possession. She thought solely and incorruptibly of what was best for the things; she had surrendered them to the presumptive care of the one person of her acquaintance who felt about them as she felt herself, and whose long lease of the future would be the nearest approach that could be compassed to committing them to a museum. Now it was indeed that Fleda knew what rested on her; now it was also that she measured as if for the first time Mrs. Gereth's view of the natural influence of a fine acquisition. She had adopted the idea of blowing away the last doubt of what her young friend would gain, of making good still more than she was obliged to make it the promise of weeks before. It was one thing for the girl to have heard that in a certain event restitution would be made; it was another for her to see the condition, with a noble trust, treated in advance as performed, and to be able to feel that she should have only to open a door to find every old piece in every old corner. To have played such a card was therefore, practically, for Mrs. Gereth, to have won the game. Fleda had certainly to recognize that, so far as the theory of the matter went, the game had been won. Oh, she had been made sure of!

She couldn't, however, succeed for so very many minutes in deferring her exposure. "Why didn't you wait, dearest? Ah, why didn't you wait?"—if that inconsequent appeal kept rising to her lips to be cut short before it was spoken, this was only because at first the humility of gratitude helped her to gain time, enabled her to present herself very honestly as too overcome to be clear. She kissed her companion's hands, she did homage at her feet, she murmured soft snatches of praise, and yet in the midst of it all was conscious that what she really showed most was the wan despair at her heart. She saw Mrs. Gereth's glimpse of this despair suddenly widen, heard the quick chill of her voice pierce through the false courage of endearments. "Do you mean to tell me at such an hour as this that you've really lost him?"

The tone of the question made the idea a possibility for which Fleda had nothing from this moment but terror. "I don't know, Mrs. Gereth; how can I say?" she asked. "I've not seen him for so long; as I told you just now, I don't even know where he is. That's by no fault of his," she hurried on: "he would have been with me every day if I had consented. But I made him understand, the last time, that I'll receive him again only when he's able to show me that his release has been complete and definite. Oh, he can't yet, don't you see, and that's why he hasn't been back. It's far better than his coming only that we should both be miserable. When he does come he'll be in a better position. He'll be tremendously moved by the splendid thing you've done. I know you wish me to feel that you've done it as much for me as for Owen, but your having done it for me is just what will delight him most! When he hears of it," said Fleda, in desperate optimism, "when he hears of it—" There indeed, regretting her advance, she quite broke down. She was wholly powerless to say what Owen would do when he heard of it. "I don't know what he won't make of you and how he won't hug you!" she had to content herself with lamely declaring. She had drawn Mrs. Gereth to a sofa with a vague instinct of pacifying her and still, after all, gaining time; but it was a position in which her great duped benefactress, portentously patient again during this demonstration, looked far from inviting a "hug." Fleda found herself tricking out the situation with artificial flowers, trying to talk even herself into the fancy that Owen, whose name she now made simple and sweet, might come in upon them at any moment. She felt an immense need to be understood and justified; she averted her face in dread from all that she might have to be forgiven. She pressed on her companion's arm as if to keep her quiet till she should really know, and then, after a minute, she poured out the clear essence of what in happier days had been her "secret." "You mustn't think I don't adore him when I've told him so to his face. I love him so that I'd die for him—I love him so that it's horrible. Don't look at me therefore as if I had not been kind, as if I had not been as tender as if he were dying and my tenderness were what would save him. Look at me as if you believe me, as if you feel what I've been through. Darling Mrs. Gereth, I could kiss the ground he walks on. I haven't a rag of pride; I used to have, but it's gone. I used to have a secret, but every one knows it now, and any one who looks at me can say, I think, what's the matter with me. It's not so very fine, my secret, and the less one really says about it the better; but I want you to have it from me because I was stiff before. I want you to see for yourself that I've been brought as low as a girl can very well be. It serves me right," Fleda laughed, "if I was ever proud and horrid to you! I don't know what you wanted me, in those days at Ricks, to do, but I don't think you can have wanted much more than what I've done. The other day at Maggie's I did things that made me, afterwards, think of you! I don't know what girls may do; but if he doesn't know that there isn't an inch of me that isn't his—!" Fleda sighed as if she couldn't express it; she piled it up, as she would have said; holding Mrs. Gereth with dilated eyes, she seemed to sound her for the effect of these words.

"It's idiotic," she wearily smiled; "it's so strange that I'm almost angry for it, and the strangest part of all is that it isn't even happiness. It's anguish—it was from the first; from the first there was a bitterness and a kind of dread. But I owe you every word of the truth. You don't do him justice, either: he's a dear, I assure you he's a dear. I'd trust him to the last breath; I don't think you really know him. He's ever so much cleverer than he makes a show of; he's remarkable in his own shy way. You told me at Ricks that you wanted me to let myself go, and I've 'gone' quite far enough to discover as much as that, as well as all sorts of other delightful things about him. You'll tell me I make myself out worse than I am," said the girl, feeling more and more in her companion's attitude a quality that treated her speech as a desperate rigmarole and even perhaps as a piece of cold immodesty. She wanted to make herself out "bad" —it was a part of her justification; but it suddenly occurred to her that such a picture of her extravagance imputed a want of gallantry to the young man. "I don't care for anything you think," she declared, "because Owen, don't you know, sees me as I am. He's so kind that it makes up for everything!"

This attempt at gayety was futile; the silence with which, for a minute, her adversary greeted her troubled plea brought home to her afresh that she was on the bare defensive. "Is it a part of his kindness never to come near you?" Mrs. Gereth inquired at last. "Is it a part of his kindness to leave you without an inkling of where he is?" She rose again from where Fleda had kept her down; she seemed to tower there in the majesty of her gathered wrong. "Is it a part of his kindness that, after I've toiled as I've done for six days, and with my own weak hands, which I haven't spared, to denude myself, in your interest, to that point that I've nothing left, as I may say, but what I have on my back—is it a part of his kindness that you're not even able to produce him for me?"

There was a high contempt in this which was for Owen quite as much, and in the light of which Fleda felt that her effort at plausibility had been mere groveling. She rose from the sofa with an humiliated sense of rising from ineffectual knees. That discomfort, however, lived but an instant: it was swept away in a rush of loyalty to the absent. She herself could bear his mother's scorn; but to avert it from his sweet innocence she broke out with a quickness that was like the raising of an arm. "Don't blame him— don't blame him: he'd do anything on earth for me! It was I," said Fleda, eagerly, "who sent him back to her; I made him go; I pushed him out of the house; I declined to have anything to say to him except on another footing."

Mrs. Gereth stared as at some gross material ravage. "Another footing? What other footing?"

"The one I've already made so clear to you: my having it in black and white, as you may say, from her that she freely gives him up."

"Then you think he lies when he tells you that he has recovered his liberty?"

Fleda hesitated a moment; after which she exclaimed with a certain hard pride: "He's enough in love with me for anything!"

"For anything, apparently, except to act like a man and impose his reason and his will on your incredible folly. For anything except to put an end, as any man worthy of the name would have put it, to your systematic, to your idiotic perversity. What are you, after all, my dear, I should like to know, that a gentleman who offers you what Owen offers should have to meet such wonderful exactions, to take such extraordinary precautions about your sweet little scruples?" Her resentment rose to a strange insolence which Fleda took full in the face and which, for the moment at least, had the horrible force to present to her vengefully a showy side of the truth. It gave her a blinding glimpse of lost alternatives. "I don't know what to think of him," Mrs. Gereth went on; "I don't know what to call him: I'm so ashamed of him that I can scarcely speak of him even to you. But indeed I'm so ashamed of you both together that I scarcely know in common decency where to look." She paused to give Fleda the full benefit of this remarkable statement; then she exclaimed: "Any one but a jackass would have tucked you under his arm and marched you off to the Registrar!"

Fleda wondered; with her free imagination she could wonder even while her cheek stung from a slap. "To the Registrar?"

"That would have been the sane, sound, immediate course to adopt. With a grain of gumption you'd both instantly have felt it. *I* should have found a way to take you, you know, if I'd been what Owen's supposed to be. *I* should have got the business over first; the rest could come when you liked! Good God, girl, your place was to stand before me as a woman honestly married. One doesn't know what one has hold of in touching you, and you must excuse my saying that you're literally unpleasant to me to meet as you are. Then at least we could have talked, and Owen, if he had the ghost of a sense of humor, could have snapped his fingers at your refinements."

This stirring speech affected our young lady as if it had been the shake of a tambourine borne towards her from a gypsy dance: her head seemed to go round and she felt a sudden passion in her feet. The emotion, however, was but meagerly expressed in the flatness with which she heard herself presently say: "I'll go to the Registrar now."

"Now?" Magnificent was the sound Mrs. Gereth threw into this monosyllable. "And pray who's to take you?" Fleda gave a colorless smile, and her companion continued: "Do you literally mean that you can't put your hand upon him?" Fleda's wan grimace appeared to irritate her; she made a short, imperious gesture. "Find him for me, you fool—*find* him for me!"

"What do you want of him," Fleda sadly asked, "feeling as you do to both of us?"

"Never mind how I feel, and never mind what I say when I'm furious!" Mrs. Gereth still more incisively added. "Of course I cling to you, you wretches, or I shouldn't suffer as I do. What I want of him is to see that he takes you; what I want of him is to go with you myself to the place." She looked round the room as if, in feverish haste, for a mantle to catch up; she bustled to the window as if to spy out a cab: she would allow half an hour for the job. Already in her bonnet, she had snatched from the sofa a garment for the street: she jerked it on as she came back. "Find him, find him," she repeated; "come straight out with me, to try, at least, to get at him!"

"How can I get at him? He'll come when he's ready," Fleda replied.

Mrs. Gereth turned on her sharply. "Ready for what? Ready to see me ruined without a reason or a reward?"

Fleda was silent; the worst of it all was that there was something unspoken between them. Neither of them dared to utter it, but the influence of it was in the girl's tone when she returned at last, with great gentleness: "Don't be harsh to me—I'm very unhappy." The words produced a visible impression on Mrs. Gereth, who held her face averted and sent off through the window a gaze that kept pace with the long caravan of her treasures. Fleda knew she was watching it wind up the avenue of Poynton—Fleda participated indeed fully in the vision; so that after a little the most consoling thing seemed to her to add: "I don't see why in the world you take so for granted that he's, as you say, 'lost.' "

Mrs. Gereth continued to stare out of the window, and her stillness denoted some success in controlling herself. "If he's not lost, why are you unhappy?"

"I'm unhappy because I torment you, and you don't understand me."

"No, Fleda, I don't understand you," said Mrs. Gereth, finally facing her again. "I don't understand you at all, and it's as if you and Owen were of quite another race and another flesh. You make me feel very old-fashioned and simple and bad. But you must take me as I am, since you take so much else *with* me!" She spoke now with the drop of her resentment, with a dry and weary calm. "It would have been better for me if I had never known you," she pursued, "and certainly better if I hadn't taken such an extraordinary fancy to you. But that too was inevitable: everything, I suppose, is inevitable. It was all my own doing—you didn't run after me: I pounced on you and caught you up. You're a stiff little beggar, in spite of your pretty manners: yes, you're hideously misleading. I hope you feel how handsome it is of me to recognize the independence of your character. It was your clever sympathy that did it—your extraordinary feeling for those accursed vanities. You were sharper about them than any one I had ever known, and that was a thing I simply couldn't resist. Well," the poor lady concluded after a pause, "you see where it has landed us!"

"If you'll go for him yourself, I'll wait here," said Fleda.

Mrs. Gereth, holding her mantle together, appeared for a while to consider.

"To his club, do you mean?"

"Isn't it there, when he's in town, that he has a room? He has at present no other London address," Fleda said: "it's there one writes to him."

"How do *I* know, with my wretched relations with him?" Mrs. Gereth asked.

"Mine have not been quite so bad as that," Fleda desperately smiled. Then she added: "His silence, *her* silence, our hearing nothing at all—what are these but the very things on which, at Poynton and at Ricks, you rested your assurance that everything is at an end between them?"

Mrs. Gereth looked dark and void. "Yes, but I hadn't heard from you then that you could invent nothing better than, as you call it, to send him back to her."

"Ah, but, on the other hand, you've learned from them what you didn't know—you've learned by Mrs. Brigstock's visit that he cares for me." Fleda found herself in the position of availing herself of optimistic arguments that she formerly had repudiated; her refutation of her companion had completely changed its ground.

She was in a fever of ingenuity and painfully conscious, on behalf of her success, that her fever was visible. She could herself see the reflection of it glitter in Mrs. Gereth's sombre eyes.

"You plunge me in stupefaction," that lady answered, "and at the same time you terrify me. Your account of Owen is inconceivable, and yet I don't know what to hold on by. He cares for you, it does appear, and yet in the same breath you inform me that nothing is more possible than that he's spending these days at Waterbath. Excuse me if I'm so dull as not to see my way in such darkness. If he's at Waterbath he doesn't care for you. If he cares for you he's not at Waterbath."

"Then where is he?" poor Fleda helplessly wailed. She caught herself up, however; she did her best to be brave and clear. Before Mrs. Gereth could reply, with due obviousness, that this was a question for her not to ask, but to answer, she found an air of assurance to say: "You simplify far too much. You always did and you always will. The tangle of life is much more intricate than you've ever, I think, felt it to be. You slash into it," cried Fleda finely, "with a great pair of shears, you nip at it as if you were one of the Fates! If Owen's at Waterbath he's there to wind everything up."

Mrs. Gereth shook her head with slow austerity. "You don't believe a word you're saying. I've frightened you, as you've frightened me: you're whistling in the dark to keep up our courage. I do simplify, doubtless, if to simplify is to fail to comprehend the intensity of a passion that bewilders a young blockhead with bugaboo barriers, with hideous and monstrous sacrifices. I can only repeat that you're beyond me. Your perversity's a thing to howl over. However," the poor woman continued with a break in her voice, a long hesitation and then the dry triumph of her will, "I'll never mention it to you again! Owen I can just make out; for Owen *is* a blockhead. Owen's a blockhead," she repeated with a quiet, tragic finality, looking straight into Fleda's eyes. "I don't know why you dress up so the fact that he's disgustingly weak."

Fleda hesitated; at last, before her companion's, she lowered her look. "Because I love him. It's because he's weak that he needs me," she added.

"That was why his father, whom he exactly resembles, needed *me*. And I didn't fail his father," said Mrs. Gereth. She gave Fleda a moment to appreciate the remark; after which she pursued: "Mona Brigstock isn't weak; she's stronger than you!"

"I never thought she was weak," Fleda answered. She looked vaguely round the room with a new purpose: she had lost sight of her umbrella.

"I did tell you to let yourself go, but it's clear enough that you really haven't," Mrs. Gereth declared. "If Mona has got him——"

Fleda had accomplished her search; her interlocutress paused. "If Mona has got him?" the girl inquired, tightening the umbrella.

"Well," said Mrs. Gereth profoundly, "it will be clear enough that Mona *has*."

"Has let herself go?"

"Has let herself go." Mrs. Gereth spoke as if she saw it in every detail.

Fleda felt the tone and finished her preparation; then she went and opened the door. "We'll look for him together," she said to her friend, who stood a moment taking in her face. "They may know something about him at the Colonel's."

"We'll go there." Mrs. Gereth had picked up her gloves and her purse. "But the first thing," she went on, "will be to wire to Poynton."

"Why not to Waterbath at once?" Fleda asked.

Her companion hesitated. "In *your* name?"

"In my name. I noticed a place at the corner."

While Fleda held the door open Mrs. Gereth drew on her gloves. "Forgive me," she presently said. "Kiss me," she added.

Fleda, on the threshold, kissed her; then they went out.

CHAPTER XIX

IN THE PLACE at the corner, on the chance of its saving time, Fleda wrote her telegram—wrote it in silence under Mrs. Gereth's eye and then in silence handed it to her. "I send this to Waterbath, on the possibility of your being there, to ask you to come to me." Mrs. Gereth held it a moment, read it more than once; then keeping it, and with her eyes on her companion, seemed to consider. There was the dawn of a kindness in her look; Fleda perceived in it, as if as the reward of complete submission, a slight relaxation of her rigor.

"Wouldn't it perhaps after all be better," she asked, "before doing this, to see if we can make his whereabouts certain?"

"Why so? It will be always so much done," said Fleda. "Though I'm poor," she added with a smile, "I don't mind the shilling."

"The shilling's *my* shilling," said Mrs. Gereth.

Fleda stayed her hand. "No, no—I'm superstitious."

"Superstitious?"

"To succeed, it must be all me!"

"Well, if that will make it succeed!" Mrs. Gereth took back her shilling, but she still kept the telegram. "As he's most probably not there—"

"If he shouldn't be there," Fleda interrupted, "there will be no harm done."

"'If he 'shouldn't be' there!" Mrs. Gereth ejaculated. "Heaven help us, how you assume it!"

"I'm only prepared for the worst. The Brigstocks will simply send any telegram on."

"Where will they send it?"

"Presumably to Poynton."

"They'll read it first," said Mrs. Gereth.

"Read it?"

"Yes, Mona will. She'll open it under the pretext of having it repeated; and then she'll probably do nothing. She'll keep it as a proof of your immodesty."

"What of that?" asked Fleda.

"You don't mind her seeing it?"

Rather musingly and absently Fleda shook her head. "I don't mind anything."

"Well, then, that's all right," said Mrs. Gereth as if she had only wanted to feel that she had been irreproachably considerate. After this she was gentler still, but she had another point to clear up. "Why have you given, for a reply, your sister's address?"

"Because if he *does* come to me he must come to me there. If that telegram goes," said Fleda, "I return to Maggie's to-night."

Mrs. Gereth seemed to wonder at this. "You won't receive him here with me?"

"No, I won't receive him here with you. Only where I received him last—only there again." She showed her companion that as to that she was firm.

But Mrs. Gereth had obviously now had some practice in following queer movements prompted by queer feelings. She resigned herself, though she fingered the paper a moment longer. She appeared to hesitate; then she brought out: "You couldn't then, if I release you, make your message a little stronger?"

Fleda gave her a faint smile. "He'll come if he can."

Mrs. Gereth met fully what this conveyed; with decision she pushed in the telegram. But she laid her hand quickly upon another form and with still greater decision wrote another message. "From *me,* this," she said to Fleda when she had finished: "to catch him possibly at Poynton. Will you read it?"

Fleda turned away. "Thank you."

"It's stronger than yours."

"I don't care," said Fleda, moving to the door. Mrs. Gereth, having paid for the second missive, rejoined her,

and they drove together to Owen's club, where the elder
lady alone got out. Fleda, from the hansom, watched
through the glass doors her brief conversation with the
hall-porter and then met in silence her return with the news
that he had not seen Owen for a fortnight and was keeping
his letters till called for. These had been the last orders;
there were a dozen letters lying there. He had no more information to give, but they would see what they could find
at Colonel Gereth's. To any connection with this inquiry,
however, Fleda now roused herself to object, and her friend
had indeed to recognize that on second thoughts it couldn't
be quite to the taste of either of them to advertise in the
remoter reaches of the family that they had forfeited the
confidence of the master of Poynton. The letters lying at
the club proved effectively that he was not in London, and
this was the question that immediately concerned them. Nothing could concern them further till the answers to their
telegrams should have had time to arrive. Mrs Gereth had
got back into the cab, and, still at the door of the club, they
sat staring at their need of patience. Fleda's eyes rested, in
the great hard street, on passing figures that struck her as
puppets pulled by strings. After a little the driver challenged
them through the hole in the top. "Anywhere in particular,
ladies?"

Fleda decided. "Drive to Euston, please."

"You won't wait for what we may hear?" Mrs. Gereth
asked.

"Whatever we hear, I must go." As the cab went on
she added: "But I needn't drag *you* to the station."

Mrs. Gereth was silent a moment; then "Nonsense!" she
sharply replied.

In spite of this sharpness they were now almost equally
and almost tremulously mild; though their mildness took
mainly the form of an inevitable sense of nothing left to say.
It was the unsaid that occupied them—the thing that for
more than an hour had been going round and round without naming it. Much too early for Fleda's train, they encountered at the station a long half-hour to wait. Fleda
made no further allusion to Mrs. Gereth's leaving her; their
dumbness, with the elapsing minutes, grew to be in itself a

reconstituted bond. They slowly paced the great gray platform, and presently Mrs. Gereth took the girl's arm and leaned on it with a hard demand for support. It seemed to Fleda not difficult for each to know of what the other was thinking—to know indeed that they had in common two alternating visions, one of which, at moments, brought them as by a common impulse to a pause. This was the one that was fixed; the other filled at times the whole space and then was shouldered away. Owen and Mona glared together out of the gloom and disappeared, but the replenishment of Poynton made a shining, steady light. The old splendor was there again, the old things were in their places. Our friends looked at them with an equal yearning; face to face, on the platform, they counted them in each other's eyes. Fleda had come back to them by a road as strange as the road they themselves had followed. The wonder of their great journeys, the prodigy of this second one, was the question that made her occasionally stop. Several times she uttered it, asked how this and that difficulty had been met. Mrs. Gereth replied with pale lucidity—was naturally the person most familiar with the truth that what she undertook was always somehow achieved. To do it was to do it—she had more than one kind of magnificence. She confessed there, audaciously enough, to a sort of arrogance of energy, and Fleda, going on again, her inquiry more than answered and her arm rendering service, flushed, in her diminished identity, with the sense that such a woman was great.

"You do mean literally everything, to the last little miniature on the last little screen?"

"I mean literally everything. Go over them with the catalogue!"

Fleda went over them while they walked again; she had no need of the catalogue. At last she spoke once more: "Even the Maltese cross?"

"Even the Maltese cross. Why not that as well as everything else?—especially as I remembered how you like it."

Finally, after an interval, the girl exclaimed: "But the mere fatigue of it, the exhaustion of such a feat! I drag you to and fro here while you must be ready to drop."

"I'm very, very tired." Mrs. Gereth's slow head-shake was tragic. "I couldn't do it again."

"I doubt if they'd bear it again!"

"That's another matter: they'd bear it if I could. There won't have been, this time either, a shake or a scratch. But I'm too tired—I very nearly don't care."

"You must sit down, then, till I go," said Fleda. "We must find a bench."

"No. I'm tired of *them:* I'm not tired of you. This is the way for you to feel most how much I rest on you." Fleda had a compunction, wondering as they continued to stroll whether it was right after all to leave her. She believed, however, that if the flame might for the moment burn low, it was far from dying out; an impression presently confirmed by the way Mrs. Gereth went on: "But one's fatigue is nothing. The idea under which one worked kept one up. For you I *could*—I can still. Nothing will have mattered if *she's* not there."

There was a question that this imposed, but Fleda at first found no voice to utter it: it was the thing that, between them, since her arrival, had been so consciously and vividly unsaid. Finally she was able to breathe: "And if she *is* there—if she's there already?"

Mrs. Gereth's rejoinder too hung back; then when it came—from sad eyes as well as from lips barely moved—it was unexpectedly merciful. "It will be very hard." That was all, now; and it was poignantly simple. The train Fleda was to take had drawn up; the girl kissed her as if in farewell. Mrs. Gereth submitted, then after a little brought out: "If we *have* lost—"

"If we have lost?" Fleda repeated as she paused again.

"You'll all the same come abroad with me?"

"It will seem very strange to me if you want me. But whatever you ask, whatever you need, that I will always do."

"I shall need your company," said Mrs. Gereth. Fleda wondered an instant if this were not practically a demand for penal submission—for a surrender that, in its complete humility, would be a long expiation. But there was none of the latent chill of the vindictive in the way Mrs. Gereth pursued: "We can always, as time goes on, talk of them together."

"Of the old things?" Fleda had selected a third-class compartment: she stood a moment looking into it and at a fat woman with a basket who had already taken possession. "Always?" she said, turning again to her companion. "Never!" she exclaimed. She got into the carriage, and two men with bags and boxes immediately followed, blocking up door and window so long that when she was able to look out again Mrs. Gereth had gone.

CHAPTER XX

THERE CAME TO HER at her sister's no telegram in answer to her own: the rest of that day and the whole of the next elapsed without a word either from Owen or from his mother. She was free, however, to her infinite relief, from any direct dealing with suspense, and conscious, to her surprise, of nothing that could show her, or could show Maggie and her brother-in-law, that she was excited. Her excitement was composed of pulses as swift and fine as the revolutions of a spinning top: she supposed she was going round, but she went round so fast that she couldn't even feel herself move. Her emotion occupied some quarter of her soul that had closed its doors for the day and shut out even her own sense of it; she might perhaps have heard something if she had pressed her ear to a partition. Instead of that she sat with her patience in a cold, still chamber from which she could look out in quite another direction. This was to have achieved an equilibrium to which she couldn't have given a name: indifference, resignation, despair were the terms of a forgotten tongue. The time even seemed not long, for the stages of the journey were the items of Mrs. Gereth's surrender. The detail of that performance, which filled the scene, was what Fleda had now before her eyes. The part of her loss that she could think of was the reconstituted splendor of Poynton. It was the beauty she was most touched by that, in tons, she had lost—the beauty that, charged upon big wagons, had safely crept back to its home. But the loss was a gain to memory and love; it was to her too, at last, that, in condonation of her treachery, the old things had crept back. She greeted them with open arms; she thought of them hour after hour;

they made a company with which solitude was warm and a picture that, at this crisis, overlaid poor Maggie's scant mahogany. It was really her obliterated passion that had revived, and with it an immense assent to Mrs. Gereth's early judgment of her. She too, she felt, was of the religion, and like any other of the passionately pious she could worship now even in the desert. Yes, it was all for her; far round as she had gone she had been strong enough: her love had gathered in the spoils. She wanted indeed no catalogue to count them over; the array of them, miles away, was complete; each piece, in its turn, was perfect to her; she could have drawn up a catalogue from memory. Thus again she lived with them, and she thought of them without a question of any personal right. That they might have been, that they might still be hers, that they were perhaps already another's, were ideas that had too little to say to her. They were nobody's at all—too proud, unlike base animals and humans, to be reducible to anything so narrow. It was Poynton that was theirs; they had simply recovered their own. The joy of that for them was the source of the strange peace in which the girl found herself floating.

It was broken on the third day by a telegram from Mrs. Gereth. "Shall be with you at 11.30—don't meet me at station." Fleda turned this over, but was sufficiently expert not to disobey the injunction. She had only an hour to take in its meaning, but that hour was longer than all the previous time. If Maggie had studied her convenience the day Owen came, Maggie was also at the present juncture a miracle of refinement. Increasingly and resentfully mystified, in spite of all reassurance, by the impression that Fleda suffered more than she gained from the grandeur of the Gereths, she had it at heart to exemplify the perhaps truer distinction of nature that characterized the house of Vetch. She was not, like poor Fleda, at every one's beck, and the visitor was to see no more of her than what the arrangement of luncheon might tantalizingly show. Maggie described herself to her sister as intending for a just provocation even the understanding she had had with her husband that he also should remain invisible. Fleda accordingly awaited

alone the subject of so many manœuvres—a period that
was slightly prolonged even after the drawing-room door,
at 11.30, was thrown open. Mrs. Gereth stood there with a
face that spoke plain, but no sound fell from her till the
withdrawal of the maid, whose attention had immediately
attached itself to the rearrangement of a window-blind and
who seemed, while she bustled at it, to contribute to the
pregnant silence; before the duration of which, however, she
retreated with a sudden stare.

"He has done it," said Mrs. Gereth, turning her eyes
avoidingly but not unperceivingly about her and in spite of
herself dropping an opinion upon the few objects in the
room. Fleda, on her side, in her silence, observed how
characteristically she looked at Maggie's possessions before
looking at Maggie's sister. The girl understood and at first
had nothing to say; she was still dumb while Mrs. Gereth
selected, with hesitation, a seat less distasteful than the one
that happened to be nearest. On the sofa near the window
the poor woman finally showed what the two past days had
done for the age of her face. Her eyes at last met Fleda's.
"It's the end."

"They're married?"

"They're married."

Fleda came to the sofa in obedience to the impulse to
sit down by her; then paused before her while Mrs. Gereth
turned up a dead gray mask. A tired old woman sat there
with empty hands in her lap. "I've heard nothing," said
Fleda. "No answer came."

"That's the only answer. It's the answer to everything."
So Fleda saw; for a minute she looked over her companion's
head and far away. "He wasn't at Waterbath; Mrs. Brigstock must have read your telegram and kept it. But mine,
the one to Poynton, brought something. 'We are here—what
do you want?' " Mrs. Gereth stopped as if with a failure of
voice; on which Fleda sank upon the sofa and made a movement to take her hand. It met no response; there could be
no attenuation. Fleda waited; they sat facing each other like
strangers. "I wanted to go down," Mrs. Gereth presently
continued. "Well, I went."

All the girl's effort tended for the time to a single aim—

that of taking the thing with outward detachment, speaking of it as having happened to Owen and to his mother and not in any degree to herself. Something at least of this was in the encouraging way she said: "Yesterday morning?"

"Yesterday morning. I saw him."

Fleda hesitated. "Did you see *her?*"

"Thank God, no!"

Fleda laid on her arm a hand of vague comfort, of which Mrs. Gereth took no notice. "You've been capable, just to tell me, of this wretched journey, of this consideration that I don't deserve?"

"We're together, we're together," said Mrs. Gereth. She looked helpless as she sat there, her eyes, unseeingly enough, on a tall Dutch clock, old but rather poor, that Maggie had had as a wedding-gift and that eked out the bareness of the room.

To Fleda, in the face of the event, it appeared that this was exactly what they were not: the last inch of common ground, the ground of their past intercourse, had fallen from under them. Yet what was still there was the grand style of her companion's treatment of her. Mrs. Gereth couldn't stand upon small questions, couldn't, in conduct, make small differences. "You're magnificent!" her young friend exclaimed. "There's a rare greatness in your generosity."

"We're together, we're together," Mrs. Gereth lifelessly repeated. "That's all we *are* now; it's all we have." The words brought to Fleda a sudden vision of the empty little house at Ricks; such a vision might also have been what her companion found in the face of the stopped Dutch clock. Yet with this it was clear that she would now show no bitterness: she had done with that, had given the last drop to those horrible hours in London. No passion even was left to her, and her forbearance only added to the force with which she represented the final vanity of everything.

Fleda was so far from a wish to triumph that she was absolutely ashamed of having anything to say for herself; but there was one thing, all the same, that not to say was impossible. "That he has done it, that he couldn't *not* do it, shows how right I was." It settled forever her attitude, and she spoke as if for her own mind; then after a little she added very gently, for Mrs. Gereth's: "That's to say, it shows that he was bound to her by an obligation that, however much he may have wanted to, he couldn't in any sort of honor break."

Blanched and bleak, Mrs. Gereth looked at her. "What sort of an obligation do you call that? No such obligation exists for an hour between any man and any woman who have hatred on one side. He had ended by hating her, and now he hates her more than ever."

"Did he tell you so?" Fleda asked.

"No. He told me nothing but the great gawk of a fact. I saw him but for three minutes." She was silent again, and Fleda, as before some lurid image of this interview, sat without speaking. "Do you wish to appear as if you don't care?" Mrs. Gereth presently demanded.

"I'm trying not to think of myself."

"Then if you're thinking of Owen, how can you *bear* to think?"

Sadly and submissively Fleda shook her head; the slow tears had come into her eyes. "I can't. I don't understand—I don't understand!" she broke out.

"*I* do, then." Mrs. Gereth looked hard at the floor. "There was no obligation at the time you saw him last—when you sent him, hating her as he did, back to her."

"If he went," Fleda asked, "doesn't that exactly prove that he recognized one?"

"He recognized rot! You know what *I* think of him." Fleda knew; she had no wish to challenge a fresh statement. Mrs. Gereth made one—it was her sole, faint flicker of passion—to the extent of declaring that he was too abjectly weak to deserve the name of a man. For all Fleda cared!— it was his weakness she loved in him. "He took strange ways of pleasing you!" her friend went on. "There was no obligation till suddenly, the other day, the situation changed."

Fleda wondered. "The other day?"

"It came to Mona's knowledge—I can't tell you how, but it came—that the things I was sending back had begun to

arrive at Poynton. I had sent them for you, but it was *her*
I touched." Mrs. Gereth paused; Fleda was too absorbed in
her explanation to do anything but take blankly the full,
cold breath of this. "They were there, and that determined
her."

"Determined her to what?"

"To act, to take means."

"To take means?" Fleda repeated.

"I can't tell you what they were, but they were powerful.
She knew how," said Mrs. Gereth.

Fleda received with the same stoicism the quiet im-
mensity of this allusion to the person who had not known
how. But it made her think a little, and the thought found
utterance, with unconscious irony, in the simple interrogation: "Mona?"

"Why not? She's a brute."

"But if he knew that so well, what chance was there in
it for her?"

"How can I tell you? How can I talk of such horrors? I
can only give you, of the situation, what I see. He knew it,
yes. But as she couldn't make him forget it, she tried to
make him like it. She tried and she succeeded: that's what
she did. She's after all so much less of a fool than he. And
what *else* had he originally liked?" Mrs. Gereth shrugged
her shoulders. "She did what you wouldn't!" Fleda's face
had grown dark with her wonder, but her friend's empty
hands offered no balm to the pain in it. "It was that if it
was anything. Nothing else meets the misery of it. Then
there was quick work. Before he could turn round he was
married."

Fleda, as if she had been holding her breath, gave the sigh
of a listening child. "At that place you spoke of in town?"

"At the Registrar's, like a pair of low atheists."

The girl hesitated. "What do people say of that? I mean
the 'world.'"

"Nothing, because nobody knows. They're to be married
on the 17th, at Waterbath church. If anything else comes
out, everybody is a little prepared. It will pass for some
stroke of diplomacy, some move in the game, some out-
witting of *me*. It's known there has been a row with me."

Fleda was mystified. "People surely knew at Poynton," she objected, "if, as you say, she's there."

"She was there, day before yesterday, only for a few hours. She met him in London and went down to see the things."

Fleda remembered that she had seen them only once. "Did *you* see them?" she then ventured to ask.

"Everything."

"Are they right?"

"Quite right. There's nothing like them," said Mrs. Gereth. At this her companion took up one of her hands again and kissed it as she had done in London. "Mona went back that night; she was not there yesterday. Owen stayed on," she added.

Fleda stared. "Then she's not to live there?"

"Rather! But not till after the public marriage." Mrs. Gereth seemed to muse; then she brought out: "She'll live there alone."

"Alone?"

"She'll have it to herself."

"He won't live with her?"

"Never! But she's none the less his wife, and you're not," said Mrs. Gereth, getting up. "Our only chance is the chance she may die."

Fleda appeared to consider: she appreciated her visitor's magnanimous use of the plural. "Mona won't die," she replied.

"Well, *I* shall, thank God! Till then"—and with this, for the first time, Mrs. Gereth put out her hand—"don't desert me."

Fleda took her hand, and her clasp of it was a reiteration of a promise already given. She said nothing, but her silence was an acceptance as responsible as the vow of a nun. The next moment something occurred to her. "I mustn't put myself in your son's way."

Mrs. Gereth gave a dry, flat laugh. "You're prodigious! But how shall you possibly be more out of it? Owen and I—" She didn't finish her sentence.

"That's your great feeling about *him*," Fleda said; "but how, after what has happened, can it be his about you?"

Mrs. Gereth hesitated. "How do you know what has happened? You don't know what I said to him."

"Yesterday?"

"Yesterday."

They looked at each other with a long, deep gaze. Then, as Mrs. Gereth seemed again about to speak, the girl, closing her eyes, made a gesture of strong prohibition. "Don't tell me!"

"Merciful powers, how you worship him!" Mrs. Gereth wonderingly moaned. It was, for Fleda, the shake that made the cup overflow. She had a pause, that of the child who takes time to know that he responds to an accident with pain; then, dropping again on the sofa, she broke into tears. They were beyond control, they came in long sobs, which for a moment Mrs. Gereth, almost with an air of indifference, stood hearing and watching. At last Mrs. Gereth too sank down again. Mrs. Gereth soundlessly, wearily wept.

CHAPTER XXI

"It looks just like Waterbath; but, after all, we bore *that* together:" these words formed part of a letter in which, before the 17th, Mrs. Gereth, writing from disfigured Ricks, named to Fleda the day on which she would be expected to arrive there on a second visit. "I sha'n't, for a long time to come," the missive continued, "be able to receive any one who may *like* it, who would try to smooth it down, and me with it; but there are always things you and I can comfortably hate together, for you're the only person who comfortably understands. You don't understand quite everything, but of all my acquaintance you're far away the least stupid. For action you're no good at all; but action is over, for me, forever, and you will have the great merit of knowing, when I'm brutally silent, what I shall be thinking about. Without setting myself up for your equal, I dare say I shall also know what are your own thoughts. Moreover, with nothing else but my four walls, you'll at any rate be a bit of furniture. For that, you know, a little, I've always taken you—quite one of my best finds. So come, if possible, on the 15th."

The position of a bit of furniture was one that Fleda could conscientiously accept, and she by no means insisted on so high a place in the list. This communication made her easier, if only by its acknowledgment that her friend had something left: it still implied recognition of the principle of property. Something to hate, and to hate "comfortably," was at least not the utter destitution to which, after their last interview, she had helplessly seemed to see Mrs. Gereth go forth. She remembered indeed that, in the state in which they first saw it, she herself had "liked" the blessed

refuge of Ricks; and she now wondered if the tact for
which she was commended had then operated to make her
keep her kindness out of sight. She was at present ashamed
of such obliquity, and made up her mind that if this happy
impression, quenched in the spoils of Poynton, should
revive on the spot, she would utter it to her companion
without reserve. Yes, she was capable of as much "action"
as that: all the more that the spirit of her hostess seemed,
for the time at least, wholly to have failed. Mrs. Gereth's
three minutes with Owen had been a blow to all talk of
travel, and after her woeful hour at Maggie's she had, like
some great moaning, wounded bird, made her way, with
wings of anguish, back to the nest she knew she should
find empty. Fleda, on that dire day, could neither keep her
nor give her up; she had pressingly offered to return with
her, but Mrs. Gereth, in spite of the theory that their
common grief was a bond, had even declined all escort to
the station, conscious apparently of something abject in
her collapse and almost fiercely eager, as with a personal
shame, to be unwatched. All she had said to Fleda was that
she would go back to Ricks that night, and the girl had lived
for days after with a dreadful image of her position and her
misery there. She had had a vision of her now lying prone
on some unmade bed, now pacing a bare floor like a lioness
deprived of her cubs. There had been moments when her
mind's ear was strained to listen for some sound of grief
wild enough to be wafted from afar. But the first sound, at
the end of a week, had been a note announcing, without
reflections, that the plan of going abroad had been abandoned. "It has come to me indirectly, but with much appearance of truth, that *they* are going—for an indefinite
time. That quite settles it; I shall stay where I am, and as
soon as I've turned round again I shall look for you." The
second letter had come a week later, and on the 15th Fleda
was on her way to Ricks.

Her arrival took the form of a surprise very nearly as
violent as that of the other time. The elements were different, but the effect, like the other, arrested her on the
threshold: she stood there stupefied and delighted at the
magic of a passion of which such a picture represented the

low-water mark. Wound up but sincere, and passing quickly from room to room, Fleda broke out before she even sat down. "If you turn me out of the house for it, my dear, there isn't a woman in England for whom it wouldn't be a privilege to live here." Mrs. Gereth was as honestly bewildered as she had of old been falsely calm. She looked about at the few sticks that, as she afterwards phrased it, she had gathered in, and then hard at her guest, as if to protect herself against a joke sufficiently cruel. The girl's heart gave a leap, for this stare was the sign of an opportunity. Mrs. Gereth was all unwitting; she didn't in the least know what she had done, and as Fleda could tell her Fleda suddenly became the one who knew most. That counted for the moment as a magnificent position; it almost made all the difference. Yet what contradicted it was the vivid presence of the artist's idea. "Where on earth did you put your hand on such beautiful things?"

"Beautiful things?" Mrs. Gereth turned again to the little worn, bleached stuffs and the sweet spindle-legs. "They're the wretched things that were here—that stupid, starved old woman's."

"The maiden aunt's, the nicest, the dearest old woman that ever lived? I thought you had got rid of the maiden aunt."

"She was stored in an empty barn—stuck away for a sale; a matter that, fortunately, I've had neither time nor freedom of mind to arrange. I've simply, in my extremity, fished her out again."

"You've simply, in your extremity, made a delight of her." Fleda took the highest line and the upper hand, and as Mrs. Gereth challenging her cheerfulness turned again a lustreless eye over the contents of the place, she broke into a rapture that was unforced but that she was conscious of an advantage in being able to feel. She moved, as she had done on the previous occasion, from one piece to another, with looks of recognition and hands that lightly lingered, but she was as feverishly jubilant now as she had formerly been anxious and mute. "Ah, the little melancholy, tender, telltale things: how can they *not* speak to you and find a way to your heart? It's not the great chorus of Poynton; but you're not, I'm sure, either so proud or so broken as to be reached by nothing but that. This is a voice so gentle, so human, so feminine—a faint, far-away voice with the little quaver of a heart-break. You've listened to it unawares; for the arrangement and effect of everything—when I compare them with what we found the first day we came down— shows, even if mechanically and disdainfully exercised, your admirable, infallible hand. It's your extraordinary genius; you make things 'compose' in spite of yourself. You've only to be a day or two in a place with four sticks for something to come of it!"

"Then if anything has come of it here, it has come precisely of just four. That's literally, by the inventory, all there are!" said Mrs. Gereth.

"If there were more there would be too many to convey the impression in which half the beauty resides—the impression, somehow, of something dreamed and missed, something reduced, relinquished, resigned: the poetry, as it were, of something sensibly *gone*." Fleda ingeniously and triumphantly worked it out. "Ah, there's something here that will never be in the inventory!"

"Does it happen to be in your power to give it a name?" Mrs. Gereth's face showed the dim dawn of an amusement at finding herself seated at the feet of her pupil.

"I can give it a dozen. It's a kind of fourth dimension. It's a presence, a perfume, a touch. It's a soul, a story, a life. There's ever so much more here than you and I. We're in fact just three!"

"Oh, if you count the ghosts!"

"Of course I count the ghosts. It seems to me ghosts count double—for what they were and for what they are. Somehow there were no ghosts at Poynton," Fleda went on. "That was the only fault."

Mrs. Gereth, considering, appeared to fall in with the girl's fine humor. "Poynton was too splendidly happy."

"Poynton was too splendidly happy," Fleda promptly echoed.

"But it's cured of that now," her companion added.

"Yes, henceforth there'll be a ghost or two."

Mrs. Gereth thought again: she found her young friend suggestive. "Only *she* won't see them."

"No, 'she' won't see them." Then Fleda said, "What I mean is, for this dear one of ours, that if she had (as I *know* she did; it's in the very taste of the air!) a great accepted pain—"

She had paused an instant, and Mrs. Gereth took her up. "Well, if she had?"

Fleda still hesitated. "Why, it was worse than yours."

Mrs. Gereth reflected. "Very likely." Then she too hesitated. "The question is if it was worse than yours."

"Mine?" Fleda looked vague.

"Precisely. Yours."

At this our young lady smiled. "Yes, because it was a disappointment. She had been so sure."

"I see. And you were never sure."

"Never. Besides, I'm happy," said Fleda.

Mrs. Gereth met her eyes awhile. "Goose!" she quietly remarked as she turned away. There was a curtness in it; nevertheless it represented a considerable part of the basis of their new life.

On the 18th The Morning Post had at last its clear message, a brief account of the marriage, from the residence of the bride's mother, of Mr. Owen Gereth of Poynton Park to Miss Mona Brigstock of Waterbath. There were two ecclesiastics and six bridesmaids and, as Mrs. Gereth subsequently said, a hundred frumps, as well as a special train from town: the scale of the affair sufficiently showed that the preparations had been complete for weeks. The happy pair were described as having taken their departure for Mr. Gereth's own seat, famous for its unique collection of artistic curiosities. The newspapers and letters, the fruits of the first London post, had been brought to the mistress of Ricks in the garden; and she lingered there alone a long time after receiving them. Fleda kept at a distance; she knew what must have happened, for from one of the windows she saw her rigid in a chair, her eyes strange and fixed, the newspaper open on the ground and the letters untouched in her lap. Before the morning's end she had disappeared, and the rest of that day she remained in her room: it recalled to Fleda, who had picked up the newspaper, the day, months before, on which Owen had come down to Poynton to make his engagement known. The hush of the house was at least the same, and the girl's own waiting, her soft wandering, through the hours: there was a difference indeed sufficiently great, of which her companion's absence might in some degree have represented a considerate recognition. That was at any rate the meaning Fleda, devoutly glad to be alone, attached to her opportunity. Mrs. Gereth's sole allusion, the next day, to the subject of their thoughts, has already been mentioned: it was a dazzled glance at the fact that Mona's quiet pace had really never slackened.

Fleda fully assented. "I said of our disembodied friend here that she had suffered in proportion as she had been sure. But that's not always a source of suffering. It's Mona who must have been sure!"

"She was sure of *you!*" Mrs. Gereth returned. But this didn't diminish the satisfaction taken by Fleda in showing how serenely and lucidly she could talk.

CHAPTER XXII

HER RELATION with her wonderful friend had, however, in
becoming a new one, begun to shape itself almost wholly
on breaches and omissions. Something had dropped out
altogether, and the question between them, which time
would answer, was whether the change had made them
strangers or yokefellows. It was as if at last, for better or
worse, they were, in a clearer, cruder air, really to know
each other. Fleda wondered how Mrs. Gereth had escaped
hating her: there were hours when it seemed that such a
feat might leave after all a scant margin for future acci-
dents. The thing indeed that now came out in its simplicity
was that even in her shrunken state the lady of Ricks was
larger than her wrongs. As for the girl herself, she had
made up her mind that her feelings had no connection with
the case. It was her pretension that they had never yet
emerged from the seclusion into which, after her friend's
visit to her at her sister's, we saw them precipitately retire:
if she should suddenly meet them in straggling procession
on the road it would be time enough to deal with them.
They were all bundled there together, likes with dislikes and
memories with fears; and she had for not thinking of them
the excellent reason that she was too occupied with the
actual. The actual was not that Owen Gereth had seen his
necessity where she had pointed it out; it was that his
mother's bare spaces demanded all the tapestry that the
recipient of her bounty could furnish. There were moments
during the month that followed when Mrs. Gereth struck
her as still older and feebler, and as likely to become quite
easily amused.

At the end of it, one day, the London paper had another

piece of news: "Mr. and Mrs. Owen Gereth, who arrived in town last week, proceed this morning to Paris." They exchanged no word about it till the evening, and none indeed would then have been uttered had not Mrs. Gereth irrelevantly broken out: "I dare say you wonder why I declared the other day with such assurance that he wouldn't live with her. He apparently *is* living with her."

"Surely it's the only proper thing for him to do."

"They're beyond me—I give it up," said Mrs. Gereth.

"I don't give it up—I never did," Fleda returned.

"Then what do you make of his aversion to her?"

"Oh, she has dispelled it."

Mrs. Gereth said nothing for a minute. "You're prodigious in your choice of terms!" she then simply ejaculated.

But Fleda went luminously on; she once more enjoyed her great command of her subject: "I think that when you came to see me at Maggie's you saw too many things, you had too many ideas."

"You had none," said Mrs. Gereth: "you were completely bewildered."

"Yes, I didn't quite understand—but I think I understand now. The case is simple and logical enough. She's a person who's upset by failure and who blooms and expands with success. There was something she had set her heart upon, set her teeth about—the house exactly as she had seen it."

"She never saw it at all, she never looked at it!" cried Mrs. Gereth.

"She doesn't look with her eyes; she looks with her ears. In her own way she had taken it in; she knew, she felt when it had been touched. That probably made her take an attitude that was extremely disagreeable. But the attitude lasted only while the reason for it lasted."

"Go on—I can bear it now," said Mrs. Gereth. Her companion had just perceptibly paused.

"I know you can, or I shouldn't dream of speaking. When the pressure was removed she came up again. From the moment the house was once more what it had to be, her natural charm reasserted itself."

"Her natural charm!" Mrs. Gereth could barely articulate.

"It's very great; everybody thinks so; there must be something in it. It operated as it had operated before. There's no need of imagining anything very monstrous. Her restored good humor, her splendid beauty, and Mr. Owen's impressibility and generosity sufficiently cover the ground. His great bright sun came out!"

"And his great bright passion for another person went in. Your explanation would doubtless be perfection if he didn't love you."

Fleda was silent a little. "What do you know about his 'loving' me?"

"I know what Mrs. Brigstock herself told me."

"You never in your life took her word for any other matter."

"Then won't yours do?" Mrs. Gereth demanded. "Haven't I had it from your own mouth that he cares for you?"

Fleda turned pale, but she faced her companion and smiled. "You confound, Mrs. Gereth, you mix things up. You've only had it from my own mouth that I care for *him!*"

It was doubtless in contradictious allusion to this (which at the time had made her simply drop her head as in a strange, vain reverie) that Mrs. Gereth, a day or two later, said to Fleda: "Don't think I shall be a bit affected if I'm here to see it when he comes again to make up to you."

"He won't do that," the girl replied. Then she added, smiling: "But if he should be guilty of such bad taste, it wouldn't be nice of you not to be disgusted."

"I'm not talking of disgust; I'm talking of its opposite," said Mrs. Gereth.

"Of its opposite?"

"Why, of any reviving pleasure that one might feel in such an exhibition. I shall feel none at all. You may personally take it as you like; but what conceivable good will it do?"

Fleda wondered. "To me, do you mean?"

"Deuce take you, no! To what we don't, you know, by your wish, ever talk about."

"The old things?" Fleda considered again. "It will do no

good of any sort to anything or any one. That's another
question I would rather we shouldn't discuss, please," she
gently added.

Mrs. Gereth shrugged her shoulders.

"It certainly isn't worth it!"

Something in her manner prompted her companion, with
a certain inconsequence, to speak again. "That was partly
why I came back to you, you know—that there should be
the less possibility of anything painful."

"Painful?" Mrs. Gereth stared. "What pain can I ever
feel again?"

"I meant painful to myself," Fleda, with a slight impatience, explained.

"Oh, I see." Her friend was silent a minute. "You use
sometimes such odd expressions. Well, I shall last a little,
but I sha'n't last forever."

"You'll last quite as long—" Here Fleda suddenly hesitated.

Mrs. Gereth took her up with a cold smile that seemed
the warning of experience against hyperbole. "As long as
what, please?"

The girl thought an instant; then met the difficulty by
adopting, as an amendment, the same tone. "As any danger
of the ridiculous."

That did for the time, and she had moreover, as the
months went on, the protection of suspended allusions.
This protection was marked when, in the following November, she received a letter directed in a hand at which a
quick glance sufficed to make her hesitate to open it. She
said nothing, then or afterwards; but she opened it, for
reasons that had come to her, on the morrow. It consisted
of a page and a half from Owen Gereth, dated from Florence, but with no other preliminary. She knew that during
the summer he had returned to England with his wife, and
that after a couple of months they had again gone abroad.
She also knew, without communication, that Mrs. Gereth,
round whom Ricks had grown submissively and indescrib-
ably sweet, had her own interpretation of her daughter-in-
law's share in this second migration. It was a piece of calculated insolence—a stroke odiously directed at showing

whom it might concern that now she had Poynton fast she was perfectly indifferent to living there. The Morning Post, at Ricks, had again been a resource: it was stated in that journal that Mr. and Mrs. Owen Gereth proposed to spend the winter in India. There was a person to whom it was clear that she led her wretched husband by the nose. Such was the light in which contemporary history was offered to Fleda until, in her own room, late at night, she broke the seal of her letter.

"I want you, inexpressibly, to have, as a remembrance, something of mine—something of real value. Something from Poynton is what I mean and what I should prefer. You know everything there, and far better than I what's best and what isn't. There are a lot of differences, but aren't some of the smaller things the most remarkable? I mean for judges, and for what they'd bring. What I want you to take from me, and to choose for yourself, is the thing in the whole house that's most beautiful and precious. I mean the 'gem of the collection,' don't you know? If it happens to be of such a sort that you can take immediate possession of it—carry it right away with you—so much the better. You're to have it on the spot, whatever it is. I humbly beg of you to go down there and see. The people have complete instructions: they'll act for you in every possible way and put the whole place at your service. There's a thing mamma used to call the Maltese cross and that I think I've heard her say is very wonderful. Is *that* the gem of the collection? Perhaps you would take it, or anything equally convenient. Only I do want you awfully to let it be the very pick of the place. Let me feel that I can trust you for this. You won't refuse if you will think a little what it must be that makes me ask."

Fleda read that last sentence over more times even than the rest; she was baffled—she couldn't think at all of what it might be. This was indeed because it might be one of so many things. She made for the present no answer; she merely, little by little, fashioned for herself the form that her answer should eventually wear. There was only one form that was possible—the form of doing, at her time, what he wished. She would go down to Poynton as a pilgrim might go to a shrine, and as to this she must look out for her chance. She lived with her letter, before any chance came, a month, and even after a month it had mysteries for her that she couldn't meet. What did it mean, what did it represent, to what did it correspond in his imagination or his soul? What was behind it, what was beyond it, what was, in the deepest depth, within it? She said to herself that with these questions she was under no obligation to deal. There was an explanation of them that, for practical purposes, would do as well as another: he had found in his marriage a happiness so much greater than, in the distress of his dilemma, he had been able to take heart to believe, that he now felt he owed her a token of gratitude for having kept him in the straight path. That explanation, I say, she could throw off; but no explanation in the least mattered: what determined her was the simple strength of her impulse to respond. The passion for which what had happened had made no difference, the passion that had taken this into account before as well as after, found here an issue that there was nothing whatever to choke. It found even a relief to which her imagination immensely contributed. Would she act upon his offer? She would act with secret rapture. To have as her own something splendid that he had given her, of which the gift had been his signed desire, would be a greater joy than the greatest she had supposed to be left to her, and she felt that till the sense of this came home she had even herself not known what burned in her successful stillness. It was an hour to dream of and watch for; to be patient was to draw out the sweetness. She was capable of feeling it as an hour of triumph, the triumph of everything in her recent life that had not held up its head. She moved there in thought—in the great rooms she knew; she should be able to say to herself that, for once at least, her possession was as complete as that of either of the others whom it had filled only with bitterness. And a thousand times yes—her choice should know no scruple: the thing she should go down to take would be up to the height of her privilege. The whole place was in her eyes, and she spent for weeks her private hours in a luxury of comparison and debate. It should be one of the smallest things because it should be one she could have close to her; and it should be one of the finest because it was in the finest he saw his symbol. She said to herself that of what it would symbolize she was content to know nothing more than just what her having it would tell her. At bottom she inclined to the Maltese cross—with the added reason that he had named it. But she would look again and judge afresh; she would on the spot so handle and ponder that there shouldn't be the shade of a mistake.

Before Christmas she had a natural opportunity to go to London; there was her periodical call upon her father to pay as well as a promise to Maggie to redeem. She spent her first night in West Kensington, with the idea of carrying out on the morrow the purpose that had most of a motive. Her father's affection was not inquisitive, but when she mentioned to him that she had business in the country that would oblige her to catch an early train, he deprecated her excursion in view of the menace of the weather. It was spoiling for a storm; all the signs of a winter gale were in the air. She replied that she would see what the morning might bring; and it brought, in fact, what seemed in London an amendment. She was to go to Maggie the next day, and now that she had started her eagerness had become suddenly a pain. She pictured her return that evening with her trophy under her cloak; so that after looking, from the doorstep, up and down the dark street, she decided, with a new nervousness, and sallied forth to the nearest place of access to the "Underground." The December dawn was dolorous, but there was neither rain nor snow; it was not even cold, and the atmosphere of West Kensington, purified by the wind, was like a dirty old coat that had been bettered by a dirty brush. At the end of almost an hour, in the larger station, she had taken her place in a third-class compartment; the prospect before her was the run of eighty minutes to Poynton. The train was a fast one, and she was familiar with the moderate measure of the walk to the park from the spot at which it would drop her.

Once in the country, indeed, she saw that her father was right: the breath of December was abroad with a force from which the London labyrinth had protected her. The green fields were black, the sky was all alive with the wind; she had, in her anxious sense of the elements, her wonder at what might happen, a reminder of the surmises, in the old days of going to the Continent, that used to worry her on the way, at night, to the horrid cheap crossings by long sea. Something, in a dire degree, at this last hour, had begun to press on her heart: it was the sudden imagination of a disaster, or at least of a check, before her errand was achieved. When she said to herself that something might happen she wanted to go faster than the train. But nothing could happen save a dismayed discovery that, by some altogether unlikely chance, the master and mistress of the house had already come back. In that case she must have had a warning, and the fear was but the excess of her hope. It was every one's being exactly where every one was that lent the quality to her visit. Beyond lands and seas and alienated forever, they in their different ways gave her the impression to take as she had never taken it. At last it was already there, though the darkness of the day had deepened; they had whizzed past Chater—Chater, which was the station before the right one. Off in that quarter was an air of wild rain, but there shimmered straight across it a brightness that was the color of the great interior she had been haunting. That vision settled before her—in the house the house was all; and as the train drew up she rose, in her mean compartment, quite proudly erect with the thought that all for Fleda Vetch then the house was standing there.

But with the opening of the door she encountered a shock, though for an instant she couldn't have named it; the next moment she saw it was given her by the face of the man advancing to let her out, an old lame porter of the station, who had been there in Mrs. Gereth's time and who now recognized her. He looked up at her so hard that she took an alarm and before alighting broke out to him: "They've come back?" She had a confused, absurd sense that even he would know that in this case she mustn't be there. He hesitated, and in the few seconds her alarm had completely changed its ground: it seemed to leap, with her quick jump from the carriage, to the ground that was that of his stare at her. "Smoke?" She was on the platform with her frightened sniff: it had taken her a minute to become aware of an extraordinary smell. The air was full of it, and there were already heads at the window of the train, looking out at something she couldn't see. Some one, the only other passenger, had got out of another carriage, and the old porter hobbled off to close his door. The smoke was in her eyes, but she saw the station-master, from the end of the platform, recognize her too and come straight to her. He brought her a finer shade of surprise than the porter, and while he was coming she heard a voice at a window of the train say that something was "a good bit off—a mile from the town." That was just what Poynton was. Then her heart stood still at the white wonder in the station-master's face.

"You've come down to it, miss, already?"

At this she knew. "Poynton's on fire?"

"Gone, miss—with this awful gale. You weren't wired? Look out!" he cried in the next breath, seizing her; the train was going on, and she had given a lurch that almost made it catch her as it passed. When it had drawn away she became more conscious of the pervading smoke, which the wind seemed to hurl in her face.

"Gone?" She was in the man's hands; she clung to him.

"Burning still, miss. Ain't it quite too dreadful? Took early this morning—the whole place is up there."

In her bewildered horror she tried to think. "Have they come back?"

"Back? They'll be there all day!"

"Not Mr. Gereth, I mean—nor his wife?"

"Nor his mother, miss—not a soul of them back. A pack o' servants in charge—not the old lady's lot, eh? A nice job for care-takers! Some rotten chimley or one of them portable lamps set down in the wrong place. What has done it is this cruel, cruel night." Then as a great wave of smoke half choked them, he drew her with force to the little waiting room. "Awkward for you, miss—I see!"

She felt sick; she sank upon a seat, staring up at him. "Do you mean that great house is lost?"

"It was near it, I was told, an hour ago—the fury of the

flames had got such a start. I was there myself at six, the very first I heard of it. They were fighting it then, but you couldn't quite say they had got it down."

Fleda jerked herself up. "Were they saving the things?"

"That's just where it was, miss—to get *at* the blessed things. And the want of right help—it maddened me to stand and see 'em muff it. This ain't a place, like, for anything organized. They don't come up to a *reel* emergency."

She passed out of the door that opened toward the village and met a great acrid gust. She heard a far-off windy roar which, in her dismay, she took for that of flames a mile away, and which, the first instant, acted upon her as a wild solicitation. "I must go there." She had scarcely spoken before the same omen had changed into an appalling check.

Her vivid friend, moreover, had got before her; he clearly suffered from the nature of the control he had to exercise. "Don't do that, miss—you won't care for it at all." Then as she waveringly stood her ground, "It's not a place for a young lady, nor, if you'll believe me, a sight for them as are in any way affected."

Fleda by this time knew in what way she was affected: she became limp and weak again; she felt herself give everything up. Mixed with the horror, with the kindness of the station-master, with the smell of cinders and the riot of sound, was the raw bitterness of a hope that she might never again in life have to give up so much at such short notice. She heard herself repeat mechanically, yet as if asking it for the first time: "Poynton's *gone?*"

The man hesitated. "What can you call it, miss, if it ain't really saved?"

A minute later she had returned with him to the waiting-room, where, in the thick swim of things, she saw something like the disk of a clock. "Is there an up-train?" she asked.

"In seven minutes."

She came out on the platform: everywhere she met the smoke. She covered her face with her hands. "I'll go back."